You Cake My Breath Away

A novel
TOBIE CARTER

Copyright © 2025 by Tobie Carter

All rights reserved.

No part of this publication may be reproduced, distributed, or transmitted in any form or by any means, including photocopying, recording, or other electronic or mechanical methods, without the prior written permission of the publisher, except as permitted by U.S. copyright law. For permission requests, contact Rising Phoenix Publications LLC.

The story, all names, characters, and incidents portrayed in this production are fictitious. No identification with actual persons (living or deceased), places, buildings, and products is intended or should be inferred.

Book Cover by Tobie Carter

Character Illustrations by Emsdrawsthingson IG. Emyd92@gmail.com

This book is dedicated to four very special people.

Ben & Kris

My brothers in Heaven.

Yaya & Nonna

Two mothers who live every day with hearts too heavy with sadness to carry.

Content Warning

Hi reader! Thanks for picking up my book! I know not everyone needs content/trigger warnings before reading a book, but I want to be mindful of my readers who would like one. If that's not you, feel free to skip this page as I'll be listing them below:

-Grief(spousal death)
-Death of sibling(on-page, in the past gun violence)
-Mention of drug use
-Touch starvation
-Pregnancy
-Open-door intimacy

Contents

1. Tilly — 1
2. Tilly — 7
3. Archer — 11
4. Tilly — 19
5. Tilly — 25
6. Tilly — 33
7. Archer — 41
8. Tilly — 44
9. Archer — 50
10. Tilly — 57
11. Archer — 70
12. Tilly — 74
13. Archer — 83
14. Tilly — 88
15. Archer — 96
16. Archer — 99
17. Tilly — 103
18. Tilly — 106

19. Archer	116
20. Tilly	119
21. Archer	128
22. Tilly	131
23. Archer	143
24. Tilly	149
25. Tilly	155
26. Archer	165
27. Archer	168
28. Tilly	170
29. Tilly	176
30. Tilly	185
31. Tilly	193
32. Archer	198
33. Tilly	203
34. Archer	212
35. Tilly	215
36. Archer	226
37. Archer	229
38. Tilly	236
39. Tilly	247
40. Tilly	258
41. Archer	264

42.	Tilly	273
43.	Archer	280
44.	Tilly	288
45.	Archer	296
46.	Tilly	302
47.	Archer	310
48.	Tilly	316
49.	Archer	321
50.	Tilly	328
51.	Tilly	335
52.	Epilogue	339
Thank You		341
Acknowledgements		342
Chapter		344
About the author		345

Chapter One
Tilly

Today, I will make the bed.

I've told myself this repeatedly for the last six months. Yet, the soft fibers of the wool carpet pull me into its depths as I stare at my biggest foe. In its defense, it did nothing to warrant my ire. The smooth bamboo sheets and sage green duvet are soft and welcoming, and even though I've washed them plenty, they still manage to hold my husband's scent within the threads. Or at least that's what my brain tells me.

It's been too long since I've been able to make Jessie's side of the bed, to pretend that the covers aren't disheveled because he overslept and was late for work or that he's simply in the bathroom brushing his teeth.

Pillows are piled up in the middle, a makeshift mountain range that curves in the exact way he used to hold me. One pillow between my calves where he'd sneak his cold feet for warmth, one nestled around my rear where our bodies met, one where his broad chest met my back, and a smaller one, long and round, where his arm wrapped around me, making me feel safe.

When I close my eyes, I can almost imagine it's him.

But the sunlight streaming in through the window highlights the empty space where the love of my life took his last breath.

I promised myself—and my therapist—that I'd make progress in restarting my life. Plenty of philosophers and entrepreneurs wax poetic about how making the bed first thing in the morning can set your day on a positive path, but by the way my stomach aches just looking at the space, I think they're wrong.

"Tilly?" Shantel's chipper voice echoes from the living room, snapping me from my daze.

Tears prickle behind my closed eyes, pushing over the rubbed raw lids and streaming down my cheek. I wipe them away and scurry into the closet, so Jessie's sister thinks I'm making actual progress sorting through the clothes I told her I'd donate months ago.

Her keys jangle loudly as she nears the bedroom, and the nutty notes of her hazelnut coffee hit my nose as she enters the space I shared with her brother. "Where are you?"

"In here." My voice is scratchy as it claws its way up my tight throat. I wave a hand outside the closet and stand in front of Jessie's clothes trying to gain my bearings before I see the disappointment etched into her features.

"Are you naked?" Shantel's eyes are closed as she enters the closet, munching on one of the glazed lilac scones I baked last night. Her smooth brown skin is flawless and glowing, and I'm envious that she wears minimal makeup yet looks like she's about to step onto a runway.

"No," I reply, gaze moving to the row of band t-shirts Jessie loved to wear. He was all business outside of these walls, a regular Shemar Moore, but at home with me he was the guy who loved to karaoke and grill out on the weekends in sweats and slides.

"Phew." Her eyes pop open and a smile breaks on her face. "Wow, you're already doing it!"

I heave a sigh at her excitement. Donating Jessie's clothes has been on my to-do list for months, but every time I've tried to let go of the items, I find myself curled up in a ball on the closet floor.

What can I say? I'm an expert at avoidance.

Shantel decided to appoint herself as my very own Marie Kondo when I let it slip that I was having trouble parting with the items. I'm already regretting my decision. I don't *need* the space where his clothes hung for any reason. I rather liked being able to walk into the closet and rustle his old t-shirts where his bergamot cologne still clings to the material, greeting me like an old friend.

But I know it's time.

I'm ready.

I think.

"How can I help?" Shantel sets down her cup and walks into the closet, careful not to touch me as she passes.

Stretching my neck side to side, I will the tension away from my shoulders. If I don't do this now, I'll stay stuck, unable to move forward after life ripped the carpet out from beneath me and stole my husband away.

To some people, moving on means selling a house or signing up for a dating profile, but to me it's trying to make the damn bed and force myself to donate clothes that are just gathering dust.

I inhale a deep, calming breath and infuse my spine with steel nerves. "Grab me a trash bag."

One anxiety attack and three hours later we've managed to pack all of Jessie's suits and shoes, his undergarments, and most of his t-shirts—sans the one I'm wearing and the ones I refuse to part with. All that's left are a few boxes piled in the corner.

"These scones are so good," Shantel says around a mouthful. One benefit to my procrastinating is that I've been trying out new flavor profiles. The citrusy taste of lilac was a perfect addition to my mom's old scone recipe. "Are you gonna take some to your dad?"

The mention of my dad sours my somewhat uplifted mood. We've been two ships in the night, and when I drop off my confections to him to sell in my parents' restaurant, he's always rushing me out like he doesn't have time.

"No," I reply, throwing my curly brown hair into a sloppy bun atop my head. "Maybe once I perfect the recipe."

She thankfully doesn't push me on my distant relationship with my father and snags the last scone as I pull the first box toward me. A rubber duck, an Astros bobblehead, a few old action figures and some random tchotchkes from Jessie's childhood fill the cardboard box.

"That butthead." Shantel snatches a rabbit's foot keychain from my hand, holding it up to the light with drawn eyebrows and tight lips. "I knew he stole my lucky charm, but he would never fess up to it."

I scoff. "A lot of luck it gave him." Wishing I could shove the words back inside, I cover my mouth, hopeful Shantel didn't hear my crass comment over her chewing. My cheeks immediately flame when I look up and find her jaw unhinged. "Oh my gosh, I'm sorry." As if shame is exuding from my being, I cover my face.

Grief is a weird thing. One day life is going along as planned—you go to work, grab groceries, cook out over the holiday—and the next you're sitting in the shower crying so your sobs are muffled by the spray of water on the tile. Since Jessie died, I've cried, I've screamed until my throat was raw, and I've thrown more items than I can count. What I haven't done is laugh.

"Don't apologize." Shantel reaches out as if to comfort me, but I pull back, still unable to withstand her touch.

Shantel shrugs with a wry smile on her face. "If you can't joke with your dead husband's sister, then who can you joke with? Amiright?"

"There's something very wrong with us." I sigh and close up the box with the trinkets. "Thanks for doing this with me."

"What are sisters for?"

I try to smile at her, but I'm bone tired, my energy zapped from the roller coaster of emotion I've been riding this morning. I'm about to call it a day when a sleek black box tucked behind the fire extinguisher on the floor catches my eye. It's no wider than a standard notebook with gold embossed letters.

"Malacko, Zook, & Pierce?" I muse aloud, running my hand along the raised writing.

"What's that?" Shantel sidles up next to me on the floor, and her forehead crinkles as she reads over my shoulder. "A law firm?"

I bristle at her closeness, and she backs off, moving to sit in front of me with her legs crossed. Sliding a sweaty palm down my jeans, I try to ignore the nausea now wreaking havoc in my stomach. My mind spins with a thousand reasons why he could've needed to consult a law firm—and why he hid the paperwork.

"Are you gonna open it?" she asks just before I allow myself to spiral. With clammy hands and a pounding heart, I lift the lid. As if she's not staring at the same pad of papers on my lap, she adds, "What is it?"

I sigh heavily, ignoring her question as I flip through the stack, scanning each line for some idea of what I'm looking at. The papers are all out of order, as if Jessie dropped them and scrambled to put them back together. A memory from a few weeks before he passed slides to the front of my mind.

Shantel and I watched cheesy rom coms, making it into a drinking game any time the love interests stared longingly at the other, while Jessie hung out in his mancave with his best friend, Archer. It'd been a long time since we all hung out as a group, something that seemed to occur less and less since Jessie and I started dating. After our third movie, I was ready to climb into bed. Jessie followed not long after that, creeping into the dark room, trying not to wake me. I slid out of bed to check on him when he was in the bathroom too long and found him on his knees in the attached closet. He startled, but when I asked him what he was doing, he told me he tripped over his shoes. In my drunken state, I didn't question it.

Maybe I should've.

"Looks like a contract for something." I organize the papers by number, hoping that reading them in order will enlighten me to the content. My heart thrums in my ears, bringing heat to my chest as I thumb through the pages on the closet floor. I touch the base of my neck, shaking my head as my gaze lands on words that make no sense.

Asset: Property. Establishment. Purchase price.

There was no mention in Jessie's will about any other businesses or estates. Our house was paid off thanks to his sales commissions, and my scholarships took care of most of my student loans from culinary school. Outside of those expenses, we had nothing.

Jessie wouldn't have bought something without talking to me beforehand, or at least I don't think he would've. My gut churns, worried there's an outstanding bill I've missed payments on.

I flip the page and my gaze lands on the familiar swoop of the letter 'J' in Jessie's signature, right beside the 'buyer' line. I flinch back, blinking when I read the name next to the seller.

Archibald Wilson.

My husband's best friend.

Chapter Two
Tilly

"Can I see it?" Without waiting for an answer, Shantel tugs the paperwork out of my hands.

Glancing around the closet, I search for answers I know aren't there. We didn't keep secrets from each other. *Did we?* Doubt creeps in the longer Shantel reads, and I scrutinize her face for any hint of understanding. Slowly, her lips pull in, crinkling at the corners as she purses them.

"What?" I ask.

"I dunno." I catch what I think is a flutter in her jaw, but she shakes her head and lifts her shoulders in a shrug. "You'll have to ask Archer."

I roll my eyes, blowing out air through my nose. That's the last thing I want to do. Where there used to be camaraderie and mutual respect between us, it dwindled to grunts and scarce eye contact once Jessie and I started dating. I thought Jessie's passing would've brought us closer, maybe evened out the terrain where our friendship hit rough patches, but it's done nothing except increase the distance.

"I haven't seen or talked to Archer in weeks," I reply, toying with a fuzzball from the carpet. It's not a lie, but it's also not the full truth. I've seen Archer a handful of times in passing, but like always, he gives me the cold shoulder, barely able to look at me or speak in full sentences.

"You know how he is." She sighs, unfolding herself and standing with her hands on her hips. "I'm sure he'll be at your birthday dinner this weekend. You can talk to him then."

I open my mouth to remind her that I don't want a birthday dinner—or to talk to Archer—but she speeds out of the room at a breakneck pace. Dragging myself from the comfy floor, I follow her into my bedroom. Her purse is already slung over her shoulder, and she grabs three bags for donation.

"What's the rush, Shanti?" I ask. "Thought you were staying for breakfast."

Her gaze flits off to the side, and she rolls her lips between her teeth before spouting off, "I...uh, forgot Mom needed me to pick up something she made from the pottery shop, and if I'm going to drop this stuff off for you before work, I've gotta get going."

I cock my head to the side, unsure of why she's rambling. My forehead bunches, but I force myself to smooth out my features and paste on a smile. Shantel and my mother-in-law, Nora, have been so good to me. After Jessie's passing, they could've let our relationship dissolve, but they've managed to draw me closer, absorbing me into their family.

I pick up the other two bags as she backs out of the room, nearly bumping into the door jamb. My ring snags on the stretchy plastic, and I curse as it splits, spilling a few items onto the ground.

Maybe you're not supposed to donate those, my brain helpfully supplies. Gathering the few items into my hands, I expertly throw them back into my room without Shantel noticing. After grabbing a new bag and shoving the contents inside, I follow her downstairs, my arms—and chest—heavy as I lug Jessie's belongings to her car. Heat pours off the concrete, but I'm frozen as I stare at the bags. Ropes of anguish circle my throat, pulsing like the emotions I've kept clamped inside all morning are ready to boil over.

I dig my fingernail into the skin on my thumb, fixating on the black fabric holding what's left of him.

The love of my life.

My best friend.

Tears prickle my eyes as I expel a breath, suddenly too weak to even lift my feet to move. My heart aches—pulverized by the thought of letting go of another piece of the man I thought was my forever—yet there's a vague numbness that settles over my body.

I promised myself I would do this, that I'd honor Jessie by living my life instead of succumbing to the riptide of grief that's always so close to the surface, ready to pull me into the current and swallow me whole.

A fresh start.

"Guess I'll see you on Sunday," Shantel says, severing the tendrils of grief threatening to suck me under.

I nod and say goodbye, watching as she slides into her car. Words form at the back of my throat, urging me to stop her before she leaves. I press my tongue against the roof of my mouth and clench my teeth, not allowing myself to go back on my word.

Her car slowly inches out of the driveway, the noxious stench of exhaust fumes following her as she disappears from my view. I inhale a calming breath and walk into the house, closing the door on the past and looking forward to the future.

***

Inside the closet, the black box draws my attention. It's been days since I found it, yet I haven't been able to muster up the courage to reach out to Archer. I called the law firm, but they couldn't find anything under Jessie's name, and because of client confidentiality, they wouldn't tell me why Archer's name was on the paperwork.

Just send him a text, Tilly.

I huff out a breath and slide the hair band off my wrist, tying my brown hair into a loose bun.

Archer's phone number glows on my contacts list. My hands tremble as I tap out a sentence, practicing what I want to say before deleting it all again. The squeal of the trash truck outside startles me, and my thumb accidentally swipes the screen, scrolling the display. Texts from years ago, when talking with Archer was as easy as breathing, flood the screen.

Most of the time we talked in the group chat between me, him, and Jessie, conversing about the Chemistry project we were teamed up for our sophomore year in college. A friendship bloomed between us, and we spent junior and senior year as The Three Musketeers.

That is, until things got weird between me and Archer after a drunken kiss. Our friendship was strained from then on, and when Jessie asked me out on a date not too long after that, I had no reason to say no.

I roll my neck and shake out my hands, inhaling a deep breath like the therapist taught me to expel the anxious thoughts. I thought getting rid of Jessie's clothes would be my undoing, but it's the little black box inside the closet that throws me for the biggest loop.

And the still unmade bed.

Ignoring the disheveled heap of covers and pillows, I muster up some courage. If I want answers about what the paperwork is, I can't keep pretending Archer doesn't exist—or better yet, I can't keep allowing him to pretend *I* don't exist.

I quickly type a message and send it off.

A stream of air flows through my parted lips as I release my held breath. I did it. I made the first step in hopefully reopening the lines of communication.

Chapter Three

Archer

Present

There should be a law against requiring a person to listen to stodgy old city council members on the weekends, yet here I sit, beckoned by Mr. Brahm. After listening to the head of the council list all the reasons why I need to open the bakery, I'm ready to pull my hair out. He acts like I don't know the historic, yet vibrant community of The Pearl is prime real estate. It's the exact reason I chose to buy a building there.

Clamorous chatter about parking tickets thunders around the hall, and I take it as my opportunity to slip out the door and find an open bar to nurse the ache starting at the back of my head. Between managing my own employees and attending stupid meetings like this one, I almost missed the deadline to submit my application to the TV network looking for a carpenter to host a reality show.

You could be the next Ty Pennington, the agent who stumbled upon me giving a woodworking seminar my parents roped me into at the local college said. At this point, I'd sign up to become a rodeo clown if it meant getting out from under my father's thumb.

"Wait a minute, Archer." Mayor Stevens follows me out, stopping me with a hand on my shoulder. As much as I'd like to ignore him and keep walking, pissing off the mayor is probably not the best idea when he can make life more difficult for my businesses.

I grit my teeth and turn his way, nearly choking on the noxious scent of his Brut cologne. "What can I do for you, Mayor?"

He tilts his head, and a breeze lifts the back of his brown toupee. "We both know old man Brahm isn't going to stop harping on you to get that location open."

"Brahm can kiss my ass for all I care," I reply, stretching my neck.

He sighs. "I don't want to have to force you either, but having an empty building in the heart of The Pearl is the equivalent of a storefront in Times Square being empty. It's bad for business."

I throw my head back and run my tongue along my teeth, sucking in a calming breath. When I bought the building, I had big plans to expand my carpentry business. My hardware stores are already successful, and I wanted to open a woodworking shop where people can learn how to use tools to complete their own projects. But when your best friend needs a location for his wife's bakery, sometimes you have to make sacrifices.

"I know." I slide a hand into my pocket and ball my fist.

"I know you've had a rough year." He winces.

I scoff. Losing your best friend, the man who saved your life, isn't just a *rough* year. It's the second worst fucking year of my life. Add in the fact that I messed shit up with Tilly years ago, and it's pouring salt in the wound.

"I can give you until the beginning of the year—"

"It's already September," I nearly holler before I remember who I'm speaking to. Mayor Stevens might hold a soft spot for me solely because he loved my brother Sebastian and plays golf with my father, but to the people no doubt eavesdropping on our conversation from the other side of the door, I'm sure they'd take my disrespect as another reason to oust me.

"—or else I'll have to heavily suggest that you sell the location. Unless you want Brahm and his crew to start picketing and riling up the community even further."

My jaw aches as I stifle the retort about where Brahm can stick his picket.

"That's only four months away," I reply, pushing my toes into the soles of my work boots, trying to expel the anger bubbling to the surface.

He claps me on the shoulder with a grimace on his face. "It's been more than a year since you bought the building."

He's got me there. In my defense, I didn't expect that Jessie would die just as we made the deal. Grief takes a really fucking long time to deal with. It's been years since my brother passed, and I'm still not over it.

"Fine," I grit out through clenched teeth.

"Thanks, son."

We shake hands and he returns inside to listen to the rest of the town's dilemmas while I head three streets over and stand in front of the apparently offensive vacant building. My heart thumps a wild rhythm thinking of the last time I was here, a few weeks before Jessie and Tilly's first wedding anniversary.

I shake the memory away before it has a chance to form. I should be relaxing in my garage workshop with a cold beer in my hand and rock music blaring through the speakers, not being forced to open wounds that have barely healed.

Damp, musty wood greets me as I pry open the plywood door with calloused fingers. I step forward and am assaulted by cobwebs. Silvery webs stick to my neck as I bat the woven strands away and spit out the pieces that got inside my mouth. Ensuring no spiders are hanging around to attack, I take stock of the place.

Outside of a thick layer of dust clinging to every visible surface, the place isn't much different than it was when I first bought it. Exposed wooden beams, a beautiful bay window, and enough space to segment the place into a café with a full kitchen in the back.

Exactly what Tilly needs to open her bakery.

A pang strikes my chest when I think of my late best friend's wife. It's been weeks since I've seen Tilly, a fact my pseudo-mother, Nora, reminds me of every time I visit her. It's not that I don't want to see her, but every time we're around each other I can't help but push her away. Maybe it's a defense mechanism, a wall I subconsciously built when my two best friends ended up dating each other, but at this point, I'm sure I'm the last person she wants to see.

But you promised Jessie you'd help get her bakery in order.

I inwardly chastise myself. Jessie asked me to handle the construction aspect of Tilly's bakery, but I've let it go to shambles—similar to mine and Tilly's friendship.

My nostrils flare, and my nails bite into my palms. I have four months to keep my word to my best friend and get this place up and running, and I'll be damned if I go back on that promise.

***

Hot water sluices down my body, warming my aching muscles and tinging the water pink from my blood-caked knuckles. After clearing all the cobwebs and dust, I pulled up the eyesore that was the puke-green linoleum flooring from the previous owner. I have a crick in my neck, but working with my hands helped me ignore the voice in my mind insisting I need to tell Tilly about this.

Jessie was supposed to do that.

These days I can barely get more than twenty words out of my mouth around her without finding a way to drive the wedge between us even further. It's my own fault. I'm a coward who managed to turn one of my best friends into an enemy because I couldn't handle my own feelings. But the fact remains that I want to see Tilly happy and thriving—as I always have—and right now the only way I can do that is to make good on my word and get her shop ready to open.

I just need to find the courage to tell her about it.

I will...after I finish some work.

Shutting off the water, I towel dry and run a comb through my hair and beard. I grab my journal from the dresser and write a quick note to my brother about the day before dressing and heading outside to my workshop. My cell rings the second I flip on the lights, illuminating the various tools in disarray on the countertop and Mr. Johnson's car propped up on the ramps, ready for an oil change.

"What's up, Shanti?" I ask Jessie's sister, putting her on speaker as I organize the tools.

"Tilly knows about the bakery," she blurts out without a hello. Ice pours into my veins, and I curse the council for causing a stink. That's got to be the reason she found out about it. Before I have a chance to ask, Shantel continues rambling. "I didn't know what it was when she opened it, and I didn't see it when we were going through the clothes to donate. I'm sorry, Arch. I should've found it first."

"Whoa, Shanti. Calm down." I lounge against the table, propping myself up on my elbows. "Take a breath and repeat what you said but slower."

Her gulp of breath is audible, and I find myself seeking the same calming breath I'm coaching her to take.

"I was helping Tilly sort Jessie's clothes for donation when she found a black box that had a bunch of legal paperwork with yours and Jessie's names on it. I didn't tell her what it was for, but she said she was going to call the firm to find out."

"Fuck," I exhale. I thought for sure it would've been Brahm and his cohort that ruined the surprise.

A surprise Jessie should be giving her.

I slide a hand along my beard, tugging at the stray strands. This bakery was his gift to her for their anniversary, but he didn't make it. It was my responsibility to make sure what needed to be finished was completed.

I failed him.

I'm no stranger to being a failure—at least in my parents' eyes—but knowing I let down my brother, and also my best friend, stings in a way I can't describe.

"Arch?" Shantel's wavering voice grabs my attention. "What are you gonna do?"

"What I have to," I reply, pulling a large sheet of draft paper down to start a blueprint for Tilly's bakery.

"How can I help?" she asks just as the network's entertainment agent's number flashes across the screen. Goosebumps raise the hair on my arms. What could they possibly be calling about? Did I mess up something on the application for the carpentry show?

I snap from my daze, sweat forming on my brow. "You can't, but hey—"

"There's gotta be something I can do."

The vibrations in my hand continue.

"Listen, Shanti. I gotta run. Love you"

"No, Ar—"

I swap to the other line, hoping and praying I didn't miss the call. "Hello?" My heart thunders in my chest, and a few beats pass where

I hear nothing but silence. I hold my breath, cursing myself for not hanging up on Shantel sooner.

"Hello, Mr. Wilson?"

A rush of air releases from my lungs. "Yes, I'm here."

"Oh great! We've read over your application and would love for you to come in and do a live audition for the show. Any chance you could be here this weekend?"

I rear back, surprised at her offer. I hadn't expected to even get a call, seeing as I was so close to the cut-off time. Flying out to Tennessee on short notice isn't ideal, but I can make it work.

"Yes," I reply, already tapping out a message to my hardware store employees letting them know I'll be gone. "I can be there. What time and where?"

As I'm sending the message, another one from Tilly comes in. She texted earlier saying we needed to talk, but I thought it was a perfunctory message spurred by Nora's meddling. I start typing out a response but stop myself—again. Now that I know she found the sale paperwork, I need to make sure I have my story in order before I talk to her.

"I'll send you an email with all the details," the woman says with a chipper voice before hanging up.

All the tension releases from my body, and I sag into the aluminum chair in front of the worktop. This opportunity could be my big break, a way to prove I don't need to be a doctor—like the rest of my family—to be worthy of the Wilson last name.

Her email comes through five minutes after the call ends. I open the attachments, noting the outgoing flight they booked for me on Saturday and a return flight for Monday morning. I'll miss Sunday dinner, and Tilly's birthday celebration, but I need this. She won't care that I'm not there, and I'm not sure I'm ready to see her yet either. At least not until I can think through what I need to say to her.

My footsteps are lighter as I stroll into my office, drop my phone on the desk, and unroll the draft paper along the surface. Photos of me, Jessie, and my brother Sebastian are hung on the wall, memories of laughter and the chaos of three young boys growing up in the suburbs of South Texas. My gaze slides to another picture—one I hate looking at yet can't manage to let go—of me, Jessie, and Tilly. The Three Musketeers. Jessie's in the middle of us—like he's always been—but while they're both staring at the camera with big smiles on their faces, I'm captivated by Tilly's effervescent charm.

A knot lodges in my throat as I stare down at the picture, and shame washes over me. It's been more than five years, but my heart still does that funny thing when I think about what could've been years ago had I not felt this overwhelming debt to Jessie.

My ribs squeeze tight, and disgust pours into my sternum. I shake my head, lip curling at myself for letting envy seep into my thoughts. Jessie saved my life. And I made him a promise long ago that I wouldn't interfere, that I would let these feelings I've had for Tilly since we met dissolve.

Just because he's gone doesn't mean she's meant for me now.

Blinking away the wetness on my lashes, I grab a pencil and get to work on a blueprint, ensuring I can at least keep the promise of constructing Tilly's bakery by the beginning of the year.

Chapter Four
Tilly

Life may be about dancing in the rain, but only for those fortunate souls who have never encountered an unexpected storm in San Antonio. The ceaseless rain nearly topples me over as I cross the street, seeking refuge under the sun-bleached awning of my favorite coffee shop. The familiar scents of hazelnut and cinnamon flow out of the small café as I head inside, heralding a sense of peace to what has been a chaotic morning. A new patchwork tapestry hangs on the wall beside a dozen bedazzled crosses, the muted sound of mariachi music playing through the stereo behind the barista.

"Caramel macchiato," Violet says, placing the cup on the counter for another customer. My mouth waters picturing the flavors bursting on my tongue. Usually I'd love a frothy drink like that, but on a day like today, where I *need* to feel close to Jessie, simply drinking his favorite flavored latte draws his memory so close I can almost imagine he's there beside me.

My phone vibrates in my hand, and I catch a glance of the notification.

Shantel: Boy, do I have a present for you!

I roll my eyes, still perturbed at her for the subterfuge leaving my house the other day. Curious, I swipe the screen and am ambushed by another dating profile she deemed good enough to send me. It's like ever since I made the decision to get my life back on track, she assumes that means I'm ready to start dating again.

"Tilly?" Violet calls, snapping my attention away from the shirtless, blond-haired man on my phone.

"Yeah?"

She shakes the cup with her thick brows raised. "Here's your drink."

"My drink?" I ask, dumbfounded. "I didn't order yet."

She stares at me like I'm talking gibberish and says, "Traffic light earrings, hair in space buns, comes in Tuesdays and Thursdays around ten for a peppermint latte." She shrugs. "Figured it was easier to just have it ready."

My cheeks heat. Have I become that predictable? I step forward and grab the cup, warmth encompassing my hand as I wordlessly offer her the debit card from my pocket.

"It's on the house," Rosie, the elderly owner says with a wide smile, highlighting the deep wrinkles at the corner of her brown eyes as she comes to the counter. "Did you bring me more cupcakes?"

"Thank you." Appreciating the kind gesture, I tuck my card into my pocket. Jessie's life insurance policy left me with more than enough to live on for the rest of my life, but I won't touch it. I'd rather use the money I get baking desserts for my parents' restaurants to supply any needs I might have. "I need to pick up some ingredients, but I'll bring some by tomorrow."

"When are you going to stop dragging your ass and finally open your own bakery?" She pins me with a cold stare and pinched lips, the look of a woman who means business. "I need my mango habanero cupcakes daily."

I laugh at her bluntness, reminded of something Jessie said before he passed. This was his favorite coffee shop. He always said the owner reminded him of his mother and her candor, never one to blanch away from speaking their mind. My heart simultaneously warms and withers with the memory.

"Maybe one day." I sigh and gulp down a swig of the latte, allowing the overly sweet peppermint drink to sooth my rain-chilled bones. Since graduating culinary school, I've made ends meet by supplying the bakery cases in my parents' restaurants with old-fashioned pies, red velvet cakes, and an assortment of cookies, but I can't lie that I die a little more inside each time.

"One day soon, por favor." She frowns at a overcooked pan dulce in her small display.

Stifling a chuckle, I stop a moment to thank her again before leaving. With the surprise rainstorm now over, sunlight glistens on the ground as I head toward my car. My phone rings the moment I'm safely inside.

I don't have to check my Bluetooth to know it's Shantel calling.

"Happy Dirty Thirty," she yells before I even have a chance to say hello, drowning out the slap of my windshield wipers.

I quickly lower the volume. "Thanks, Shanti. What's up?"

"Did you see the picture I sent?" The giddiness in her tone makes me cringe. Setting your brother's widow up on a dating app surely can't be normal.

"I did." I check my mirrors, catching sight of a couple locked in a passionate embrace in the car behind me. A lightning bolt shoots through my chest at the memory of Jessie's kiss. Opening the glovebox, I shove my hand inside in search of a pair of sunglasses to block out the sun—and the couple.

A tire pressure gauge, old chargers, and a bunch of folded papers tumble out of the messy compartment. The last time Jessie borrowed my car when his was in the shop, he told me I should clean it out, said it looked like a Buc-ee's exploded inside it. I never got around to emptying it. I gather the contents to shove them back inside when my gaze lands on the disheveled paperwork. Flipping it open, I find a loan application from a bank I've never been to.

Where did this come from?

"And?" Shantel's exasperated voice steals my attention, huffing as if she's asked this twice. "What did you think?"

I think it's been less than two years, I mouth, trying to keep my tongue in check.

"He's alright, I guess." Paperwork forgotten, I merge onto the road, headed toward my mother-in-law's house. "If you like guys who can, and I quote, 'bench-press you better than your ex.'"

She snorts. "Alright, you got me there. But that doesn't negate the fact that we need to get you back out there."

"Shantel," I chide.

"Tilly," she sighs. "It's time."

"*I know*," I emphasize. "But—"

"No buts. I miss Jessie too. Every damn day. But he'd want you to move on and keep this momentum," she pauses, static filling the air when I don't reply. "You deserve to be happy and for all your dreams to come true, but you've gotta get out of this...this cycle you're stuck in."

Sunlight peeks through the clouds, and the cake charm on my bracelet shimmers—a reminder of the man who loved me with his entire soul. A thousand tiny knives stab at my throat. Jessie always encouraged my hopes and dreams. We'd lay out on the deck at night, talking about me starting a bakery where I could try out new flavors along with some of my mom's old recipes. But between him starting his business, and me finishing culinary school, it never seemed to be the right time.

Shantel's right, but I can't find the words to reply. Her brother was everything to me. How can she expect me to move on when no one can ever measure up to the man he was?

"I just want to help," she says. "You've been a hermit lately, and with Archer working so much..."

My selective hearing kicks in the moment she mentions Archer's name. He still hasn't messaged or called me back.

"Where are you anyway?" she asks.

"Just left Rosie's."

A humming noise comes through the speaker as if she's contemplating something. "Jessie loved that old lady and her peppermint lattes. What'd you get?"

My mouth fills with sand as I try to come up with a lie to tell her. She knows I don't like peppermint lattes, but it's become part of my routine, a way to feel closer to Jessie when the days feel particularly hard to get through.

Like my thirtieth birthday he should be here to celebrate.

I struggle to come up with anything but a lie. "I dropped off some cupcakes and she yelled at me about opening my own bakery. You know, a typical Tuesday."

She harrumphs. "Well, she's not wrong. But that'll all be solved soon enough."

"Huh?" I ask.

"Shit..." She pauses, talking to someone I can't hear in the background. "I gotta go get ready, but I'll see you at Mom's for your birthday dinner."

"Uh, okay." My forehead creases at her abrupt change in subject and the way she's hustling me off the phone.

"Hey Til," she says before hanging up.

"Yeah?"

"Do something special for yourself today."

Even though she can't see me, I roll my eyes. What's the point of doing something special when the one person you want to spend your birthday with isn't here anymore?

"Sure," I reply. "I'll see you later, Seester."

Rain starts up again, pelting the windshield as I wait for the light to change, contemplating Shantel's words. Her heart is in the right place, but I'm not sure I'm ready yet. How does one know they're ready to move on after something tragic happens? If there's an answer to that question, I have yet to find it.

Rosie's comment about dragging my ass comes back to mind. I'm not sure how she even knew owning a bakery was a dream of mine, but if I could do something for myself, give myself one gift, it would be the bakery Jessie and I dreamed up under the stars.

That thought follows me the entire way to Nora's driveway. Snatching the old loan paperwork from my glovebox, I Google what it would take to get a business loan. I'm not as business savvy as Jessie was, but I'm sure it shouldn't be too difficult.

Chapter Five
Tilly

I'm all blues and no clues as I leave the bank, stuffing the thick stack of paperwork into my floral crossbody purse. My head spins with everything necessary to acquire a simple small-business loan, and there's a small chance the fluttering inside my stomach isn't excitement but nausea. When Jessie was alive, we calculated start-up, equipment, and overhead costs for my dream bakery location. I had my business plan all in order, my dreams so close I could taste the sweet icing of success, but we could never find a good location.

A soft chiming emanates from my purse. I shuffle through it to grab my phone and slice my finger along the loan paperwork, cursing at the sting. This day keeps getting better. Without glancing at the caller, I answer.

"Hello?" I cringe at the brashness in my voice.

"Hey sweetpea," my mother-in-law says.

My shoulders curve in, immediately embarrassed by the tone I answered with. I clear my throat, trying to shake away the tension riding my vocal cords. "Hey Nora."

"Are you home?" she asks.

A frown tugs at the corners of my mouth. "Just left the bank downtown."

"I hope everything's okay."

I inhale, hoping disappointment doesn't seep into my voice. "It's fine. I talked to someone about getting a loan to start a new bakery location."

Her sharp gasp melds my feet to the cement. "No," she breathes.

"No? What do you mean *no*?"

The phone crackles in my ear like she's holding it against her chest. Her animated voice muffles as she argues with someone in the background.

"We can talk about it at dinner tonight," she says. "Would you mind picking up my pottery since you're already downtown?"

"Didn't Shantel pick it up the other day after she left my house?"

"She had a meeting she couldn't be late for, and if the bowl isn't picked up today, I'll have to wait until next month when the owner is back from vacation," Nora says, coughing into the speaker.

I sigh into the phone, inwardly cursing my sister-in law. Nora doesn't ask me for much. She could have cut ties after Jessie passed, but she and Shantel have been my rock and support system through everything. This is the least I can do, even if I'd rather go home and wallow in my misery with a pint of ice cream.

"You know what," she interrupts my negative thoughts, "don't worry about the bowl. I can ask Archer to pick it up."

Archer's name twists the knots in my stomach even tighter.

"No," I reply too harshly. "I'm already down here."

"Okay." Her voice fades, mumbling words to someone else, another uninvited guest to the conversation like my late husband's best friend. "I'll see you soon."

Thankfully, the pottery shop is just a few blocks away from where I'm at now, and I get to pass by the building I always dreamt would be my bakery—had someone not nabbed the space before I could.

Canopies and wide umbrellas are set up in preparation for the weekend farmers market, but thankfully it's early enough there aren't a ton of people congregating in the area. I pass a few owners opening their stores, but otherwise encounter only delivery drivers hauling beer from their trucks.

The warmth from the red brick seeps through my worn sandals, the Texas heat bearing down on my exposed neck. I creep toward the plywood covering the door of the building. Whoever leased the building never opened it, a dick move in my humble opinion. I listen closely for any chatter or tools clanking together. When the only sounds I hear are the cars passing behind me, it's clear no one is here.

Standing in front of the spot where I imagined my career would start, I place a hand over my stomach and will the knots to loosen. I close my eyes and my dream bakery comes alive. Black and white checkered floors leading to the counter with a built-in bakery case. Persimmon lemon pinwheel cookies, dark chocolate habanero cupcakes, and my mom's favorite pie flavors lining the shelves beside a metal, old-school register that makes the 'ca-ching' sound when opened. Tea cups and saucers to dip fig biscotti and Italian cookies, an area to teach kids' baking classes off to the side...basically everything I've dreamed of.

Nearly two years ago, I passed by this exact spot with my husband and made a wish that I could open my own bakery here.

Today, I stand in front of it as a widow with only a desperation that the last year never happened—that I could change my stupid wish of starting my own business to one that would give me Jessie back.

A voice in the back of my head reminds me that though there's no magic that can reverse time, it's still possible to make my dream of owning a bakery come true—even if it's not in the location I originally wanted. I don't care how difficult the loan process is. I *will* get my life back on track and complete the dreams I set out for myself, the ones Jessie knew I could achieve.

My hand hangs heavy at my side, the comforting weight of my wedding ring drawing my attention. I bat away tears that threaten to fall and spin it around my finger, soothed by the good memories it brings to mind.

With one last look at the building where I should be selling sweet treats, I head down the road. Hair raises on my arms when I see the mass of people hanging around the square. I scan the crowd for a way to pass through without touching anyone—even the thought of someone accidentally bumping me chafes—but there's no space. I'm embarrassed and frozen on the outskirts, waiting for a clear path as I try to calm my jitters. A walkway opens near the food hall, and I breathe a sigh of relief as I scurry toward the entrance.

Careful not to set off my touch anxiety, I stay away from the more densely packed area in front of the jazz bar, skirting the crowd, and make it to The Tiny Finch without being touched; in my book, that's a success.

The ceramic shop is thankfully empty of patrons. Quicker than expected, I pay for Nora's avant-garde bowl and get on the road to Sunday dinner. Traffic is light as I drive toward Alamo Heights, where the homes range from luxurious mansions to quaint one-story houses with high price tags.

I turn onto Nora's street and find Archer's green F-150 parked in my usual spot in her driveway. Sweat coats my palms and I consider driving back home to pretend I came down with a stomach bug. Only it's pointless. I have to face him eventually—he has the answers I need.

Grabbing the box of treats and Nora's pottery, I climb out of the car and nudge the door shut with my hip. Archer isn't inside the truck, but the leatherbound journal he carries around like a Bible sits on the dash along with a pair of sunglasses.

My stomach knots standing on the front porch as I rehearse the answers to the questions I know they'll ask. *Yes, I'm eating. No, I don't want to swipe right on his profile. And yes, I totally made his side of the bed.* That last one would be a lie. I still haven't managed to fully make the bed.

Put your big girl pants on, Tilly, I grumble, still considering leaving the treats and pottery on the doorstep and going home so I don't have to deal with Archer's awkward silence across the dinner table.

"Are you gonna go in or stand there all day?" I startle backwards at Archer's gravelly voice—as unmistakable as it is unwelcome—and trip over the lip in the concrete.

The bowl and desserts slip from my hands, and I dive for Nora's pottery, saving it from an untimely demise on the cement steps. The same can't be said for my lemon bars. My freshly scraped knuckles sting, but that's nothing compared to the ache of discovering the bracelet Jessie bought me lying in their ruins. Thank God it can be cleaned, though.

"Where the hell did you come from?" I yell, voice a touch too high as I crouch to pick up the mess, clutching my bracelet and the lemon bar goo now on the chain.

"My truck." The sarcasm in his voice makes me grit my teeth. "Are you okay, Space Buns?"

I jerk back at his use of the nickname he gave me in college. It used to be endearing, making me feel part of the cool crowd, but now it grates on my already worn-down nerves.

I clear the majority of the lemon goop off my bracelet and reattach it to my wrist while counting backward to calm down. Once upon a time, I would've laughed about this with him, maybe even punched him in the shoulder playfully, but those times are long gone, swept away like our caps on the windy day Archer, Jessie, and I graduated from UTSA.

I grab the dessert box and clean up the remnants of my hard work.

"I'm fine," I reply, dusting off the gravel embedded in my palms.

"What're these?" He collects the papers that fell out of my purse.

"They're nothing." Heart thundering inside my chest, I snatch the papers from his hands without looking at him. "You know, you could help, seeing as it's your fault."

Even I bristle at the bite in my voice. I have no clue how to navigate this weird dynamic between us where we're either snapping at each other or ignoring each other completely.

He grunts. "It's not my fault you're so jumpy."

Tension bunches at the back of my neck. I should bill him for the massage I'll be needing after this interaction. "Why have you been ignoring my messages?"

"I don't know what you're talking about."

I glance up at him with fire in my eyes, but he's looking off to the side with his tongue in his cheek like he can't even manage to make eye contact while he lies to me.

"You know, I thought you'd outgrow your asshole routine after graduation, but I guess not." I throw a piece of a lemon bar at him and divert my eyes back to the mess. When Jessie and I started dating, Archer distanced himself. At first, I thought it was because he felt like a third wheel, but it became more apparent as time went on that it was me he had a problem with.

He shrugs. "I was busy. Must've forgotten."

"Sure, you did. Like you forgot my birthday party." The words slip out before I filter them, and my cheeks burn at my admission.

His voice softens as he crouches down to help me clean. "I didn't think you'd want me there."

Swallowing would be a good idea, but my tongue is too heavy in my mouth. *Did* I want him there? College me would've said yes in a split second. But me after years of cold shoulders where there used to be nothing but warmth hesitates.

He fills in the silence. "I had important stuff I needed to get done."

"It's fine if you didn't wanna come." Unable to meet his gaze, I keep my eyes focused on the ground. "You don't have to make an excuse."

"I'm not making an excuse. Some of us have to work for a living."

I bite down on my lip, half trying to stop myself from cursing him out and half trying to stop myself from crying. Letting Archer see he's affecting me in any way is the worst possible thing I could do. He's only happy when he knows he's pissed me off.

Foregoing a remark, I open the door to Nora's and swing it shut behind me. Archer curses. I smile knowing I managed to hit him, as intended. Serves him right.

"Is that you, Tilly?" Shantel yells from the kitchen. "Mom, she's here."

Nora shuffles into the entryway, her long gray braids swinging behind her. Her smooth brown skin is devoid of any wrinkles, and the smile she beams at me takes over her whole face. As far as mothers-in-law go, I hit the jackpot.

"Tilly, my dear. You look beautiful." She tilts her head in acknowledgment to me and moves toward Archer, embracing him in a long hug. Even a year after Jessie's death, she knows I still can't bear to be touched. No skin-to-skin contact, not soft hugs or handshakes.

When your husband dies with his arms wrapped around you, it makes it hard to ever want anything else to brush along your skin.

I nearly gave the EMTs a heart attack when I screamed as they tried to assess me at the scene, and then I refused to allow the doctors or nurses to touch me at the hospital. I thought the desire for human touch would eventually return, but it never did. The therapist called it "touch starvation," but to me it's more like memory saving.

"I brought dessert bars, but *someone* scared me outside and they went everywhere." My eyes dart to Arch, but his focus is on the ceiling.

"As long as they didn't fall into the mud they're fine." Nora waves a hand in the air. "Why don't you take them in to Shantel while I chat with Archer."

Recognizing the dismissal, I head into the kitchen.

"Are those your new recipe?" Shantel steps away from the steaming pot and reaches for the box in my hands before pulling her hands back. I place the box on the counter so she can pick through them.

Her eyes close and she does a little shoulder shimmy. "These are absolutely yummy." She reaches for another but the pot boiling over steals her attention. "Did I hear Arch out there too?"

"Yeah," I grumble. "He parked in my spot then had the audacity to scare the shit out of me on the front porch."

"I'll never understand y'alls relationship." She snorts. "I'm sure working on the bakery will help you guys hash out your problems."

I blanch at her insinuation. Nora must've told her about our conversation from earlier. "I'd rather dip my hands in acid than be forced to work with the iceman out there."

The creak of the wood floor and the exasperated sigh are the only indicators we aren't alone. The man in question stands with his lips pinched, eyebrows furrowed, and an emotion I can't place in his eyes.

With a frown, he turns and leaves the room, taking all the air in my lungs with him.

Chapter Six
Tilly

Sunday dinners used to be filled with a table set for seven, lots of laughter, and a feast that could rival any holiday celebration. Shantel would bring her husband, I came with Jessie, and Archer would bring whatever flavor of the week suited his fancy, at least until Deidre, who surprisingly stuck around. We'd sit around the table slinging jokes, eating good food, and playing a game or two of poker until we were filled with fun and family.

The new four-person table is swallowed by the large room, no longer filled with spouses and laughter. I should probably feel guilty, but I'm relieved I'm no longer subjected to Archer's dates, all placating me with "I'm sorry" and "It must be hard to be a widow" and "I can't imagine how sad you are."

In all honesty, the smaller table makes me grit my teeth because I have to be more aware of my body so as not to touch anyone. But there are no more empty seats. No seat beside me to remind me that I shouldn't be at this table alone.

"Can you say the prayer, Archer?" Nora asks.

"Sure." Archer nods and lays his poker chip on the table. He carries that token with him everywhere, like he's holding onto a souvenir from a wild night gambling with a woman. I'd bet he never got her name, and that the chip is the only thing he has left to remember her by. But Archer isn't the sentimental type. He doesn't look back at situations and wish they could be different.

"Amen." My momentary lapse is snapped by Archer's voice.

"How was your week, Tilly?" Nora spoons fragrant collard greens onto her plate before passing the bowl my way.

"It was fine." I shrug, surprised that she didn't immediately bring up the loan discussion. I had planned on telling them more about the process, but with Archer here I don't need to hear his negative comments on my business prowess. I'll wait until the end of the night to corner him and ask him about the paperwork I found. "I dropped some of my new lemon bars off at the restaurant."

"I'm glad you're baking new items again," she says. "I bet they're fantastic."

Getting back to my passion took a lot longer than I expected after Jessie died, but therapy is helping me climb out of that hole of grief, reminding me it's okay to still enjoy things from my old life.

Jessie loved when I baked, pretended he was eating at Laduree in Paris any time I set a new recipe in front of him. After he passed, I spent months in a haze of grief, missing him and sick to my stomach any time I tried to bake.

"What did everyone think of your new bars?" Shantel asks around a mouthful of salad.

"They loved them."

"They probably have no taste buds," Archer teases.

"Archibald Wilson," Nora chides just as Shantel mutters, "Ass."

I grip my fork, willing it to stay in the juicy piece of ham I've skewered rather than lodging it into his eye. As best friends, me, Archer, and Jessie would playfully gibe each other, but that was the past and the camaraderie to carry a remark like that hasn't existed between us in a few years.

"Not everyone has a child's palate like you do." I meet his stare and hold it. I haven't taken the time to truly look at him since he scared me on the doorstep. My lips snap together when I take in the beard he's grown, the soft wrinkles at the corner of his green eyes, and the splotches of paint covering his flannel shirt.

He looks a wreck.

The little voice in my head reminds me that I'm not the only one who might still get smacked by the waves of grief, sometimes unable to take care of myself.

"I have a very sophisticated palate," he replies, then adds, "For good food."

"Be nice, you two," Nora chides.

Archer holds his hands up in surrender like he's doing me a favor when he's the one slinging insults. I roll my eyes and shove a forkful of potatoes into my mouth just as a notification from a dating app—one of the three Shantel downloaded—dings on my phone.

"Someone's got a match," Shantel singsongs.

My face heats as Archer and Nora's wide eyes land on me. With a swipe, I mute the sound and look down at my plate as if the mashed potatoes are a piece of artwork.

"A match?" Archer asks.

"It's noth—"

"Dating app match," Shantel interjects unhelpfully.

Flames lick at my cheeks and I inhale a sharp breath. Archer's bunched eyebrows and pinched lips cause my throat to dry. Does he—like me—feel like I'm betraying Jessie by considering dating so soon after he passed?

I ignore the obvious tension in the air and focus my attention on Shantel. "Did you get that meeting you were working for?"

"Of course." She sets her fork down and tells an animated story about the high-profile hair stylist she's been trying to get to come work at the salon that fills the awkward silence.

The side of my face is hot, and I know Archer, with his perpetual frown, is staring at me.

After dinner, I focus on tidying the dining area while everyone else cleans the kitchen. My mind floats back to the mysterious paperwork and the loan. If I can't get it, what will I do? What location should I pick since my dream one is already leased?

Raised voices lead me to the swinging kitchen door. My name floats through the thin wood, Archer's sharp tone urging me to put my ear against it to listen.

"When are you going to tell her?" Shantel whispers.

"When I'm finished," Archer sternly replies.

"No, Archer." Nora's tone is brisker than I've ever heard it. "She needs to know now. For Pete's sake, she spoke with a loan officer already."

My heart thuds in my chest, and a sinking feeling ekes into my stomach. *What are they talking about? Me?* I look down at my feet, willing them to move from the spot where they've cemented themselves.

"She'll want to have a say in it," Shantel chimes in just as I'm about to confront them.

"I know what she'll want, and it'll get done."

"What happens when you leave?" Nora talks over Shantel who says, "What makes you think you know what she wants?"

"She won't care that I'm leaving," Archer says. "I already pissed her off by missing her birthday dinner last week."

My brain short circuits and steals my breath. Blood pounds in my ears as I push through the door.

"You're leaving?" I ask, incredulous. "To where?"

Three pairs of eyes focus on me.

Archer's hands are perched on his hips, and he sucks his teeth in annoyance. "Tennessee."

"For what?" A weird feeling slides into my chest, trying to find a place to settle. I shouldn't care that he's leaving. He's basically been a ghost in my life since his sister's wedding four years ago, and if I'm honest, since Jessie and I started dating, so why do I feel like he's another person abandoning me?

My mom was my best friend, and cancer took her away before we had a chance to know each other as adults. It took Dad's spirit with her. The man I grew up with, the one who supported and encouraged me, became a shell of who he was. He threw all his energy and attention into managing the restaurants he ran with my mother.

I never understood it until I lost Jessie.

Routine is key to keeping the grief at bay. You can almost trick your mind into thinking everything is normal, that your spouse is simply at the store or away on a business trip. It's why it's been so difficult to make his side of the bed, or to even consider removing my wedding ring.

When no one answers me, I demand again, "Why are you leaving?"

"I have an opportunity for a carpentry position," is all he says, eyes filled with...is that regret?

"Oh, that's great." My neck throbs, pain accompanying the dry swallow I force myself to take. "So, what's the issue?"

"Tell her." Shantel's brows rise to her hairline.

"Tell me what?"

Archer's knuckles crack as he leans on the counter and silently hangs his head.

"Tell me what?" I repeat.

"Archer," Nora pleads.

He curses and shakes his head like he's being forced to give up the nuclear codes.

"Before Jessie…" Archer pauses and his shoulders lift with a deep breath. "Before he passed, he asked me to fix up your bakery."

"I don't have a bakery." I add the *yet* inside my mind.

"You do," Shantel says, a wide smile on her face.

Frustrated, I press my fingers into my temples and rub. My head throbs as I roll the tension from my shoulders and speak through gritted teeth. "Stop talking in circles and just tell me what you mean."

Nora walks toward me like she's going to embrace me, but instead she fists her hands at her side to stop herself. "The bakery spot you wanted at The Pearl. It's yours."

"I'm so confused. What do you mean it's mine?" I cross my arms and dig my fingers into my ribs, staving off the weird feelings bouncing around my chest when I look at Archer.

"It was supposed to be a surprise." A muscle flutters in his jaw. "He took care of everything."

Emotions overload my throat, and tears burn my eyes.

The paperwork.

"Is that what the paperwork is for?" I ask Archer before turning to Shantel. "And you knew the other day when you saw it?"

Her lips roll in, and her eyes fall to the floor as if she's ashamed. Archer does nothing except nod.

"No." I force the word out, but I don't even know what I'm saying no to. Spots dance behind my eyes and cotton clogs my ears. A gasp fills the room, and it takes a moment before I realize the sound came from me.

Nora lays a hand on my arm, and I recoil, wiping the wetness from my cheeks. Through tear-filled eyes, Shantel and Archer share a look that conveys a message I'm not privy to, but all I can think about is Jessie.

Visions of us standing in front of my bakery, large shears in hand to cut the red ribbon signifying I'm finally open for business, sneak into my mind. People chatting at wooden tables with colorful cupcake liners resined into the top, sharing a slice of cake and coffee. Flour-nosed children laughing as they pipe icing onto each other during my kids' baking classes.

Every dream I had for my bakery explodes out of the tiny box I tucked them into when I found out the location had been taken. The bittersweet feeling is overshadowed by the betrayal sinking to my gut.

They kept this from me...for almost two years.

Anger swells in my gut. I stagger backward, pushing against the swinging door, almost falling to the ground as I run to the table to grab my keys.

"Wait," Nora begs.

"He wanted to give it to you for your first wedding anniversary," Shantel yells to my retreating back.

"Tilly." Archer's voice sounds off behind me but I've already made it to the driveway, unlocking my door with expert speed. The quiet of the car envelops me, and I cough, sputtering out the breath I've been holding. Archer flies down the front steps and over to my car.

"Til," he rasps like emotion has his throat in its clutches too, but why would it? Why does he care how I feel? He hasn't cared about my feelings or dreams since he dogged my baking to his friends at his sister's wedding then disappeared from my life after Jessie died.

"Leave me alone, Arch."

He knocks on the window, eyes wide and worried. "Please, don't leave."

Swiping snot and tears away, I turn the ignition and crack my window. "I just need some space and fresh air." I put the car into gear and back up. In my rearview mirror, Nora and Shantel hold each other on the porch, and Archer stands in the spot where I left him, where I left the remnants of my already tattered heart.

Chapter Seven
Archer
Present

*D*ear Seb,

I used to think you were cheesy for writing me encouraging letters while you were away at college, but I can't deny rereading the letters has helped me miss you less. It's probably why I finally started writing back. I know it's been a few weeks since I wrote in this book, but I've been busy trying to figure out what the hell to do with my life. You'd forgive me if you were here, right?

You probably don't care, but Tilly's so mad at me. In her defense, I'm mad at myself too. I didn't want to miss her birthday dinner, but I had to take the meeting with the producers. It was perfect because I needed the morale boost after my meeting with the City Council went south. Mr. Brahm is still the same stickler he was when you and I got in trouble for TP'ing the principal's house that one Halloween. He got the whole council riled up and the mayor got involved. He told me if I don't open the bakery by December he's going to highly suggest I sell it.

I've been working to the bone trying to get Tilly's bakery up to code, but without Jessie, it's just me. I'll have to balance working on the bakery with the jobs I'm already contracted for, along with flying out to Tennessee for interviews with the network's people.

I'm excited for what feels like the first time in years, and I know how pathetic that sounds, but I am. This HGTV carpentry job could set me up *for life, make my carpentry business a household name, and maybe I'll even be able to hire another guy or two to run a workshop. But Tennessee is far away. I don't want to abandon Nora. She's already lost so much. She told me yesterday she was glad she still had one son to dote on. Why couldn't we have parents like that? Ones that loved us despite the idiotic mistakes we made.*

I guess you don't really have to deal with that anymore, right? Fuck, I'm an ass. Anyway, Tilly's been her usual old self, giving me the cold shoulder, and it's bothering me more than it should. Most times I've been able to brush off her lack of interaction, but with me potentially leaving, it's getting harder.

And now I have Brahm and the mayor up my ass about opening the bakery. Had I known there'd be a deadline to open the location, I wouldn't have bought it.

Who am I kidding? I would've bought the building beside it so she could have more space. Even though I try to hide it, I hate the chasm that's opened between us since Jessie died. It's like he was the gravitational pull that held us together when all we wanted to do was push apart. Now that he's gone, Tilly and I can't manage to stay in our own orbits, constantly bumping into each other, causing unintentional, and sometimes intentional, damage any time we're around each other.

I guess that's just part of my personality. I'm always the one ruining things. Or at least that's what our parents think. Can you believe during dinner last week Dad told me I'm damaging the family image? Like because I'm not a surgeon I'm sullying the Wilson name. Like always, Mom and Claire didn't defend me. They sat rigid in their seats, forcing roasted cauliflower into their mouths so they didn't have to speak up. They're still just as scared of him as you were, but I'm sick of it.

Why'd you have to be an idiot? Why couldn't you have just told them you were struggling? Why do I have to bear the brunt of the anger that should be directed at you? Fuck, man. Why do I have to be angry at you?

I'm so mad at you for leaving me. For making dumb decisions for people who only wanted to use you. I miss you and our late-night talks. Smoking weed and drinking on the roof when Mom and Dad were on call. I wish we would've made better decisions. Maybe I wouldn't be the fuck up I am now, and you'd be sitting here sharing a beer with me.

If I get this job in Tennessee, I'm leaving this whole city behind. I won't have to come to dinner and be berated for decisions you made or sit across from Tilly at Nora's and wonder why you thought I didn't deserve her. I'll meet new people, ones who don't know me as Archibald Wilson or look at me and feel nothing but disdain. Maybe I'll settle down and have a family. I legit just had a cold chill at the thought. That'd be somethin' right? Me, a husband? A dad? I don't deserve any of that if you aren't here to have it too.

Alright, I'm too drunk to be making any sense, but know I love you and miss you bro. Hope you're doing some fancy surgery that'll give you endless praise up in Heaven.

-Arch

Chapter Eight
Tilly

A knocking at the front door grows louder, nearly overpowering the whiny voice of Bella Swan begging Edward Cullen not to leave her in the forest alone. Clad in fluffy dinosaur slippers with a piece of raspberry chocolate truffle cake, I open the door to Shantel standing on my front porch.

"You look a wreck." She pauses, taking in the state of my messy bun and the Curious George pajamas I haven't changed out of in two days. "And I mean that in the nicest way possible."

"Thank you for lavishing such compliments on my attire," I deadpan and keep the door cracked. If she thinks that about my appearance, she'd pass out if she saw my living room.

Whoever said there's beauty in the breakdown lied.

Sometimes it takes more effort than I have to even change my shirt, let alone clean the house. I've been told it's normal to fall into these spells, but I thought I was getting better. All it took to set me back was for Archer to show up again and throw a wrench in my plans by telling me about the bakery.

"Come on, Til. Let me in." Shantel holds up a grocery bag. "I brought Dutch Bros. and frozen pizza."

Pizza. The secret passcode to enter. Damn she's good.

"No judging." I inch the door open.

"Scout's honor." She salutes me in a definite *not* Scout's honor, and I laugh, ushering her in before Mrs. Jackson across the street senses I've opened the doors. I am not ready for her to come pester me again about joining whatever neighborhood club the widows of Alamo Heights have formed.

Her sharp intake of breath shows me just how far down the rabbit hole I've fallen. I take in the state of my living room, the stack of cups, the crusted over plates filled with food I couldn't force myself to eat, the pile of clothes in the corner.

My internal messiness has spilled over to my surroundings.

"Umm," she starts, opening and closing her mouth like she's unsure what to say. "How can I help?"

The tension inching my shoulders to my ears releases, and I hang my head and rub away the tears prickling my eyes. "Honestly, I don't know."

She points to the couch. "Finish Depressing Moon while I pop this pizza in the oven."

I fall to the cushions and press play on my comfort movie. She busies herself with cleaning while I struggle to focus on the scene in front of me. My life is a mirror image of the main character sitting on a chair staring out the window as months pass. The hole inside my chest didn't just tear open when Archer told me Jessie bought my bakery.

It exploded.

Every defense against the sucking tendrils of grief I've cultivated disappeared in the snap of a finger, and the remnants of what I had—of what I lost—came barreling in, knocking me back to the moment I woke up with Jessie's stiff arms around me.

By the time the ding of the oven sounds, my living room is clean, the dishes are done, and the smell of pepperoni, sausage, and Canadian bacon wraps itself around me like a warm blanket.

"Shower, then pizza." Shantel turns off the TV and hitches her thumb over her shoulder.

Grumbling, I rise and shuffle toward my room.

"You'll thank me when you smell better," she yells down the hall.

Inside the master bathroom, I stare at the random bottles of cologne, aftershave, and lotion I've yet to be able to part with. Sometimes a scent is enough to trick my brain into thinking Jessie's going to walk through the door at the end of the day.

I know it's time to 'get back out there' but moving on in life isn't as easy as it sounds. I pick up a bottle of his cologne and hold it to my nose, inhaling the scent as if it's his life force. My throat aches, and I clench my jaw as my eyes brim with tears.

On my side of the sink, a new pair of pajamas, aloe-infused fuzzy socks, and a stress-relief body wash are laid out for me. I slip into the shower and let the hot water beat down on my neck. Two days' worth of shame and sadness slip away, swirling down the drain with the last of my self-control. Tears and snot mix with water as I crumble to the shower floor, arms wrapped around my knees, crying into the crevasse of my thighs.

Why me? It's the same thing I chanted over and over again when the doctor told me there was no way to stop the unimaginable from happening.

It was just our luck of the draw.

I scoff.

Luck is finding a ten-dollar bill in your car console, or realizing you finally caught your favorite TV show before it's midway through.

It's not having an aneurysm.

Dying before you even knew you needed to say goodbye.

"Tilly?" Shantel's voice floats through the door. "You okay in there?"

"I'm fine," I croak. "I'll be out in a minute."

Grabbing Jessie's body wash, I lather the wash cloth and spread my favorite scent over my body. Bergamot and spice fill the steamy air as I shut off the water and towel dry. My eyes land on the pajama pants Shantel bought me, but without thought my hands reach for the faded Hawthorne Heights shirt Jessie loved. It reaches the tops of my thighs, so I grab a pair of shorts to wear under it and slip into the comfy socks.

I clasp my bracelet back onto my wrist, eyes snagging on the marquise diamond ring sliding down my finger. Jessie picked the perfect jewelry, a testament to how well he knew me. If not for the thin ring guard keeping it secure, the weight I've lost would prevent me from wearing it.

"Feel better?" Shantel asks when I plod into the now spotless living room.

I survey my surroundings. How did she complete all that within an hour when I haven't been able to complete one task for two days?

"I do. Thanks."

Shantel plops onto the sofa and pats the seat beside her. "Sit."

I oblige her request but sit on the far edge with my legs pulled to my chest so we're not touching. She smiles, but her eyes are filled with pity.

"Why are you here?" I ask.

"Because you need me." She shrugs, gaze bouncing around the room. "Why else?"

"I know you've got something to say, so just say it."

She pouts and crosses her arms. "You know me too well."

I tilt my head, urging her on. "What's wrong?"

"Archer needs your help at the bakery."

Instantly my throat closes.

He kept Jessie's gift a secret from me.

They all did.

In the moments when I needed to feel close to him, to remember I still had a portion of him with me, the bakery could've been my solace.

It wasn't listed on any of his will documents. Jessie was the financially smart one and paid all our bills. I never had any need to look through our financials, nor a reason to touch the life insurance money left over after his funeral.

Now not only do I have to deal with the influx of grief and frustration I was going through trying to get a loan for something I apparently already have, but also with the fact that Archer is leaving too. I'm not sure why, but thinking about it gives me indigestion.

"What do you want me to say?" I ask. "Y'all kept this from me for almost two years!"

Shantel blanches at my raised voice and throws her hands in the air. "You stopped baking. Archer went back and forth on what to do with the place because we never thought you'd get back to that person who came alive in the kitchen. Just...please go check it out. He's done a lot of renovating."

"I bet it looks like a dungeon, not a bakery."

A pillow hits me in the face. "It's beautiful. But he needs you to show him where you want things hung."

"I'll show him where he can hang himself," I mumble. Shantel wields another pillow and I throw up my hands. "Okay, okay. I'll stop."

My mind pushes forward like a freight train carrying all the questions I refuse to speak out loud.

Why is he doing this? He doesn't care about me or my feelings. He made that clear at his sister's wedding when he instigated and egged on his friends to give my desserts a bad review. He never had a problem telling Jessie he didn't want to do something, so why is he working on a bakery for a woman he can't stand to be in a room with more than once a week?

His gentle face when he stood outside of my car and begged me to stay pops into my mind. It was the face of the Archer I knew back in college. The one who asked to be my partner in Chemistry. The one who brought me my favorite caramel macchiato on the nights we all stayed up cramming for finals. I saw the caring man I used to call a friend come through the person I've learned to put up my defenses around.

A fluttery feeling wreaks havoc on my stomach, but I push it away. He may have finally told me about the bakery, but it doesn't make up for the way he's pushed me away or his dishonesty over the last year.

Chapter Nine
Archer
Ten Years Ago

Brisk air creeps through the cracked window, sending goosebumps down my arms as I fan the pungent smell of marijuana toward the small opening. Jessie tosses me the empty pizza box like it'll help eliminate the smell faster than the fan already in my hands. Grease from our supreme pizza trickles down my arm, and I lick it up, savoring the taste of garlic, peppers, and onions.

"I think I hear someone." Jessie's eyes shift to the door.

My arms pump faster, and the fear drains away some of my high. If Mom finds out we were smoking again, she'll rip me a new one. Never mind the fact that I got it from her best friend's son, who says he took it from his mother's stash.

Footsteps move closer, someone coughs, and Jessie joins me with a pillow. We move in tandem, arms frantically flapping as we try to push out the smell.

"I told you we should've smoked at the park," I whisper-yell.

His brown eyes narrow in my direction. "We couldn't order pizza to the park."

"Have you ever tried to order pizza to the park?" I cough through the burn in my chest.

"No, but—"

"Kids, kids," a voice says behind us.

Spinning around, I find my brother standing in the open doorway, his blonde hair sticking up like he's done nothing but run his hands through it all evening. His laptop case is haphazardly slung around his shoulder, black slacks looking as fresh as they did this morning when he went to class, but the dark circles under his eyes have reappeared. I don't know how he manages working while attending medical school.

"Dude, you scared the shit out of me." Jessie pulls him in for a bro-hug.

Sebastian falls to the bed, resting his head on the pillow as he shoots off rapid-fire texts. "What're you slackers doing?"

"Slackers?" I ask. "Mom had me fix the garage door since *someone* ran into it the other night."

Jessie groans. "Come on, man. I'm sick of hearing you moan and groan about it."

Sebastian's phone goes off, triple dings echoing through the small room. His attention shifts to the screen, mouth pressed into a pout. He sits up and taps out another message.

"Damn it," he says.

"What's wrong?" I ask, eyes drifting to the TV where a carpentry show I'd love to host is on HGTV. "Your Friday night fling cancel on you again?"

Jessie chuckles. "Who stood you up, Seb?"

"No one," he grunts out.

With his frustration increasing, I take notice of his appearance in a new light. I thought he'd quit taking the pills after the last time, but I guess I was wrong. The state of his disheveled hair shows me he's been dragging his fingers through it, agitated about something, and the dark circles mean he hasn't been sleeping. I told him not to let the pressure of our parents' expectations to be at the top of his class weigh on him, but Sebastian only knows how to be the best.

"What's wrong?" Jessie asks Sebastian.

Sebastian slaps his hands on his thighs and rises from the bed, and the frustration that plagued him a moment ago vanishes. "You stoners wanna go see a movie? I need to chill."

My shoulders relax, but the niggling in the back of my mind keeps me on edge.

"Yeah." I close the window and turn off the TV. "What do you wanna see?"

"An action flick," Sebastian says. "I need to not think for a while."

Jessie karate chops the air. "Hell yeah."

We barrel down the stairs but stop cold when Dad says, "And where do you think you're going?"

I know he's not talking to me because why would he? Ever since I told him I wasn't going to med school he's frozen me out. Having dreams of being the next Ty Pennington isn't a worthy career in his mind. No, it's not me he cares about anymore, but his prized child. The one he's putting so much pressure on that he takes uppers just to stay awake so he can cram more knowledge than required of him into his brain.

A pang shoots through my heart knowing that the full brunt of my parents' expectations are now the anvil weighing down Sebastian. Carrying the family name by becoming a doctor was apparently my responsibility, something I failed at miserably enough I almost flunked out of college before I found what I loved to do.

I sigh. "We're going to a movie."

His focus stays on Sebastian. "Don't you have your second licensing exam coming up?"

Sebastian taps his finger on his head. "It's all crammed in here. I won't let you down."

Dad's frown is more pronounced, but Mom strolls into the room and slips her arm in his. "Let them have a night of fun, Archie. We can relax a little before we're on call."

She shimmies her shoulders in a suggestive move that brings the pizza back up my throat.

"Eww," Jessie says.

"Ditto," Sebastian and I reply simultaneously.

Piling into the car, I relax into the seat and put on some music. Sebastian and Jessie play rock, paper, scissors to decide who'll ride shotgun. Jessie wins.

"We watching the new Tom Cruise flick or the new Statham one?" Sebastian leans between the center console, long arms resting on the backs of our seats.

We all share a look of agreement. "Statham."

We're nearing the theater when traffic comes to a standstill due to an accident. Sebastian types away on his phone while Jessie tries to get the girls in the car next to us to give him their number. My eyes keep flitting back to Sebastian, trying to note any symptoms of withdrawal.

Last time he was a wreck, barely able to focus on a thirty second conversation without fidgeting and sweating.

"Hey...uh, can we stop by the gas station on Wurzbach?" Sebastian asks, gaze not lifting from his phone. "I have to pee."

I groan. "We're almost to the theater."

"Dude, just piss in a bottle," Jessie says.

"I'll fill up your tank and pay for the snacks at the movies," Sebastian replies.

"And we'll get three separate bags of popcorn so there's no weird hand touching going on," I say.

Sebastian nods. "Whatever you want. Just take me to the Corner Store."

Flicking on my blinker, I shift lanes, throwing up a thank you to the nice elderly couple driving twenty miles less than the speed limit for letting me over.

I pull up to a gas pump and Sebastian hops out and heads inside. Jessie comes around the side and leans against the trunk as I set the pump.

"Think he's going to make it to finals without the pills?" he asks.

"Doubt it."

His shoulders droop. Jessie grew up with Sebastian and me. Our families met at the country club, and naturally we became The Three Musketeers. We played sports together, had the same crushes, and even occasionally beat the shit out of each other for fun.

Sebastian's addiction doesn't affect only me.

I know if it wasn't for my parents' expectations he would have made it through med school without any issue, but he's always been a people pleaser. Even the tiniest bit of disapproval from Dad sends him reeling, and Dad wields his power over him as often as he can.

Raised voices off to the side of the convenience store steal my attention. I'd know Sebastian's voice anywhere. Twisting the cap onto the gas tank, I jog to check on my brother while Jessie moves to the front of the car.

A man with baggy clothes is arguing with Sebastian, and instantly I know the reason why he wanted to come to this specific location.

He wanted to score.

"Seb." I come up beside him.

"Go back to the car, Arch." Sebastian waves me away, but I can tell the dealer is tweaking. He's scratching at his skin, pulling at the collar of his shirt, and his eyes look like they're fighting to stay open.

"Here," Sebastian says, handing the man a wad of cash before turning around and walking toward me.

"Really, man?" I ask as we walk back toward the parking lot. "One night. You couldn't wait one night before getting high again?"

He shrugs. "I have a study session tomorrow night with the chick who might beat me for valedictorian. I can't be nodding off. I need to be sharp."

My stomach clenches, twisting tighter. I despise my parents for the pressure they're putting on my older brother, and I wish he had the strength to stand up to them like I did, but that's not him. He's the *good* kid.

Rounding the corner, Jessie comes into view. He's moved the car into a parking space so someone else could use the pump and is leaning on the hood.

Sebastian bumps my shoulder, a slick smile on his face. "After this exam, all I have is Residency then boards. I'll be fine."

I roll my eyes but bump him back.

Jessie rises from the hood of the car, his hands flying in the air, mouth open. Time slows as he lunges toward me and Sebastian. Fear ricochets through me as a loud bang echoes around us. My ears pop, pain bursting at the back of my head when Jessie slams me to the ground.

Disoriented, I scramble to get up, but his body is too heavy. I turn on my side and press my shoulder to the ground, trying to lift him off of me, but my brain is scattered. Blood pools in the gravel where I've just lifted my head, and instinctively my hand reaches behind me to feel the torn skin of my scalp as I stare out at the crowd forming, pointing their fingers at us.

Jessie's scream breaks the fog clogging my ears, and I finally notice Sebastian's limp form beside me, a circle of red spreading out on his shirt.

"Seb," I yell, but my voice sounds far away.

My heart is in my throat, my lungs refuse to fill, and my brain can't process what my eyes are seeing.

Sebastian's breathing is raspy, but he reaches for me and places my hand over the wound. "Put pressure on it."

Tears mix with the blood dripping from my head as I place my hands over his ribcage and press down. He inhales sharply, and all I can do is keep chanting, "Please don't die. I love you, Seb. Please stay."

Sirens wail around us, but my focus is singular. The paramedics and Jessie have to pry me off of Sebastian as I'm sobbing and telling him I love him. I'm shuffled into another ambulance and promised I'll see my brother at the hospital after he's out of surgery.

Chapter Ten
Tilly

No one realizes how dirty ceiling fans can get until they're lying beneath one, watching dust particles float around. I've laid here since last night, contemplating what to do and how to feel about the bakery. All I've been able to come up with is anger.

Anger at everyone for keeping this from me, anger at myself for spending the last year so out of it that I didn't notice something was going on right under my nose, and anger at Jessie for doing something so sweet and then leaving me before I had a chance to show him how happy his gift made me.

Happiness is what I want to feel, but betrayal crowds my chest, pressing against my ribs as I struggle to breathe through the tears. I stare at my wedding ring, lifting it to my first knuckle as if I'm ready to take it off then slamming it back into the webbed part between my fingers.

My phone dings beside me, and thinking it's a text message from Shantel, I grab it and swipe the screen. My social media app opens to the *memories* page. Pictures of me from a decade ago, covered in flour as I baked cookies for a school bake sale with my mom, flood the screen, bringing a smile to my face.

She always believed I had what it took to become a baker, always urged me to chase after my dreams even if someone told me I'd never measure up. It's her voice in my head that reminds me this bakery is a blessing. I just need to get out of my feelings about it being kept a secret.

I continue scrolling and my breath catches in my chest when a picture of me and Archer slides onto the screen. We're sitting beside each other in the library, books spread across the wooden table, laughing about something. The knot in my chest loosens as I think about how easy things used to be between us, how comfortable we were in each other's presence.

We were baby-faced college students hopped up on caffeine and delirious with exhaustion during finals. We spent every waking moment together, and I remember being enraptured by him and his good looks, like every other girl in our graduating class. He was charismatic, funny, and nice to me. He didn't ostracize me for memorizing the periodic table or for my funky clothes, he made it a point to include me in everything he and Jessie did.

The reminder of Jessie barrels through me and I'm right back where I started, wallowing in my grief. On a whim, I delete all the dating apps from my phone. Right now, the only thing I should be focused on is the bakery my husband left me.

Shantel told me before she left that if I want the bakery, it has to be opened by the end of the year or else the city council is going to petition to have me evicted from the spot. I doubt they can actually do that, though I wouldn't put it past them to try.

I remind myself of all the positive things that can come from this: the freedom to make the desserts I want, a store I can decorate however I please, and the chance to make my mom and Jessie proud. It'll all be worth it once I see the open sign in front of my bakery.

My phone chimes with messages from Nora telling me to come over. I force myself to get out of bed and dressed. She doesn't live far, so at least the drive is short.

Nora's house smells of apples and cinnamon—her favorite fall scents—when she opens the door with a wide smile. Inside the foyer, a cascade of white pumpkins are stacked on and around two vintage suitcases, and by the splash of maroon and burnt orange décor across the fireplace mantle in the living room, it's apparent Nora is ready for Autumn—even though temperatures don't get below sixty until at least January in San Antonio.

"Thanks for stopping by." Nora ambles toward the hallway, waving me over with a weathered hand. "Shantel said you might want to check through some of these boxes."

"Boxes?" I set my keys on the hook and follow her.

She ignores my question, continuing to Jessie's old room. A loud thump in the garage startles me. I glance at the closed door, worried her pipes may be about to burst when the clonk sounds off again above me.

"Is something wro—"

"Here you go, pumpkin." She opens Jessie's door, and my mouth pops open at the boxes stacked neatly against the wall.

His entire childhood fits in ten boxes.

"You inspired me to go through his stuff to donate to the local shelter." She stares at the room with a forlorn look, as if the now bare walls are an exact replica of her heart after losing her son. She blinks away a tear, and the corners of her mouth lift as she inhales a cleansing breath. "I've needed to do that for a while now."

Warmth spreads through my chest at the light in her eyes. It wasn't only me that was living with the past, shackled down by the weight of loss, unable to move forward in a life where half of my heart was missing.

Another thump from the ceiling startles me. "What is that?"

Nora huffs. "A leak in the ceiling. Found it the other day when it rained all over my car...inside the garage. Had to call the best handyman in town." She stops outside the doorway and turns back, placing a box of tissues on the long dresser. "If you need anything, let me know."

I watch her walk into the garage, curious as to what handyman she called. Normally, Archer would've been the one summoned, but seeing as his car wasn't in the driveway when I pulled up, she must've hired someone else.

Before I have a chance to get grumpy about everything that happened, I let my gaze fall to Jessie's belongings. My fingers twitch, and heat prickles my skin as I step toward the first box. Last time I went through his stuff, I found paperwork that led to the discovery of the bakery.

What secrets will I find this time?

With a deep breath, I open the first box. Sketch after sketch of characters from Jessie's favorite anime show are piled inside, the orange and yellow colors still vibrant years later. Imagining him lying on his bed watching the cartoon, trying to get the exact curve of Goku's hair correct, makes me smile. I lay a few of my favorites to the side and move on to the next box. Business certificates, licenses, and employee records are inside, and I grab it to drop off to his old business partner who bought his portion of the company after he passed.

Between his retro console collection—a Sega Genesis, an Atari, a Super Nintendo, an N64, an Xbox, and two different Playstations—and his baseball card collection, some kids will be very happy to receive these items. I spend the next hour filtering through his favorite band t-shirts, his educational awards, sports memorabilia, and more trinkets like the box he kept at our house. My husband was very good at organization for his business, but apparently not so much when it came to getting rid of things he didn't need anymore.

A small box in hand, I take one last look at what was my husband's teenage room. It feels different than I expected. There isn't a weight on my shoulders, nor did I need to reach for the tissues the entire time I was rifling through the boxes. A sense of peace overwhelms me, as if he's up in Heaven, cheering me on for keeping my promise to restart my life.

I step out into the hall, closing the door behind me. I don't look back but forward, heading away from the past and toward the future.

A clang inside the garage stops my feet outside the door. Nora's laugh chimes loudly, and I can't help but look inside to see what's going on. She stands at the foot of a ladder with her head tilted toward the ceiling where half of a body disappears into the attic access. The man stretches, and the black tee beneath his flannel shirt rises enough to reveal smooth tan skin covering a ripped abdomen and a deep V disappearing into his pants. Tight Wrangler jeans showcase muscular legs and a round butt, and places I thought long dormant awaken in the pit of my belly.

I'm too busy salivating over the bottom half and how the denim strains against his muscles to realize the handyman is moving down the ladder.

The box slips from my hands, clattering to the ground when my gaze lands on the face attached to the physique I was just admiring. A pair of luminous green eyes ensnare mine, and vomit shoots up my throat as I'm frozen in place.

What the fuck?

Holy shit.

My cheeks heat, and I immediately admonish myself for checking him out. Objectively, I've always known Archer was good-looking. He's an all-American type of guy, and we shared one drunken, passionate kiss in college where he made it clear he wasn't interested in more than friendship. But it's been years since I noticed him in *that* way.

That's what I get for my social media scrolling session this morning. Maybe I should take Shantel up on the offer to set me up on a date.

I blink rapidly, trying to convince myself this isn't happening—that I wasn't just drooling over my husband's best friend.

Snapped from my daze by a cleared throat, I drop to the floor and gather the contents of the box.

"Need some help?" Nora crouches to pick up the items that flew into the garage, and my skin flames in embarrassment.

"Thanks," I murmur, shuffling through excuses that would explain what just happened. *The earth tilted and I tripped. There was a banana peel on the ground. I had a momentary lapse in judgment and checked out Archer.* None of those reasons seem to convey the shame I feel, and for some reason all I blurt out is, "Sweaty hands."

"Here you go." Archer holds one of Jessie's sketches out for me to grab, and for once his face is devoid of the usual smirk he wears like a second skin. "He could've been an artist."

"Uhh..." I stammer, still unable to formulate coherent sentences. "Yeah, he could've." I look down at the box, fighting the urge to flee the house—and maybe move to another state. I turn to Nora, hoping she can't see the sweat on my forehead. "Sorry, I didn't mean to interrupt. I'll get out of your hair."

"You didn't interrupt anything, Puddin'." She turns to Archer with a raised brow as if to inconspicuously convey a message. "I'll go pour us some sweet tea."

"Oh, no need." I hike a thumb over my shoulder. "I've gotta get going."

She ignores me and continues into the kitchen. Archer toes the floor with his brown cowboy boot, clearly wanting to say something but holding back. I secure the box under my arm and turn. As I reach for the handle, I realize something and spin around.

"Where's your truck?" I ask. "I didn't see it in the driveway."

He chuckles, flashing the smirk I've grown accustomed to. "Heard that spot was reserved."

Surprised at his candor, I bark a laugh. "Ahh, I see."

"Parked up the street when Nora told me you were stopping by." He shrugs, rolling a flannel sleeve to his bicep. A moment passes between us where neither of us knows what to say, but it's Archer that breaks the silence. "I'll be at the bakery location tomorrow, if you want to stop by."

The mention of the bakery shatters the chaotic swirling of my mind. Twisting my ring around my finger, all I manage to do is nod before escaping out the front door. Inside my car, I press a shaky hand to my forehead. Though my skin feels like it's on fire, my head is cool to the touch.

Maybe I'm coming down with something.

I shift my car into gear and head home to take a long shower.

***

The last time I stood in front of this building Jessie let me think it had been purchased out from under me. I cursed the owner for taking my dream location, dashing any hopes I had of selling my desserts. This time, I'm filled with pride knowing the bakery I've dreamt about since I was a kid is finally going to be mine.

As long as I don't kill the carpenter before the work is complete.

Loud banging emanates from behind the new door Archer must've hung, and I steal a few short breaths, hyping myself up to finally see what the inside looks like. I wrap my hand around the knob, but my gaze snags on the glinting diamond I've yet to be able to remove from my finger. I close my eyes against the threat of tears. I should be stepping through this threshold with Jessie, but instead, the only thing that accompanies me through the doorway is the ache of his loss.

The tarp-covered floor shifts under me as I stare in awe at the place I'm going to make into my bakery. I inhale the sappy scent of wood shavings, allowing the aroma to bring a smile to my face.

"Hello?" I choke out over the thunk of a hammer.

"Over here," Archer's muffled voice sounds from behind a toolbox.

Breath ekes out of me when he lifts his head and I catch the first sight of his trimmed facial hair. The dark circles under his eyes are more pronounced, and the brown hair beneath his backwards hat has more strands of gray than I remember. After chatting with my therapist last night about my reaction to checking out Archer, she assured me that it's human nature to appreciate the opposite sex, that it most likely has nothing to do *who* he is, but that I'm slowly healing and opening my heart to potential like we talked about—even though the thought makes me want to barf.

"Anyone ever told you staring is rude?" Archer slams the toolbox lid, leaning on top with a smirk I haven't seen for ages. He spins his poker chip in his fingers, and his eyes take a journey from my bright yellow rainboots to my rainbow leggings and land on my solid blue top. "Haven't seen you wear an outfit like this in a long time."

If it was anyone else, I'd assume that comment was a come-on, but not with Archer. Him being attracted to me would be like cats being attracted to dogs.

I'm trying to get back a piece of myself and improve my mood by wearing clothes that make me happy, and if he has something snarky to say, he can shove it where the sun don't shine. I shift my attention away from him and take in the room. It smells of cedar and pine, but soon the air will be filled with the slightly sweet, yeasty aroma of baked goods.

The exposed beams running along the ceiling make the room seem larger, perfect for hanging holiday and event decor. Three long shelves are placed behind what I assume will be the checkout counter, and I can't wait to fill them with colorful take-out boxes with my bakery's name in script across them. I imagine tables packed with people, mouths happily devouring my delicious treats.

"I can smell you thinking from over here," Archer says with a more playful tone than I've heard in a while.

"Why are you so weird? Who says that?"

He shrugs and turns away from me, and I focus my attention on the work he's done. My imagination runs rampant with all the ideas I had for this bakery, a blueprint of where I wanted every single shelf, counter, and table.

My eyes land on a shelf adhered to the side wall. "Oh no."

"What's wrong?"

"That's not where that goes." I stifle the urge to be angry that he's made decisions in my bakery without consulting me. After talking with Shantel, I realize they were all just trying to wait it out but still keep my dream alive if they could.

He grunts. "Where what goes?"

I point and his gaze follows. "That should be on this wall."

"What are you talking about?" He pulls a rag from his back pocket, lifts his hat and wipes along his brow.

I clomp over to the shelf and wave my hands like Vanna White. "This doesn't belong here."

Heat invades my space as Archer leans down to meet my eyes. I'm 5'7, and he's only about seven inches taller than me, but the weight of his stare makes me feel like a garden gnome he's about to kick over.

"Yes, it does." He stares at me for a second with narrowed eyes, biting down on his lip like he's debating whether he should say whatever is brewing behind his emerald eyes. Pushing back from the shelf, he walks to the counter. "You said you wanted a space to hold kid's baking classes, and if that shelf was on the opposite wall or moved, you wouldn't have room to do that."

Brain malfunctioning, I find myself at a loss for words. The weird feeling snaking around my chest is unwelcome, but I don't know how to stop it. I haven't talked about my dream of teaching kids to bake since college, before he froze me out.

"How do you remember that?" I ask, curious if Jessie gave him instruction on how I'd want things done.

"You mentioned it the night we all went to Enchanted Rock before finals," he says, gaze focused on the level before him.

"Oh." How he remembers that night is beyond me. We all drank too much under the stars. He picks up a hammer, and I scramble to follow. "What can I help with?"

"I don't need your help." He crouches down to grab a slab of wood flooring.

I shrug off my jacket and kneel beside him. Goosebumps raise the hairs on my arms, and pressure settles onto my chest just from the sheer closeness of him. I wiggle away, putting distance between us.

"What are you doing?" he asks.

I pretend to push up my invisible sleeves with a smile. "I'm helping."

He closes his eyes and inhales like it's taking everything in him not to throw me out. "I don't need your help."

Frustrated, I throw my hands in the air. "What the hell, Archer?"

"Don't start," he says.

I nearly laugh. Has any woman ever actually stopped after a man made it a point to tell her whatever she's about to say is going to start an argument? I think not.

"No. You—" I point at him, "—don't start. This is *my* bakery."

"It's not *yours* yet." He covers his mouth as if he didn't mean to say that.

But he's right. Up until recently I had no idea about this building Jessie bought—because they kept it from me. I swallow against the sour taste in my mouth.

"It's not a bakery until everything is finished," Archer adds when I don't speak, trying to walk back his statement. "And I'm the one doing the work on it."

My voice lowers. "Then I'll find someone else."

"No," he growls.

A weird warmth floods my stomach and launches my heart into my throat.

"End of conversation," he snaps.

My shoulders fall, and I ball my fists at my side. He pauses what he's doing and sighs loudly before handing over a slab of flooring. I figure it's best not to poke the bear when he's finally decided to stop pawing at me, but inside I'm doing a happy dance.

I slide the lip of the flooring under another one, and the victorious snap of them locking in place makes me grin. I chance a look at him, but the minute he notices me looking, his half smile falls.

"Good job." He stands and walks to another part of the room. "You can finish that while I...uh work over here."

Coffee curdles in my stomach, and I run my tongue across my teeth, trying not to feel the sting of rejection. I didn't particularly want to work beside him either, but knowing he deems being around me such a burden makes my heart twist.

When Jessie was still alive, Archer would at least crack jokes or be semi-cordial; now he can barely stand to be in the same room without making me feel two inches tall.

Ignoring the stab of embarrassment, I finish the row where Archer stopped. Music blares to life, a rock song I'm vaguely familiar with, as I set my focus on another row of flooring. No words are spoken in the time it takes me to make it halfway to the door, and I don't pay attention to the grunting man lifting shelving over his head in front of me. With sweat sliding down my spine, I sit back on my heels and groan as I try to get up.

"You okay?" Archer asks.

I huff, placing my hands on the floor and pushing up to my feet. "Yeah, I just haven't been on my knees like that in a while."

His snicker alerts me to the innuendo I didn't intend.

"I didn't mean…What I meant was I haven't been on my knees since…oh my god, stop talking Tilly." My cheeks heat and I cover my face with my hands since I can apparently no longer string together a coherent sentence.

Archer laughs again, and a weight lands on my shoulder. My mouth parts, lungs seizing when I realize it's his hand.

On my shoulder.

"Sorry." He recoils, staring at his hand like it's a sentient being rather than the first thing that has touched my body in two years and not doubled me over in crushing anxiety.

I almost forgot how soothing touch can be, how it can bring back memories long forgotten. Tingles spread down my collarbone and convene in my chest, reminding me of my wedding day, the last time Archer ever hugged me. My eyes are glued to the spot where the heat from his hand has burned through my shirt and branded itself on my skin. The adrenaline flooding my system makes me dizzy.

"I've got to…drop off desserts for the restaurant." I stumble backward, nearly tripping over the box of flooring.

"Tilly." Archer's voice is strained, but I can't stop.

"It's fine." I turn toward the door. "I'm fine."

Outside the bakery, the door a barrier between us, I realize I'm not fine.

Not one bit.

"It's just a reaction, Tilly," I coach myself as I walk to my car. "Anyone would react that way to being touched after not having felt human contact in so long."

I hear the words I'm speaking aloud, but I know they're only a sliver of the truth. If I was fine, I wouldn't have wanted him to touch me again. My heart wouldn't be doing a conga line around my lungs thinking about how the first touch I crave since my husband's death is his best friend's.

Chapter Eleven
Archer
Present

Dear Seb,

I thought the longer I went without seeing Tilly, the easier it would be to eventually leave. Spoiler alert: it won't be. I'm not sure any time or distance will be enough to get her out of my system. Well, I guess she's never technically been in my system, but you know what I mean. She wore those damn space buns with chopsticks like she did in college, and I swear it transported me back in time to when I first saw her.

When she got with Jessie, she stopped wearing all her cool outfits, lost the spunkiness and effervescent bubbliness she always brought around. And I hated it. I wanted to tell her not to change, but it wasn't my place. Jessie didn't care one way or the other what she wore, but I would've made it a point to buy her the clothes she loved.

Do I sound like an asshole for comparing myself to him? He treated her right, made sure she was taken care of and loved. He was always like that, taking care of us like a mother hen when we'd get too drunk or trying to bring up our spirits after Dad dashed them down. He was a good guy, the best.

But seeing her...man, it was like water being poured over my head after a long day working in the sun. And I feel horrible saying that. I wanted to embrace her, to tell her I was sorry for missing her birthday and the dinners thereafter, but I couldn't muster up the courage to tell her why. She overheard Nora and Shantel pesterin' me to tell her, and when I finally did, she reacted like I'd orphaned a bunch of puppies.

What kind of asshole keeps a surprise like that from someone? She would've been so happy to know about the bakery sooner, but the selfish part of me knew her happiness wouldn't be directed at me. I shouldn't care. I DON'T care. She's still Jessie's wife.

I keep telling myself that, like if I say it enough, eventually my heart and head will finally align, and the attraction will subside. But it's been five years and my blood still hums anytime she's near. Hell, any time I hear her name I get a spike of adrenaline straight to my cock.

I'm sure you'd say, "But Arch, you promised Jessie you'd back off."

And I did. I found a way to keep her as far from me as possible, even at the expense of our friendship. I never once crossed a line or made him worry I still wanted her. I owed my life to him, because of your dumb ass, and his happiness was more important than mine. You made sure of that, right? I knew you were laughing up in heaven the moment the poker chip landed.

But that's neither here nor there. Both of you assholes left me. And Tilly seems hellbent on making me break every promise I made to Jessie about her. I accidentally touched her today, and the look she gave me was almost...hungry. I know that sounds absurd, but it was like she wanted me to touch her again. I'm sure it's just my brain twisting everything about our interaction.

She doesn't think about me like that. And keeping the bakery stuff a secret didn't win me any points either. She hightailed it out of there quicker than a kid caught out after the streetlights came on. Guess I was wrong, as I usually am, about what Tilly truly wants. Good for me I probably won't have to worry about it much longer. Once I'm done with her bakery, I'm moving. HGTV job or not. The hardware stores manage themselves at this point, and it's not like Mom, Dad, or Claire will miss me.

The second interview went well, or at least I think it did. They asked me about those wooden signs I made for the bakery and if I'd be interested in doing a segment on woodworking if I get the job. I think that means I'm still in the running. The lady on the video chat was real nice, exactly your type of woman. All business and no play. I'm just joshin' ya. She was a real sweet lady who wouldn't have given your butt a minute of her time. Mom and Dad would have loved her.

I still haven't spoken to Mom since dinner the other night, and I don't plan to. I'll never forget overhearing Dad say it happened to the wrong son, that your life was destined for something more. Something great.

They were right. It should've been me. It's my fault you're not here, even if it wasn't me that put the pressure on your shoulders to succeed or me that gave you the pills. I never should've pulled into that gas station. I should've seen the signs for what they were rather than hoping you'd keep your word. Jessie had a split second to decide who to save when he lunged for us.

He chose wrong.

I know, I know. Family is important and we're all each other has...yada yada yada. Don't you ever get sick of being the righteous voice in my head? Could you take a break for a minute and just give me some brotherly love? If you were here, they'd still look at me as the black sheep of the family because of my job. Their noses would still be turned up when they spoke about me to their hoity toity friends at the country club.

The most I can hope for is that with this job, the Wilson name won't just be known in the medical field but with households all over the country. Because of my hard work. They won't be able to look down on me when all of their friends watch the show and see me. They'll eat their words, and I for one can't wait for that day.

If I'm chosen, I'll have to be in Knoxville at the end of the year. I haven't told Nora or Shantel about the second interview yet, but I'm sure they'll *be excited for me. I just have to finish all the work on Tilly's bakery before I leave. I'm not sure how the next three months are going to go, but if I can make it nearly five years without crossing a line, I can do just about anything.*

-Arch

Chapter Twelve
Tilly

"Don't make it weird, don't make it weird, don't make it weird," I chant, standing outside the bakery with the paper plate filled with a chocolate pistachio cake and chai pinwheel cookies. With the key Archer made me, I came here to see if I could get a jump on taking measurements for my menu board. I didn't expect him to still be here so late, but the light spilling from beneath the door shows me I was wrong.

I quietly peek around the corner. He's hunched over the counter with his notebook in front of him. His brows are scrunched, a crease formed on the smooth skin of his forehead as he rubs the stupid poker chip he keeps with him in his other hand. I imagine he's checking off his to-do list of things he needs to complete before he leaves.

The thought leaves a sour taste in my mouth.

"Hey." I squeeze the rest of the way through the door.

Archer startles and slams the notebook shut like a kid caught reading a nudie magazine. His face flushes pink. "What are you doing here?"

I laugh and move closer to the counter. "I thought we went over this earlier."

He rolls up the notebook and stuffs it into his back pocket along with the poker chip. "You know what I meant."

"I do." I lay the plate of treats down, and my charm bracelet scrapes across the countertop. Archer's eyes flit to my wrist, and I catch his brief smile before he frowns and looks back up at me. "I made a new recipe I'm thinking about adding to the menu. I brought extra for you."

He nods but doesn't move to take one. I'm hurt, but not surprised. Apparently, eating my desserts would prevent him from entering heaven, and he's quite worried about his soul. I snort at my inner thoughts, and he gives me a confused look.

"Are you worried I poisoned them?" I arch an eyebrow playfully, hoping to break the tension. "I promise you can't taste the arsenic."

He stifles a laugh and shakes his head like he can't believe I just said that. When he still doesn't speak, I go to his toolbox and pull out the measuring tape. "Fine, suit yourself. One of us has to get to work."

In need of a pencil, I walk back and grab the one he keeps nestled on his ear, careful not to touch him. His eyes heat my back as I mark the wall exactly where I want the oversized chalkboard to be hung.

"What do you think about putting wallpaper behind this?" I turn around to find him with his hands propped on the side of the counter and his head hung. For a moment, I wonder if he fell asleep, but he moves his head from side to side before lifting it and piercing me with his stark green eyes.

Cement forms around my feet as he pushes off the counter and crouches down. Did I make him mad? It usually doesn't take much, but nowadays every little thing seems to set him off. Papers shuffle together, and before I know it, he's laying out colorful rolls of wallpaper, all with different designs.

"What's all this?" I ask, cheeks stretching wide in delight.

He shrugs. "I knew you'd want some funky designs on the wall, so I picked up some rolls when I went to the store the other day."

The tiny people controlling my brain clock in for the day, take an elevator down to my heart and pick up their chisels to start hacking away at the ice around it. The ice Archer put there by constantly freezing me out.

"That's so..." *Sweet. Worrisome. Surprising.* I scan each roll before landing on a chevron design. Unable to find an appropriate word, I land on, "Thank you."

He rubs the back of his neck, shrugging like it's no big deal. "They were on clearance by the checkout register."

He doesn't meet my eyes when he says that, and there's a tiny part in the back of my mind that imagines he actually spent time looking through different wallpapers he thought I'd like.

"Do you think this color will look okay?" I hold up the wallpaper.

He shrugs. "Anything you pick will be perfect."

He walks to the far wall and starts measuring. Like a child, I follow. "What are you measuring for?" I ask.

I can tell I'm annoying him by his deep sigh, but for some reason it makes me happy to pluck his nerves.

"I assume you want a wall between the front of the house and the kitchen, correct?"

I nod before I realize he can't see me. "Yes, that would be perfect."

"Great, then I need you to get out of my hair so I can get finished."

Defeated, I back up a few steps. "You don't have to be such an asshole, you know. I'm getting excited about this place."

He snorts. "Darlin', you've never seen me as an asshole."

"I beg to differ." I lean against the counter, trying not to let the many times he's pushed me away with his words bubble back to the surface. Agitation rises in my chest, making my skin itch as I lock the memories away behind a mental door. "The man I knew in college never treated me like I was scum beneath his shoes."

His measuring tape thuds to the ground, and he throws his head back, hands tensed at his sides. "Can we not do this right now?"

"No!" I yell, slamming my hands onto the counter. "I'm sick of it, Arch."

"Here we go."

The inhale I take is fueled with fire. "I've had enough of the side eyes and cutting remarks to last me a lifetime. If I've done something to you then be a man and tell me instead of having a shitty attitude all the time and treating me like a pariah. We *used* to be friends. Jessie would..." I struggle to get the words out. "Would want us to be in each other's lives. What the hell happened?"

Archer picks up the measuring tape and stomps back to his toolbox. Slamming the lid closed, he takes it and starts moving toward the door.

"You're leaving?" I ask, incredulous.

"Yup." His reply is short and delivered with a sharpness that cuts through me.

"Fine," I yell. "No one asked for your help anyway."

Faster than I thought humanly possible, Archer is back in my space, so close the mint on his breath burns my nose. His throat bobs and sweat slides down into his shirt when he leans closer.

"Someone *did* ask for my help," he grits out. "And that man was your husband."

The muscle jumping in his jaw makes me think he's holding back his emotions, and the ache in my throat becomes more prominent.

"So you honor him by treating his wife like trash," I seethe. "Got it. Duly noted. Jessie was the only person who mattered to you, and now that he's gone, you can't wait to get away from me."

He blinks like he's clearing away a haze. "No, Til."

"Forget it." Tears prickle my eyes, and I turn away from him, chest painful and tight. "I'll find someone else to finish the work."

A hand lands on my arm, the touch achingly soft. The small dose of what I've been missing floods my system and steals my breath. It's quickly pushed away as anger and hurt simmer beneath my skin. I yank my arm out of his grasp and wipe away the tears I can't stop from falling. "Don't touch me."

"Tilly, that's not what I—" Archer's voice is strained, but I don't let that deter me from my retreat. "I didn't mean to make you feel like that."

"Just go." I walk toward the bathroom, a thread at my back pulling taut as if this moment isn't finished. Anger, bitterness, and something like yearning swell behind my ribcage. I shouldn't want him to stay, to try to make up for all the things he's said and the ways he's made me feel, but there's a part of me that does.

With the closed door, I finally break down and allow the conflicting emotions to overwhelm me as I scrub at my arm, trying to remove his touch. Tears run down my face, mixing with snot and sadness as I lean against the stall and wait to hear the telltale sign of Archer's departure. If I want my bakery to succeed, I'll have to find a new carpenter or learn how to do it myself.

***

A loud scraping noise jolts me to awareness. Through heavy lidded eyes, I scan my surroundings and a cloud of confusion forms. Bright light spills into the room from the opened door, and like cogs shifting, my mind wakes up to the fact that I'm on the bakery floor, covered with strips of wallpaper.

"Did you sleep here?" Archer sets a thermos and his toolbox on the bay windowsill.

I swipe my arm across my mouth and catch the sliver of drool left from my chaotic dreams. My bones crack as I rise from the floor and roll up the wallpaper, careful to not bend it.

"Tilly?" Archer asks, a hint of worry to his voice.

Emotion I thought I beat down last night bubbles back to the surface, and the ache in my chest flares again. I ignore him and place the rolls underneath the makeshift table as he moves around the room.

My gaze follows him as he takes in all the work I did last night: the top half of the wall now covered in blue chevron paper, the tape along the walls where the wainscoting panels will go, the bookshelf that gave me gray hair overnight.

Archer's wearing a tight, green shirt that hugs his toned biceps and pants that look entirely too good around his ass. He stands in front of an admittedly poor excuse for a bookshelf with his hands on his hips and my stomach flips. Like a string cut from a marionette, his head falls.

Shame rushes up my spine and curls around my collar.

"Did you do this by yourself?" he asks.

I bite my cheek to stop from saying what I really want to say, which is that I don't trust anyone else to bring Jessie's vision—our vision—of the bakery to life.

When I don't respond, Archer moves in front of me. "Tilda."

"Don't call me that," I say.

"Tilda St. James, look at me."

His use of my full name sends a chill down my spine and lights a fire in my bones. Lightning zips through my veins at his gravelly voice. My shoulders rise, but the embarrassment keeps my head down.

Soft knuckles push against my chin, sending zaps of electricity down my throat.

"Til." Archer pins me with a look I've never seen on his face before.

Pain.

"What?" I rip my chin away and wipe the touch from my skin with the sleeve of my dusty shirt.

Three times he's touched me, and three times my body has reacted in a way I don't want it to. I still haven't figured out why his touch affects me differently than others, why it makes me feel the opposite of pity and grief. Maybe it's because he and Jessie were alike in so many ways my mind is tricking itself into thinking it's my husband's touch.

Arousal isn't the emotion my body has been conditioned to feel when it's around Archer. It's used to hurt, to always being on defense for whatever words or looks he's going to sling my way, but it also remembers the smiles and camaraderie of those early college years.

"You did a good job." He leans down to meet my eyes with a smile on his face.

Blinking away the tears, I look up at him, confused by the proud look in his eyes. "No, I didn't."

"Yes, you did. I bet that was the first shelf you've ever put together, right?"

I gnaw on my bottom lip, forcing myself to keep eye contact instead of looking at my shoes. "Yeah, it's terrible."

He walks over to it and knocks on the side. It wobbles, and Archer shrugs like it's no big deal. Like if I put mugs inside it, they wouldn't topple to the ground or knock a patron on their head, effectively landing me with worse luck than I've been dealt.

"It needs a few more screws, but it's good." He walks over to the toolbox and pulls out a cordless drill and screws. "Come help me."

Uneasy, I trudge over to the other side of the wonky shelf.

He shows me where to place my hands. "Let's move it closer to the wall and I'll screw it in."

My eyes catch on the cords of his biceps tensing as he lifts the side. I tear my eyes away, confused by the weird flip inside my stomach. The moment we lift, the boards shift, slamming onto one another before the entire thing caves and comes apart.

Nervous laughter bubbles out of me. "See what I mean?"

Archer tries to stop himself from laughing, but he doesn't succeed. His laugh is loud, hearty, but it's cut off before I have a chance to really enjoy it, almost like he hasn't laughed in so long that he's truly surprised by the sound.

"Probably a manufacturer's defect." He gives me a half-smile, rubbing the back of his neck as he kicks around the boards.

"More like a user error."

"Come on, Til." He reaches out for me but must think better of it because he pulls his arm back as quick as he offered it.

He doesn't know my body now craves the same touch he's denying me. A touch I shouldn't want from my husband's best friend. It's a headspin I've yet to understand, no matter how many times my therapist tells me it's normal, that I can crave touch yet feel disgusted by the thought of it too.

I haven't so much as batted an eye at anyone except Henry Cavill in his Witcher get-up, so why is Archer the first person I've *wanted* to touch me?

My therapist urged me to try cuddle parties, which are popular in the grief community for those with touch starvation, but I couldn't go. Laying down with someone for a certain amount of time just to curb the skin hunger didn't sound fun to me. If I couldn't even deal with familiar touch, how would I respond to a stranger holding me without bursting into tears?

I blow out a breath and rub my arms for comfort. "Yeah, maybe the screws they sent weren't long enough."

"That's the spirit," he says, neatly piling all the boards onto one another. "Now let's get this shelf back together."

I nod but can't find the motivation to start again. Spending all night split between missing Jessie and wishing it was us doing this together and watching how-to videos zapped every ounce of energy. What happens when we inevitably butt heads again? Will we be able to play nice? Or is our deadline going to come quicker than we're able to hash out the issues between us?

Chapter Thirteen
Archer
Present

There's nothing better on a rainy day than Nora's country fried steak and mashed potatoes with gravy. When she asked me to come fix a few busted wall panels in her garage, I knew I could sweet talk her into making my favorite meal. After the way the past few days have gone, her comfort food is my only saving grace.

I didn't think it'd be this difficult to be around Tilly on a regular basis.

The more I work with her, listening to her hum songs and dance (something I haven't seen her do in years) and arguing with her over shelf space and décor, I realize I'm in hell. Not the college version of hell where I longed for her sunshine and peppiness after a grueling week of football three-a-days, but genuine hell where I'm burning up—in equal parts anger and longing—for something to change between us.

Closing her out is a knee jerk reaction, a coping mechanism I've developed. I push her away when all I want is to pull her closer, and it's bitten me in the ass. I so badly want to beg her to forgive me for all the shitty things I've said to her and the distance I created, but I know there's no excuse. I have to prove to her I can change, and helping her get her bakery opened is the first step to becoming friends again.

"Do you want a second helping?" Nora asks, sliding her reading glasses up her wide nose. Her silver hair is pulled back into a tight bun and she's got a light smattering of blush on her umber skin.

"Nope." I pat my stomach. "You've spoiled me already, might have to roll me out like an Oompa Loompa."

She laughs, and the crinkles at the corners of her eyes deepen. "I've gotta take care of my boy. You, Shantel and Malik, and Tilly are all I have left."

My stomach torpedoes into my throat at the honesty in her voice, the longing for how things used to be. The backs of my eyes burn with tears. I rise from the chair and clean off my plate in the sink. "You've taken plenty care of me. It's time someone takes care of you."

"We all need someone to take care of us, son. Even when we think we're doin' just fine on our own."

I chuckle. "You gonna let Mr. Hawkins finally take you out?"

A dishtowel hits me in the side of the head and drops to my forearm. Nora stands propped against the island with her arms crossed and a playful look on her face.

"I'll let Hawkins take me out when you finally make things right with Tilly."

I choke on the baseball lodged in my throat, sputtering as I turn off the water and dry my hands, heading to the island. Nora's been a buffer between us since Jessie passed, but she's never been one to meddle in her kids business. I'm not sure if Jessie ever told her how he ended up being the one to ask Tilly out, and I'm not going to be the one to tell her.

"Things between Tilly and me are fine."

Her weathered hand rests upon mine. "Son, I may not be your actual mother, but I'm still a mother, and I know when something is wrong with one of my babies."

I squeeze her hand. "I'm fi—"

"Don't lie to me, boy," she reprimands. "I'm not blind. You looked like a lovesick puppy when she tore outta here that night."

Heat rushes to my cheeks, my chest, my neck, suffocating the tiny vessels of my heart. I thought I masked my surprise well during dinner when Shantel mentioned Tilly getting back into the dating field, but I guess not. It shouldn't matter to me—she deserves happiness more than anyone I know—but it does. And the way my heart twists every time I think about her being happy with someone other than me shows me I'm nowhere near unbothered enough to pretend like it doesn't affect me.

Stunned by her words, I struggle to find something to say.

"You know," she says, "sometimes things don't work out the way we want, but that doesn't mean we can't change our path."

A strangled laugh finds its way out of my mouth. "Ok, Confucius."

She whacks me again. "I'm serious, Archer. Time is fleeting, and you never know when you may miss an opportunity to tell someone how you truly feel about them." She pauses, gulps. "I'm part of a club no parent wants to be in, but having you and Tilly still in my life helps me on the hard days. You'll understand when you have kids of your own, but when someone is important to you—" she pins me with her sharp gaze "—you don't waste another second allowing them to feel like they're anything but that."

Her words convict me, reminding me of all the times I wanted to divulge my feelings but chickened out. An image of Tilly—the most important woman in my life outside of Nora, the one I've made feel like she's inconsequential to me—pops into my mind like a pesky jack-in-the-box. I shake my head, clearing the image away. "There's no point in trying to repair our friendship when I'm probably leaving anyway. I've got another interview coming up."

"We don't always get a chance to fix what we've broken, or to make things clear to those we love."

My skin prickles with her comment. There's so much I wish I could've said to Seb, so much I wish I could've changed or made right with him before he passed, but I don't feel like that with Jessie. We were best friends, brothers by choice. I made a promise to him about Tilly, and he made one to me too. We both knew the score, and I lost.

"Your relationship with Tilly is worth repairing." She gives me a wry smile then shrugs. "And maybe it won't just be friendship that you find."

Shock hardens my stomach, and a cold sweat breaks out over my body at her insinuation there could be anything more than friendship between me and Tilly. As Jessie's mother, I feel like she should be angry at me, worried that I wasn't being a good friend to her son, but all I see in her eyes is hope.

After she blew up on me about how I was treating her, there's no way Tilly sees me as anything but the person helping her get her bakery ready for opening. But if there's some chance of repairing our friendship, then I need to try.

"Okay." I ignore her comment, grab my tool kit, and head to the garage to clear my head. "Now, how did these panels get busted?"

Nora shuffles behind me. "I think the foundation shifted some, because those panels weren't that close to the side the other day."

I laugh, and she punches me in the shoulder. Grasping my arm, I play like I'm hurt, and she threatens me with another knuckle sandwich.

"Don't start, boy."

I get to work fixing the wall Nora ran into, and my mind buzzes with everything we spoke about. If anyone knows how short time is, it's me. There's nothing I wouldn't give up for another day with Sebastian and Jessie, and knowing my time might be limited to make things right with Tilly, I can't risk pushing her away anymore.

Slipping my phone out of my pocket, I shoot her a text to see what time she'll be coming to the bakery in the morning. Tomorrow I'll start repairing what I've broken.

Chapter Fourteen
Tilly

The aroma of cocoa tempts me toward an indie bookstore a few blocks from where my bakery will be. Outside, the birds chirp loudly, the sun bathes my skin, and there's a lightness in my chest that feels suspiciously like...hope. It's been so long since I've been able to see out from under the blanket of grief, to see that there is something to look forward to each day, and I'm realizing that for me, it's the bakery. I told Archer I'd be there at ten o'clock sharp but seeing as I'm fifteen minutes early, I can spare a few moments to peruse the selection. Excited for the closeness of a fellow entrepreneur, I head inside to introduce myself.

"Hello?" A ding above me announces my arrival, and a melodic voice floats from the back area.

"I'll be right out."

Small tables are tucked into the corners of the bookshop, and there's a counter with an espresso machine and a selection of treats. I knew I'd smelled chocolate, but I assumed it was from coffee, not cookies and pastries. A blip of jealousy creeps into my mind like only one of us can be selling delectable treats, and it's going to be me.

Enchanted by the smoky vanilla scents of crisp paper and dust, I run my fingers along the spines of the classics on the shelf and wait to see who my competition is going to be. Will it be a cute old lady, using the last of her pension to keep a dying bookstore alive, or is it a hipster who doesn't know the difference between a romance and a love story?

The door swings open, and my heart promptly falls to the ground. Deidre.

Archer's ex is the last person I thought I'd encounter in a place like this. There's no way a woman as cold as her owns such a lovely, warm place. Hell, the temperature of the room dropped by at least a cool twenty degrees the moment her eyes locked on me standing with a wide smile at her counter.

She's always disliked me for some reason, making snarky comments when she thought I wasn't listening, and she never tried to get to know me when Archer would bring her to family dinners.

"Tilly," she says, a hint of amusement in her tone.

"Deidre." I give her a curt smile. "I didn't know you worked here."

She nods like a person does when someone is telling them something they couldn't care less about. "I've owned this place for three years."

I vaguely remember her prattling on about opening a business back when Jessie would force me to go on double dates with her and Archer, but I was so focused on being nice to her that I forgot. A weird feeling snakes its way around my chest, and I spin my ring around my finger to refocus.

Deidre always had this perpetual frown on her face if I entered a room. I thought she'd be the one to lock down Archer. He had a series of women he filtered through, but when he met her, she stuck around. She was always over-the-top touchy feely with him, and a small part of me hated her for it.

Looking back, I wonder if instinctively my brain was picking up on something I've yet to even admit to myself. That I knew, even back in college, my life could've gone a very different way had a drunken kiss with Archer meant something to him.

"It's a beautiful bookstore," I say. "Quaint."

Her smile is pasted on, stale. "Thanks."

Awkward tension hangs in the air between us. "Well," I start to speak but struggle to find words, "I just wanted to introduce myself to some of the shop owners down here."

"Oh." She arches a brow. "Why?"

Straight to the point.

"My bakery is going to be on the next street over."

Her forehead crinkles, a frown forming on her face. "Oh right, I forgot about the little shop Archer's been working in."

A stickiness coats my mouth at the mention of Archer. Did everyone but me know Jessie bought this bakery? Has Archer invited her inside my shop?

"Yeah," I croak, face heating when she doesn't respond with any questions. I scramble to find a way out of this awkward encounter. "Umm, ok. Well, if you need anything I'm just around the corner."

She smiles. "I doubt it, but thanks."

Her words follow me out the door, my footsteps sluggish as I head to the bakery.

The October sun is unusually blistering today, and my pits are already damp from the short walk from Deidre's storefront to mine. Okay, I started sweating bullets when she walked out from the back room, but that's beside the point. My bare legs slide against each other, and I curse my mother for my juicy thighs as they rub. In hindsight, wearing a skort to work in wasn't my brightest idea, but I'll be climbing up ladders today and tight denim was an even worse option.

Music blares through the thin wooden door. I knew he'd be here, but it still takes my heart a moment to catch up to my quickened breath. Yesterday felt like a turning point for us, a kind of truce. But with each new day, I wonder how long it'll be until we're back at each other's throats.

"Hey." I skirt through the door.

He doesn't look up from the table he's hunched over, a level and a pencil in hand. "One moment," he says, drawing a line down the two by four he's about to cut. The table saw blares to life, screeching as he splits the wood. Now covered in dust, Archer turns to me, a toothpick hanging from the side of his mouth. Dressed in a tight black t-shirt that clings to his abs and denim jeans, Archer is the epitome of a bad boy. A regular James Dean. If only he drove a muscle car instead of a larger-than-life truck.

"Did you bring your camera?" he asks.

"No. Was I supposed to?"

"A picture lasts longer."

My stomach riots and a wave of shame flows over my face after being caught checking him out. I fight the urge to look guilty, embarrassed. He'd love to see me flinch away, but I'm in the mood to challenge today.

"My memory works just fine," I reply, toying with the cake charm on my bracelet.

Archer is good-looking. He knows this. He knew I was attracted to him back then, and just because I fell in love with his best friend doesn't mean I didn't still find him attractive.

Any red-blooded person would.

Even though we've only been working together a short amount of time, it reminds me of college when we were Chemistry partners and I found it exceedingly difficult to keep my eyes on my work.

I seem to be having the same problem now.

Doing projects together was something Jessie and I did. Okay, well watching Jessie put together the IKEA items we bought was more my thing, but I at least provided the caramel balsamic mochis to keep our bellies filled as we laughed over him putting it together wrong.

That must be what it is.

Working with Archer makes me miss Jessie. I've been so wrapped up in his gift to me that I haven't gone for my monthly visit to his grave site. Maybe that's my problem. I need to remind myself of the man I married.

"What do you want to work on today?" he asks.

My self-control. "Painting."

He nods and pulls a keyring of swatches from his toolbox.

"Are you prepared for everything?" I ask, surprised as he hands me the paint samples.

They're all bright colors. Not a dark one in sight, like he knew I wouldn't dare put a muted color on the walls.

"I was a Boy Scout, of course I am." He laughs and goes back to marking up another two by four.

I search through the swatches, noting I have clothes in every shade he's provided. Jessie probably picked out the swatches before he passed.

"I'll pick up whatever color you choose while I'm out." He places clear protective glasses over his eyes.

Archer makes safety sexy.

I chastise myself for the errant thought. Why, after years of indifference, is my brain trying to reconnect the pathway to my heart, and below, to *Archer*, of all people. Annoyed, I grab the roll of light blue chevron wallpaper, holding a lilac swatch against it. The tones are complementary, and an image of the bakery in all its glory fills my mind. White decorative paneling splitting the wall, a splash of color on the top half, and three or four tables for patrons to come for a quick treat and a cup of coffee. It'll be amazing. Much better than the bookshop around the corner.

Briefly, I imagine a display case filled with Bundt cakes and small bundtlets for the people who want a quick treat rather than a full dessert. The thought brings me back to when I made the wedding cake for Archer's sister's wedding, the one he dogged to his friends, and immediately my mood tanks.

"This one is fine." I throw the swatch on the counter and make a line where the paneling will go.

"Uh, okay." Archer picks up the paper. "This color will look good with the blue."

Anger simmers beneath my skin. "I know."

His face scrunches up like he wants to say something, but he stays mum and goes back to cutting wood. We work in silence for the next two hours, barely speaking to one another. An alarm goes off and Archer slides his phone out of his pocket, his face going from a smile to a slight frown.

I stop myself from asking why he looks like that. We aren't friends, and his life outside of this building is none of my business. For all I know, he may be meeting someone for an afternoon date.

My shoulders curl inward, drawn by the pulling sensation in my gut.

"I've got a meeting." He unplugs the saw like I can't be trusted with power tools. "I'll pick up your paint and a can of primer for the paneling. Anything else you need while I'm out?"

"Nope." My answer is short, like my fuse at this point.

He leaves, and my entire body sags to the ground. I thought I had to worry about Archer bailing on our project because of how much he dislikes being around me, but I'm dangerously close to pulling the plug because I can't get a grasp on my own feelings.

A train of envy chugs around my chest, but a prickling in the back of my mind slows the train on its tracks. The only logical answer for the way I feel is that maybe I am ready to get back into the dating field and I'm jealous that dating comes easier to everyone else.

Yeah, that's gotta be it.

A shrill ring stops my self-destruction, my dad's ringtone.

"Hey Dad."

"Tilda," he says, an air of sadness in his tone. "Where have you been?"

Anxiety curls in my stomach. I hate how he makes it seem like I've been avoiding him when he's the one being sketchy.

I still haven't told him about the bakery.

Eventually I will, but I'm not ready for him to have an opinion about it yet. I could stay making boring desserts for my parents' restaurants for the rest of my life, but I need to do this for myself. And Rosie. She'd never forgive me if I gave up making her cupcakes.

My desserts should be in the hands of the people, talked about during school events and birthday parties, maybe even weddings one day.

"Baking." I run my hands up and down my arms.

"I can tell by the amount of treats," he laughs. "Shantel dropped off more than your usual haul yesterday, but I haven't seen you since last week."

You'd think he would've called sooner, but I'm sure it slipped his mind. He's a busy man, after all. Hell, every time I come to the restaurant I feel like he's rushing me out, like he doesn't want to see me. Why is he worried about where I've been now?

"I've been busy helping Archer with some work at—"

"Archer?" His interruption sets me on edge. "What are you doing with him?"

"I just told you I'm helping him—"

"I thought you were going to start helping Shantel at her salon?"

"Not until the beginning of the year."

Damn it, Dad. Would you just shut the hell up?

He continues. "I can find something for you at one of the restaurants."

"No, Dad." I sigh. "I'm fine."

I wish things were different between us, that losing my mom didn't create this chasm where it feels like we're on different continents.

"Okay. I'll see you for dinner this weekend?" he asks with a weird tinge of something akin to hope lacing his tone.

"Sure."

With a stale 'I love you' the line goes silent.

I stare down at the ring I've told myself multiple times I'd take off, yet each time I think about doing it, I'm reminded of how alone I feel, and the comfort of having the ring on my finger fills my chest with a sense of peace.

Love is supposed to fill you, but it seems like someone broke the tab on my tank and it's all spilled out of me, never able to refill. The love Jessie showed me is like droplets clinging to the side of the tank, moments away from evaporating and leaving me dry.

Chapter Fifteen
Archer
Jessie and Tilly's First Anniversary

Dear Seb,

Whoever made the gift list for wedding anniversaries had to be a businessman. Paper. Who buys their significant other paper to say, 'I love you?' Rich people who send memos on special stationary or military wives sending their deployed husbands a love letter sealed with a kiss.

How do I know this, you ask? Well, Jessie asked me to come with him to buy Tilly a 'first anniversary' present. I should've known, since he always asks my opinion, but something this important should be from him and him alone. The woman at Tiffany's was really nice. Even though it could've potentially lost her a sale, she told Jessie the first anniversary wasn't a huge diamond but a slab of tree. I tried to tell him a diamond wasn't the way to go, but he never listens.

Remember when he decided he wanted hair like Justin Timberlake, blond ramen noodle waves and all? He wouldn't hear any reason. Sometimes I wonder how Tilly puts up with it, if he railroads her into his wishes like he used to do with us. Then I slap myself silly because he's my best friend and I want him to be happy. They're perfect for each other. They fit in with each other's family, they're both smart and funny, down for go-kart races and cooking out on a whim.

He dragged me from the jewelry store to the car dealership. Tilly's car wasn't new, but it wasn't old by any means either. It was the same one she *drove every day in college to meet us at the coffee shop before class, but it was old by Jessie's standards. You'd think we came from different sides of the tracks by the way we look at money. Even though we were both brought up around it, it disgusts me to have that many zeros to my bank account. It makes him proud. I'm not knocking him, he's worked hard to build his wealth, but the same money that comforts him strangles me. Mom and Dad lord it over me, like I need their funds to be part of the family.*

Every penny I have, I've earned by blood, sweat, and very manly tears. I didn't need their checks to buy the buildings for my construction business or my hardware stores, and it's driven an even bigger wedge between us. Money creates more problems than it solves.

Jessie was so excited when he found a car for Tilly, but I knew it wasn't the right gift for her. Tilly doesn't like flashy gifts. I once bought her a funny magnet and a tiny gnome holding a dandelion from her favorite online shop and she gushed over it for weeks. I wish you would've gotten a chance to meet her. We used to scribble notes and pictures to each other in class, and one time she made me and Jessie come to a picnic lunch where she made these tiny sandwiches and an overload of baked goods. She loves to bowl, loves karaoke (even though she sings off-tune), and Christmas is her favorite holiday because she loves to give gifts even though she hates receiving them.

Gosh, I sound like an asshole listing all the things I've noticed about Tilly but shouldn't have. Jessie is a good man. He treats her right, takes care of her, and I know he loves her. But I love her, too. And I can't stop my brain from greedily storing every tidbit of information about her even though it'll never get used.

When Jessie grabbed his checkbook, I couldn't stay mum about it anymore. Buying a sixty-thousand-dollar SUV wasn't going to make Tilly's eyes light up. He was looking for a reaction to his gift, and he wouldn't get it with that. He looked at me like I was crazy when I told him to sublet the building I chose for my new venture for Tilly's bakery. He was the only person who knew I was expanding my business to include rentable workshop space, but the location was perfect, and I knew Tilly had been looking in the area for a while. Maybe I subconsciously leased it to be near her. I own a few other hardware stores across the city now, so it wouldn't be a huge hit to me to lose this location to see her happy.

Jessie gave me a weird look, but it only took a moment before he was telling me I was the smartest man alive and that he'd have his realtor send me the paperwork. It pissed me off that he was going to get the mega smile for his gift, even though it was me who gave him the idea, but all that mattered was that she'd be happy. Having her own bakery was her dream, a place where she could teach kids to bake and rework some of her mom's old recipes. She'd finally have a place to sell the pineapple cinnamon rolls she used to bring us for weekend study sessions. They were my favorite thing she made, but I refuse to allow myself to eat the treats she makes anymore. It's just one more thing that makes it impossible to not love her. One more thing that reminds me she's not—nor will ever be—mine to love. The girl can bake, and a woman who makes life sweeter is one you keep.

I just wasn't meant to keep her.

-Arch

Chapter Sixteen

Archer

The day after Jessie's Funeral

*D*ear Seb,

Jessie's gone. Jessie's gone. Jessie's gone. Jessie's gone. Jessie's gone. Jessie's gone. Jessie's gone.

FUCK!!!! No matter how many times I write it, it still doesn't feel true.

Jessie.

My fucking best friend, my brother.

He's gone.

Last week we were standing inside the building, talking about our plans to surprise Tilly with her dream bakery, and now he's...he's just...gone.

Why!? Why does everyone that matters to me die?

There's this ache inside me that won't let up, a constant reminder that I'm...alone. I couldn't save either of you. I failed.

My eyes burn like I've rubbed sandpaper all over them from how much I've cried. Fuck, I just want this pain to go away. I want my best friend back. I want you back.

The minute I heard Shantel's panicked voice on the phone, I knew something happened. An aneurysm. A stupid fucking blood vessel that popped in his brain overnight took my best friend. Losing you was heartbreaking, but I was able to tell you that I loved you. I was able to say goodbye because in my own way I knew I was losing you. He left me.

He left her.

Tilly.

God, Seb.

Getting the phone call and not being able to run to her was torture. If we'd still been close. If I hadn't driven a wedge between us because of my own stupid feelings, I could've been there for her. How could I try to console her with words of comfort when for the past few years I made it a point to pretend she was inconsequential to me? I ~~was~~ *am a coward.*

His funeral was yesterday. It wasn't much different than yours, except instead of doctors filling the room, businessmen crowded in beside each other. They memorialized Jessie with tales of mergers and takeovers, things that didn't fucking scrape the surface of who he was. He wasn't some suit who ate thousand-dollar meals and jetted off to tropical islands every chance he got. He had Sunday dinners with his family. Played poker better than any card shark I know.

He was the best fucking friend in the world.

He saved my life, and I didn't even have a chance to save his.

It's stupid to pray for a sickness. I know that. But why couldn't he have needed a fuckin' kidney or something? Something I could've given to him. Repaid him in some way for everything he's done for me.

Hell, I would've taken his place if I could've. My life isn't worth anything. I'm a carpenter. Whoop dee freaking do. He was meant to change the world.

At the wake, I sat beside Nora. Three chairs away from Tilly. She was dressed in all black with her arms wrapped around her. Jessie's coworkers offered their condolences with awkward smiles to the family. My entire body ached with the need to punch something, to rage and throw things against the wall. But I'm supposed to be stoic, the strong man not allowed to cry. I don't have you. I don't have Jessie. And the one person I want to grieve with hates me. Rightfully so.

How could he leave me when we had so much life left to live? So many more things to experience together?

How could he leave her?

Tilly's vacant eyes didn't leave his casket the entire service. I wanted to hug her and tell her we would get through it. Jessie did that for me when you died. But something held me back from approaching her. Nora confided in me that Tilly didn't want to be touched. Every time someone touched her, she screamed. Tilly was always affectionate. I used to call her Touchy Tilly to mess with her, even though I secretly loved it when she'd playfully hit me. Nora called it something like touch aversion. I had to Google it. It tears me up to know she's hurting so bad she can't be touched. I wish I could say it was that knowledge that held me back, but the truth is, I knew I'd be the last person she'd ever want comfort from.

I've done nothing but cause her pain.

Fuck man, I don't know what to do. I've made sure to be around for Nora and Shantel for whatever they need help with, but what can I do for Tilly? She won't answer phone calls or texts and she hasn't left the house except for the funeral. I drive by every night and sit outside, trying to convince myself to knock. I doubt she'd open the door for me, and if she did, I have no clue what I could say that would even touch the depth of remorse I feel for treating her so poorly that she feels she can't turn to me during this time.

In college, I promised Jessie I'd back off in his pursuit of Tilly, but yesterday I made him another promise as I stood on the loamy soil where they laid him to rest. I told him I'd find a way to make things right with her. I just don't know how. This chasm between us feels too deep to fill with apologies that should've come years ago.

I wish I could ask him what to do. Fuck. I wish both of you were still here so I wasn't alone.

Take care of him up there for me. And tell him I'll do my best to take care of his mom and sister, and that I'll make sure ~~our~~ his girl gets the bakery of her dreams.

-Arch

Chapter Seventeen
Tilly

S plinters are the devil's confetti.

In hindsight, attempting to move a few pieces of wood that are much larger than my tiny arms can handle wasn't the best idea. I try to grab the little sucker with my tweezers but wince as I rip a crevasse in my fingertip. Abandoning the effort to remove it, I discard the tweezers with a huff. Glutton for punishment that I am, I blink away the tears and reach for another slab of wood.

Sweat coats my skin, dripping down into the tank top I changed into after Archer left. My mouth is parched, and the droplet of saltiness cresting my upper lip is the only thing I've consumed other than my morning chorizo, egg, and avocado stuffed yam. Arms wide, I clear the doorway and am almost to the table when a wave of dizziness hits me. I waver, nearly tumbling over the extension cord on the ground.

"Whoa, Tilly," Archer shouts as he comes up behind me, arms reaching to meet mine on the wood.

His solid stomach is against my back, his breath hot on my neck as he walks me forward and I bend over to place the wood down. Exhausted, I nearly collapse onto the table. A strong arm bands around my stomach, and I nearly lose it. The tightness of his arm holding me against his firm chest, my ass nestled in a spot I've dreamt about too often the past couple days, the breath coasting along my neck.

One by one my touch receptors explode.

Archer's body weight presses the corner of the table between my legs, and the feeling rips a moan from me. There's a sharp intake of breath, but I'm unsure if it's his or mine, because before I know it, there's a weight settled between my ass, and the pressure from the table is there again, causing me to whimper.

My mind does overtime catching up to the rest of my body. It screeches to a halt and downpours disgust into my veins. I rip Archer's hands from my body, inwardly whining as I do so, and push him back.

"Fuck." He throws his hands up in surrender then reaches for me with a pained expression. "Tilly."

Snagging a bottle of water, I move as far away from him as possible. "I'm okay," I lie, fighting the urge to move closer. "I'm going…I'm gonna use the bathroom."

Inside the sanctuary of the bathroom, I lean my exposed back against the cool tile wall. I chug water, not stopping when it spills out of my mouth and down my chest. My skin is on fire, nerves that haven't been activated in forever thrown into a tailspin. The tile at my back sends a chill down my spine, the water rolling down my breasts makes my nipples hard, and slowly, so slowly, my hand makes its way down my body.

Arousal continues to overtake my system; my skin is hungry for any touch I'm willing to give it now that it remembers what it's been missing. In a daze, I slide my fingers along my stomach where he touched me and try to replace the image of him behind me with Jessie.

My heightened senses beat their wings like a butterfly finally free from its chrysalis as I circle the pulsing need between my legs, but instead of uttering my husband's name, Archer's name slips from my lips on a moan.

Flooded with shame, I slump against the wall. My cheeks are ruddy in the mirror, my hair messy and clinging to my skin. Tension stretches the muscles of my neck and shoulders, and my normally calm stomach twists in knots.

Frustrated, I head back out to the workspace. The silence is what I notice first. No loud saws or hammers banging, no rock music blaring through the speakers.

Only silence.

Questions batter my brain, and of course it takes the worst road possible. Archer must be disgusted by what happened too.

Damn it, Tilly.

We were just starting to get along. Almost.

I ball my hands into fists, frustrated at the conflicting feelings bouncing around my chest. Archer hasn't given me any indication there are unresolved feelings on his side, so it's ridiculous to feel rejected over something so small.

Trying to take my mind off the fact that Archer left me here, I slide a roll of nails in the nail gun and begin the wood paneling. An hour passes, then two, and still no sign of Archer. Part of me wants to call him to check in, but I won't.

Chapter Eighteen
Tilly

Grandma Tilda, my namesake, used to tell me hate was like drinkin' poison and expecting the other person to die, but I beg to differ. Hate is indifference.

It's the ability to look at someone and no longer feel weighed down by the expectations that come with love, or in my case, attraction.

Her words used to soothe me when I was a child, but as I sit on my back porch, pondering what could've transpired between me and Archer yesterday, they're no longer a balm but a spiked cord wrapping around my heart.

Sunday dinner is today, and I'm not sure I can muster up the energy to go. I spent the last two days working at the bakery and scrolling through dating websites, trying to keep my mind off Archer while simultaneously hoping he'd walk through the door with his crooked smile and tight shirt. I used to think what happened between us was normal third wheel tension, but add that in with the shade I overheard him throwing about my cake at his sister's wedding, and I'm not sure why I even tried keeping him as a friend in my life.

It's been years since Claire's wedding, but I can still hear him saying those same words to a group of friends talking about my baking. *Tilly's only successful because she has supportive parents, that's it. I bet she's never had a bad review,* he'd uttered while refusing to eat my dessert. Next came the little jabs from his friends, *I can't believe your parents paid for this, you're right, her cake isn't all that good,* and *she's about to get her first bad review.*

It almost felt like he'd asked his parents to hire me so he could prove to others that my baking wasn't that good. It wasn't enough that he didn't eat my desserts anymore, he wanted to ruin my reputation with everyone else.

I couldn't stand to listen to them bash me any longer, so I left. No bad reviews were posted, but Jessie said he dealt with it, and Archer still had a black eye a week later when I passed him in the grocery store. It was what I needed to forget any lingering attraction I had to him when Jessie and I first started dating.

After being the one to constantly try to rebuild the bridge that was broken between us all those years ago, I'm not going to be the one to reach out now. I'm thankful for all the work he's completed in the bakery, but it's time to find someone else to help me finish, even if the thought of working with someone else to bring my vision to life gives me indigestion. I rub at the ache in my chest and focus on cleaning my kitchen.

My phone vibrates on the table, and I sigh when I see it's Shantel.

"Hey Seester."

"Where are you?" she asks. "You usually beat me to Mom's."

Chewing on my lips, I try to come up with an excuse. "I'm not feeling good."

"Are you sick? Need some soup?"

"No, it's just my period." The minute I say it I realize the mistake I've made. There are many benefits to being close with my sister-in-law but having synced up cycles is not one of them.

"What's going on, Til? You don't get your period for another two weeks."

"Nothing." I sigh.

"What did he do?"

"Who?" I ask, knowing damn well who she's talking about.

"Archer." Nora's voice sounds in the background, and I wonder, is he there? Is he listening in on this conversation and wondering how I could be so stupid to think he was attracted to me?

"Nothing," I repeat.

"If neither of you are going to tell me what happened I'm going to assume the worst."

A million questions speed through my mind.

What did he say when she asked him? How did she know there was something wrong between us? Would me having feelings for Archer be the worst thing? In my heart I know the answer. It's a betrayal. I was married to her brother. In love with him. How could I so easily forget all we shared just because my body and brain are confused?

"There's nothing going on," I say, my voice a little too high.

She laughs. "Mmhmm. So why aren't either of you coming to dinner?"

Like the idiot that I am, I shrug like she can see me. "I don't know. I guess you'll have to ask him why he's not there, but as for me, I don't feel up to it. I'm sorry if that disappoints you, but I can't..." My voice wavers, emotion clogging my throat. "I can't deal with it right now."

"Okay." The fight leaves her as quickly as it ramped up.

"Thanks, Seester."

Nora sighs in the background when Shantel tells her I'm not coming before the line goes dead, and I know my absence hurts her. I hate how much she's had to go through with losing Jessie, and I know if Archer gets this job and leaves, it'll be like another son lost too. I've been trying to keep my mind off his impending departure, but I can't deny the nausea that wracks my stomach any time I think of it. One by one everyone I care about leaves.

Instead of spiraling, I refocus my thoughts like my therapist taught me and decide to bake.

Nothing sounds good though.

I need fresh flavor profiles.

Anytime I was stuck on a new recipe, Jessie would tell me manual labor always seemed to push him into a new headspace to work through problems, something about using different parts of the brain. While I primed and painted the wainscoting, new recipe ideas popped into my head.

Music fills the kitchen as I throw my hair up into space buns, wrap an apron around my waist, and grab the flour, eggs, sugar, and baking powder for the multiple desserts I intend to bake. Even though it's not necessarily fall weather in Texas, a cranberry, pear, and apple tart seems like a good recipe to start with.

Relaxing into the moment, I sift flour into a bowl, mixing all of the dry ingredients before adding the applesauce to keep my cakes moist. With each scrape of the bowl into a cake pan, my shoulders ease down from my neck.

Twenty minutes pass, and a knock at my door has me walking to the front window with my rolling pin in hand. I relax when Shantel's beaded braids come into view.

"What are you doing here?"

"We figured you needed some company for your mental bakedown."

I snort. "My what?"

"You know," she shrugs, "like a breakdown but instead of crying you're baking."

Nora slams the car door shut and pops her head around the garage. "Hi, sweetie."

Her smile brings a tear to my eye, but I blink it away. She's the best mother-in-law a girl could have, and Shantel isn't too bad either.

"You guys didn't have to come all the way over here."

"We drove like six streets over," Shantel replies, pushing through the doorway. "It wasn't a burden, I promise."

A part of me wants to embrace them, and it terrifies me. Having Archer's hands on me changed something, but the fear still lingers. Will the next person I allow to touch me leave their imprint on my skin? Will my brain no longer be able to differentiate Jessie's—and Archer's—touch from others?

"We brought more flour and sugar." Nora holds up a grocery bag.

"How did you know I was baking?"

Shantel laughs. "You're stressed, and baking makes you happy. We assumed and were correct."

"Touché," I reply.

Crowded around the kitchen island, we each take on a dessert. I hand off the tart to Shantel while Nora gets working on a cardamom and apricot cookie. Baking specialty cakes is where my heart truly lies, but my parents' restaurants are more laid back. They wanted the typical chocolate cake so they could pair it with vanilla ice cream, not a decadent triple layered pineapple and blueberry sponge cake with buttercream icing and a walnut dusting on the side. I've never been one to get excited for weddings, but I can get behind eating wedding cake any day of the week.

"Can you pass the brown sugar?" Shantel asks, gathering the ingredients for the tart's crumble.

Like a teacher, I check over their work to make sure they're measuring correctly and mixing in the right order. Baking is chemistry—I'm phenomenal at Chemistry. It's the whole reason I met Jessie and Archer.

I slip into a memory of sitting at the lab table alone, surrounded by the smell of bunsen burners. In every class I've ever taken, I've always been the last one chosen to be a partner for any kind of project, but this time I wasn't. A hand raised in the back of the room as the teacher was explaining the end of the year project, and out came a voice asking if there could be a group of three. My neck spun like the girl in The Exorcist, and my eyes landed on Archer and Jessie. They were lounging in their chairs, notebooks closed like they hadn't been writing down the important instructions the teacher was doling out.

When the teacher asked Archer to repeat the question, he pointed at me and said, "The numbers for partners are uneven. Can we be a trio?"

He was ruggedly handsome, played on the football team, and drove a big truck. I couldn't lie, I had a small crush, but I wasn't the type of girl he'd have noticed. I'd passed him chatting with friends in the hallway plenty of times, but he'd never acknowledged me before this moment.

In the back of my head, I dreamt he'd picked me because he wanted to, not because he wanted to copy off my work. Study sessions filled with snacks turned into Friday night karaoke and the occasional farmers market trip, but somewhere during that semester we all became legitimate friends. Or at least I thought we did.

"Are you gonna take these to your parents' restaurant?" Nora asks, rolling cookie dough.

Sadness tugs down my shoulders. "I don't know. Dad's been acting weird lately, and I don't want to approach him about changing the menu."

"He's missing out," Nora replies. "These are going to taste so good."

"I hope so," Shantel says.

I bump her shoulder playfully, and like a record scratch, everyone stares at me, waiting to see what I'm going to do. Tingles spread down my arm and up my neck, and I itch to brush the sensation away. But I don't. I focus on the feeling, chasing the euphoria instead of the despair. A half smile pulls at the corner of Shantel's mouth and Nora openly beams. Feeling self-conscious, I look back down at the cake pans and place them in the oven.

"Are you going to go to that singles mixer this weekend?" Nora asks.

I choke on my spit, sputtering out an incoherent sentence as my gaze snaps to Shantel. She's been urging me to get out and meet someone, but I didn't think I was ready. Half the time I still wake up thinking Jessie's going to walk out of the bathroom in his boxers and socks with a toothbrush in his hand. I doubt someone would want to sleep with a woman who still wears her husband's old band shirts and can't manage to make his side of the bed.

"No," I reply, inwardly cursing Shantel for telling Nora.

"Why not?" Nora asks.

Having this conversation with my husband's mother is the last thing I imagined I'd be doing today.

"He's only been gone a year." Chest tightening, I press my fingers into the marble countertop.

"Yes, he has," she says. "And he wouldn't want you to spend any more time lonely."

I quickly reply, "I'm not lonely."

Her side eye is the equivalent of a teacher smacking a student's hand with a ruler.

"I'm fine alone."

Shantel chooses this moment to insert her two cents. "Archer says the same thing."

Something passes between Nora and Shantel, and a sickness takes root in my stomach.

"Don't you dare even think it." I struggle to fill my lungs.

"What?" she asks, innocently, though I can clearly see what she's aiming at.

"Tilly." Nora moves in front of me, her eyes soft and inviting. "Your fire has come back."

"It's because of the bakery."

"Jessie would want you to be happy."

"Not with his best friend," I yell, unaware I just voiced my thoughts outside of my head.

Nora steps back, and I feel the heat staining my cheeks. I've never raised my voice to her, and it's not like she was insinuating that Archer was the reason my fire has come back. Shame rolls in like a storm ready to batter the tattered shelter I've built around my heart.

"I'm sorry," I say, head down. "I'm not in the right headspace to have company right now. Maybe you guys should go."

"No, Til." Shantel sidles up next to me and bends to meet my gaze. "We're sorry. We didn't mean to be pushy. Let's change the subject."

I release a stream of air through my nose, shoulders relaxing from my neck as I nod. Staring down at my flour covered ring centers me. Jessie knew me better than anyone else, knew the things that would make me laugh and smile, and he was the best at giving gifts. The dainty marquise on my finger is a perfect example. With unlimited funds, he could've bought a flashy diamond, but he didn't. He chose something that was more me than him.

He wouldn't want me to move on with someone who didn't cherish me the way he did. And Archer could never love me the way I deserve. He had his chance years ago, and he didn't want it.

He didn't want me.

The thought feels like having a musket shoved into my stomach and fired. The blow ripples through my core, tearing up everything in its path. I beat back the stupid tears pushing against the backs of my eyes and move on to the next dessert.

"We were able to get the licensing to expand into a full nail salon, and that stylist I was poaching decided to come on board," Shantel says, clearing the awkward tension from the air.

Nora and I erupt. "Congratulations! That's amazing news."

"When did it happen?" I grab a bottle of wine from the fridge. "And why didn't you tell us sooner?"

She gnaws on her bottom lip, and I grab the corkscrew. "It happened a few weeks ago, but everything kind of blew up at that Sunday dinner, so I didn't want to ruin the moment."

"Oh my gosh, Shantel." I stop fiddling with the cork and stare at her. "I'm so sorry my meltdown ruined your surprise."

She waves off my apology and grabs the wine bottle. "No apology needed. I'm glad you overheard us talking. It was about time someone told you about the bakery."

Wine glasses filled, I pick one up and let the fruity flavors burst on my tongue. "How long has he been working on it?"

"I think they bought the building a week or two before Jessie passed," Nora replies when Shantel takes too big of a gulp.

A sharp twist in my chest renders me breathless.

"But Archer didn't start back working on it until the mayor told him he needed to get the shop open or forfeit the lease."

A thought occurs to me, and I wrack my brain trying to remember certain moments from after Jessie passed. "Why wasn't I notified of the bakery lease when Jessie's will was read?"

"I'm not su—"

A loud blaring goes off at my neighbor's house. For a moment I'm frozen, unable to think past the whooshing in my ears and my thumping heart. It happens every time I hear sirens, a lingering effect of going through my own tragedy. All thoughts of Archer and my dream bakery are whisked away with the cacophony of sirens and fire engines.

Chapter Nineteen
Archer
Present

D*ear Seb,*
   I am the biggest asshole on the planet. You're probably saying, 'I knew that years ago,' but I finally made sure Tilly knew it too. Oh my god what did I do! Fuck! I don't know what to do, bro. I did something, and I know if you were here, you'd punch me in the balls. I deserve it, too. Hell, I busted my knuckles trying to inflict as much pain on myself as I could.

   I let a moment where Tilly was vulnerable turn into something it shouldn't have, but the feeling of her warm body curved around mine was too tempting. She smelled like lemons. Her hair brushed against my beard when I helped her lay down the wood, and I swore I heard her moan. Like, literally moan. I tried to keep my body as far from her as possible while I helped but then she nearly collapsed, and I couldn't stop myself from wrapping my arm around her stomach and pulling her into me.

   Her body came alive under my touch, and her ass moved back into my territory. You remember what that's like, right? I was instantly stiff the moment I heard her moan, but then she pressed into me hard and I lost all coherent thought. I ~~wanted~~ *needed her to feel what she was doing to me.*

   She came to her senses much faster than I did and ran to the bathroom. It took me a few moments to situate myself and gain my bearings, but I went after her. I pressed my ear to the door, worried she was crying and trying to figure out if I should go in and console her or pretend like it never happened. But that's not what was happening in that bathroom, bro. She moaned my name and it went directly to my dick. I was no good after that. Hell, I basically ran out of there like I was being chased by an axe murderer.

What do I do? What the hell do I do? I can't go back into that bakery and look at her without hearing the way she moaned my name echoing through my brain. That's Jessie's wife. And I know you don't want to hear this, but my cock doesn't care. It doesn't care that my heart twists, stabbing me through every single time I think about her, even when it's not a sexual thought. It screams, 'if you weren't scared, she would've been yours,' but I know it's not true. And even if it was, she wouldn't be available to me.

I've done enough damage to our relationship that there's no way Tilly could look at me and not see all the hurt I've caused her. Realistically, I know her body reacted to me, not her head, but it still created a sliver of hope that she wanted me. That I hadn't ruined any chance of making her mine. But I don't deserve her, and even though I re-flipped your chip, it still lands on tails. You still don't think I deserve her either.

I came home and obliterated a thirty pack over two days, leaving her to work at the bakery alone. I was too ashamed. And maybe if I keep pushing her away, like I have been since she and Jessie got together, she'll eventually stop talking to me altogether, and it won't hurt so much when I actually do leave.

That's not true. It's going to hurt like a bitch, but as with all wounds, sometimes to heal, you gotta put pressure on it and suffer through the pain. And it'll be painful to let her go, but it'll help me stop hurting her in the long run.

Now that I've confessed, I wish I could say I feel better, but you're a terrible ghost priest. You don't talk back, you make me talk and tell you all my secrets, but you couldn't even trust me with yours. I wish I could say

I forgive you, but I don't. I'm still mad as hell. More at myself than you, but still a whole bunch toward you.

Anyway, I meant to write this to let you know how my recent interview went. I'm supposed to meet with the producers in Knoxville in the middle of next month. There was another guy and a couple there to interview before me, but they were more focused on flipping houses instead of carpentry work. We still haven't been told what the show will be about exactly, but I have an inkling it'll be a competition-based show, or maybe we'll be consulting on big projects like Ty from Extreme Home Makeover.

The next meeting isn't until mid-November, so I just have to make it through a few more Sunday dinners before I leave for good, whether or not I get the job. Nora asks me weekly if I've heard anything, and each time it breaks my heart. I know they'll come visit, but I'll miss having the access to them that I do now. I haven't told Mom or Dad yet, but I doubt they'll care. Claire is the only one who shows a modicum of attention to me, and even that is behind Dad's back.

One of these days he'll realize I'm not a fuck-up. That my work is just as important and worthy of praise as their craft. It probably won't be any time soon, but it'll happen. And I know you'll be smiling up in Heaven when I tell him to shove it. Miss you man.

-Arch

Chapter Twenty
Tilly

The brisk November air stuns me the minute I step outside of the house, and immediately I go back inside to change. In Texas during fall, the weather changes at the drop of a dime. The chilly mornings turn sweltering by mid-afternoon, leaving you sweating in a long sleeve t-shirt. Today's attire, a lime green flannel shirt with vertical pink stripes and denim jeans, will suit me just fine if I wear a tank top beneath it.

Shuffling the box of treats for my parents' restaurant to the side, I wave hello to my elderly neighbor, the one who is thankfully okay now and sitting on her front porch. I was grateful for the interruption to the awkward conversation Shantel and Nora started in the kitchen, but my blood pressure took entirely too long to even out after that.

Any sirens bring back memories of the day Jessie died.

Like an ad popping up in my mind, the memory of that morning assaults me as I walk down the stairs. The ambulance and fire engines came blaring in, worried because I kept screaming at the 911 operator on the phone to help me save Jessie.

November isn't just a month on a calendar to me anymore.

It's the month we were supposed to be celebrating two years of marriage, the month my life irrevocably changed. If I didn't have things to do at the bakery, I'm sure I'd be looking for something to keep my mind busy. Instead, I get on the road to my parents' restaurant with my eyes stinging and an ache behind my ribcage.

"Morning, Til," one of the cooks says when I arrive at the back door of the restaurant.

"Morning," I reply.

Dad isn't in the office when I peek my head in, and immediately I'm on edge. That's his nest, the place he goes to hide from the customers and eat a Snickers. I go on a search mission and find him standing in front of the dessert case with an older woman in a flowing dress. Her hand is on his forearm and they're laughing like they've known each other all their lives. An odd feeling thumps inside my chest before it thuds to the pit of my stomach.

"You're here early."

I hear Dad's voice, but my mind is far away. The box is removed from my hands, and I snap back into focus. Dad's mouth is pinched tight, his expression one of uneasy tension. I clear my throat and answer.

"I couldn't find you in the back, so I came to put the desserts away."

"I'm glad you're here." He motions to the woman standing off to the side. "This is Gloria."

Gloria sticks out her hand but then yanks it back, her cheeks taking on a pink hue. "Oops, I'm sorry. Your dad told me you don't like to be touched."

He told her that? When? Just this morning when she came into the restaurant? That uneasy feeling swirling around my stomach gathers into a storm.

"Nice to meet you," she says, smiling like my world isn't tilting.

The way my dad looks at her, the slight spark in his eye, makes me wonder if I'm missing something. This woman couldn't be...no, she isn't. I'm misreading the situation.

"This is my girlfriend."

His voice sounds far away due to the pounding in my ears and the loud ripping sound that is my paper heart. His girlfriend? But he's...married.

"Tilda," Dad says. "Did you hear me?"

I nod, blinking rapidly like I have the power to rewind time and stay in that sweet moment before he uttered those words. All of the times he's rushed me out of the restaurant, the distance he's created between us comes into focus. He had a secret girlfriend. "Yeah."

"It's nice to finally meet you, Tilda," Gloria says.

"Tilly," I say. "It's Tilly."

Only my parents call me Tilda, and one surly carpenter when he's angry, but this woman? This interloper? She doesn't get that right.

Gloria's worried gaze moves to my dad, who clears his throat to bring me back to the present.

"Yeah," I reply. "You too."

Words evade me, and too many emotions pelt my armor. I turn and walk away, ignoring Dad's voice as I head to my car.

Not now.

I can't.

How could he move on? Did his and my mom's love mean nothing to him? My own conscience chastises me the minute I think it. Not long ago I was pressing myself against Archer's body, desperate for his touch. A touch I've apparently harbored a desire for since my husband passed. How am I any better?

Vomit pushes its way up my throat, and I force myself to pull over and get some fresh air. Sucking in large gulps of gas station air infused with the smell of burnt hot dogs, I finally find some clarity.

His eyes were shimmering.

Dad was full of life again.

He had a smile on his face and he was laughing. It's been so long since I've seen him happy that I didn't recognize it. Didn't recognize something was changing over the past few weeks when he'd rush me out of the restaurant or not want me to linger after dropping off my desserts. Or was it me who didn't want to linger? In his defense, he did always ask what I'd been up to, but he still kept *this* from me.

A girlfriend.

My dad has a girlfriend, and she's pretty. I'm sure she's kind too, but I didn't even give her a chance. I swept out of there so fast you'd only know I was there because of the treats I left behind.

My Bluetooth alerts me to a missed call once I get back into the car. Swiping the phone from my center console, I see two missed calls from my dad. I'm not ready to talk to him just yet. I'm not even sure what I'd say if I did call him back, but until I can process this, it's better for me to stay silent.

***

The door to the bakery is propped open when I arrive, and the tell-tale sound of rock music drifts into my ears. A shiver works its way up my spine, and the hairs on my arms raise. What is he doing here?

Slipping in through the door, I find Archer on a step ladder nailing drywall. The entire wall separating the back of the house from the front is erected, and my breath whooshes out of me.

"What the hell?"

Archer doesn't turn around, so I walk to where his phone is beside the speaker and lower the volume.

"Hey," he yells, nearly falling off the ladder when he sees me. "Tilly," he breathes.

"What the hell are you doing?"

His teeth clamp down over his lips like a child who said a bad word.

I repeat myself.

The ladder creaks as he descends and wipes the caulking from his hands. "What does it look like?"

"You can't come back after you deserted me for almost a week." My voice cracks, and any chance I had to pretend I'm not affected is out the window.

"I'm sor—"

"Nope." I halt his words, pulling an envelope from my bag and handing it to him. "I don't want to hear it. I've got another carpenter due here in half an hour, so please grab your stuff and leave."

"What's this?" he asks.

"Checks."

His annoyed sigh and the accompanying eye roll nearly bring a smile to my face.

"For what?"

"For every week up until the end of the year."

"Absolutely not," he replies, anger replacing the previously apologetic look on his face.

A laugh wholly unrecognizable to me leaves my mouth. "Absolutely yes."

"I don't want your money," he gruffs out.

He throws the envelope onto the worktable, and my hands clench at my sides. "I know you said Jessie paid you for what you've done already, but this is for any job you had to turn down to take on this one. You're free to do whatever job you want now."

My heart slingshots inside my chest when Archer strides my way, the set of his jaw screaming determination and destruction. The sharp angles of his face make the first cut through the defenses I've built the last few days, and poison seeps into his irises.

"Not happenin', darlin'." His minty breath freezes my heart inside my chest, and he turns his back to me. "I'm not taking the money. Call whoever it is and tell them the job's taken."

It takes a beat for me to gather my bearings. "Why?"

He stops. "What do you mean why?"

Forcing my bottom lip to stop wavering, I bite it, causing a blast of pain to spread down my neck.

"Being around me is such a struggle for you, so why continue the job? This is an easy out." My charm bracelet jingles as I throw my hands in the air.

His muscles flex as he presses down on the countertop, and his shoulders inch up to his neck. "It has to be me."

"No, it doesn't."

"Yes, it does." His voice is pained.

"Gosh darnit, Archer." I stomp my foot. "No, it doesn't. Jessie is gone. He's not going to come back to haunt you if you stop helping me."

"It's not about him." Archer increases the volume on his music app and climbs back up the ladder with a drill in hand. "Call the other carpenter and tell him the job is taken."

His words, and the pain cinching his eyebrows together, leave me breathless.

If it's not about Jessie, then it's about me, and nothing about that equation makes sense. We can barely tolerate each other. Had this been four years ago, I would've accepted his insinuation that he's here for me. But friends do favors for friends, and we're barely amicable.

Something in the back of my head urges me to let him help, like Jessie is there scolding me for being mean to his friend who's only trying to help bring his dream for me alive. Frustrated, I type out a message thanking the other carpenter for his help and promising to pay him for his time even though he didn't actually do any work.

Screws puncture the drywall, the whirring sound drawing my attention to Archer. That same fluttering in my stomach returns, and I try to squash it by reminding myself why we'd never work. Outside of the obvious issue of him being my late husband's best friend, Archer is surly, childish, and can be notoriously bad at communication.

During college, me, Jessie, and Archer would text all the time. Even on holiday breaks, Archer would call to check on me. But after Jessie and I started dating, Archer got a new girlfriend and fell off the face of the earth. He rarely came to anything I invited him to, and when he did, it was like we barely knew each other anymore.

Jessie knew me. The way I liked things, the things that made me happy or sad, knew when to back off before an argument made us too flustered.

But why is your body reacting this way?

The thought rams through my defenses, rendering me stunned. With Jessie, our lovemaking was sweet, sensual. Candles and music, soft words spoken. I didn't have to worry about love marks on my neck or having to check my hair before I met friends. It wasn't the tear your clothes off type of feeling I get while fighting with Archer, but it was...us.

Sick to my stomach, I admonish myself and the obscene thoughts running through my head. Archer and I are wrong for each other. Always have been.

"Knock knock," a woman's voice cuts through the room.

A volcano spurs to life inside my chest.

"Hey, Deidre." Archer comes down from the ladder and leans on the counter. "What's up?"

Deidre walks inside, and I can't help my eyes from moving to Archer. Is he happy to see her? Excited? Filled with lust? A green ball of envy settles in my chest, and I find myself angry she was able to touch him, to know his innermost thoughts, and to wake up with his arms wrapped around her.

Stunned by my own thoughts, I stumble to the side, accidentally tripping over the drill cord and sending a closed paint can rolling her way. Her blue eyes snap to me awkwardly standing there, and her previously pasted on smile falters.

"Tilly." Her lips pinch, but she forces that smile back on and looks at Archer. "I forgot you were helping her with this...place." She waves her hand around like she can't quite put her finger on what it is. In her defense, it's kind of chaos right now.

Large swaths of cloth protect the new vinyl flooring from any paint splatters, a countertop in the middle of the place serves as our makeshift workstation, and the wall Archer is working on is half complete. It's a wreck.

But it's my wreck.

"Yeah." Archer rubs the back of his neck, his eyes bouncing between us like he's uncomfortable.

I decide it's easier for us both if I leave. I need a breather anyway.

Shoulders back, I search for my keys. "I'm going to Rosie's. Want your usual, Arch?"

Deidre's jaw tenses, and I know I've pissed her off. I don't want Archer to think all is squashed between us, but I need to remove myself from the situation and clear my head. Rosie will be happy to hear an update on my bakery adventures, and I need caffeine if I'm going to survive another day in close quarters with him.

"Uh, yeah," Archer replies, a hint of light now back in his eyes and a half-smile turned my way.

Damn it. Don't smile at me like that.

A familiar tune plays through Archer's speakers as I'm gathering my bag.

"Jessie's Girl." Deidre smirks, looking down her sharp nose in disgust. "How ironic."

Everything I've eaten or drank today moves into my throat. I clamp my cheeks in between my teeth and try to keep the tears at bay. The stabbing sensation in my chest moves to my stomach, and I wrap my arms around myself to try to stop from breaking down. In this moment I could use Archer's comfort, but when I look to him, he's stone. He's not blinking, his body is rigid, and I'm not sure he's breathing at all.

I don't wait for either of them to speak. Stepping outside, I suck in the largest breath possible and sprint to my car, seeking a quiet place to break down. Shame is a weight on my chest as I pull into traffic and put the bakery, and my pesky feelings for my husband's best friend, in the rearview mirror.

Chapter Twenty-One
Archer
Jessie and Tilly's Wedding

*D*ear Seb,

Can you hear bells up in heaven? What about hell? Because that's where it feels like I am right now. Today was the day I've dreaded the past six months. It's their wedding day, my two best friends. I know it doesn't seem like Tilly is my friend, let alone my best friend, but she was at one point. She was the first person I wanted to talk to in the morning, even if all she chatted about was the periodic table or the new traffic light earrings she bought. She knew our parents were assholes, even if she didn't know why, and she still consoled me when I had a bad day after fighting with them. She even encouraged me to follow my dreams of becoming a carpenter instead of doing what they wanted me to. College would've sucked without BOTH of them.

Without Jessie I probably wouldn't have graduated and gotten into that apprenticeship with Mr. Banner. After you passed, Jessie kept my head on straight, didn't let me get drunk every day, and made sure on the days I did drink, that I didn't go too far. We looked out for each other and spent as much time together as possible.

So when he asked me to be his best man at his wedding, how could I say no? I couldn't. I couldn't look my best friend, my brother by choice, in the eye and tell him I couldn't stand beside him while he married the woman of his—our—dreams. He deserved that type of happiness, and I didn't.

The shitty part is that I flipped your poker chip, like I always do, and asked if I should stop the wedding. Would you find a way to convince God to make her feet cold, give her a sign that it wasn't Jessie, but me who she was meant to be with? Unsurprisingly, it landed on tails. You, in your own way, had spoken. It wasn't going to happen, and I just needed to get over it.

I know this, yet I can't figure out what it is about her I can't get over. I bought her a bracelet with a mixing bowl charm and left it on the gift table along with all the other gifts. I didn't sign it. I didn't want her to know it came from me because with how I've avoided her the past two years she would've thrown it away.

I love Jessie, and I know he's the right person for her—even though he doesn't truly know her like I do. I just need to make a promise to myself to quit cold turkey. I'm done being a terrible friend.

I thought watching them get married would be the most excruciating pain in the world, but it wasn't. She looked beautiful in her wedding dress; it was tight to her curvy body, the lace highlighted her beautiful brown skin, and her hair was straight and had one single braid with flowers in it. I missed her curls, the natural unruliness they seem to carry with their bounce. She stood in front of Jessie with a big smile on her face and tears in her eyes. She was...happy. Did I still imagine she was reciting the vows to me? Yes. Did my lungs cease working when her eyes locked on mine right before she said, "I do?" Also, yes.

But something happened in the moment after the pastor declared them husband and wife. Something that felt earth shattering. I felt at peace, like she was where she was meant to be. Her happiness was more important than anything, and I knew Jessie would treat her right. She'd never want for anything, she'd have a mother-in-law that was kind and warm, not like our mother. She'd be able to sleep at night without someone waking up with nightmares or refusing to come to bed because they couldn't stop their mind from whirring, the spiraling that happens when I start thinking about you.

Tilly doesn't deserve that. She deserves someone whole. Someone who wouldn't tarnish the light she has pouring out of her. And the person for that job is Jessie.

Watching them, so in love, made me think about my future. Deidre's back in town, and she wants to get together. I know I told you she was annoying and bitchy, but she only left me because she caught on to my attraction to Tilly and didn't want to be second fiddle. I couldn't blame her, and it wasn't right for me to string her along, but I don't want to spend life alone.

I want a wife and kids. Even if they only have me and their mom as a family because our parents suck. I'm sure Nora would be a great surrogate grandmother, and Shantel and Jessie...and Tilly, will be great aunts and uncles to my kids. Like I would've been to yours, if you were still here.

Facing down a future where you don't get to meet my family sucks. It's the worst, and I loathe myself for the anger I still harbor in my heart toward you. Will I ever get rid of it? Or is it destined to live in my heart like a poison waiting to seep into my bloodstream and strangle me?

I'm making myself a promise, making you a promise. This time next year I'll be happy again. I'll be doing a job I love, and I'll be dating someone I genuinely care about. I'll be going on double dates with Tilly and Jessie because I'll have moved on, and maybe I'll even find a way to fix things with Mom and Dad.

Okay, that last one is a lie. I'm not going to try with Mom and Dad. Bite me. They deserve every bit of my contempt, and if you don't like it then you should convince God to rewind time, so your dumb ass doesn't get yourself killed. I gotta run. But just know that I'm going to make you proud.

-Arch

Chapter Twenty-Two
Tilly

I'm a coward.

I couldn't go back into the bakery and pretend like nothing happened. I've been sitting inside Rosie's cafe for an hour trying to convince myself I wasn't upset by Deidre's appearance, or that my heart didn't break a little bit when I imagined him embracing her after I left.

I'm a married woman.

Or, I was.

None of the therapy groups I went to after Jessie died covered the part of grief where your heart starts to beat again. They didn't tell me it'd hurt like a broken-down machine coming back to life, the cogs and gears rusted over, whining as they shift back into motion.

If this is what moving on without the person I thought I'd have forever with feels like, I don't want it. It's like I have the flu; my skin is constantly feverish, muscles achy from being so tense, and my stomach is on a carousel, spinning too fast.

"Want another?" Violet stops by the table, jolting me from my self-loathing.

I'm on a pathway that's splitting. I can go back to the bakery and pretend like nothing happened and get back to work, or I can call Shantel for some emergency girl time and text Archer an excuse.

Fear wins out and my fingers swiftly move across the screen typing out a message to my sister-in-law.

"No, thank you." I rise from the booth and pitch my half empty cup into the trash, stopping a moment to leave a tip in the jar.

I flip through the radio, trying to find something to take my mind off what I'm driving away from. Archer texted back that he hoped I'd get some rest and feel better and that he'd finish up the wall today so we could start setting up the front of the bakery.

His kindness creates another hole in my armor and reignites my reasoning for getting away from him. The more I'm around him and the nicer he is to me, the harder it is to fight the attraction.

"Hey girl hey," Shantel chimes when I arrive at the salon.

She's mid-way through shaving the side of an elderly lady's hair. The woman is tattooed and has purple streaks going through her braided hair. She's everything I hope I'll be when I grow up.

"Hey." I sit in the empty stylist's seat beside Shantel's area.

"Why the long face?" the elderly woman asks. "Rough day?"

I snort. "You could say that."

Shantel's eyes narrow, pinning me to the chair and wrapping themselves around me like zip ties. "What happened with Archer?"

I cock my head, eyes darting to the woman she's trimming. "Nothing."

"I presume you're Tilly," the woman says.

My mouth pops open, eyes burning a hole into the side of Shantel's face. Unbothered, she shrugs. "She was here last time he came in bitching about me threatening to tell you about the bakery."

"That man is one fine hunk of real estate." She fans a hand in front of her face. "If only I was forty years younger and didn't live in a retirement village."

I chuckle. "I'm sure he'd love you no matter what age you are."

"So, what did he do?" she asks while Shantel turns on the electric shaver and presses the blade to her head. "He didn't cheat on you, did he?"

I sputter out a cough. "Oh, no. We're not...we're not together."

"But you want to be," she supplies.

"No." My nervous laughter betrays me.

"Til," Shantel halts her buzzing and gives me a side-eye.

"Don't start." I suck in a breath, reminded of the way Deidre smirked as the Rick Springfield tune played. I am—and will always be—Jessie's girl.

"Well," the woman says, "go on. Tell me what he did."

"He didn't do anything," I mutter.

"Then what's got you in such a tizzy?" she asks.

I can tell I'm not getting out of here without answering, so I hunker down and decide there's no better place to air my dirty laundry than the stylist's chair. One of Shantel's other stylists comes over and asks me if I want her to do my hair.

"Give me something new," I say. "I need to get out of this funk."

"Say less, babe."

"Stop stalling," Shantel's client says. "I'm on pins and needles here."

With a cape wrapped around my shoulders, I close my eyes and let the stylist get to work. I don't want to see what she's doing, and to be honest, I don't know if I can meet Shantel's eyes when I say what I'm about to say.

"I'm attracted to my late husband's best friend." I wince, waiting for the grief and shame to pummel me, but instead all I find is lighter shoulders and more room in my chest to breathe.

"What's the problem with that?" Shantel's client, who eventually introduces herself as Zevia, replies.

"Did you not hear what I said?" I ask, eyes popping open and fixed on her face. "He's my husband's best friend, and an asshole."

"I may be old, but I'm not deaf." Shantel brushes the woman's neck free of the buzzed hairs and starts coloring her hair. I glance at her, hoping to catch some type of reaction to my confession, but her face is clear of anything but concentration on what she's doing. "You're a widow who's ready to get back in the dating game. There's nothing wrong with moving on."

Emotion rises in my throat. "Not with his best friend."

"The heart chooses who it chooses."

"He treats me like a pariah," I reply. "We can barely keep eye contact, and stay on opposite sides of the building."

"Ever think he might push you away because he's dealing with the same conflicting feelings?" Zevia says.

"Mmhmm," Shantel chimes in.

"How could you say that?" I meet her eyes in the mirror. "Archer loved Jessie."

"You're right," Shantel says. "They were thick as thieves, and nothing could separate them. Even you. Just because Archer may or may not have had feelings for you, he never would have done anything to jeopardize his friendship with Jessie."

"Being a jerk to his best friend's wife, someone he used to call a friend, doesn't qualify?"

"Til, is he being a jerk or is there some place inside you that recognizes you were hurt when he pushed you away after you and Jessie got together?" Shantel sighs. "I'm not saying it's right, but maybe he's been trying to protect his heart and keep his integrity intact, and to do that he couldn't be close to you any more."

Her insight ushers in a hurricane of emotions and memories that knock me down. Every smile, hug, or congratulations he gave is torn down and a new light shed on them. Every jab, smart remark, or missed celebration takes on a new look.

One that paints a picture I'm not ready to look at too closely.

I close my eyes, struggling to gain my composure. "I don't want to talk about this anymore."

"Suit yourself, pumpkin," Zevia says. "When you're ready to open your heart to happiness again, love will find you."

I want to laugh at her fortune cookie way of looking at life and love, but the simplistic words are too true for my liking.

"Thanks for the sick new do'," she says to Shantel.

Music softly plays in the background as the stylist applies a new color to my hair. I peek an eye open and catch Shantel staring at the ground as she sweeps up the remnants from Zevia's haircut. Her face is relaxed, and she's humming. If I found out my brother's wife harbored a secret attraction to his best friend, I'd be upset. But Shantel? She's living her best life, shaking her butt to Rick Astley.

"I love you, Seester," I say.

"And I love you, Til."

Surprised when a hand clasps onto mine, I squeeze back and look at her. "Always."

"Forever," she replies.

An hour passes while Shantel does a few more customers and chats with me while the stylist washes and blow-dries my hair. I've managed to not look into a mirror the entire time, but as the minutes inch closer, my heart rate moves into a dangerous territory. What color did she do? Will I look okay? What will Archer think?

I admonish myself for that last thought and let the stylist spin me around.

"Holy shit." My breath rushes out of me, quick like a popped balloon. "I love it."

"So do I." Shantel stands behind me with a smile, snapping a picture of my hair.

The base color is a tad darker, more luscious than my natural mousy brown, and the dark blue to teal ombre makes my skin pop. Curtain bangs frame my face, and I can imagine how awesome it'll look when I put my hair up in my signature space buns and add some funky earrings.

I look like…me.

Well, the me I used to be. The happy girl from college who wore funky clothes, danced everywhere, and sang karaoke as loud as possible.

"Archer's tongue is going to be on the floor when he sees you," Shantel says.

"Yeah, okay," I reply. "Besides, it doesn't matter what he thinks."

She raises her hands in surrender. "I only want you to be happy, you know that, right?"

"So you tell me all the time."

"You never listen though."

I shrug. "How can you be happy that there's a spark between us? That's a betrayal to Jessie, and you're his sister."

"Which means I knew him quite well," she interjects. "And he'd want the two most important people in his life to be happy, even if it meant being with each other."

My throat closes, a chill sweeping up my neck. I hadn't thought about it like that, hadn't considered what Jessie would've hoped my life looked like without him.

An image of my mom and dad pops into my head, a slight nudging to talk to the one person who understands what it's like to move on after a spouse passes.

I swallow the discomfort rising in my chest. "I've gotta go face my dad, so I'll talk to you later."

"Will do." She winks at me. "And let me know how Archer reacts when he sees you tomorrow."

"Okay." I laugh and walk to my car.

It's been a long day, and I know the conversation I've been putting off with my dad is only going to drain me further, but it needs to happen.

Gloria pulls out of the driveway when I approach, and waves her hand out the window with a big smile. "Hi, Tilly. Sorry I missed you. Hope to see you next time," she yells.

She seems sweet, and I feel bad for how I reacted the other day. It's not her fault I was feeling betrayed by the men in my life. I wave and pull into the spot she vacated.

"Tilda," Dad says when I enter the house. "I'm so glad to see you."

The tension is made even more awkward when he puts his fist out for me to bump. I stare at it a moment. After Archer broke the touch barrier, everyone else's touch doesn't seem so...scary. I inhale a deep breath and put him out of his misery by bumping my knuckles against his.

"I love the new hair." He smiles, but it doesn't reach his eyes. It's tentative, like he's worried I'm going to bite off his head.

I sweep some loose hair into a bun. "Thanks."

His gaze falls to my outfit, and surprisingly his mouth doesn't turn into a frown.

"You look nice," he says. "Cool rain boots."

I puff out my cheeks, unsure how to respond to this new version of my dad. He never comments on my outfits with actual words but with facial cues.

"Thanks." I point to his head. "Your haircut looks nice."

The level of awkwardness is taut like a guitar string, one strum away from exploding off the fret and curling into itself. Sick of tiptoeing around the men in my life's feelings, I go right for the jugular.

"Why didn't you tell me you were dating?"

He sighs and waves me into the kitchen. Pulling out a stool at the island, he pats on it and tells me to sit. He silently puts a kettle on the stove and pulls out our cups and tea bags. Mom used to use "teatime" as an excuse to weasel her way into learning all the new dramas of teenagers in high school. As I was on the outside of the popular clique, I rarely had any tidbits of information for her, but she filled in the silence with questions that made me feel seen.

I've never seen Dad use the kettle, or drink tea, for that matter. I guess Gloria's making a bigger impression than I expected.

"I didn't know how to tell you." His attention is on the kettle, and the way his shoulders slump makes me realize how hard this is for him too. "You were still grieving, and I'd finally started dating and reconnected with Gloria. It felt a little like rubbing it in your face, and I didn't want to add to your pain."

Understanding settles over me, right along with guilt that my father hid his happiness for so long because he was worried about me. "I was a wreck when Jessie passed. I still am."

The kettle whistles, and Dad pours the hot tea into a mug and squeezes a lemon inside it. Just like Mom did.

"I'm sorry you felt you had to hide it, and I'm even sorrier for how I acted when I met Gloria. She seems really nice."

"She's amazing." We both take a sip of tea, letting the warm liquid seep into our bones. "But I'll always love your mom, sweetheart."

I sigh. "I know."

"And I'll always love you, too. I know I've done a horrible job of showing you that, but I'm trying to get better. There's no excuse for it, but I didn't know how to love you when I was hurting so bad. I was scared I'd mess things up and hurt you too. And when you lost Jessie, we were both still in that place of hurt and couldn't see past it."

I prepare for the tension to inch back into my muscles, but it doesn't. Who figured talking about these things would actually help? I remind myself to reach out to my therapist for an appointment to hash out everything that's transpired this week.

"Gloria came into my life at my lowest and showed me what I was giving up by keeping everyone at arm's length." He chuckles, a small smile tugging at his cheek. "She chastised me the other day for how unfair I was being to you with trying your new recipes."

"I'm glad you found each other." I slide my finger around the mug rim, trying to decide if I want to bring up whatever is going on between me and Archer.

"Me, too," Dad says after a moment. "She's great."

The worry about how this conversation with my dad would go seeps away from my chest. My lungs expand, pressing against my ribcage as I inhale what feels like the deepest breath, and when I exhale, relief pours into my veins, spreading out to all my tense muscles.

"How did you meet?" I ask.

"We went to college together." He smiles, pours himself another cup of tea. "She was the girlfriend of the quarterback, and I was just the weird band kid she sat beside during the pep rallies. She was nice, but I knew I had no chance up against the school's saving grace."

I laugh. "I bet that quarterback flunked out of college because he couldn't stop binge drinking at the frat parties."

He chuckles. "No, he's actually pretty successful now. But they weren't meant to be long term. God had other plans in store for all of us."

"That's lovely, Dad." And it is. I like to think God has another plan for my life through this bakery Jessie set up for me, that he knew he'd be taking Jessie and wanted me to have something that would always be an extension of him.

"What about you, pumpkin?" he asks, pinning me with sympathetic eyes.

My head throbs with the words threatening to burst forth. Dad would understand the dilemma I'm in with my feelings for Archer. He has firsthand experience moving on after losing the love of your life. But my mom passed years ago, and it's been less than two years since Jessie died. That's too soon to be feeling like this for someone else, right? The fear of his disappointment keeps my lips zipped shut.

"Uh..." I struggle to come up with something to reply. This thing with Archer is confusing to me, and I'm not sure I'd even be able to explain it to him when I don't have a good grasp on what's happening yet. Figuring a half-truth is better than a lie, I say, "I'm just focused on baking right now."

His shoulders slump, and his brows furrow, making the wrinkles at the corners of his eyes more prominent. "I know it's not easy to think about dating again."

"Dad." I sigh, trying to ignore the uneasy feeling bouncing around my chest.

"Pumpkin." He reaches for my hand again before pulling it back. "Jessie, like your mother, will *always* have a piece of your heart that will never belong to anyone else." He bends forward, making sure he has my full attention. "But, eventually you wake up one day and it's not an immediate gut punch when you realize they aren't there. One day it won't hurt to simply draw a breath or to make the bed or even to smile. There might even be a day when you find the butterflies you thought were long dead in your stomach start to flap around again."

Heat warms my cheeks, and I think about how spot on my dad is with his words—minus the making the bed part.

"I never thought it would happen for me. Your mom was my everything, and there's not a single day that goes by where I don't see her in the little things, the flowers she planted out front, the broken off knob on the stove," he says, chuckling as he glances toward the stove before turning his attention back to me. "And the beautiful daughter she blessed me with."

I press my tongue into my cheek, begging the tears to stay trapped behind my eyelids.

"I pray you find the happiness I know Jessie would want you to have, like your mom wanted for me."

"Damn, Dad." A stray tear sneaks out, sliding down my cheek. I wipe it away before it reaches my chin. "I did not expect this conversation tonight."

He chortles. "If it makes you feel any better, I didn't expect to be talking about this tonight either. But I'm glad I got the chance to see you. It's been too long since I got some time with my girl."

I open my mouth to mention that it was him that put distance between us but think better of it.

Tonight is a fresh start for both of us.

"Gloria wants to try some of your new desserts," Dad says sheepishly.

"Oh, really?" I narrow my gaze, casually settling back into my chair.

"I know, I know," he says, head hung. "I was stuck in the past, trying to keep everything the same way your mom and I did when we opened the restaurants. I was clinging to anything I could to keep a piece of her when all I needed to do was let go. Gloria told me I wasn't just holding myself back from moving forward but also holding you back."

Excitement rushes through my bloodstream, and I itch to get home and into the kitchen. After another cup of tea, I speed home, ready to prove my desserts are worth the hype.

Chapter Twenty-Three
Archer
Present

Cracked and moisture ridden, my old phone screen stares at me with a sharp look of disdain, clearly admonishing me for not only keeping it alive though it's on its last leg, but for scrolling through text messages I've never been able to delete from six years ago. I should've gotten rid of the old Motorola Razr after college but reading Sebastian's old messages helps me relax.

A timer dings, and I get up from the couch and head to the kitchen to check on my Dr Pepper pulled pork in the crockpot. The scents of garlic and paprika float into my nose, and the liquid smoke I used gives the pork a hint of smoky flavor. Once it's shredded, I grab the BBQ sauce and a cold beer before sitting at the table with the old phone in my hand.

Between mouthfuls, I scroll down memory lane, reminding myself of all the stupid shenanigans me, Jessie, and Sebastian used to get into: TP'ing our teachers' houses, the massive bubble fan we stuck inside the principal's office, and even taking our parents' car out for a joyride.

Thumbing through the phone, I land on a thread of messages from a number I haven't seen in years. Opening it, I realize it's conversations between me and Tilly. We stopped texting daily after she and Jessie got together, and not too long after that I deleted her contact from my old phone. It was too much of a temptation, and I figured I could trick my brain into forgetting it was her number.

Deidre's comment from the other day bounces around my head like a spiky ball, digging into the soft tissue and poisoning my thoughts. I grit my teeth, wondering if that song was sent to the radio at that exact moment by Sebastian up in heaven, his version of a joke. He would've gotten a kick out of embarrassing me like that in front of a woman, but that wasn't the emotion I felt. A mixture of shame, confusion, and uncertainty swelled in my stomach, but on the tails of that came a blip of hope.

I nearly choke on my pork when my scrolling produces a picture of Tilly covered in yellow goo from head to toe. Laughing, I download the picture and send it to the phone I use now so I can forward it to Tilly.

She didn't come back to the shop after Deidre left, and as much as I want to delve into the potential reasons why, I know it wouldn't be good for me to go down that path. We're barely on friendly terrain now, I don't want to mess it up by insinuating she's feeling something other than apathy.

I try to quiet the frenetic thoughts in my head as my finger hovers over the send button. Slowly, the ice between Tilly and me has started to thaw, but I know she's like an iceberg. On the surface she's been calm, fun to work with, easygoing as usual, but I can see there is still a glacier of hurt beneath the still waters from when I pushed her away. Like a schoolyard crush, I purposefully ignored the girl I liked because I was too scared to man up and tell her my feelings, and I regret it.

Suck it up and do it, I coach myself as I stare down at my iPhone, hovering over Tilly's name on the screen.

Me: *In my humble opinion, the yellow elephant toothpaste was one of your best looks.*

The swoosh of the sent message immediately brings a bead of sweat to my neck and I lay my phone down. After taking a few more bites I pick it up again, shoulders falling when there isn't a new message or any hint she even received it. I've always hated when people talk about turning on the "read" feature to see when someone reads their messages, but the temptation to do it now is almost unbearable.

Stomach now satisfied, I clean the dishes. A ding steals my attention, and the clatter of the plate inside the sink rings loudly in the empty house. I wipe my soapy hands on my jeans without sparing a look to make sure the plate isn't broken and pick up my phone.

Tilly: *If I remember correctly, we ended up getting a B on that project because you and Jessie kept trying to put extra stuff in the solution.*

I laugh out loud, allowing a wide smile to take over my face. Jessie and I loved playing pranks on the goody-two shoes teacher's pet. Unfortunately, our prank backfired when he and Tilly swapped containers because she wanted the yellow one.

Me: *You can't deny the prank was funny, even if it backfired.*

Tilly: *BACKFIRED?!?! It took three days to get it completely out of my hair!*

Me: *I told you to stick with the blue container I gave you.*

Tilly sends me a gif of a little girl giving a massive side eye to the camera.

Me: *But you looked adorable in your shower cap when you came to the study session.*

Shit. I can't believe I just told her she looked adorable. Could I make it any more awkward?

Tension inches up my spine as I try to decide whether to take it back or to pretend like it never happened. Three dots appear, and it feels like the countdown at New Year's where I'm simultaneously thankful the year is over and terrified at what's about to happen in the next. My phone dings.

Tilly: *Umm...thanks.*

Fuck.

How the hell do I fix this?

Another ding.

Tilly: *I think I'm owed some retribution for the hardship of having to wash my hair three times in a row.*

Me: *I'll wash your hair.*

What the hell, Archer? That is not what you were supposed to say. I smack my forehead, cursing myself for making things uncomfortable again. How can we ever get closer if I can't even talk to her like a normal human being?

A vibrating on the table breaks my pity party, and my heart rate takes off like it's at the races when Tilly's name flashes on the screen. With sweaty palms, I pick up the phone and debate on letting it go to voicemail. Is she calling to yell at me? To tell me I've crossed a line and she doesn't want to work with me anymore?

I muster up the courage and press answer.

"Hello?"

"You know, in some cultures offering to wash someone's hair is a declaration of marriage," Tilly says.

I swear my gulp is audible. Flooded with images of Tilly standing across the aisle from me, beautiful in a lace dress and long veil, I forget to speak.

"I'm kidding, Arch." She laughs, and it's like walking into a warm room after being outside in the freezing cold. I haven't heard that beautiful noise in far too long.

Pots and pans clank around in the background as I try to formulate a coherent sentence.

"What are you doing?" I ask, scoffing at the unoriginal statement.

"Getting my baking materials ready for tomorrow."

I walk over to the couch and get comfortable. "What are you making?"

"I'm not really sure yet, but I was thinking about doing a cake or some cookies...maybe I'll try out a new recipe for a cheesecake or..." My eyes drift shut listening to the smooth timbre of her voice. I can tell she's excited by her nervous but cute rambling, and the fact that she called me makes my heart stutter like a kick drum. "What do you think about that?" she asks.

I was so entranced by the sound of her voice that I forgot to listen to the actual words she said. "Uh, yeah. That sounds great."

She laughs. "You weren't listening."

"Yes, I was," I reply, lying down on the couch to get more comfortable.

"Oh yeah? Then what did I ask?"

Chewing on my lip, I stifle a smile she can't see. "Something about cheesecakes."

She growls, and I swear a swarm of butterflies fills my chest. "Should I make sticky toffee or cheesecake?"

I run a hand along my beard and try to squeeze the stupid grin off my face.

"Hmm...sticky toffee for sure," I reply.

I want to ask her to dinner, but I know we're not there yet. I haven't proved I'm worthy of being her friend, let alone anything more. I'm no stranger to having to prove myself—a carpenter's success relies on his work and word of mouth—but when you've spent so many years pushing someone away, making sure they don't get close enough to see the pain in your eyes, it's a chasm too daunting to cross.

While Tilly seems to have forgiven me for some of my actions, it's not as easy to forgive myself. I want to be the type of man that deserves her love. Someone she wants to be around because she enjoys my company, not because she feels obligated. The fear of being a burden to her—like I am to my parents—makes my throat burn.

"Oh crap. I've gotta run to the store before it closes, but I'll see you tomorrow?" she asks.

"I'll be there."

We hang up, and I rest my hands on my stomach and sink into the couch cushions. There's a part of me that wonders if she's forgiven me because I'm helping with her bakery and she's just thankful, or if it's because she feels what's been brewing between us—what was there so many years ago left unkindled.

Chapter Twenty-Four
Tilly

An assortment of desserts from every country I've ever wanted to visit fills the kitchen island. There's Polvorones, a Spanish shortbread cookie, a play on an English sticky toffee pudding with a hazelnut cinnamon chip sponge cake, and a Boston cream style cake with a caramel glaze inside.

Baking is an art. The way you knead dough out for breads, or how you must serve the souffle at the precise time so the air that is whipped into the egg whites doesn't cool too quick or risk it crumpling in on itself.

I stare at the desserts I stayed up all night baking, and a sense of pride I haven't felt in a long time...well, almost ever, rises inside my chest. These treats show I have what it takes to run my own bakery. My mind is filled with more unique flavor profiles and extravagant cakes, and given the opportunity, I think I can wow this town.

I gather the supplies I need to work at the bakery, I head out into the brisk November air. Thanksgiving is two weeks away, and my grand opening date inches closer.

"Hey Dad," I say, walking in through the front door. I texted to let him know I'd be dropping off some new desserts today. He's sitting at a booth looking through schedules.

"Hey, sweetheart." He stares at my work boots and denim jeans. "You're dressed differently."

Worry takes root in my chest. With everything going on lately I haven't had the time to tell him about the bakery Jessie bought for me.

"Uhh...yeah," I start. "About that."

His bushy gray eyebrows bunch. "What's going on?"

Sweat beads my palms as I slide into the booth. Better to rip off the band-aid quickly.

"Jessie rented me a bakery location..." I clear my throat, stifling the emotions threatening to arise. "Before he passed."

Dad's lips part like he wants to say something, but I know if I don't tell him everything before the tears start, I may not be able to finish.

"Archer and I have been working to get it ready for the grand opening in December." His eyes widen when I mention working with Archer, but he doesn't interrupt. For the first time since my mom passed, I feel the bridge between us shrinking. "I'm sorry I didn't tell you."

He reaches for my hand with a smile on his face but when I don't immediately reach out, he slowly brings it back to fold his hands on the table. Because I've gone so long without touch, I'm still wary of allowing even little touches. The synapses in my brain seem to fire off at random times as they reconnect to my heart.

"That's amazing, sweetheart," he says when I'm finished and out of breath. "You've always wanted your own spot, and I know I've limited you by what you can sell here, but I'm glad you'll be able to spread your wings."

"I'll still supply your restaurants with sweet treats."

"No way. It's time to follow your own dreams."

I smile. "Thanks, Dad. We'll see how we do after opening."

"If you need anything you'll let me know, right?"

"Yup." I leave the treats with him to try while I'm not there. I can't bear to watch while he decides if he likes them or not.

Heading to the bakery, I wonder if Archer's already there. Shantel let it slip that he's got another interview for that job soon, and I can't deny the sadness I feel thinking about it. Once the bakery is finished, I won't see him anymore, unless he comes to Sunday dinners at Nora's. With his plan to leave, I'm not holding my breath. I think it's why I'm still trying to deny these feelings bouncing around my chest. I don't want to give someone else my heart and then have to watch them leave me.

I wouldn't survive it.

I stop by the cafe and grab a latte for me and Archer. We haven't spoken outside of a few texts since last night, and the last time I actually saw him, I left him there with Deidre. To be honest, I'm worried. He said Jessie wasn't the reason he was still working at the bakery, which means he's there because of me. It was the most I've gotten him to open up, the most honest he's been in years. But if he can't be transparent and talk to me, how do I tell him I'm interested but scared?

Screamo blares through the speakers as I approach the bakery, and pedestrians move to the other side of the street to get away from the sound. He's already scaring off my customers before I even open. Pushing through the door, I speed walk to the radio and turn it down.

"What the heck was that?" I ask.

It takes a beat to realize his shirt is off, the ripped muscles of his abs stealing my breath. He's covered in sweat, and my tongue darts out like it can taste the salty flavor of his skin.

"I brought you a coffee." I hold up the paper cup, my gaze refusing to lift from where his muscles take a sharp curve down his hips and into his jeans.

"My eyes are up here," he says.

Heat rises to my cheeks as he chuckles and grabs his shirt.

Stopping myself from booing takes superhuman effort.

"You didn't have to do that." He takes the drink from my hands. "But thank you."

"Don't mention it. What's on the agenda today?"

"Your hair looks beautiful."

I struggle to contain my grin by chewing on the side of my lip. "Thanks."

He takes the lid off the cup and chugs the latte. A thin strip of foam is left on his lips and without thought I reach up and swipe my thumb across it, the pad of my finger brushing against his soft lips. His sharp gasp makes my center clench. He steps back like I've hit him and brings his hand to his mouth.

"Sorry." Electricity zings around my chest, and my cheeks flame. *Why did I do that? What on Earth made me reach out and touch him like he was...mine?*

"No, it's fine." He looks down at his shoe, and I curse myself for making it awkward. My first time initiating any physical contact with him, and I ruined it.

I'm such an idiot.

I clear my throat. "Thanks for the compliment, though."

"You're welcome."

Silence descends over us. My eyes bounce around the room, taking in all that still needs to be done. I've ordered the metro shelves, stainless steel tables, and coolers for the back of the bakery. Thankfully there was already a stove and some cabinets from whatever company was here prior.

"The wall looks great." I gesture to the freshly painted wall with shelving hung and a cabinet beneath it. "All it needs is a sign."

He rubs the back of his neck and pulls out the poker chip he keeps with him, flipping it a few times. I imagine it's an obsessive trait at this point, but I keep my thoughts to myself.

"There are a few signs you can choose from at my garage," he says, kicking the toe of his boot against the wood pile.

"Jessie had signs made?" Giddiness takes over my emotions and I smile wide.

His expression doesn't match mine and I realize I've somehow offended him. I know it's difficult for him. He planned to work on this place with Jessie, and instead, he got me. I've tried not to give what Shantel and Zevia said too much thought, but could they have been right? Could Archer have been pushing me away all this time because he's been attracted to me and felt bad? Would he be honest if I asked him?

"Let me show you." He walks past me and out the door to his truck.

"Now?" I ask, following him.

He opens the passenger side door and shuts it when I get inside. Leather mixes with Archer's cologne to make the sexiest scent in the world. I close my eyes, inhaling like I want that smell to become part of my DNA. He gets in, pulling his notebook from his pocket and placing it on the dash. The truck roars to life, vibrating beneath me.

Something about a loud engine, a sexy man, and a vibrating seat gets me hot. My nipples firm beneath my top, and my center pulses in time with the music he turns on.

Archer's mouth moves but I can't hear him over the whooshing in my head and the thumping of the bass. Instead of turning the music down, he reaches over me, brushing his arm against my already sensitive chest, and secures my seat belt.

"Thanks," I yell over the tunes.

He doesn't respond but focuses on maneuvering through traffic on the frontage road to the interstate. Archer lives on the outskirts of town, far enough out he has some land for a large three car garage he uses as a workshop. I've never been to his house, but Jessie always talked about the beautiful wood carvings he does in his secret lair.

Archer doesn't speak the entire time we drive, choosing instead to tap his thumbs on the steering wheel along with the music. I yawn and rest my head on the seat, letting my mind roam. We have a little over four weeks to get the bakery opened, and we still have so much to do. Can we make it through the rest of it without acting on these feelings bubbling to the surface daily?

Chapter Twenty-Five
Tilly

Something soft brushes my cheek. "We're here, Tilly."

Opening my eyes, I blink away the haze of sleep I must've fallen under during the forty minute ride across town. A craftsman-style, two-story home with a large porch takes over my vision and I gasp. "This is your house?"

He chuckles and gets out of the truck, running around to open my door. "It needed some work, but it was a good investment."

I live in the small two-bedroom house Jessie and I bought after we got married. I'd imagined moving to a larger one with some land once we had a child, but that never happened. We weren't afforded that much time. Part of me wishes we had a kid so I could still have a piece of him, but that same part knows how that kid would feel. Probably the same way I did growing up after my mom passed and my dad checked out of parenting.

The thought leaves a sour taste in my mouth, and I press my hand against my stomach.

"Want something to drink?" Archer asks once we're inside.

"Sure."

I'm not sure what I imagined the inside would look like, but it wasn't this. His sleek black couches look like they've never been touched, and the monochrome artwork on his walls doesn't really fit with the man I've come to know over the last five years.

"Deidre decorated." It's the only response he gives to my unasked question, but it has the effect of an anvil being dropped into my stomach. Of course, she decorated. She lived here with him, cooked meals for him, slept in his bed.

Unbidden, an image of me waking Archer up with soft kisses to his naked chest pops into my head. I touch my lips like the smooth skin has the memory and is just keeping it from me.

"Water or tea?" Archer asks, pulling me from my daydreaming.

I laugh. "Is that even a question? We're Texans."

"True." He pours a sweet tea, adding a few cubes of ice before he passes it to me. Our hands touch and a lightning bolt courses through my arm and heads south. "Let's go to the garage and I'll show you the signs."

I follow him back out the door with my glass, touching it against my neck to cool myself down. His ass looks amazing in the jeans he's wearing. I catch a glimpse of his taut obliques when he grabs the key from above the door and his shirt rises. I take a quick sip to cover my low groan.

The door opens to a large garage with three massive bays. There's an older Mustang up on a ramp in the closest bay to the door, and the other two are filled with long tables and items covered by sheets. He leads me over to the work area, crossing his arms and scuffing his shoe like a kid who's embarrassed to show his teacher his artwork.

"May I?" I ask, touching one of the sheets.

"Go ahead."

A wooden cross is unveiled when I lift the cover. It's intricately woven between the center of what looks like a rock. My mouth parts, stunned by the beauty.

"These are...amazing, Arch."

He purses his lips like he's uncomfortable with the compliment.

I continue down the line. There are animals, furniture, tables, and even tiny doll houses. Imagining Archer bent over, his chisel working away at a Barbie bed so a little kid can play, warms my heart and turns it into a puddle of mush. I don't even know if he wants kids, but I'm sure he'd be a phenomenal father.

I'd always hoped Jessie and I would have a girl. A little mini-me I could bake Christmas cookies with at the kitchen island while Jessie decorated the tree.

I bite my tongue, hoping the pain will keep the tears away. I tried to make the bed again this morning. I was so close to turning a new leaf, to restarting my life in a new way. I was sure it was finally time—that I could muster up the courage to smooth out his side of the bed, to fluff the pillows, to take the empty tea cup he left on the nightstand the night before he passed to the kitchen—but I couldn't bring myself to do it.

I'm just not ready yet.

"The signs are over here," he says, snapping my attention to a dark office.

Following, I squeeze through the pathway lined with stacks of wood, side projects, and car parts. Light flickers on and Archer's office comes into view. It's large and has a distinct feel of the man standing in front of me. Pictures of Archer and Jessie, Archer and Shantel, and Archer and who I presume to be his brother are haphazardly hung on the wall. Yesterday's coffee cup sits beside the computer on the spacious mahogany desk. Archer moves in my line of sight, blocking the rest of the desk with his broad shoulders.

He points to the other side of the office. "Jessie picked out a few."

I slowly approach the covered signs, peeking over my shoulder to gauge Archer's reaction. He's busy putting something into the desk, his back turned to me. I shake out the nervousness making my fingers tingle.

Three signs are lined up against the wall when I pull off the cover. The first is a Hollywood style marquee where I can change the words to say whatever I want, maybe add a special or two. The next is a fold-out chalkboard sign that I can write on, and the other has a slot for me to put a poster style board inside. I imagine them sitting in front of the bakery on the sidewalk, people passing by and able to look at our menu, but I can't help but feel disappointed.

It's not that either of the signs are bad, but they aren't the type of sign I imagined in front of my shop.

The last sign reads, *St. James Bakery*, and it's large. So large I doubt it'll fit on the small space between the door and the awning. I blow out a breath, steeling myself before I turn and meet Archer's eyes. I feel horrible that I hate every sign Jessie chose for my shop, but none of them feel like...me. They're more his personality, his style.

I slump as my ribs grow tight, fighting the grimace pulling at my face. Jessie was always so good with gift-giving. My ring, my bracelet, the house with the massive island and double ovens. He knew what made me tick, all the little ways that a spouse should. How did he miss the mark on this when he's gotten it right so many times before?

"Knock knock," a voice says from the garage.

I spin, taking note of Archer's relaxed form leaning on the desk. He rises and looks through the window, a smile appearing on his face.

"I'll be right back." He moves toward the door. "I need to load up Mr. Robinson's car, so it'll be a few minutes."

"That's fine." *Totally fine.*

Taking advantage of the alone time, I walk back to the picture wall and inspect the faces. Archer's smile is what sticks out to me. It's been years since he smiled so wide, happy and carefree. My eyes float to the desk and a blip of curiosity rises in me. What did he shove into the drawer he didn't want me to see? I pull the blinds down a smidgeon and see him in front of the car with the hood up, taking Mr. Robinson through something about his car.

Curiosity overtakes me and I grasp the drawer handle, slowly pulling it out. Younger versions of me, Jessie, and Archer stare back at me from the ornate frame. Jessie is between me and Archer with his arms around our shoulders, but Archer's gaze is focused on me, a smile clear on his face.

A swirl of nostalgia convenes in my stomach as I think back to the night before everything changed. A night I'm not sure would have made a difference in the long run.

Slammed by the sudden onslaught of emotions, I drop the frame onto Archer's desk and back away like a cornered animal. Why does he have this picture on his desk like it's...meaningful to him? He has plenty of pictures of him and Jessie laughing, skiing, and fishing. Why keep this particular picture? A memento of better times? Times he maybe wishes he could go back to.

Still backing away from the offending photo, I stumble into his cabinet and knock into another section of signs. The covers come off and I scramble to pick up the signs, eyes catching on the beautiful wooden one hidden under Archer's desk. I lay them down and crawl across the room, ducking under the desktop to grab the one with my name on it.

I sit back on my heels, admiring the simple yet stunning sign. It's a dark cherry wood, smooth and lacquered. I run my hands along the curves, wondering how Archer managed to manipulate the wood into the cursive form of my name. It's...perfect.

Wetness slides down my cheek. I close my eyes and let the wave of emotions crash over me.

"Tilly?" Archer's voice sounds closer, but it takes a moment before he pops into view. His mouth parts and shuts quickly, his hand automatically moving to the back of his neck to rub like the sheer sight of me makes him tense.

"It's perfect, Arch." My thumbs skate along the sign in my hands as I stare down at it, tears still burning my eyes. "Can I have it?"

"Yeah...yeah, of course." His voice sounds different, a tad too high. "Let me load it up for you."

He waits until I lay it down and get up from the floor before he moves toward it, not meeting my eyes. His gaze catches on the picture I put back on the desk, but he doesn't say anything and diverts his attention back to picking up the sign.

Needing a moment to gather my thoughts, I don't follow him. I pick up the stuff I knocked over and manage to get the covers back over the signs Jessie bought. Covering them almost feels like I'm also trying to shield him from seeing the feelings sparking between me and Archer.

"I made another sign," Archer says, leaning against the door jam. "If you want to see it too."

"Lead the way."

"I made it before Jessie bought the others, but it's okay if you don't want it." Archer opens the door to a walk-in closet style room at the back of the garage. It's like the land of lost wood, filled to the brim with broken pieces and woodworking tools and saws—a scene from Final Destination if I've ever seen one. Archer moves a few boxes out of the way and unearths a small sign that he plugs into the outlet. A heart shaped glass tube in neon colors.

"You Cake My Breath Away?" I ask.

He shrugs, cheeks staining a red hue. "It's a play on words."

I chuckle. "I know that."

He kicks some pieces of wood to the side. "I figured you could use it as wall decor but forget it. I know it's stupid."

"It's not stupid at all. It's amazing."

He reaches up, hand frozen right in front of my face like he's debating touching me or not. My chest, head, and neck throb, blood pushing through my veins faster than a freight train. In my head I know this is the moment where everything can change. The moment where the inkling of attraction becomes desire or the death of our truce.

"Is this...okay?" he rasps, hand still hovering.

Lungs desperate for air, spots dance in my vision until I release my breath and inhale another.

"Yes." My fingers tremble as I lay his hand on my cheek. The brush of his thumb is like fire against my skin, yet it sends a shiver down my back. My tongue is gummy in my mouth, and I struggle to swallow down the emotions battering against my mental wall. I haven't been touched—caressed—like this, in almost two years. My face burns as if I've sat in the sun too long, the blood boiling and rushing through my system trying to flush out whatever poison my brain associated with touch.

"Tilly." Archer's chest rises in time with mine, and his tongue darts out to wet his lips.

My whole body explodes when his hand skates down my arm and lands on my hip. Our eyes meet, bodies so close we're sharing breath. Brain fizzling out, my eyes close and I tilt my head in anticipation for his lips to meet mine.

He moves first, fingers tightening on my hip as he pulls me closer. His lips brush mine in a ghostly touch just as a familiar voice yells, "Archer, you in here?"

Stunned by Nora's appearance, I quickly move back, heart whining at the loss of Archer's touch as I bump into a pile of wood and knock it down.

"I'm so clumsy," I grumble, reaching down to collect the wood.

Archer is still standing, frozen in the moment. Fear hitches a ride on the wave of adrenaline pushing its way through my system. Is he already regretting what just happened? Should I be regretting it too?

"Archer?" Nora's voice calls out again.

I punch his leg. "Earth to Archer."

"Huh?" He blinks out of his daze. "Shit."

"Yeah," I retort. "Shit."

He leaves me to clean up the closet.

Should I go out there and say hi to Nora? What will she think about me being here? Too many questions ping pong through my head, and I press my fingers into my temples and massage.

You have a perfectly good excuse for being here, and for being caught in the closet with Archer, I coach myself as I grab the sign and head out to meet Nora.

"Tilly." She smiles, and Archer moves to take the sign out of my hands then lays it on a worktable nearby. I try to decipher the look on his face, but Nora steps into my view. "I love your new hairdo. Shantel said it was pretty, but she undersold it. It's beautiful."

My smile is genuine, and the love for this woman overflows into my chest and wraps around my ribs. How did I get so lucky to marry a man with such an amazing mom?

Guilt wiggles its way back into my chest. Nora said Jessie wanted me to be happy—even insinuated that Archer could be that person for me—but knowing the reality of seeing me and Archer together like this might hurt her shears my heart. Even though she seems supportive of me moving on, the last thing I'd ever want to do is cause her pain or unintentionally disrespect her.

"Thank you, Nora." A chill sweeps through the garage and I shiver, rubbing my arms and wishing I brought a jacket.

"I just came to bring Archer a casserole," she says. "This old lady has to make it back home before dark."

"We were just grabbing some signs for the bakery," I offer, even though she didn't ask. Heat warms my cheeks when Archer's eyes flit to me, his brows scrunched like he's wondering why I mentioned it. I'm a nervous babbler, he knows this.

Unfortunately, so does Nora.

"Sure," she says with a mischievous smile. "I'll see you both at Sunday dinner."

I wave and Archer walks her out to her car. In the quiet moments after they leave the garage, a heaviness settles on my chest and my stomach twists. What would've happened if Nora hadn't stopped us? Would we have crossed the line and ended up regretting it? Would it shatter the tenuous truce we've come to silently agree upon?

Anxiety and excitement coalesce inside my stomach, creating a cocktail of emotions I'm not ready to acknowledge. I run my hand along the signs, smiling at the wall decor with the pun. It's exactly the type of fun sign I'd want in the shop, and knowing Archer made it fills my stomach with butterflies.

A slammed door and the crunch of gravel alerts me to Nora's retreating car. Standing with his arms stretched above the doorway, Archer's gaze is locked on me. Something passes over his face, and the curiosity about what the almost kiss meant is cleared up when he says, "Let's get you home."

We gather the two signs and blankets to lay them on, placing them in the bed of his truck. I don't wait for him to open my door and instead heave myself up with the running board and handle. In the side mirror, Archer's reflection shows me he's not as unaffected as he wants me to believe. His hands clench by his sides, and he swivels his neck in a move that looks like he's trying to dispel tension before he gets inside.

Leaning back against the headrest, I close my eyes and don't open them until we arrive back at the bakery. No words are exchanged as we move in tandem, each taking a sign into the shop and laying it on the floor.

"I've gotta get going," Archer says, toying with his keys.

"Cool."

"Cool," he parrots.

I fold my lip under my teeth, trying not to let my disappointment show. "I have work to do. Guess I'll see you tomorrow."

He doesn't try to stop me as I walk through the stainless-steel door and into the back.

Chapter Twenty-Six
Archer
Three Years Ago - Ring Shopping

Dear Seb,

Remember how we used to spend every weekend at the mall as teenagers, hanging out with our friends in the food court and dropping pennies off the balconies trying to see if we could hit someone? Yeah, we were dickheads. I don't say this because I may or may not have been the victim of a little shithead pelting me with a penny from said balcony, but because now that I'm a more adultier adult, I understand how annoying we were back then.

I thought Jessie dragging me out to the mall to go "shopping" meant that we'd look at some new golf clubs or tools, maybe even stop in the sports store for some new jerseys for football season. But nope. He meant RING shopping.

FML, I know, right? I almost think he made it seem like a bro date so I wouldn't flake out on him. We've only ever talked about that night once before, but we were both tipsy, and I doubt he even remembers. But I do. I remember telling him to treat her right, making him think I'd moved on and wasn't hot for his girlfriend anymore. What else was I supposed to say? Should I have told him I think about kissing her more often than I should? That every time I try to move on and sleep with someone else that it's her I'm imagining beneath me?

Pfft. That would've gone over well, I'm sure. But it's beside the point. I started talking to this new girl, Deidre. She's smart, has a good sense of humor, and comes from a good family. Apparently, Deidre's mom plays tennis with Mom occasionally, and they orchestrated their own little "meet-cute" as Mom called it. At least Deidre isn't an airhead, and she's pretty, too. She's not Tilly, but I know no one ever will be, so it's time to move on.

Anyways.

After being attacked with pennies, Jessie and I stopped by a store in the mall. He looked around at a few sets, and each time my stomach did a spin when he chose the largest ring. I could imagine Tilly's dainty fingers being swallowed by the diamond, weighed down at her side. She wouldn't be able to lift her hand to wave at anyone. He'd get pricing on the ones he liked and move on to the next store to repeat the process.

We went to three more jewelry stores before he decided it was time to go to Tiffany's. The rich smell of the store was nauseating. It reeked of the expensive perfume Mom wears, like Saint Laurent or Dolce & Gabbana. A woman in a sharp looking pantsuit approached us with a toothy smile, and my teeth nearly cracked returning it. It was uncomfortable, but I guess I've always been the one uncomfortable around wealth because of how our parents throw it around.

The day wore on me, emotionally and physically, and I couldn't see straight. Jessie kept showing me rings, asking what I thought about each of them, and the saleswoman would huff every time I said they looked "fine." Like how dare I use such a lackluster word to describe a rock that cost more than my truck.

I broke. I couldn't watch him keep picking things I knew she'd hate. She always commented on rings any time a celebrity got engaged and received a massive ring. "Such a beautiful ring. I think I just want a simple solitaire with a band when I get married," she'd say. He never picked up on it, and I didn't want her to be walking around with a ring she disliked.

I helped him choose a marquise solitaire I thought she'd like, and even though there was a hint of a frown on his face, he handed over his card. I think somewhere in his mind, he knew that I knew her better, understood her more. But that doesn't change the fact that she fell for him.

There was no doubt she was going to say yes to his proposal, but at least I'd know she was getting something that was about her, not about what he wanted.

I feel like if you were still alive, you'd be writing one of those "Am I the asshole" posts about me on Reddit so people could comment and tell me how awful of a friend I am. How undeserving of her affections I'd be if she chose me.

I'm about to leave for the big proposal dinner Jessie disguised as a get together for his birthday. A few other co-workers and their wives will be there along with Shantel and Nora. I doubt Tilly will catch onto what's happening beforehand. She hates huge crowds or attention on her, so she'll probably try to hide in the background. Wish me luck.

-Arch

Chapter Twenty-Seven
Archer
Three Years Ago - Proposal

Dear Seb,

No one realizes how awkward proposals are until they're forced to sit and watch one happening in real time. Declaring your love in front of a table of twelve and then asking someone to give you an answer right then and there is nerve-wracking for the spectators. I can only imagine how Tilly felt with all eyes on her as Jessie started his speech and ended it with his knee on the ground and a ring box in his hand.

Deidre leaned over and started gushing about how adorable the entire thing was, and it made me sick to my stomach. Cheers and champagne were passed around as everyone congratulated the happy couple. Shantel squeezed my shoulder and pulled me in for a hug. For a minute I worried she knew my dirty little secret, but then she whispered, "I'm so drunk I can't see straight, will you take me home?"

I congratulated Jessie on his proposal and told him I was going to take his sister home before she made a fool of herself. Malik had to work late on a merger, so he stayed home. I hadn't expected Tilly to wrap her arms around me, elation written all over her face as she told me how much she loved her ring, how perfect it was. She'd had a few drinks by then and was a little more open than normal. Fire exploded in my chest when she squeezed me tight. Her hair smelled of lemons, and I couldn't help planting a soft kiss onto the top of her head as I congratulated her.

Deidre's frown had me pulling away from Tilly quicker than I wanted, but it wasn't right for me to be holding her anyways. She wasn't mine, and she never would be. But holding her close seemed to shatter my world completely.

I dropped Deidre off at home with a promise to give her a call tomorrow, and Shantel's drunk ass couldn't make it up the steps to her house, so I called Malik to come get her. He came out in Jack Skellington pajamas and threw her over his shoulder with a thanks. It was pretty funny to see when everything she drank exploded down the back of his shirt and he started cursing. I wish I could say I was a nice guy and helped him clean it up, but I was strung tight and needed to unwind.

I should be sleeping, but instead I'm writing to you telling you all about my shitty week. Mom and Dad begged me to do some construction work at one of their friends' houses tomorrow. It's funny how they look down on my career until it benefits them in some way. But the money is good. It's better than good, so I keep my trap shut like you taught me and do the work right. My construction company is really starting to grow, and if I keep on this upward trajectory, I'll be able to put a down payment on that fixer-upper with the three-car garage you and I saw on the outskirts of town. It's far enough away from Mom that I won't have to worry about her stopping by to gather information for Dad disguised as "I miss my boy" visits.

So many things are starting to happen for me, and I wish you were here to celebrate. I'll do a few shots in your honor tonight while I drown my sorrows about Tilly. Come tomorrow, I'm starting on a new plan. One that involves moving up and moving on.

-Arch

Chapter Twenty-Eight
Tilly

Grocery shopping for baking materials is my favorite part of the week. With Dad's approval of the sticky toffee pudding cake and the apple-pear crumble I made, I'm feeling excited about the prospect of opening my bakery in a month. Nearly all of the construction work outside of a few shelves are complete, so I can finish decorating the inside and prepare for a soft opening. The front area is all painted, and I'm waiting on a delivery of tables and light fixtures this week. I've yet to find a bakery case I love, but I'm holding out hope I'll find one soon. I'd rather not open without one, but I also don't want to be forced into buying one I absolutely hate either.

I've managed to avoid Archer the last three days because he was away doing a construction job, but I know he's returning soon for the Thanksgiving break, and I'm not sure what the new dynamic will be between us.

It's equal parts exciting and anxiety-inducing.

On autopilot, I pay for my groceries, drop them off at my house, and head to Nora's for Sunday dinner. I note the absence of a particular green truck when I park my car, and an uneasy feeling settles in my chest.

"Hey chickadee." Nora greets me at the door with her silver hair pulled into a bun and a fall inspired apron around her neck. "Dinner's almost done. Shantel needs help with dessert."

"Oh no." I hold up the pie in my hand and she laughs.

"Thank God you brought that. We'll probably need it."

Shantel's braids are a crazy nest on top of her head, and she's buzzing around the kitchen making messes as she goes. She's always been a frazzled type of baker, but this is next level.

"Want some help?" I ask, placing the pie I made into the fridge.

"I swear if that's dessert I'll chop off your fingers." She wields a knife, pointing it my way like a crazed killer. "I told you I was going to try to make something this time."

"You'd likely cut your own fingers off before you managed to get anywhere near me."

She huffs. "You're probably right, but we're not opening yours until we at least try mine."

I surrender. "No problemo."

A familiar noise outside grows louder, and in turn my heart rate increases. Archer's truck has a distinct sound I'd know anywhere. Wiping my sweaty hands on my skirt, I grab a knife and chop cucumbers for a salad beside Shantel.

"Hey ladies." Archer's dressed in a tight black sweater and dark jeans. His beard is trimmed, and he looks like he's gotten a haircut sometime in the last few days.

It takes a moment before I realize my mouth is parted and I'm breathing too heavy. Shantel bumps my arm, and I accidentally slice into my finger.

"Damn it," I say.

"Shit, I'm sorry, Til." Shantel grimaces, an apology written on her face.

Archer's warm body encroaches on my space. He takes my hand and leads me to the kitchen sink. "Let me see how deep it is."

It's not the pain at the forefront of my mind but the firm grasp he has on my fingers. The nerves in my body light up like fireworks, and

I struggle not to lean more into him. I'm vaguely aware of Nora and Shantel chatting, but the man diligently cleaning my wound has my full attention.

His green eyes are paler today, like he's tired and in need of a good night's sleep, and his lips are slightly chapped, most likely from the wind San Antonio's known for. He's much more attractive than I remember him being five years ago when I first met him.

A cleared throat pulls my attention to the two women standing off to the side with grins on their faces. I roll my eyes and pull my hand back from Archer's.

"Thanks, but it's not that deep."

"Give me your hand." He reaches into the cabinet and pulls out one of Nora's fingertip band-aids. Like I'm a child, he wraps it around my finger then places the trash in my hand and tells me to go throw it away.

The room is near silent, but there's a buzzing energy floating around the table when we finally sit down to eat. Shantel and Archer chat about a new contract her husband negotiated for his company, and I piledrive pot roast into my mouth. Nora's eyes bore into the side of my face, and even though I try to fight the urge to turn and meet her eyes, I royally fail. She's got a smug look on her face like she's proud of something, but I can't quite figure out what that something is yet.

"Archer and Shantel can set up the table while you and I do the dishes," Nora says to me.

The silence that descends over the room is shocking. I always set up Jessie's poker table, and if Nora is beckoning me to the kitchen, it's to talk in private. And I'm not sure I'm ready to hear what she has to say. Has seeing the change in the dynamic between me and Archer made her reconsider her thoughts on whether we belong together? Is she now disgusted at the thought?

My throat tightens and I chance a look at Shantel. She shrugs like it's no big deal. Archer's eyes are wide and filled with worry. I imagine it's what I'd see if I looked into a mirror. Nora's humming a tune and scrubbing the dishes when I finally make my way into the kitchen. She throws me a dish towel to dry with.

"How's your finger?"

"It's fine. Just a cut." She hands me a bowl to dry.

"You know Archer is like a second son to me, right?"

Whoa. Right in for the kill. Nora doesn't waste any time getting to the point.

"I do."

"And I want him to be happy just as I wanted Jessie to be happy."

Fear spikes through me, raining down shards of dread.

"Yes?"

"I want Archer to be as happy with you as Jessie was."

The bowl tumbles from my hand, clanking against the countertop but not breaking. I send a thank you to Heaven, and a question of 'why' to God. Why did my mother-in-law just tell me she wants me to be happy with my husband's best friend?

"It's okay, Tilly," she says when I don't respond.

"How? Why?" I fumble my words. "I don't understand."

"Yes, you do." She leaves the dishes in the sink, dries off her hands, and turns to me. "I haven't seen you smile in months, yet the minute you started working with Archer you've done nothing but smile."

"He's helping me with the bakery."

She charges on. "You didn't flinch away from his touch."

A tear slides down my cheek. "The pain from the cut was all I felt."

She smiles and shakes her head like she can't believe I'm trying to defend myself when it's so achingly clear what's going on.

"You've come alive again, and so has he."

"But I'm married to Jessie," I choke out.

She reaches out for my hand on the counter, and I nearly pull it back, a kneejerk reaction I'm trying to curb as I work on my touch issues. I know she needs the comfort just as much, if not more than me.

"You loved Jessie with all your heart while he was on this earth, but he's not here anymore. He's up in Heaven probably yelling at you to stop getting in the way of your own happiness."

"I feel like I'm betraying him, betraying you and Shantel."

She squeezes my hand and grabs a paper towel for me to dry my eyes. "You're not. You're only betraying yourself by neglecting to give your heart what it needs."

"He's made it pretty clear I'm not what his heart needs."

"Oh pish posh," she says. "He's fallen head over heels for you. Who wouldn't? You're amazing."

"No, he isn't," I reply. "You don't treat people you love like they don't matter for years."

"I think he knows he didn't handle his…feelings properly," she says.

I scoff. "That's an understatement."

"But," she interjects, pinning me with her sad eyes. "If there's something…there…forgive before it's too late for growth to happen." My brain can't wrap around the fact that my husband's mother thinks his best friend is in love with me, yet she's unbothered. "Jessie would want you to be happy, and so do me and Shantel. If Archer is the person to do that, we want you to know we approve."

She doesn't give me time to reply and heads out to the table to play poker. Stunned, I take a moment to try and digest everything she said. Was this what she was trying to tell me the day I yelled at her? How would things be right now if I had stopped worrying about what others thought about my attraction to Archer and let things unfold?

Nausea swirls around in my gut. I know my heart was true when it came to Jessie. I loved him more than life itself, even if there was a part of me attracted to Archer years ago when we met. But how do we move forward if neither of us can stop looking back?

Chapter Twenty-Nine
Tilly

Lightning slices through the sky, followed by a foundation shaking rumble as I clean up the poker chips and cards. Shantel shrieks when the lights flicker, and I can't contain my laughter. Her evil eye doesn't scare me, but the crack of thunder that comes after makes me jump.

"This looks like it might be a bad one," Archer says, leaving the kitchen. "I'm going to stop by the bakery and make sure it's locked up tight."

"I'll come with," I say, bouncing with unspent energy. Even though things are kind of weird between us, being home alone during a thunderstorm doesn't sound fun either. At least if I'm at the bakery I can get a jumpstart on unloading shipments. "I need to inventory some of the materials that came in."

Unboxing sprinkles, icing, and wooden rolling pins may not seem fun to some, but I'm nearly overcome with excitement that I'm finally at the point of organizing materials for our soft opening.

"Y'all better go now before the storm breaks." Nora hands us each a tub of Country Crock filled with leftovers.

She embraces Archer and tells him good luck, but I'm not sure if she's telling him that about us or his job. We haven't talked about it much, and to be honest I've tried to stay away from bringing it up. There are enough unsure feelings between us without adding in the stress of him leaving.

The drive to the bakery takes less than ten minutes, and I spend each of those minutes nervously tapping against the steering wheel. I haven't been alone with Archer since the wood closet at his house, and not much has been solved since then. As in, nothing really. It feels exactly like the last time we shared a kiss, when I could feel him pulling away even before it ended, like he knew he was making a mistake. It's why I never brought that kiss up, and also why I won't force him to acknowledge this one. I'm not ready to hear the rejection.

Somehow, I beat him to the bakery. I park and go inside, hoping to get as much done as possible before the sky is no longer happy with just making noise. The lights flicker on, and my chest expands when I see the quirky sign hung behind the countertop. Archer must've hung it before he came to Nora's because it wasn't there when I left earlier. He even added a few neon cupcake lights around it to highlight the sign.

I fight back the tears welling up. He's done so many small things to make this bakery my home. The one place I can be myself. He hasn't batted an eye at the crazy wallpaper or the funky light fixtures. He's only accepted me for who I was, and that's the Archer I miss from all those years ago.

Twenty minutes pass before Archer arrives. I'm on the floor counting an inventory of sprinkles and icing when he slides through the swinging door.

"I picked up some sandbags for out front in case it starts to flood." He leans against the wall, the sleeves of his sweater pushed up and baring his strong forearms.

"Thanks for thinking about that." I lay the clipboard down. "And thanks for putting up the sign and everything. I couldn't have done it without you."

Sitting on the floor and having the weight of his stare on me makes me shift and my lungs scream for air. Lips parched, I get up and walk to the fridge to grab a bottle of water. I feel his eyes follow me, but I can't bring myself to turn around. My stomach boards a roller coaster as I stand in front of the fridge.

I'm struggling to gather my thoughts when Archer comes up behind me and reaches into the fridge. "Thanks for the offer." He grabs a bottle for himself. "I'd love some water."

His breath is hot on the back of my neck and the heat of his body makes goosebumps break out down my arms. Cool air from the opened fridge wafts our way and I shiver.

"Sorry." I try to step back.

He doesn't take the cue and move.

He grunts when my back collides with his chest, and his arm bands around my stomach to keep me from tumbling over. Releasing his hold on me, he lets out a breath and steps back.

"Sorry," I say.

"Stop apologizing." Archer laughs, rubbing his hand along his beard.

There are words stuck in my chest, all scrambling to climb up my throat and out of my mouth, but I can't open my lips to let them out.

"We have unfinished business." A tug on my space buns lifts my eyes to meet Archer's. His lips are curved into a smile, and his tongue darts out to wet them.

My core twists watching his lips moisten. "I know," I groan, hoping my voice doesn't waver. "I have to finish the inventory, organize the metro shelves, and—"

Firm lips crash onto mine, stopping my list of to-dos and stealing my breath. Brain lagging to catch up, it takes a beat for me to realize this is happening. He's finally kissing me. And it's everything I expected it to be.

Demanding. Passionate. Consuming.

One hand cradles my head while his other pulls me closer. The cadence of my heart is erratic as he swipes his tongue across the seam of my lips, begging for access. My back meets the fridge, slamming the door as his tongue plunges into my mouth, tasting, teasing, claiming.

"Arch," I groan, pressing my chest closer to him.

"I know," he breathes, releasing my mouth and pressing heated kisses to my collarbone and up my neck.

My skin is alive, synapses connecting the nerves I've left to die because of my touch starvation. His fingertips digging into my hips are like kerosene on a bonfire, and my hands wrap around his neck, pushing into his thick dark hair.

Firm hands snake down my ass and grasp my thighs before I find myself lifted off the ground and my legs wrapped around Archer's waist. The thick bulge pressing against my center rips a moan from my lips and I swear he growls as he sets me on the stainless-steel table.

"God, you smell like lemons," he says in between kisses. "It's always driven me crazy."

I laugh and he nips at my neck, sending a thrill down my core. Our lips meet again, limbs tangled, touching, feeling, absorbing every movement. The burning sensation of my skin has changed into a throbbing hum as Archer's hands skim down my sides before yanking me to the edge of the table.

A tub of sprinkles falls to the ground, exploding rainbow candies all over the floor, when Archer moves against me. His erection brings me closer to the edge of insanity. Stars dance in my eyes, and I nip at his lip to quell the rising arousal in my core.

A loud crack of thunder pulls us apart, chests heaving, lips red and swollen. Darkness envelops us as the lights go out.

Even in the darkness, the shame I thought I'd feel after finally kissing Archer isn't there. Instead, a feeling of satisfaction fills my body. Like I've been dehydrated and have finally received the water I needed to live again.

Archer slides his fingers into the loops of my jeans as if they're handcuffs preventing his fingers from roaming to other landscapes. His teeth close against the burning skin at my neck, and I can't help the needy moan that spills from my mouth.

"More," I whimper, confident in my need though my body trembles.

He responds by releasing the loop and moving his hand to the apex of my thighs. Over my jeans, his thumb rolls in soft circles, alternating light and firm pressure. With the lights out, no electricity humming in the room, all I can hear and feel is his breath against mine, his soft groans as he sucks on the flesh at my collarbone.

He captures my bottom lip between my teeth as he cups me, putting firmer pressure exactly where I need it. An atom bomb of pleasure explodes in my core, and I throw my head back, letting the euphoria wash over me. Minutes pass where nothing but our panting is audible, and before I have a chance to reach for Archer to return the favor, the lights return and he breaks the silence.

"We made a mess." He chuckles, looking around at the sprinkle-covered floor before his eyes meet mine. They're bright and blazing, and the smile he flashes me sends butterflies fluttering through my chest.

"I'll get a broom." Seeking a moment to process, I hop down from the table and scoot past him into a back closet. Placing my hand along the cool wall, I let my head fall back and inhale a deep breath. At the edges of my mind, fear and guilt try to breach the border of my happiness, but I push them back, not allowing them to sour this moment.

Another flash and bang shakes the building, dumping buckets of rain out of nowhere. I return to the front to quickly clean the floor and empty the dustpan into the trash, smiling as I think about what we just did—what I let him do—on my bakery table.

"I'm glad I got those sandbags." Archer walks toward the door. "I'll drive."

"I'll be fine," I reply.

"The water is coming down too quickly, and you know the roads are going to flood."

I sigh, but it doesn't hold any weight. "Okay."

I didn't wear my rainboots today because as much as they say we're going to get rain in San Antonio, it's a rare day when it actually happens at the aforementioned time. Archer's hand rests on the small of my back as I gather my jacket and purse. Even though we crossed a boundary tonight, I still fight the urge to pull away.

Sheets of rain pelt us as we run to Archer's truck. He opens the door for me and lifts me up into the seat before running around to his side. Shaking the droplets from his hair, he turns to me with a bashful smile. The weight of holding myself back finally lifts and I return his smile. I wait for the awkwardness to settle in, to be knocked down by all the what ifs and questions of the future, the shame of finding comfort—and pleasure—in the arms of my husband's best friend.

But it doesn't come.

I'm filled with a sense of peace when his hand lands on my thigh. He shifts the truck into gear, and his wipers groan, oscillating as they try to clear the rain fast enough so he can see out of the windshield.

Streetlights pass quickly as we head towards my house and fight the rising waters. He was right, my car would've been swallowed beneath the underpasses. When the rain blankets the window and there's no chance of moving forward safely, Archer pulls off the side of the road and into a bank parking lot.

"We'll wait it out here," he says, turning the heat on low.

I unclick my seatbelt and rest my head on the seat, listening to the rain striking the window. It's peaceful sitting here with Archer as chaos ensues right outside the door. Horns blare, tires screech, splashing water up and over the truck, but all I can focus on is Archer's hand on my leg, his fingers inching up closer to my hand. Making the first move has never been my strong suit—the one time I did, I ended up sending our friendship down a completely different path—but I move out of my comfort zone and entwine our hands.

"There's an estate sale up in Waco I'd like to check out."

"Really?" I ask, an edge of worry to my voice. "Are you looking to buy another house?"

"No." He pulls my hand onto his lap. My gold bracelet glows against his denim pants as he fingers the charm on there, and my wedding ring pulses around my finger, reminding me it's still there. A flutter of muscle in Archer's jaw works, and I wonder if seeing Jessie's ring still on my hand hurts him. "I thought we could go see if they have a display case. It's an old bed and breakfast that ran a deli out of the bottom floor."

A smile cracks my cheeks. "That would be awesome."

"I'll drive in case you actually find one and need a way to bring it home."

"Thank you." I squeeze his hand. "For everything."

He lifts our conjoined hands to his lips and kisses the back of my hand. "My pleasure."

In the back of my mind, I know the closer we get to the soft opening next month means it's closer to the time Archer might be leaving if he gets the spot on the show, but I try to push it away and focus on the here and now.

The storm slows enough to where we can safely get back on the road, and a whine bubbles up in my throat. I squash it down, thankful to the heavens that we had this time together.

Archer walks me to my front door. "I'll pick you up tomorrow at eight."

Part of me wants to invite him inside, to finally shed the shackles I've placed on myself since Jessie died, but the shame I didn't feel earlier rears its ugly head, chastising me for even thinking about sleeping with Archer so soon after losing my husband, and in his house.

Hell, if I can't even manage to make the bed without breaking down there's no way I'd be able to welcome someone else between the sheets.

He leans down to kiss me, but disgusted with myself, I turn my head so he meets my cheek.

"Time," I breathe. "I need time."

He steps back and shoves his hands into his pockets. "I'm sorry, I didn't mean to overstep."

"You're fine, you didn't," I ramble and shake my head, unable to look at him. "I just don't know how to navigate whatever this is."

"Neither do I, but we'll figure it out together." A firm squeeze on my fingers has me looking up at him. His eyes are soft, and the apples of his cheeks are slightly pink. "We go at your pace and see where it goes."

"Thank you." I squeeze his hand back.

"I'll see you soon."

"See you then." I head inside the dark house, foregoing turning on the lights.

I struggle to look myself in the mirror as I brush my teeth and put on my favorite shirt of Jessie's. Normally the worn edges of the Silverstein shirt bring me comfort, but all I feel is disgrace sliding down my back. I fooled around with my husband's best friend and then came home to sleep in the bed we used to share together. Nausea seeps into my core, and I gather covers to sleep on the couch. Without the endorphins from being around Archer bouncing around inside my head, anxiety seeps into my core, spreading out over my shaky limbs. My heart rate climbs, my stomach cramps, and a heavy weight settles on my chest as I struggle to catch my breath. Every potential outcome of this thing with Archer spins inside my mind on a carousel.

Heavy rain and an emergency call with my therapist are the only things I can count on to help me calm down enough to finally fall asleep.

Chapter Thirty
Tilly

I'm entirely too well dressed and caffeinated for a four-hour adventure to Waco for an estate sale, but I needed the confidence boost to get through today. After speaking with my therapist, she helped me understand that sometimes my emotions will feel erratic, even causing panic attacks, when it comes to moving on in the next portion of my life without Jessie. That even though I can feel happiness and excitement about this new thing with Archer, I might still have lingering guilt about moving on, but that there's nothing wrong with that. It'll take my mind and heart a bit of time to catch up to each other.

My long, flowy dress whips around me as I putter throughout the house, cleaning up in an effort to appease my nerves. Sun streaks through the bay window inside my kitchen, and I fight the urge to close the curtains and darken up the place, an exact replica of the warring emotions inside my body.

A knock at the door makes me still. I check the clock on the stove and do a quick inventory of my appearance. Effortlessly styled bun with my favorite chopsticks piercing the center, a light dusting of blush on my cheeks, pumpkin earrings, and my denim jacket in case it gets too chilly. It's the most effort I've put into how I look since Jessie passed.

With my hand on the doorknob, my gaze is drawn to my sparkling ring. Slowly, I lift my hand in front of me, admiring the exquisite diamond. The plastic ring guard still pushes against my finger, holding the ring in place. I roll my lips between my teeth, uneasiness bouncing around my stomach.

Taking my ring off is a statement I'm not sure I'm ready to make yet. Resolved to keep it on, I open the door.

"Morning." I swipe a loose tendril of hair behind my ear.

Archer leans on the wrought iron post, two insulated cups in his hand as he stares down at his boots. There's a brief moment where I can see the tension riding along his shoulders, the deep inhale he takes and expels like he's as nervous as I am about this new territory we're venturing into. His eyes snap to mine and the apprehension is washed away with his smile. "I brought caffeine."

Unsure of whether I should invite him in, we stand there smiling at each other like imbeciles. I open my mouth to ask how his night went, but then his lips part, preparing to ask something, so I snap mine closed. He does the same, and then we burst out laughing at the awkwardness.

"We're a pair, aren't we?" Archer chuckles, trying to hide his smile.

I fold my lips between my teeth and nod. My face is hot, the emotions inside my head boiling like lobsters, screaming to be released. He hands me my drink, and his fingers brush along mine. Tiny zaps of electricity skitter up my arm, and I fight the urge to pull away at the touch.

"Caramel macchiato," he says.

A loud sigh slips from my lips. "I haven't had one of these in forever."

He rubs a hand along the back of his neck, eyes cast off to the side. "Wasn't sure if you still drank those, but figured you were basically made of them in college, so…" He lets the sentence peter out, and I inwardly bat away at the butterflies taking flight inside my stomach.

"Thank you." I groan at the sweetness of the caramelized sugar and the nuttiness of the espresso. Archer clears his throat, bringing my eyes to the way his swallow rolls down the column of his strong neck.

I grab my purse from inside, hoping he doesn't see the slight shake of my hands as I lock the door. I probably shouldn't drink more caffeine since I'm already hyper, but the gesture sends a thrill through me.

"You look beautiful." Archer steps closer, and I can tell he's nervous by the almost hug he covers with a flick of the chopsticks in my hair. I despise this weird middle ground we're in even more than when I used to think he hated me. Every touch or look now carries a question of 'what does this mean?'

"You do, too." I mentally smack myself for the stupid remark. "You know what I meant."

He chuckles. "Lead the way."

Archer's hand grazes my lower back, barely there as if he knows I'm like a skittish animal who wants someone to pet them yet can't withstand the touch. I can almost imagine the press of his fingers into my spine. He helps me into the car and slides into his side.

"Did you print out the directions like I asked?"

I snort, handing him the papers from my purse. "Of course, I did, Mr. MapQuest."

"You say that now, but we're gonna be out in the country and your cell service may cut out."

"You're right." I make a show of screenshotting all the directions.

His smile touches his eyes, and he shakes his head like he can't believe how amazingly smart I am.

"You're something else, Tilda."

My stomach flips at his use of my first name. I dig my fingers into the side of my leg, hoping a little bit of pain will squash out the arousal gathering in my core. One touch. One freaking touch and my name on his lips has me near panting.

Get a hold of yourself girl.

"You can pick the music," he says.

I choose the least sexual music I can possibly find and end up on the classical music station. His arched brow shows me he's not a fan, but his shrug tells me he'll survive. Craving a little relaxation, I stare out at the passing trees. Archer seems at peace with everything that's happened, almost like the real him has been locked up tight since the moment Jessie and I started dating.

I've missed *this* Archer.

Over the years I've caught glimpses of the trio we used to be. Eating our body weight in Mexican food while singing karaoke on Friday nights at the bar, playing air hockey at the student community center after a long study session. The laughter we all used to share became segmented when Jessie and I got together. He and Arch had their friendship, which was solid before I ever came into the picture, and Jessie and I became a unit. There were no more Three Musketeers or friendly lunch dates.

If I was there, Archer wasn't, and vice versa.

It reminded me of my small group of friends in high school before they all scattered to attend colleges far away while I stayed close to home to ensure my dad was taken care of and to help him at the restaurants.

I wish I could find the same peace Archer seems to have about our situation, but he's not the one who was married. He's not the one who stood in front of San Antonio's high society and promised to love their spouse for the rest of their life, the one who'll be looked down on with disdain when they find out I've fallen for someone else. I need this bakery to be successful, and I can't do that if everyone turns against me.

"I know I said you could pick the music, but it's putting me to sleep," Archer says.

I pretend to be upset and pout, but I turn it to a country station to appease his uncultured ears. We stop twice to go to the bathroom and grab a breakfast taco, but the four-hour drive is spent in easy silence, listening to music, and chatting about things I want to do at the bakery.

Between the life insurance policy and my paychecks from my parents' restaurants, I've budgeted well for any extra renovations I want to complete. Archer assured me everything was already taken care of for what he'd done prior to telling me about the bakery, and even though I still write him checks for the lease and the work he's doing now, he refuses to deposit them.

A million other questions itch to be spoken, but I can't force myself to ask. There's so much I don't know about Archer, about his past with his brother—something he rarely talked about during college—and what they were all like as kids, but I know it's not the right time to ask. Jessie always shied away from the memories that included all three of them too, like talking about Sebastian without Archer there was too difficult. I've gleaned enough from Nora and Shantel to understand what happened, but it's not the same as hearing it from someone who was there.

I'm scared if I push him too hard, he'll retreat into the silent man who shut me out. Even if I'm not ready to move into relationship territory with him, I don't think I could handle losing him completely.

"We're about an hour or so out," he says after our last stop. "The sale starts at one, so we'll get there early, peruse what else is going up for sale, and grab a seat."

"Sounds good." I pull a notepad out of my purse.

"What are you scribbling there?" he asks once we get back onto the road.

"I'm just thinking of new recipes for the menu or events I could host that would bring people in."

"People are going to come in, no doubt about it."

"You don't know that." I tap my pen on the notepad. "You haven't tasted anything I've made in like four years."

His hand moves back to my knee and squeezes. "Look at me."

I fight the urge to tell him to keep his eyes on the road, but I oblige his request, a wave of uneasiness crashing in my chest.

"I know it sounds corny, but I didn't need another reason to fall for you."

His honesty wraps around my chest, squeezing the air from my lungs. I get it, I totally do. I spent many nights during study sessions trying to convince myself I wasn't attracted to him. He was a playboy who wasn't serious about anything except football, least of all his studies.

Jessie was the opposite. He was focused on business, had a five-year plan, and everything just felt easy with him. When he asked me out, I had no earthly reason to say no. He was hot, interested, and a good man. Pushing my thoughts of Archer to the side was easy because I hadn't allowed myself to make that connection. My heart was open to Jessie's advances and completely shut to Archer's.

Even though Archer seems all in on whatever is blooming between us, it's me that's still scared to give him my all. The last time I did that, I lost not only my best friend but my husband.

Feeling the tension in the truck rising, I change the subject instead of commenting.

"Dad really liked the cake I made, and I'm wondering if it would be beneficial to do a platter of 'Around the World' treats?"

He flicks on his blinker and slows down to make a sharp turn. His notebook slides down the dash and falls to the floor. My gaze floats to the cream colored pages with his slanted scrawl, and a familiar name catches my eye. Archer grabs it and shoves it between the seat and console before I have a chance to investigate why my name is scribbled inside. I've always wondered what he writes in there but have never been brave enough to ask.

"I think that would be great," he replies, changing the direction of my thoughts back to baking.

"But I also wanna try out old recipes with new flavors," I continue, eyes lingering on the notebook. "Maybe a strawberry balsamic sponge cake. The savory flavor will make the strawberries sweeter. And for those who like spicier desserts I can add the mango habanero chocolate cupcake."

He laughs. "I'm sure whatever you decide on is going to taste amazing, and I'll be your taste tester."

I can't stop the smile from creeping onto my face. Why does he have to hit me right in my most vulnerable spot? Not only Dad has come around to trying more of my desserts, and giving honest feedback on them, Archer is finally willing to give up the ghost and dig in.

A spot of clouds rolls in, and I open my phone to check the weather. Like Archer mentioned this morning, the service in this area isn't great, and I'm struggling to update my app.

"Think it's going to rain?" I ask.

He shrugs. "Fifty-fifty chance out this way."

We pass a few barns, a small gas station, and finally turn onto the long stretch of road leading back to the bed and breakfast. The parking lot is filled, so Archer parks off to the side in the grass. He helps me down from the truck, not releasing my hand once he shuts the door.

The air is breezy, but I'm warm all over when he squeezes my hand and leads me inside. I stare at our entwined hands with a sense of curiosity. Would my body have reacted this way to him years ago, or is it because I'm so deprived of touch that it feels earth shattering to me when it would feel normal to others? Has he noticed I'm still wearing my wedding band? Does it upset him?

Is this just attraction between us or something more?

We piddle around, looking at some of the other items going up for auction, but my attention is focused on the reason we came.

"Wanna sit in the front?" he asks.

I nod, not trusting my voice to come out even.

We grab a number card and find two open seats. A vibration on my leg steals my attention, and Archer reaches into his pocket for his phone. His mom's name flashes across the screen, and instead of answering it, he ignores the call.

"We're gonna start in a few minutes," the announcer says. "Remember, no fighting, cursing, or tag-teaming to raise the price."

Archer snorts, and I prepare myself for battle.

Chapter Thirty-One
Tilly

I've never been to an estate sale, but I didn't think it'd get as raucous as it does. Two naked statues bring out the claws and an elderly lady argues with a younger man over splitting them up or buying them as a set. A wrought iron chandelier goes for more money than my entire house is worth, and I realize I'm extremely out of my depth here. I came for one item, and one item only. Will I have to fight someone for it? How much am I willing to pay for a display case for my desserts?

"Looks like we might have some competition for the case." Archer points to a middle-aged man staring intently at the next item up for sale.

They wheel the case out and my heart implodes. It's amazing. The bottom half is a lighter distressed wood that could be sanded down and painted, and the sides of the case have beautiful artwork on them. Inside, the shelves are cracked, and the door to the back of the case needs new hinges, gaskets, and a glass pane, but everything is fixable.

I chew on my lip, gaze darting back and forth from the man to the bakery case. He rubs his hands together like he's got an evil plan, and the announcer tells everyone to take their seats so the bidding can begin. I hold my breath, hoping everyone else looked at the case and figured it'd be too much work.

"I can fix it up." Archer stretches his arm across the back of my chair and rubs the base of my neck. A chill runs down my arms, and I lean into his embrace. He kisses my temple, and I smile behind my number panel.

Feral Felix, as we've taken to calling him, doesn't back down on the case. What started as a nice back and forth quickly spirals into a tennis match of numbers thrown at each other.

"I don't want to pay more than three thousand for this," I say. "If it means that much to him, let him have it." I lay my hand across Archer's wrist holding the number panel. His mouth is tight, and I can tell he wants to keep going, wants to get me that case, but it's not in the budget I made. "I'll find another one."

"Four thousand," Archer yells.

My mouth drops and I smack his leg. "Archibald Wilson!"

His eyes open wide at my use of his full name.

He's lucky I didn't call him 'the second.'

"Sold to the man in the yellow and black flannel shirt," the announcer calls.

"Tilda St. James," he grits out. "There's no amount of money that I'd let get between you and your bakery."

Air rushes out of me, and my tiny heart grows three sizes too big for my chest. The announcer tells us where to pay for the case, and when I try to hand him a check, Archer places his in the cashier's hand first. I squeeze his arm, trying to hold back the tears. I know he's not trying to buy my affection, but I can't deny his belief in me—his support—has given me a piece of myself back. Slowly but surely, Archer Wilson is wiggling his way back into my heart.

We secure the case to the truck, and something takes over my body. I'm alive, jittery, filled to the brim with emotions I can't name. I leap into Archer's arms and press my lips to his. Like soft pillows, they cushion mine, forming to the curves as he returns my kiss. Arms snaking around my back, he pulls me flush to him and sucks my lip into his mouth, nibbling before he releases me and exhales.

"Get in the truck." His order, accompanied with the darkness swirling behind his eyes, lights a fire under my ass.

We get onto the road before the light rain begins. Archer's hand rests on my leg, and I play with the longer strands of hair at the back of his head. Occasionally he'll pull my hand in for a kiss, or rub my leg, other times we chat about my bakery plans. It's not lost on me that he strays away from talking about his job and the potential of him leaving.

I don't want to think about it just yet either.

A loud boom echoes through the car. My hands fly to the dashboard, heart thrashing around as Archer swerves before regaining traction. He safely pulls over to the side of the road and gets out.

"Shit," he says when he gets back into the truck.

"What happened?"

"Blowout," is all he says as he grabs his phone.

"Oh."

"Damn it." He chuckles and slams the phone down on his dashboard. "No service."

"I'm sorry, Arch." I rest my head on my hands, elbows on my knees.

"You have no reason to be sorry."

"We wouldn't be stuck out here if I didn't want that bakery case."

"We wouldn't be stuck out here if I didn't forget to replace my spare tire." He wraps an arm around my shoulder and pulls me to him. "And even if you weren't with me, I still would've come to get you that case. It was my decision, not yours."

I hear his words, but they don't have the effect I need them to. I still feel crappy that we're stuck with no service as a storm rolls into the hill country.

A truck appears behind us, their lights bright against the darkening sky.

"Stay in here." Archer gets out of the truck to meet the driver.

"Y'all broken down?" I can hear the older man ask.

He doesn't look like a serial killer, but neither did Ted Bundy. Archer sizes him up too, and I can tell he knows he could take him if something went wrong.

"What type of tire do ya need? I have a few in my barn up the road."

Him and Archer chat for a few minutes about the truck while I sit in the warmth of the cab. The wind has picked up, and the sun is speeding toward the horizon like it can't wait to go to sleep after a long day.

Archer leans through my open window. "Mr. Bob has graciously offered us use of his barn apartment for the evening if he can't find a tire."

"What if he's a killer?" I whisper.

"You think I'd let anything happen to you?"

I nod. "Any person in their right mind would save themselves."

He laughs and grabs my hand, placing a kiss on my knuckles. "I'm not sure whether to be proud or offended you would ditch me. If it helps, I'd happily fight off a pack of wolves—or a serial killer disguised as a sweet old grandpa—if it meant you made it safely home."

Bob disappears over the hill to go check his barn. Archer rests his forehead against mine, and exhales. "I'm so glad that guy backed down and you got your case."

"Me, too." I nuzzle his nose and kiss him until we're both breathless and panting. I almost forgot what it felt like to be teenagers making out in the front seat of a truck.

Too soon, Bob returns with bad news. No tire to match, and with the cell service down and night descending, calling for a tow isn't an option. Archer looks to me to decide on whether or not we are staying in Bob's barn. I nod and follow him out of the truck.

"What about the display case?" I ask. "Someone might steal it."

"We can move it into my garage for the night," Bob says. "Have y'all eaten yet? My wife Minnie cooked."

On cue, my stomach grumbles. Archer chuckles and helps Bob move the display case. We're all crammed in the front of Bob's old, two-door Chevy, and a month ago I would've hated every minute of being so close to Archer, but now? Now, I can't get close enough.

Bob's wife, Minnie, cooked a feast for us and tried to send us to the barn with extras. We politely declined, and using Bob's truck, drove the mile down to the ranch hand's apartment attached to the barn. It sits on the back half of their ten-acre property, surrounded by stables and fields of cattle. The animals are all in the pen when we walk in, and they bay, shifting around like they're greeting us.

"This way." Archer leads me up the stairs past a chest.

All my thoughts of relaxation grind to a screeching halt when he opens the door and turns on the lights, illuminating the singular bed in the middle of the room.

Chapter Thirty-Two
Archer

Five Years Ago

P icking an outfit for karaoke should not be an hours-long adventure, but Jessie and I can't stop cracking jokes, pretending like we're women putting on a fashion show for each other. He's dressed in a brown sweater and khakis paired with a lighter colored suede jacket and brown Oxfords, looking like he comes from wealth but isn't an asshole who flaunts his money.

"Your shirt looks fine, man," he says, nodding to the mirror.

I stare at the green button-up and feel underdressed beside my best friend. Taking the poker chip out of my pocket, I flip it to help me decide if I should keep this outfit on or change.

"If it lands on tails, I'll stay in this."

He laughs. "You know Sebastian isn't making these choices for you."

I quiet him with a push onto the bed and flip the chip in the air. In my head, I know flipping Sebastian's chip isn't a connection to him, but in my heart, I feel like he helps me make decisions when they feel too heavy for me. We can't chat and work through things like we used to, so this is the closest I get.

"See." Jessie smiles as the chip lands on tails. "Even Sebastian thinks you look nice in that outfit. Let's go before we're late."

Tilly hates when we're late.

The three amigos have a standing date every Friday night at the Mexican bar where we do karaoke. It's our little ritual for making it through another week of Chemistry.

"Come on, slowpoke," Jessie yells from downstairs.

I spritz myself with some cologne and take a comb through my hair. My chest is tighter than my back muscles with how nervous I am every time we hang out with Tilly. Me, her, and Jessie have been Chemistry partners for the entire semester, and with the class ending soon, I either need to make a move or lose my chance with her.

Sliding into the passenger seat of Jessie's SUV, I borrow the lint roller he keeps in his console while he checks his hair for the umpteenth time. We haven't talked about our mutual attraction to the space-bunned princess who has us wrapped around her finger, how we'll deal with it, if we will at all.

"You guys look nice," Tilly says when we arrive at our usual booth.

She's dressed in her normal attire: a pair of colorful leggings with an oversized sweater in a mismatched color scheme, her hair thrown up into messy buns with chopsticks.

I love her don't care attitude about her clothing. It makes her stand out in the best way possible. People look at her and just know she's a good time, that you could never be sad around her because even her clothing can bring up your spirits.

Jessie and I always sit on the same side of the booth, an unspoken truce so Tilly doesn't feel uncomfortable sitting beside one of us. My long legs brush against hers as we get comfortable, and my cheeks heat like a teenage boy when she playfully bumps my leg.

"The usual?" the server asks when she arrives at our table.

"Can I have a twisted margarita?" Tilly asks.

She usually doesn't drink, but I guess it's a celebration.

"I'll take a Jack and Coke," I reply.

"Same," Jessie adds. "And chips and queso, please?"

The bartender drops off our drinks and appetizer, making a point to flirt in front of Tilly. Neither Jessie or I give her our attention because it's solely fixed on the woman dancing happily across the table from us.

"How do you guys feel about that test?" Tilly asks, munching on a tortilla chip.

"It was harder than I thought," I say.

"I felt prepared for it." Jessie shrugs. "Probably because of your help."

I clench my teeth against the urge to kick him in the shin or stomp on his toe.

"Aww." Tilly smiles. "You guys would've done just fine without my help."

We all share a laugh at that, knowing she's dead wrong. Me and Jessie would've bombed this class if it wasn't for her.

Three drinks and a basket of chips and queso later, the karaoke host announces the first singer. The bartender drops off another margarita and two Jack and Cokes to our table. I'm trying to stay sober and keep an eye on Tilly's drinking, so she doesn't get too plastered, but each time I notice Jessie getting closer to her or making her laugh I order another drink.

The bar reeks of greasy tortilla chips and sweat from the bodies gyrating on the dance floor, but it's my favorite place to be because she's here. Jessie and I cheer her on as she takes the stage and tries to rap the entirety of *Ice Ice Baby* without managing to hit one note correctly. She exudes happiness, and everyone who takes the time to get to know her is immediately pulled into that happiness too.

She's out of breath, skin glistening when she hops off the stage and tumbles into the seat beside me. Beside me. My heart trips over itself when she latches onto my arm and looks up at me with her big brown eyes and pink cheeks.

"You're up next, Arch."

"Me?" My voice cracks. "I can't sing."

She boops me on the nose. "That's the whole point, silly. No one can, but it's exhilarating."

"Go on, Arch." Jessie has a shit-eating grin on his face.

"Next up on the roster is Archer Wilson." The host pauses. "Singing 'Man I Feel Like a Woman?'"

His questioning voice echoes mine. My wide eyes land on Tilly, and she's so excited and giggly I nearly kiss her right there. I know in that moment I'd do anything to make this girl smile like that every day of my life if she'd have me.

I scoot out of the booth and head up to the stage, sheepishly keeping my eyes on the ground. I grit my teeth against the hoots and hollers of the crowd cheering me on. If my parents could see me, there's no way they'd be able to hide their embarrassment at having me as a son. Everyone would finally see how much of a disappointment I am to them.

The opening chords of the song begin and the entirety of the bar joins in as I start singing. In this moment, I'm thankful Seb used to force me to listen to country music when he drove us to high school. I can't imagine the bar would be this hyped if I was stumbling over the words. I chance a look at the booth where Tilly sits with her head propped up on her hands and her eyes fixed on me. Jessie gives me the finger and I laugh, nearly missing my next cue.

After I'm finished, I head to the bathroom to splash my face with some cold water. I'm pushed up against a wall the moment I walk out of the bathroom, and Tilly's mouth is on mine. I'm so stunned it takes me a moment to react.

"That was so hot," she says, breathless.

Lips on fire, I snake my arms around her waist and spin us around until she's pinned against the wall. Lithe fingers skate across my beard and into my hair, tugging softly in a way that makes me tilt my head so she can deepen the kiss. Her soft moans warm my core, and the strawberry taste of her mouth makes me hungry for more than this kiss, this moment.

Glass crashes to the floor, and like a shotgun going off, the entire bar stops and stares at the person who dropped their drink. It takes only that split second for Tilly to slip from underneath my arms and head back to the booth.

I take a few breaths and adjust the now very awake animal inside my pants and make my way to where she and Jessie chat with a round of fresh drinks in their hands. I'm stone cold sober after that kiss, and I want to make sure Tilly and Jessie both get home okay, so I forego another, in hopes she'll want to continue what happened in the hallway.

Jessie scrutinizes me the moment I arrive at the booth, tongue pressed into his cheek like he knows we kissed. Tilly won't meet my eyes. Her gaze flits to me for a moment before Jessie grabs her attention again, and I find myself stuck between my two best friends, unsure which one my loyalty lies with. Tilly's face lights up as Jessie tells her another joke, and an uncomfortable sensation ensnares my chest.

We walk Tilly to her apartment, and I take the keys from Jessie to drive us home. My thoughts are filled with all the what ifs of tonight. What if she didn't like my kiss? What if I upset her by taking charge? What if it's not me she belongs with?

Am I repaying Jessie for saving my life by stealing his girl?

Chapter Thirty-Three
Tilly

"There's only one bed."

Archer laughs, laying his journal and car keys on the small nightstand. "You're still just as good at math as you were in college."

I push him and he chuckles. "It's not funny, Arch."

He turns to me, rubbing his hands up and down my arms. "I'll sleep on the floor, Til. No worries."

The nice person in me wants to say no, but the woman who hasn't slept with another person since her husband died with his arms around her can't bear the thought of it. Thankfully Archer, being the amazing human he is, doesn't push the subject. He takes the top cover off the bed and lays it on the floor with a pillow, grabbing his journal and pen.

"What are you always writing in there?" I lie on the bed, spinning my ring on my finger.

Like a teenage girl with a diary, Archer presses the book to his chest and gives me a scathing look. "I'm drawing pornographic images of you on that bed. Prop your head up and show me some skin so I can sketch you like a French girl."

I laugh and throw a pillow at him. We lie in silence for a few minutes before the smell finally reaches me. The inside of my nose stings with a noxious scent. "Gosh, that smell is horrid."

Archer grimaces as he looks up from his notebook. "How does the ranch hand endure this? I'm not sure I can sleep with the odor this strong."

I pinch my nose. "Me either."

He rises from the floor and peeks out the window. "It's not raining anymore. Not that it'll be much better, but maybe we can find some extra blankets in that chest in the hallway and sleep out there? The breeze might help."

I follow him out of the room, eyes lingering on the opened journal on the floor. I almost stop to steal a peek at it, but something holds me back. Archer's voice calls to me from down the hallway. He's standing with covers piled onto his arms, a smile of success on his face.

"Let's see if we can find a semi-dry spot outside."

Horses neigh and huff as he walks down the stairs and out the door. The sky is completely clear of clouds as if a few hours ago it wasn't raining. It's a tad humid, but the air isn't as heavy with the smell of manure. Archer pats the ground, searching out the least wet spot.

"What about the bed of the truck?" he asks, hopeful.

I shrug. "It's actually larger than the bed inside, and worst comes to worst, I can sleep in the front seat."

He rolls his eyes and swipes the small amount of collected water onto the ground. "We'll make it work."

He throws handfuls of clean hay into the bed of Bob's truck, making a layer over the ridges so they won't hurt our backs. I spread out the covers while Archer runs inside to get our pillows and belongings. When he returns, I'm already two covers deep staring up at the stars in the sky.

Coming from the city, it's rare to see stars. San Antonio is filled with twenty-four-hour Whataburgers and gas stations galore. There's always too much light to see anything but buildings for miles.

The truck dips when Archer climbs in and slides beneath the covers. Even with another barrier between us, I can still feel the heat from his body. He lays on his back, arm bent behind his head, and I struggle to keep my eyes from staring at his bulging biceps.

"Did you bring your camera?" he asks.

"Huh?"

"You're ogling me like you want me to take off my shirt."

"I am not," I reply, haughtily. "But I wouldn't mind it if you did."

He laughs, reaching behind him and pulling his shirt off with one of those sexy one hand maneuvers. My hands wrap around the blanket in an effort not to reach out and touch his smooth pecs or allow my fingers to trace each individual pillow of muscle on his stomach.

"Are you doing okay?" Archer turns, staring at the side of my face.

Even though the temperature has dropped, my underarms gather moisture and make the double covers unbearable. Why did I think wearing leggings under this dress was a good idea?

I slide out from the bottom layer and into the top. My brain screams, *nearly naked man beside you*, but I shut it down.

"I'm fine, just a tad hot."

"You've always been hot," he says.

I slap his chest. He catches my hand, bringing it up to his lips to kiss each pad of my fingers before he places one in the center of my palm then lays it down on his chest. The feather light kiss sends my heart on its own racetrack around my body, speeding past my stomach and moving into my core.

"Are you okay when I touch you?" His eyebrows are cinched tightly, a pained look on his face. "I just realized I never asked if this was...okay?"

Warmth rises in my chest. When he first started touching me, I thought I'd freak out, but I noticed it didn't affect me the same way I expected. His touch brings me a sense of peace.

I nod. "I like when you touch me."

The need to have him touch me in places long forgotten rises, and my thighs quiver with the restraint of keeping them closed. My fingertips tingle as I play with his small patch of dark chest hair, trying to convince myself it'd be a bad idea to kiss him again. If the lights coming on hadn't separated us at the bakery, would we have been able to stop before we went too far? Is this thing between us just something fun, or does it have potential for...more?

A tug in my chest tells me it's the latter, and that has me leaning forward and sealing my lips over his. He groans like he's been waiting for this all day, and his hands move into my hair, tilting my head so he can taste me deeper. A spark in my chest urges me closer to him, desperate for the intimacy I've denied myself.

His firm grip lands on my thigh, squeezing and pulling my leg across his body. He's hard beneath my leg, so close to where I need him but so far. Soft caresses move their way up the side of my shirt, thumb testing the underwire of my bra.

"Tilly," Archer rasps, breathlessly ripping his lips from mine. "If this is not something you want, something you're not ready for, we should stop right now."

I capture his lips in a bruising kiss and shake my head.

He smacks my ass with his other hand. "Words."

"I want you," I squeak.

His thumb slips beneath my underwire, circling my painfully hard nipple. It's overly sensitive from underuse, and the sensation drives me to the edge. My skin burns with his touch, with the need to be bare with him, for him to have all of me. I cry out when he lifts the bra and sinks his teeth into the soft flesh of my breast, nipping and tugging on the dark bud.

"More." I arch my back for him to take off my shirt and bra.

With expert hands, he removes both, barely releasing my nipple from his mouth. His hands skate down my bare sides, gripping my waist and pulling me closer. His fingertips dip beneath my waistband, softly skimming across my pelvic bone. I suck in a breath, nervous excitement stealing the air from my lungs.

"Is this okay?" Archer asks. "Do you want me to stop?"

Tension strains his voice, like it's the absolute last thing in the world he wants to do but would if I asked.

"Please don't." His touch is dopamine to my touch starved brain. I push his hand down further, chasing the feeling.

It takes all of two seconds for him to start exploring the soft hair of my mound, his fingers moving lower until he grazes my clit. I hold my breath and squeeze my eyes tight when he presses down and circles my most needy spot.

"Fuck," he breathes into my neck.

I silently agree and open my legs further. There's a small nudge in the back of my mind, reminding me we're out in the open, down the hill from Mr. Bob's house. But the thought immediately vanishes the moment Archer delves between my folds, pushing against my opening.

Thick fingers sink inch by inch into my core, twisting, plunging, greedy for my slickness. Archer's growl vibrates down my chest, and it's a moment before I realize his body is moving along with it.

"Arch." I whine when he removes his fingers, the loss of pressure driving me insane.

He stands at the edge of the truck bed, his hair disheveled, lips red and swollen.

"Hold on, baby girl." He wraps his hands around my thighs and pulls me to the edge. I squeal and the covers bunch beneath me, creating a pillow that forces my hips up into the air. He removes my leggings and panties then lowers his face between my legs, eyes locked on mine. "I'm hungry."

I bite down on the meaty part of my hand to stifle my scream when his tongue touches my clit, his beard tickling my inner thighs as he explores me. His tongue is a weapon, somehow sensual in his strokes yet explosive when he thrusts his tongue into my center. His growls of pleasure drive me insane, and when he adds his fingers to the swirling of his tongue, I shatter. Stars dance above me as my inner walls pulse around the fingers he's still moving inside me.

"I need you," I say, breathless and panting.

"Damn it." I rise up on my elbows, confused by his curse. His fingers are in his mouth, eyes locked on mine as he cleans them.

"What?" The truck dips as he climbs back up and hovers over my body to kiss me.

"No cake, no...cookie, nothing on earth could compare to how you taste."

Warmth floods my chest, and my hands find their way to the erection heavy between his legs, palming and squeezing it. He hisses against my neck and thrusts into my hand.

"Please tell me you have a condom." I nibble on his earlobe, damn near keening at the way he lavishes his tongue along my neck.

"Fuck." He stills, head falling to my shoulder. "Hold on, let me check."

Archer hops off the bed and drops to the ground where our clothes are. I can't see what he's doing, but when he pops back up with a condom in hand, I can barely contain my excitement.

He sheds his clothes, and my mouth waters.

He's glorious.

Broad, muscular chest. Cut abdominal muscles and obliques that curve into a V and disappear beneath his boxers. Strong quads that highlight the girth between his legs.

My lungs cease to expand. I touched him. Palmed his erection just moments ago. Yet, I didn't imagine he was hiding that thing.

"I don't think that's going to fit," I mutter, pulling on my lip as he fully undresses.

"We'll make it fit, darlin'." He chuckles and rips the foil packet open with his teeth, sliding it onto his erection entirely too slow. He climbs back over me, cock gliding between my legs, gathering the slickness from my orgasm and driving me wild.

"Are you sure about this?" He grips my hip to stop me from moving beneath him.

Unable to meet his gaze, I nod.

"Words, Tilda." His fingers seize my chin, and he turns my face to meet his. "Are you *ready* for this? If you need more time, we can wait."

The sincerity in his eyes makes my heart explode. We're suspended in time, a moment in between breaths where I can see the line we're teetering on. My pause isn't because I'm second guessing stepping over it, but that I'm acknowledging the healing happening in this moment. I grab his cock and line it up with my opening. His eyes track my movements, and he leans down to capture my lips for a bruising kiss.

"Yes," I say.

The word is barely out of my mouth before the first inch of him is stretching me. He groans into my neck, stilling his movements so I can adjust.

Once my lungs decide to start working again, I say, "Move."

"I can't." He curses. "I swear if you move an inch, I'm going to embarrass myself."

I laugh and my hips loosen, taking him in deeper.

"Damn it, Tilly," he growls.

"Just do it," I beg. "Don't be gentle."

I never realized how passionate the woman lurking beneath my surface was. The woman who likes to be bitten and to bite, to fight and to chase. She's begging for something I've subconsciously needed but have been too afraid to ask for. The freedom to be me.

"I don't want to hurt you," he says.

"You won't."

His hands latch onto my waist, and he pulls out and slams into me until he's fully seated. He smothers my scream with his mouth, his hands kneading the soft flesh of my ass as he thrusts into me in short spurts.

"Are you okay?"

I take a mental and physical calculation. The fire between my legs from his size slowly abates, morphing into the beginnings of pleasure.

"I'm okay." I pull him down and thrust my tongue into his mouth. "Are you?"

He shakes his head, unable to speak as his eyes glaze over with what I think are tears.

"Fuck," he says, trying to shake the tear away.

I grasp his face between my hands, clearing the wetness from his cheeks before I wrap my arms around his neck and bring him down so I can rest my chin on his shoulder. "I know," I say. "Me, too."

His spine raises as he inhales, and his breath is hot on my skin when he thrusts back into me. I'm savoring his slow movements, the short thrusts mixed with him pulling the entire way out and sliding back in, but I need more. I need all of him, as hard and deep as he can give me it.

"Harder," I beg.

Archer curses and thrusts into me, hitting the spot I need him to over and over. Waves of pleasure crash over me when his thumb presses down on my clit, hand splayed against my belly as he pistons his hips faster until I cry out, pulsing around him.

"You feel so good." Sweat slides down his chest as he speeds up, his thrusts moving my body further into the truck, the slapping sound of our flesh filling the nighttime air.

Unprepared, another orgasm blasts through my core just as Archer stills and groans, slowing his movements as he comes.

"Holy shit." My chest heaves, synapses still firing. Even with the delicious ache between my legs, the rest of my body is more relaxed than I've been in months. My shoulders aren't tight anymore, and my head is clear and empty of all the questions of 'what if?'

Lying beside Archer, with the expansive sky of stars twinkling above us, I realize not once did I feel an ounce of shame. Thoughts of what other people would think if they knew, what Jessie would think, vanished from my mind and it was only us.

Chapter Thirty-Four
Archer
Five Years Ago

*D*ear Seb,

I met my future wife. I bet you're up in Heaven laughing at that, but it's true. I was hungover and running late to the first day of the semester because Dad just had to get his little digs in about me changing my major. It's your fault, of course. If you were here, he wouldn't have been on me for the last few years to go into medicine like you were supposed to. I'm not sure he understands yet that just because I have the Wilson name, does not mean I have the Wilson passion for digging into people's bodies.

Anyway, here I was picking up Jessie, flipping your chip like a Magic 8 ball when a girl in a polka dot red dress walks past us. Imagine a beautiful caramel skinned, brunette Marilyn Monroe with space buns. I know you don't know what space buns are, but on the right girl they can be sexy instead of nerdy. I was just about to roll down the window and introduce myself when Jessie stole my attention and she disappeared. But guess what? Later, when I strolled into Chemistry class, she was sitting right there in the front row! Come on, you can't tell me that's not some good luck!

I tried to get Jessie to move tables without telling him why, but he wouldn't. The girl was spunky, had a big smile on, and was smart. She raised her hand to answer almost every question. You were always saying I needed a woman smarter than me, and here she was.

Near the end of class, the teacher told us we needed to pair up for a group project that would last all semester. I knew immediately I wanted the girl as my partner, but Jessie whined about having to find someone else. People were pairing up quickly, and she was just sitting there staring around the room. I did a quick count of how many students were in the class; it was uneven. I accidentally smacked Jessie in the face when my hand shot up to ask the teacher if we could pair up with the girl as a group of three since the numbers were odd.

She turned around, and her face lit up like Christmas morning. I'd never tell Jessie this, but I could've sworn I was the Grinch and my heart had grown two sizes bigger. It was like the ground shook, but no one else but me felt it. How couldn't they see this moment for what it was?

I left class determined to introduce myself, but Coach came barreling down the hallway with a stick up his ass. I hightailed it out of there and down to the field so fast. You know I'd never hear the end of it from Dad if I made Coach wait. He's taken to saying, 'if you're not going to do something with your life, you might as well make some money by playing football,' like blue collar jobs aren't what this country is built on. It's not like anyone from our school has made it to the NFL in the past fifty years anyway. Sure, I can't cut out an appendix, but I'm still good with my hands. Hell, I could probably build a house from the ground up. That's not good enough for him though, it never will be.

Later that night, Jessie ruined everything by telling me he thought she was hot, and you know what that meant. He wouldn't stop until he got her. Too bad, I wasn't going to make it easy on him this time. He'd have to fight me for her.

Who do you think will win? Every time I ask the universe that question and flip your chip it lands on tails, so I think that means you're on my side. But I don't know. Lately, every time I've flipped this damn thing you give me shitty stuff, and I almost wonder if it's all a joke. Is this thing weighted to always land on tails? Are you sick of me writing to you? Do you get ghost mail up in Heaven? Wait...are you a ghost or just a spirit floating around? Maybe I could convince that Kat chick from the movie Casper to use the machine to bring you back! Could you imagine all the fun we'd have? Man, I miss you.

Oh, and her name is Tilly, if you want to put a good word in with the Boss man up there. I could really use some luck.

-Arch

Chapter Thirty-Five
Tilly

Vibrations beneath my head rouse me awake, and I slam my hand down, searching around for the phone as I keep my eyes tightly closed, hidden from the bright sun spilling in through the curtains. A pungent odor hits my nose, worrying me that there's an issue with the sewer. Jessie's arm around my waist prevents me from getting up, and I wiggle, trying to create room for me to turn over. There's a pleasant ache between my legs, surrounding an insistent, throbbing desire for more as I push against the length stretched along my backside.

"Morning, darlin'," he grumbles.

Darlin'?

Slowly, the scene focuses as I open my eyes. Green pastures, pens with pigs and cows, the rusty side of the truck bed. My heart slingshots out of my chest when I turn and Archer's beard and naked stomach come into view.

Holy shit. Am I drunk? Why is Archer here? With his arms around me?

The spinning wheels of a safe inside my mind unlock, and my stomach plummets like a broken dumbwaiter. *What the fuck did I do?* My lungs shrivel behind my ribcage as I scramble to get his arms off me, backing away like a cornered animal with the blanket clutched to my chest.

No, this can't be. I couldn't have.

A hamster wheel of thoughts spins around my head, each one more devastating than the next. *I slept with Archer. I cheated with my husband's best friend. Jessie is gone, and he's not coming back.* Along the heels of the last thought comes the worst realization.

I'm vaguely aware I'm hyperventilating, clawing at my chest and arms, trying to remove Archer's touch, but it's already seared into my skin. When I close my eyes, all I can remember is his fingers digging into my hips, his teeth scraping against my neck, arms, and chest.

Jessie's kisses and soft touches are gone.

I gasp, tears pushing through my squeezed shut eyes.

How could you? It was all you had left!

I told myself not to fall asleep, not to keep staring up at the stars when my eyes were already heavy. And now, I've erased the last memory of Jessie's last touch from my brain.

"Tilly," Archer repeats, reaching out for me. "It's okay."

"No." I shake my head, knees pulled up to my chest.

Archer moves off the bed of Bob's truck and slips into his clothes, giving me the space I need to calm down. He places my pants on the tailgate and folds the covers before he takes them back into the barn.

Through damp eyelashes, I can't decipher how he's feeling, but my chest feels like it's been run through a vacuum sealer, stealing all of my air. Last night was...amazing. It was more than I could have hoped for or expected, but the lead brick sitting in my stomach sours it. Am I going to lose more bits and pieces of Jessie the longer this thing with Archer goes on? And is Archer going to push me away now that he sees how broken I still am?

God, my head is a mess.

I dress quickly, worried now that it's daylight people can see us and hoping to get back in the truck before I have to meet his eyes again. I know I can't expect him to understand how I'm feeling, or to be okay with it, but I hope he'll give me the time to figure it out.

He slides into the front seat. "Ready?"

"Yeah," I murmur, twisting my hands in my lap.

He shifts into gear and turns the truck around, heading back up the hill toward the main house. Bob greets us with a large breakfast, and I can barely manage to eat a piece of toast without wanting to throw up. Thankfully, we don't dawdle. We load my display case from the garage and head down the road.

"A friend had the tire you needed," Bob says, pulling up to Archer's truck. They get out and start moving the display case over. "He came by and replaced it for you."

"That's so sweet, Mr. Bob." I give the old man a weak smile.

"How much do we owe ya?" Archer asks.

"Nothing. We take care of our own out here." He shakes Archer's hand and then turns to me.

Already overly sensitive, my hands snake further around my body. I'm still too stunned, too raw from allowing Archer to touch me that I can't bring myself to return his gesture.

"Thank you for all your kindness," Archer says, trying to diffuse the awkward moment.

"Y'all take care." Bob waves as he drives away.

Getting into the truck takes superhuman strength. It's a four-hour drive back to San Antonio and seeing as we haven't spoken but ten words to each other, it'll be torture. I know it's my fault, that my reaction to waking up with his arms around me is what caused all this, but I'm not sure how I can fix it.

I'm scared.

Now that I've had him, will he be taken away like my mom and Jessie? If I let him into my heart, let his skin imprint on mine, and he leaves, I'll be back in the same exact position I was when Jessie passed.

"I know you're scared." Archer's voice is filled with resignation.

The fact that he knows me well enough to know that's where my head went is another reason this is terrifying. He's deeply woven into the fabric of who I am.

I can't lose him too.

I need to know if this is just fun or something...more.

My limbs are rigid, teeth clenched in preparation for this conversation.

"I'm sorry," I whisper.

He reaches out to grasp my hand, but I tense, keeping the death grip I have on my legs. My body is like a computer in safe mode, trying to protect the critical parts of my heart. I miss his touch, the familiarity I found in it last night, but my mind is a jumbled mess drowning in guilt yet reaching for the future.

"You have nothing to apologize for."

Words bubble out of my mouth, overflowing like a cauldron. "But I freaked out on you this morning and probably made you feel like shit. I didn't mean to fall asleep. I knew what would happen, and I feel terrible."

"Stop." His hand lands on top of mine, and as I pull back my ring scraps along his palm. He clenches his hand a moment then places it back on the wheel. "You don't have to explain anything to me, Tilly. I know this is hard for you. And I'm sorry if I made it more difficult."

My shoulders fall as his words soothe some of my anxiety. "You didn't do anything wrong, Arch. It's me that's broken."

"You're not broken." He turns and looks at me. "Do you understand me?"

I grumble a response.

"Words, Tilda St. James."

"Yes, fine."

"No, not fine."

He flicks on his blinker and pulls over to the side of the road. The leather steering wheel squeaks as his hands grip it, and he stares out at the open fields before turning to me.

"He was your husband and my best friend. He was a phenomenal, fun, caring guy, and it fucking sucks he's gone. But he loved you so much, Tilly."

My nose runs, mixing with the tears on my upper lip, and I steal a Whataburger napkin from his glove compartment to clear my face.

"I know." I sniffle.

He stares out the window, and I can tell by the furrow in his brow that he's thinking about his brother. "Grief is fucking hard. Doesn't matter if it's been two or twenty years. After a few years, I realized the hardest part of losing Sebastian wasn't his actual death, it was figuring out how to live afterward. Figuring out to get up every morning and not immediately reach for your phone to call them, or how to breathe—" he pauses, sucking in a shaky breath, "—when every breath reminded me that he wasn't here, that I had to go through life without him every single day of the rest of my life. But if I didn't have Jessie, and Shantel and Nora, to help lift the weight, I would've let it drown me." He grabs my hand and softly squeezes. "You're not broken. You are working through it daily, just like the rest of us."

I dab at the tears on my face and give him a weak smile. "Thank you."

A minute passes with Archer swiping his thumb along the back of my hand, drifting over the diamond still on my finger as he soothes my fraught nerves. "I know I'm not him. I'm moody, I'm not that fun, and I've treated you poorly. I'm sorry for pushing you away, it wasn't right, and I know you may not be able to forgive me. But all I'm asking is for a chance to make it up to you. To show you how much you mean to me.

I'll take it however slow you need me to, but I'm asking for my chance to make you feel like I should've been doing all these years, which is loved."

I'm standing at a fork in the road, terrified to move in either direction.

One way leads me back to the empty comfort of grief where I can still pretend I'm not alone, pretend that Jessie would've wanted me to stay true to him even as a widow.

And the other way leads to potential disaster. If Archer and I try to make a go of it and it all comes crashing down, not only will it affect us, but it'll affect Nora and Shantel, and even potentially ruin my chance at opening my bakery.

Needing air, I roll down the window and inhale the earthy smell of rain. Too many options sit in front of me, and either way I may end up alone.

But you're already alone, my conscience reminds me. And it's not wrong. I've been alone since Jessie died; that was my comfort zone. I learned how to live by myself, relying on no one to take care of me, and it worked for a while. But now that I've given a part of me to Archer, I don't think I want to be alone and scared anymore. I want someone to enjoy daily life with, someone to relax into after a long day at work, and I want that person to be Archer.

Running a bakery is a risk I'm willing to take, so why isn't putting my heart back out there worth it too?

"A chance," I murmur.

"A chance," he pleads.

My chest rises, renewed hope filling the deserted crevices of my heart. "Okay."

For the first time in a long time I crave to be held, and like always, Archer senses exactly what I need without me having to voice it and wraps his arms around me. My hands slide around his back and pull him closer, thankful he didn't freak out or make me feel bad for how I reacted this morning. I imagine it's hard on him too, to have feelings for his best friend's widow.

"Thank you," he whispers into my hair.

We get back onto the road headed home, and even though I know there's so much more we need to talk about, so many things left to hash out, I relish this time where it's only us. Before the outside world pushes its way in, ready to tell us that what we're doing is wrong.

After stopping home to shower and change into new clothes, we make it to the bakery before evening traffic commences. My entire body hums with excitement as we unload the display case, shifting it into the spot between the counter and the side hallway.

"It's perfect." I dance around on anxious feet, my dress loudly swishing around.

Archer turns on the neon 'You Cake My Breath Away' light and stands behind me, his hands on my waist, chin on my shoulder. "It's your bakery. Of course, it's perfect."

I turn my head and capture his lips. Our kiss is slow and sensual, an embrace of not only our tongues but the words we're too scared to say. The 'I need you,' 'I want you,' and the 'I'm scared this is too good to be true' statements lingering in the backs of our minds.

Archer deepens the kiss and leads me back until I'm pressed against the new display case. His fingers graze my bare arms, and the strap of my dress falls down my shoulder as his kisses on my neck become more feverish. I'm lost to the moment, lava pouring into my veins, mind a swirling abyss of pleasure. Within moments, my hands are in his hair, pushing him down to my chest.

"Tilly," he groans, pulling down the cup of my bra, alternating between nipping and licking the sensitive buds.

"More." My mind a haze of two years' worth of pent-up sexual frustration, I push him further.

I'm thankful the windows are still boarded up because his knees hit the ground and he crouches under my dress, pulling my panties down. My hand splays against the display case as he lifts my leg over his shoulder. His firm tongue slides through me, swirling around my clit before he sucks it into his mouth. I cry out, gripping my dress in my hand and trying to steady myself against the case.

A muscled arm wraps around my thigh, bringing my center closer to his mouth as thick fingers slide through my arousal. Fire sizzles down my spine when they push into me, pressing against my g-spot and ripping a whine from my throat.

"Feels so good," I pant, head falling against the case, adrenaline pumping through my system.

He grunts, adding a finger and bringing me closer to the edge. My legs quiver from the strength of holding myself up while he ravages me, and my hips buck along with his fingers, hand pressed against the back of his head as I come.

Archer comes out from under my dress and stands, his fingers still at my pulsing core. He kisses me, long and deep, swirling my release on my over-sensitive clit before he removes his fingers and dips them into his mouth. The image alone threatens to make me orgasm again.

I think of the last time I was here with him, my arousal so high I almost touched myself in the bathroom. But this time when I come, he's still there, still pressing kisses to my neck and chest, whispering adorations into my mouth.

I grab his waistband, heart thundering inside my chest as I deftly unbutton the jeans between me and his erection. Velvet skin meets my palm when I delve into his boxers and grasp his shaft, pumping a few times for good measure.

Archer's sharp intake of air as I lower to my knees is all the encouragement I need to taste him. His hand slams against the counter, gripping the edge as I lick up the vein on the bottom of his penis, swirling my tongue around the throbbing head and stealing the bead of precum settled there.

"Fuck," he groans, hand resting on the back of my head.

In a teasing mood, I lick him a few times and take his balls into my mouth. He's struggling, legs shaking, when I finally wrap my warm mouth around him. Taking him deep into my throat is near impossible with how large he is, but his groan gives me the strength to fight my gag reflex.

His hips move, shallowly thrusting as he stares down at where his cock disappears into my mouth. Our gazes meet as I take him as deep as I can and hum, vibrating his shaft in my throat.

He pulls out and reaches for me. "I need to be inside you right fucking now."

"I don't have—"

He whips a condom out of his back pocket. I laugh and roll my eyes. "Boy Scouts."

"Dress on or off?" He smirks at my comment and sheathes himself.

I think about it for all of two seconds. "On."

I've always wanted someone to be so hungry for me that they needed me right that instant, clothed and all. I bunch up my dress, and Archer lifts me up, wrapping my legs around his waist. His erection pushes against my center, easing its way in and letting me get used to the feeling of him.

There's no warning before he slams me down onto the rest of his cock, and I moan so loudly I swear Deidre can hear it a block away. His thrusts switch between fast and slow, long and short strokes, pressing me back into the display case. It shakes with our movements, and a part of me worries it'll shatter with the force of his thrusts, but like always, Archer knows exactly what I'm thinking.

"I'll buy you a new case, but I'm not moving from this position."

I laugh, and he responds by impaling me on his cock over and over again until I'm screaming my release into his neck and digging my fingers into his back. A few strokes later he's grunting out his orgasm, nipping and pulling at my lip like he can't get enough.

Archer sets my feet on the floor, and his smile morphs into a frown when his gaze lowers between us.

"Shit, it ripped." He drags a hand down his face. "I'm sorry."

The realization knocks me back a step. My cycle has always been regular, so I'm not worried about a pregnancy scare, but the idea of having a child with Archer reminds me I'll never have one with Jessie.

My throat swells at the thought, and Archer's hand is gripping his jaw so tightly I think he might crack bone. I can tell we're both about to spiral, so I try to salvage what I can.

"It's okay, Arch. I haven't been with uh...anyone since Jessie, and I'm not ovulating."

"I've always used protection and gotten tested regularly."

He stares at the condom, and I scramble to fill in the silence. "I promise, it'll be okay."

"I'm sorry." He's stuck in this cycle until I wrap my arm around his bicep, coaxing his shoulders to relax. He takes a moment to get rid of the condom and grab a warm towel to clean us up before wrapping his arms around me. "Let's order dinner and I'll finish putting up the lights."

Starry-eyed, I look up at him and sigh. "Thank you."

His eyebrows bunch. "For the orgasm or the lights?"

"For the food." I laugh, and he swats my ass and brings me in for another kiss. "I'm kidding. Thank you for everything you've done for me."

"I should've done it a long time ago," he says.

My sick mind fills in the unspoken words, *I wish so too.*

Embarrassed by my atrocious thoughts, I look down to the ground. Archer catches my chin in his hand and lifts it up. "Don't do that."

"Do what?" I ask.

"Retreat into yourself. You're doing nothing wrong," he says. "You're allowed to be happy, and you're allowed to be sad too. You can feel whatever you need to, but don't bottle it up."

Thankful he's only half a mind reader, I nod and let him kiss me once more before he goes to the back to order food.

I take a moment to meditate on his words, repeating back to myself that it's okay to be both sad and happy. That I don't have to feel like I'm betraying Jessie by finding happiness again so soon, and that it's okay if this...relationship is different than what I had with Jessie—the quiet type of passion that leaves your heart glowing. I remind myself I loved Jessie with all my heart and there was never space in there for Archer then, but there's space now, and that's okay.

"Food should be here in twenty minutes." Archer returns and slides his phone into his pocket before he grabs the box of lights from a nearby table. "Ready to light this place up?"

Chapter Thirty-Six
Archer

Present

Dear Seb,

I've spent the last five years dead inside because of you. Because instead of having you to talk to, I convinced myself if I let your stupid chip help me make decisions that it was like actually having you here with me, guiding me. But all it did was make me believe you didn't think I was good enough for Tilly, like I didn't deserve her. And hell, I probably don't. I could've ignored the chip and still told Tilly how I felt, but that's my own dumbass fault. I know helping her open her bakery doesn't make up for the past hurt between us, but it's brought us closer and given her the chance to figure out there could be something between us.

And the something between us isn't just sex. Yeah, that's fucking explosive. I knew it would be. There's so much history and tension that was built up that made the sex that much better (you better not be watching, or I'll kick your ass once I get to see you again). But now we're in this weird space, a situationship if you will, where we're not officially anything but we're spending all of our time together. If you were here I'd ask for your brotherly advice, but you're not. And neither is Jessie.

If I dwell too long on the fact that I only have Tilly now because Jessie's gone, I start to doubt that I truly deserve a chance with her and feel like a total dick for what I'm doing. But I know Jessie would want Tilly with someone who'd love her with his whole heart, and that's me.

We've spent the last week working at the bakery, putting finishing touches on the place while we wait for the coolers and door, and every night we have dinner at my house. She hasn't stayed the night yet because she still isn't able to be cuddled, which is understandable given the way Jessie passed, but I hope with time she'll eventually get there. I want to cuddle the fuck out of her. The house has never felt so...warm. It's stupid, but Tilly brings life to it. There's always music playing and food cooking and having her here just feels right. Like this is where she belongs. With me.

Nora and Shantel stopped by to have coffee the other day when Tilly was at the bakery, and even though I feel like they'd be okay with it if Tilly and I decided to make a go of it, I still couldn't tell them about us spending time together. What if I ruin things with Tilly? I'm the exact opposite of everything Jessie was. I'm gruff where he was poised, surly when he was always happy, and I'm worried deep down they know I'm not good enough for her.

Dad sure made it clear he knows I'm not good enough. Mom called the other day and, in the background, he mumbled to stop spending so much time with Tilly or I was going to tarnish her too. It's getting harder not to cut them completely out of my life. I know if you were here I'd be able to suffer through Dad's blatant disdain for me and Mom's nonchalant attitude about it, but you aren't here. You left me.

I should be hearing from the producers of the show in a few days. I haven't figured out what to do about Tilly and me if I get chosen. When I applied for the job I figured it'd be the best option for me to get out of the state, away from everything that reminded me of you and Jessie and how much I've lost. It would be the break from seeing Tilly I needed to finally move on. No chance of running into her at the store or being forced to sit across from her at Sunday dinners, because I'd be a state away. But then I started working on the bakery with her. I figured we'd get the work done, and it would be painful and motivating for me to want to leave, but the opposite happened, and I fell even harder.

We haven't made things official yet, and we should probably have that conversation soon, but there's so much up in the air right now. I'm not sure I can give up the opportunity to advance my career, and I can't ask her to move to Knoxville with me when her life is here, either. I've gotta call the lawyer so he can draw up the paperwork to change the bakery lease to Tilly's name instead of mine so it's officially hers, but that's another thing I'm struggling to do. How is she going to react when she finds out it was my building? That Jessie never had the chance to submit the paperwork to sublet it from me and that's why she found it in the closet. It shouldn't matter to her, but I know it will. We're in such a good spot that I'm terrified of rocking the boat with all the things we've pushed to the side. Each one has the potential to poke a hole in the boat we're coasting on, and I'm already sinking with the weight of everything I've got on my shoulders. Send me some good luck down here, asshole. I really need it.

-Arch

Chapter Thirty-Seven

Archer

Present

B acon could very well be considered the eighth wonder of the world. Its smoky flavor, salty goodness, and its sheer versatility should be taken into consideration by whomever is leading the search. I ponder this as I stand in front of the stove making breakfast for Tilly.

After reminding her it's okay to be happy, she's stayed with me all week. Each morning, I've made it a point to get out of bed earlier than her, so she doesn't have to go through what she did the first time. Seeing the pain in her eyes is something I wasn't prepared for, something I don't yet know how to handle. We're still new, and we haven't really talked about what's going on between us or long-term plans, but I know one wrong move and she'll bolt before I have a chance to tell her, to show her how much she means to me.

My entire world has seemed like it's been rotating the wrong way on its axis, but with Tilly in my arms, everything finally feels...right. Like it's always been this way, even though it hasn't. I try not to think about how things would've been had I asked her out sooner, had I not left life up to chance, but even I know you get what you deserve. And I didn't deserve Tilly back then. Hell, I'm not even sure I deserve her now, but I'll be damned if I look fate in the face and let go of this second chance it's blessed me with.

"Archibald Wilson." Tilly leans against the kitchen doorway in my two sizes too big t-shirt. It grazes her knees, leaving her gorgeous legs for viewing. Her chestnut brown hair is thrown into a messy bun, and the pink in her cheeks makes me want to kiss her until her lips match the same color.

"Tilda St. James," I reply, flipping the bacon.

"How'd you know I love bacon?"

I laugh, and she walks over and slinks her hands around my waist, resting her head on my back. She does this when she wants comfort but isn't ready to be touched yet. I'm slowly learning what type of touches make her draw away and which are comfortable for her. Her touch starvation is a minefield we're both tiptoeing through, but it's worth it to ease her into familiar touch again.

"I sat across from you at breakfast study group for an entire year. I'd have to have amnesia to not remember your pile of ten pieces of bacon with syrup."

She chuckles and pushes against my arm, her signal she's ready for touch. I pull her to my side, dropping my head to kiss her. She tries to deepen it, but I swat her rear end and laugh at her yelp. The last thing I need is her to get burned by some popping grease. "Go sit down and I'll bring you some."

"Aye aye, captain." She salutes me and snags the cup of green tea I made her.

Having her in my space, walking around my house in my clothes, getting to wake up next to her, almost feels like a gift I've been waiting years to unwrap. I'm still in shock at what's finally transpired between us, and I know there's so much we need to discuss, but I'm not ready to make waves in our steady sea as we get to know each other like this.

As she gets comfy at the table, I bring her a massive plate of bacon accompanied by a set of pancakes and eggs. We stare each other down over the rims of our mugs, both eager to see who is going to reach for the food first. Primly, she sets down her cup and lays her palms on the table. Confused, I tentatively reach for her hands.

"I'll pray," she says.

I bow my head and close my eyes, listening to Tilly pray.

"Thank you for the beautiful day, for the amazing creation that is bacon, and thank you for the sexy man who made it. Amen."

I snort, nearly causing coffee to shoot out of my nose. "Amen."

She draws her lip between her teeth, eyeing me across the table as she reaches for a piece of bacon. That singular look has my appetite ramping up for something else. Something I know will fill my heart more than my stomach. I've always thought of sex as a means to an end, a release until the next time, but with Tilly it's a need. I crave her body, her mind, her essence, like it's life-giving water.

"Are you ready?" she asks, pulling me back from my daydreaming.

"For?"

"To bake, silly."

***

When Tilly told me she needed help baking for the local shelter, I thought she meant we'd make a pie or something together, not two hundred coconut-grapefruit sugar cookies and a large German white chocolate cake. Standing in front of the island covered in flour, Tilly places the finishing touches on her sugar cookie icing before turning to me with a wide smile that steals my breath.

"What do you think?" she asks, using the back of her hand to push her hair back. A dollop of coconut icing drops onto her cheek, and I lean over to lick it off. She giggles and dabs my lips with the icing bag before reaching on tiptoes to steal it back with a swipe of her tongue.

"I think you're gorgeous..." I plant a kiss at the corner of her mouth. "Funny." Another one on the slide of her neck. "Talented." I pepper kisses down her jawline until I reach her chin and tilt it up. "Mine," I rasp out before my hand snakes into her hair, and I devour her sweet tasting lips.

Tilly drops the icing bag onto the island and wraps her arms around my waist, moaning when my hard as steel erection brushes against her stomach. A groan rumbles in my chest when she presses close to me and grabs the hair at the nape of my neck, deepening the kiss.

"Yours?" she asks, out of breath and panting.

My heart ramps up, grunting like a caveman at the thought of her truly being mine. Of her laughs, her kisses, her smiles being only for me. Cooking dinner for her, watching her as she bakes and dances around the kitchen, relaxing on the couch with her after a long day. I've wanted all that with her for longer than I can remember, and it's all within my grasp.

Not if you get the job and leave.

The thought barrels into me and sours the cookies in my stomach. Tilly notices when my arms go slack around her, and the middle of her brow crinkles in confusion.

"What's wrong?"

I try to shake off the thought, to bring myself back to the present instead of the future by gripping her tighter and nuzzling into her neck. I can't bear to look at the questions in her eyes when I don't have the answers yet. "You'll always be mine."

"What happe..."

My phone ringing on the island stops whatever she was about to ask. I can't say I've ever been thankful to hear from my father, but in this moment, I'd rather take whatever verbal abuse he's about to give than figure out what to tell Tilly about what just broke my concentration.

"I've gotta take this."

"Okay."

I give her one last kiss and reach for the phone. Walking into the living room, I stand in front of the picture of me and Seb hanging on the fireplace, willing him to give me strength to handle this conversation.

"Hello?"

"Archibald," my father's gruff voice comes through the speaker. "Your mother wants to know if you're going to grace us with your presence at Thanksgiving this year."

Thanksgiving? How is it that soon? And why would they want me there when I haven't attended a Thanksgiving with them since Sebastian passed?

"I hadn't planned on it," I reply.

I normally spend the holiday with Nora and Shantel, my actual family, and Tilly normally spends it with her father.

He grunts like it's the exact answer he expected me to say. "Good," he mumbles. I wait, because I know there's more. He wouldn't call me for just any reason. "Well, since you're not going to be doing anything important, Mr. Kennedy at The Dominion needs a new bar top and I told him you'd do it."

I sigh. This is typical of my father. He wants nothing to do with me, yet he wants to use me to better his standing at their country club. At least my construction company gets good word of mouth from it.

"How much?" I ask. If I'm going to do this in my spare time away from Tilly and the bakery, it better be worth it financially.

"How much?" He scoffs like I've offended him.

"Yes, Father. I don't work for free."

"I heard you've been working for free someplace else," he replies. "Everyone's been talking about you and Jessie's girl."

He knows her name. He hired her family to cater Claire's wedding, and Tilly made the cake. He's being the asshole I know him to be by not addressing her correctly to spite me.

Shards of glass stab my throat as I swallow. "What of it?"

He laughs. "Wilsons don't do sloppy seconds, Archibald. Don't tarnish our reputation by having the gossip mill running."

I dig my fingernails into the brick fireplace mantle, clenching my jaw as pain slices across the pads, ready to curse out my father for even insinuating Tilly's worth, like he knows the value of anything but pride. Warm arms slide beneath my shirt, and my abs tense as Tilly's hand ventures south. I suck in a breath and close my eyes when she sneaks below my waistband.

"Is he coming?" My mother's chipper voice floats into my ear, reminding me I'm on the phone.

I cough, sputtering at her choice of words just as Tilly's smooth hand finds me hot and heavy for her.

"I'll contact Mr. Kennedy." I disconnect the call and pull Tilly around to my front, pressing her back to the fireplace. "You're a naughty girl."

She draws her lips between her teeth. "I was lonely in there, and you seemed tense. Everything okay?"

I kiss her softly and pull her back into the kitchen, trying to figure out what to tell her. She's never really asked about my relationship with my parents, but I'm sure Jessie probably told her.

I shrug. "My parents were asking if I was coming to Thanksgiving."

"Oh." She leans against the fridge. "Are you going?"

"Hell no." I scoff. "I usually spend it with Nora and Shantel." She looks down at her shoes, not meeting my eyes. I reach over and tilt her chin up with my knuckle. "What's up, Til?"

"Would you maybe want to...spend it with me?" Her coffee-colored eyes are filled with so much hope my chest constricts. "I mean, I know we haven't really talked about what we're doing, but..."

"Yes," I cut her off. "I'd love to spend the holiday with you."

She smiles. "Really?"

I figure saying "I want to spend every holiday with you for the rest of my life" is probably too soon and will scare her off, so instead I pull her into my arms and kiss her delirious. I so badly want to ask her to let me love her, to be my everything, but if I dump the magnitude of my feelings on her so soon, she might get overwhelmed and want to take a step back. Not to mention, things are still up in the air with the hosting job. As much as it pains me to take it slow, I can't risk losing her after she's finally given me a chance.

Chapter Thirty-Eight
Tilly

Sunlight spills into the room when Shantel walks in the front door carrying the ingredients I need for my rhubarb and elderflower cupcakes. Ever since I got home and put the display case and lights up at the bakery, I've been flooded with ideas for new desserts. It's almost like my brain knows we're inching closer to the bakery opening, and it wants to be sure I've got enough ideas to tide me over. Using Archer's kitchen has been nice, but I missed my large island and double oven.

And as petty as it may seem, there's no essence of Deidre here. The thought crosses my mind that Archer may feel the same way hanging out in the house where Jessie and I lived, but at least they were friends. There's no love lost between me and Deidre.

"These better be good," Shantel says, laying the bags on the counter.

"I think they're going to be a hit."

Dad asked me to bring a dessert to Thanksgiving with him and Gloria, and my nervousness about spending time with his new girlfriend had me anxious and in need of relaxation, so I chose to try out a new recipe.

Shantel sits on the stool at my kitchen island and lines the high-sided baking tray with parchment paper so we can roast the rhubarb. I zest a few lemons and place them to the side before mixing the flour, baking powder, baking soda, salt, and almonds for the cake. Shantel works on the filling, whipping the cream to soft peaks along with the remaining roasted rhubarb, yogurt, and elderflower cordial.

I manage to get the cakes out of the oven before Archer knocks on the door. Ever since we got back from our trip, we've spent the majority of time up at his house, mainly in bed. I know there's stuff we need to talk about, like where we go from here, but I've been busy letting him rehydrate my body with his touch.

"What's Archer doing here?" Shantel asks.

I shrug, dusting my hands on my apron before going to answer the door.

"Hey, baby girl." Archer leans down to kiss me.

I shiver at his nickname and fight the urge to step back, to be worried about what Shantel will think when she sees us.

Old habits die hard.

He hands me a bouquet of flowers, and all I hear behind me is Shantel squealing.

"Did this…Did you…" She covers her face, shaking her head. "Finally!"

"Shantel." Archer's voice is a reprimand.

"I'm sorry." She laughs. "I'm just happy for y'all."

"Thanks," I grumble, walking back into the kitchen and placing the flowers in a vase.

Archer sits beside her, plucking a strawberry from a bowl I have set aside for my strawberry and Nutella cake topping. Shantel's smile reaches her eyes, and she can't stop flitting between Archer and me with a look of sheer excitement on her face.

"Would you chill out?" I throw the dish towel at her.

"I can't." She's antsy in her chair, bopping her shoulders to a tune only she can hear.

The timer dings, signaling my rhubarb cakes are finished cooling. Archer and Shantel chat, and I can't help comparing it to how we all used to convene in the kitchen when Jessie was alive. Before things went south after Archer's sister's wedding.

I push away the negative thoughts and replace them with new memories, ones where Archer has shown me he does believe in my abilities. Our little family is back together.

For now.

A niggle of abandonment twists in my stomach as I watch them, worrying how long it'll be until Archer leaves me again too. We still haven't talked about his job opportunity, and I'm too scared to approach the topic. This thing between us is so new, and I'm worried the slightest complication will snap it in half.

"I'm gonna change for dinner."

"You're going to dinner with the parents?" Shantel asks, wide eyes pointed at Archer.

"With my dad." I cringe at the thought of Gloria stepping into my mom's shoes, then chastise myself because Archer's in a slightly similar position with me being his best friend's widow.

I go down the hall to my room, leaving them to talk about me in hushed tones. Closing my eyes, I do the breathing exercises my grief counselor taught me when I first lost Jessie and so much was changing.

The slight blush on my cheeks and the light that has returned to my eyes shines back at me from the mirror, and I'm thankful. Thankful I finally found a way through the grief and the sadness, that I'm allowing myself to move on in the wake of a terrible tragedy.

"Knock knock," Shantel says from the doorway as I'm smoothing down my dress. "You look radiant."

My cheeks heat. "Thank you."

"You nervous?" she asks.

I shrug. "A little."

"Don't be." She reaches for me as if to pull me in for a hug but drops her hands before she connects. Feeling like this is one of those moments I spoke with my therapist about where people give me the opportunity to find comfort in them and I *don't* push it away because of fear, I grab her and pull her into a hug. She murmurs into my hair, "You deserve it, and so does he."

I squeeze her tight, relishing in the comfort of her arms.

"I'm glad y'all got out of your own way," she whispers and backs away before adding, "It's been a long time coming."

I roll my eyes and head back out to the kitchen.

"I'm just being honest," she yells, opening the front door. "I'll call you tomorrow."

Finally alone, Archer nuzzles into my neck and cups my butt. "I'm hungry for dessert."

"Later." I playfully push him away and take the desserts to the car. "We're gonna be late."

The imposing door of Dad's house makes my heart thump like a tribal drum. Archer's hand is on my back, and right now, it's the only thing keeping me standing.

"We probably should've talked about how to introduce me on the way over here," he whispers as we wait for someone to answer.

"Well, *someone* wouldn't keep their hands to themselves and kept risking my precious cake to get under my dress."

He laughs. "Touché."

The door opens and I'm hit with the aroma of turkey and celery and carrots. Immediately, I realize Dad is making my mom's famous stuffing. My chest aches with the memory of sneaking into the restaurant on Thanksgiving to use the kitchen so all of the desserts would be ready at the same time as the meal.

"Hey sweet pea." Dad ushers us into the foyer. He gestures to the box in my hand. "Is that your new dessert?"

"Yup." I hand the box to Archer so I can slip off my jacket. "Rhubarb and elderberry sponge cake."

Gloria walks out of the kitchen in a beautiful orange dress, a tray of sweet potatoes in her hand. My mouth salivates at the melted butter on top, and I'm smacked with the memory of the last meal I made for Jessie: harvest chicken with sweet potatoes and brussel sprouts. I used to hate any form of yams, but I've basically lived off sweet potatoes for the last year, wishing that it could bring me back to the night before my life changed, and now I can't stop eating them.

"Hi," she says, pulling me from my spiral. Her dark hair is pinned back, a welcoming smile on her face. She stops beside Dad, eyeing the cake box in his hands.

"This is Tilly's boyfriend, Archer," Dad says.

Archer coughs like there's something stuck in his throat, and I'm so shocked by my dad's assumption, correct as it may be, that I'm frozen with my mouth open.

Gloria shifts the plate and extends her hand. "Nice to meet you, Archer." She turns to me. "It's great to see you again, Tilly."

My smile can only be described as painful. Archer elbows me as we follow them into the dining area. I never imagined my dad picking up on whatever's going on between Archer and me, but I guess love recognizes love.

I nearly choke on my own thoughts. I don't love Archer. Or at least I'm not willing to admit it out loud yet. When you tell someone you love them, it gives them the power to take that love away, and since love seems to always flee from me, I'm hesitant to utter the words I know my heart feels. No matter how stupid it sounds, I know the minute I finally tell

Archer I'm in love with him, it'll give the universe an opportunity to take him away...like it did Jessie.

"How's the bakery coming along?" Dad asks as we get seated.

I'm still struggling to find my words, so Archer answers for me. "It's almost done. We're waiting on another walk-in cooler, the front door, the register, and the specialty boxes she ordered."

Finally finding my voice after a long drink of water, I say, "I need to get in there and organize some before we get the menu boards up and start posting signs."

Dad nods, taking a bite of the food. "I can't wait to see it when it's finished. I'm so proud of you."

"Thank you."

"Your mom would be too," he says, giving me a half smile.

My heart twists in my chest, and I look up at the ceiling, trying to keep the tears at bay. Archer squeezes my leg beneath the table, and as I look at him a calm presence overwhelms me.

"You two are so cute," Gloria says. "Have you been dating long?"

My dad and Archer simultaneously cough. Dad must not have told Gloria too much about Archer and me, or else she'd know the answer to that question.

"No." I take a bite of macaroni and cheese flavored with Old Bay and hot sauce, effectively cutting off the rest of my statement. The creamy cheese cuts through the heat of the sauce, and the seasoning reminds me of my mom's home state of Maryland.

"You'd never know," she replies.

I'd kill for a glass of wine right now, but instead I shovel a forkful of sweet potatoes into my mouth.

"Dessert, anyone?" Archer asks, breaking the tension.

Dad and Gloria head to the kitchen as Archer and I clear the plates.

"Are you doing okay?" He caresses my arm, stopping a moment to toy with my bracelet. His gaze moves to my ring, and there's a hint of a smile on his lips before he meets my eyes again. I can't tell if it pains him that I still wear the jewelry Jessie bought, but I'm not ready to part with them yet.

Throat thick with emotion, I nod. "I'm fine. Thank you for being here."

I sigh when his lips meet my forehead. "I wouldn't want to be anywhere else."

We crowd around the island, excited to taste my new concoction. The citrusy flavor and sourness of the rhubarb are cut by the earthy flavor of the elderberry cream in the center. It's the perfect mix of sour and sweet.

"This is amazing, Tilly," Gloria says, feeding Dad another bite.

"She's right, kiddo. It's fantastic."

My smile splits my face, and I squeak out a thank you just as Archer's hand grips my ass.

"You're amazing," he says, kissing my cheek.

My face heats, and I wink at him and divert my eyes to the cake on my plate. I can't bear to look at my dad right now. Is he frowning? Upset that I've moved on with Archer? Or is he happy I've found love again? I was so shocked he called Archer my boyfriend that I didn't take note of his tone earlier.

Dad calls Archer into the formal living room for a drink, while Gloria and I clean up the kitchen.

"Thank you for allowing me to spend the holiday with you," she says, scrubbing a plate.

I struggle to find something to say and instead give her an awkward smile and say, "Thanks for making Dad smile again. He's been way more open to my new desserts since you've come into his life, and for that, I'm forever thankful."

She laughs. "You've got talent, and his stubborn butt was holding you back."

I nod, realizing it's exactly what my mom would've said if she was still alive.

***

For Thanksgiving night, the bar is filled with loud and rowdy patrons chatting and drinking as the band gets ready on the stage. One of my favorite artists, Sylvie, is behind the piano tonight, her curly brown hair pinned up like she came from her own family dinner. Cymbals clash as the drummer sneaks onto the stage with a beer in his hand, and a giddiness overtakes my body. I love all things music, and even though I can't hold a tune, I'll sing my heart out any time I can.

A squeeze on my thigh steals my attention. "One hour," Archer repeats. "Then you're mine."

The kick drum is the soundtrack to our kiss, and the crowd disappears as our lips meld together. I sigh, thankful I decided to go out tonight instead of staying home. The first few holidays without Jessie, I locked myself in my room with a sad book and a bottle of wine. Most times I didn't remember anything about the book the next day, but I also didn't remember the puddle of tears I'm sure I cried into my pillow reliving the previous holidays spent with him.

"Archer," a woman's voice cuts through the din of the bar. "I'm surprised to see you here."

My teeth clench together so painfully I'm sure I've cracked a molar when Deidre rests her hand on Archer's shoulder.

"Deidre." Archer shrugs off her hand, keeping his gaze fixed on the stage.

Possessiveness pools in my stomach, pushing its way up and into my chest. "It's nice to see you again, Deidre," I say, making my presence known.

She smiles and nods but doesn't return the sentiment. Her eyes move back to Archer.

"I thought you'd be jetting off to shoot that little show you told me about, but I see you're still with *her*."

The snooty way she says 'her' ignites a fire in my veins, but Archer's strong hand on my thigh calms me.

"What I do with my time is none of your business anymore, Deidre. Now leave."

She rolls her eyes and throws her hair over her shoulder as she leaves the table. As glad as I am that she's gone, I can't forget her mentioning Archer will be leaving soon, leaving me to shoot that carpentry show. We haven't spoken about long-term goals, so I'm in unsure waters, drowning without a buoy.

Archer's tense frame makes me decide to leave that conversation for tomorrow.

He rises from the seat. "I'm going to get a drink."

The band starts taking requests, and I get in line to scribble my three favorite songs onto the paper and slip it into the jar. Even if I only hear one of the songs tonight I'll be happy. I turn and find Archer's eyes on me as he drinks his beer. He winks, and my shoulders relax when I see the playful side of him is back and not affected by his ex's childish remarks.

"You better not have requested Shania Twain or I'm leaving." He smiles, beer froth coating his mustache.

I reach out, sliding my finger along the white foam before sinking it into my mouth. He growls and pulls me to him, cupping my buttcheeks as he tastes my mouth. His kisses are all-consuming and passionate, and sometimes I feel like I might trade the ability to breathe if I could live off his air.

The guitarist reaches his hand into the request jar and pulls out a slip. Dancing in my seat, I cross my fingers, hoping it's my favorite Cranberries song.

"Ooo, this is spicy, but I love this song." He hands the paper to the other players in the band so they're on the same page. "This song is requested for a special someone, you know who you are."

The crowd is alive with electric energy filling the air, and Archer's hand wraps around mine and brings it to his mouth. Sometimes I almost forget it hasn't always been this way, that we didn't spend the last five years on opposite sides of a friendship that could've been more had we opened our eyes, but then I chastise myself because I know things happened the way they were meant to. I was meant to marry Jessie, and as unconventional as it is, I also feel like I was meant to reconnect with Archer in the midst of my grief.

"Here we go," the guitarist says.

If I thought Archer was tense when Deidre made her comments, he's near explosive when the band begins playing the opening chords to *Jessie's Girl*. Everything I've eaten or drank today moves into my throat, and the sick feeling rises to my head.

Deidre.

I try to keep the tears at bay by sucking my cheeks in between my teeth. The stabbing sensation in my chest moves to my stomach, and I wrap my arms around myself to try to stop from breaking down. In this moment I need Archer's comfort, but when I look to him, he's stone. He's not blinking, his body is rigid, and I'm not sure he's breathing at all.

My eyes scan the room, looking for the woman who was so hurt by being rejected that she went so low as to bring my dead husband into the picture. When I can't find her, I rise from my chair, intent on hunting her down.

"I forgot I have something I need to finish in the morning," Archer says, still staring at the stage. "Let's get you home."

I close my eyes as the happiness I felt walking in here drains from me. I thought *I'd* have a bigger problem with the tabooness of our relationship, but one underhanded dig from his ex and he's pulling away.

Chapter Thirty-Nine
Tilly

Two days have passed since the piano bar fiasco with Deidre, and outside of a few texts, I haven't seen or heard from Archer. We've been ships in the night, and with three and a half weeks until we're supposed to open, I'm starting to worry I'm not only going to lose my relationship, but also my bakery if it's not ready for opening.

Confronting Deidre has passed my mind a few times, but I know it wouldn't change anything, and even though she created this rift between Archer and me, she's not the one who's going to help close it.

It's taken me this long to realize I was selfish, only focused on my own grief about Jessie's passing and my relationship with Archer. I didn't stop to ask how he's been managing the past two years, or how he felt about the progression between us. It's easy to forget the mountain of history between us when we're in bed, but being stripped down with someone in the physical doesn't negate the fact that we've kept our emotions clothed, our scars still hidden in the deep valley of our minds for fear of it breaking this new balance between us.

Sunlight spills into the room as I gather the clothes strewn about, throwing them into the hamper inside the bathroom. My mind spins like a top, replaying the last few weeks with Archer as I piddle around, windexing the mirror, cleaning the toilet, then moving into the bedroom to organize. It's not until I'm standing at the sink with a tea-stained mug in my hand that I realize what I've done.

Limbs frozen in shock, the cup slips from my hands and clatters in the stainless steel bin. Like a VHS tape being rewound, I race up the stairs with sweat coating my skin and a silent prayer on my tongue. The thundering inside my chest heralds the storm brewing in my stomach as I near the door to my—our—room.

My eyes are closed when I pass the threshold, as if the darkness can shield me from what I know will be there when I open my eyes. A few short inhales are all my chest will allow before I force myself to look at the destruction of the last place I felt my husband's arms wrapped me.

A gale of air rushes from my lips. "Oh no."

Tears queue in the corner of my eyes, a waterfall ready to gush forward the moment I blink. I was so focused on everything changing between me and Archer, the happiness I've felt the past few months, the life I could see making with him, that without thought I made Jessie's side of the bed.

With a deep inhale, I close my eyes and let the tears slide down my cheeks. My fists clench at my stomach, hoping it'll keep the pain away.

It never comes.

There's a thumping inside my ears, my chest, and my fingertips, but no ache accompanies it. I thought I'd break down and throw stuff against the wall, that there'd be a heaviness permanently settled on my chest, but instead there's a quiet kind of peace that settles over me as if I was stuck in the last chapter of a book unable to bring myself to finish the story, and now I'm ready to turn the page and find out the ending.

To find my happily-ever-after.

Or at least I hope so.

I stare at the throw pillows stacked neatly where Jessie's head laid, no longer a mountain barricading my limbs from spreading out wide on the bed. A breeze whips along my neck, and I glance at the closed window.

A tugging sensation in my chest has my eyes going up, looking toward Heaven with a smile.

Thank you, I whisper, hoping Jessie can hear me. *I love you, too.*

There's a lightness to my steps as I back out of the room, quietly exhaling any lingering doubt and replacing it with gratitude as I grab my keys and head to the bakery—my last gift from Jessie.

***

After calling Archer a few times to let him know about the breakthrough I had and getting his voicemail, I decided to throw myself into opening day prep. There's nothing like menial work to take my mind off things I don't want to deal with, like Archer going silent after the bar fiasco. Shantel and Nora find me sitting on the bakery floor surrounded by approximately three hundred small take-out boxes.

"Hey guys."

"What's wrong?" they ask in unison.

"Nothing," I reply, voice a tad too high. Shantel's eyes narrow on me as if she knows I'm lying. A beat passes where I swear she can see into my soul, and before I know it, she turns toward the door. "Where are you going?"

"I'm going to kick his ass."

"No," I plead. "Don't do that."

She turns, a frown marring her face. "Give me one good reason why I shouldn't."

"Because he didn't do anything." I sigh. "It was all Deidre, and I'm giving him time to work through what happened."

"What happened is he's a jackass."

"Shantel," Nora chastises. "Let them work it out themselves."

I give her a half smile. "What's up? Did you need help with something?"

Shantel leans against the door, her arms crossed as she toys with the sleeve of her lace top. "We came by to see if you wanted to come have lunch with us?"

I take an inventory of the room, realizing there's not much more I can do until the walk-in freezer arrives. With the milestone I crossed in my healing journey this morning, I deserve a treat. I consider telling them about making Jessie's side of the bed, but I decide to keep it to myself, relishing in the pride I feel.

"Sure." I get up from the ground and dust off my pants. "That sounds great."

After locking up, we walk toward the main sector of The Pearl. A familiar voice steals my attention as we pass the road where Deidre's bookstore is located. Though my mind is telling me to continue, my feet have melded to the cement. Shantel and Nora's voices sound far off as I stare at *them* with a thumping inside my skull. Deidre shoves Archer's notebook into his chest and gives him the finger, and his shoulders fall slack, chin touching his chest in defeat.

A pit opens in my stomach. It's in this moment I realize the only reason I'm hurt is because I've fully fallen for him. The time we've spent together the past few weeks, the way he's encouraged me and helped me work through my own grief, was building a firm foundation for me to fall head over heels for him.

The revelation makes my knees buckle.

"Everything okay?" Shantel asks.

My hands curl into themselves, and I force myself to nod and follow her and Nora who are headed Archer's way. Deidre locks eyes with me, and with an unfriendly smile and an eye roll, she heads back into her store. Archer hasn't noticed us yet, but his low shoulders and the shake of his head show me he's upset by whatever she said. I stop myself from going down the rabbit hole of jealousy. I take a deep breath and paste a smile onto my face.

"Hey," Shantel calls to Archer.

My lungs seize and my feet slow as he turns, and his pained eyes settle on me. He rolls up his notebook and shoves it into his back pocket, greeting Nora and Shantel with a hug before he stands in front of me.

"Hi." My voice sounds like a caged animal.

"Hey."

Nora and Shantel gesture behind him that they're going to the restaurant and leave us to our own devices as we walk away from the bookstore, our pace slow and deliberate.

"Sorry I didn't come by last night." He rubs the back of his neck, gaze glued to the cement. "I had some stuff to work through and didn't want to bring my bad mood over."

"I understand." I roll my lips between my teeth. "Me, too."

He nods to the restaurant. "Having brunch?"

"Yeah." I give him a weak smile. "Did you wanna come? I'm sure they wouldn't mind."

He stops before the door, eyes sliding to where Nora and Shantel sit with their backs to us. "No," he replies. "I've got some things to take care of, so I'll catch up with you later?"

Pain strikes through my chest. It feels like he's pulling away from us. From me.

My teeth clamp down on my lip, and I struggle to swallow.

"K," is all I manage to say.

I tilt my head up for a kiss, but he presses one to the side of my head instead. "See you later."

Nausea sinks into my core as I stare at his retreating back. I can't flake out on Shantel and Nora, but I don't want to be here. I want to find Archer and beg him not to give up on what we've started.

"Where's Archer?" Shantel looks over my shoulder.

"He had stuff to get done."

Like a mother, Nora must pick up on the unsaid words. "Are you sure everything's okay?" She reaches out and grasps my hand. "You know we're always here for you, Tilly. And we know how he can be."

My brain is screaming at me to tell them, to ask them what they think about the entire situation, but my heart is still too tender and confused. Archer has been spending all of his time helping me get my bakery ready, showing up for me in ways I never expected. He's dealing with stuff I'm not sure how to help him through, and I want to show him it's not a one-way street, that he can rely on me too.

"Everything's fine," I say, though I'm not sure I believe my own words. "He's having a bad week and needs some space."

Nora smiles, and the waitress brings us menus and drops off our coffees.

"So are you guys just sleeping together?" Shantel asks, stirring cream into her cup.

I nearly choke on my coffee, eyes skittering to Nora before they turn into daggers I shoot at my unhelpful sister-in-law.

"Shantel," Nora admonishes.

"What?" she asks. "I'm just wondering if they'll be getting married soon so my baby can be a flower girl or ring bearer."

Silence encompasses the table as realization settles.

"Baby?" Nora yells excitedly, wrapping her arms around her daughter. "Really?"

My heart is in my throat, clogged by a mixture of happiness and dread. I'm happy for Shantel, but seeing Nora's excitement reminds me of the grandkids I was never able to give her.

"Congratulations, Shantel." I lift my mug in the air, ceramic clinking as they add theirs.

We spend the next hour chatting about how Shantel found out, how Malik reacted, and what her due date is, and thankfully mine and Archer's confusing relationship is forgotten.

I head to the bakery and try to stop the stupid tears from streaming down my face by reorganizing and labeling the shelves filled with icings.

A text cuts through the blaring music, and I nearly tumble from the small step ladder.

Dinner at my house, 6pm?

My cheeks puff out with a breath, and I stifle the urge to chuck my phone across the floor. If I'm going to get the answers I need about what's going on between him and me, then I have to buck up and be an adult about the situation.

Sure, I type back, looking at the clock. It gives me five hours to obsess over the conversation in my head, and that may not even be enough time to rehearse all the things I want to say.

***

Traffic during rush hour still sucks going out of the city, but at least the temperature has dropped enough that I can drive with the windows down and feel the breeze on my face. I've been sitting at the edge of Archer's property trying to coach myself to drive the rest of the way up the driveway. I'll either leave here tonight with a boyfriend or alone, and both options terrify me.

Staring down at my hand, I twist my wedding rings around my finger a few times, my heart galloping in my chest at the thought of taking them off. When Jessie put these rings on my finger I thought it was forever. I didn't expect a year later I'd be a widow. And I never expected I'd fall for someone else, least of all Archer.

It's a big step, taking off my rings, but one I feel ready to make. Even if things don't work out with me and Archer—a thought I hate even considering—it's time.

I'm ready for the next chapter.

They tell you in grief counseling to go with what feels right, to not compare your journey to others, and while I know some people take years to find happiness again, my journey has been different.

My heart skips when I think of him inside cooking me dinner, waiting for me to come home, and the butterflies still flapping inside my stomach make me think Jessie is somewhere out there telling me it's okay. Telling me I deserve to be happy again.

"Let's do this," I say, coaching myself to get the rest of the way up the driveway and out of my car.

Through the window, Archer's broad frame comes into view. He's wearing a hunter-green Henley, sleeves rolled up on his strong forearms as he stirs something on the stove. I sink my teeth into my lip and stare at the tight pants he has on, the material hugging his muscular butt and thighs. Smoothing my sweaty hands down my dress, I gather up the courage to knock.

"Wow," he says, opening the door. "You look gorgeous."

I look down at my burnt orange sweater dress and black booties. I wouldn't call the outfit gorgeous, but it definitely highlights my curves in a way I've always loved. "Thanks, you look good, too."

I follow him into the house and skitter to a halt once I'm in the foyer. Gone are the pictures and couches Deidre decorated with, and in their place are the pictures from out in the garage. Curiosity pulls me further into the room, wondering if our picture is up there or if it's still hiding on his desk.

Stomach spinning, I move closer to the wall, wondering if he's been planning to do this or if the Thanksgiving fiasco made him want to change things around just to make me more comfortable here. My fingers dance over pictures of Archer and his brother I've never seen. They look alike. Dark hair, green eyes, slim frames and tan skin, but Archer is taller. His smile is wide in every picture with his brother, and the slight twinge in my chest reminds me he basically lost two brothers. Unconsciously, my thumb swipes along my now bare ring finger, breath hitching at the weird feeling when my eyes land on the picture of me, Archer, and Jessie.

"Like the new living room?" Archer asks, startling me.

He's leaned against the fireplace, arms crossed, a smile on his face.

"I love it." If he's changing his house, moving pictures of us into the living room, maybe we *are* headed in the right direction.

"Food's done." He reaches out for my hand, and I take it with renewed spirit. His forward movement stops as if something clicked in his brain, the moment when you finally slide the last puzzle piece into place. He glances at our entwined hands, and his throat rolls with a swallow as he notes my bare ring finger.

A declaration that I'm serious about moving forward together too.

He squeezes my hand with a shy smile as leads me through the house. The aroma of garlic and oregano floats into my nose as we move into the kitchen. Archer hands me a glass of white wine and pulls the chair out for me to sit. It feels vaguely like our first official date, even though we've been out together before. There's a candle, and the table is set for two. It's casual but intimate.

He pulls a lasagna out of the oven and places it on the potholder on the table beside the homemade garlic bread. My tongue is heavy in my mouth with all the words I want to say, but I swallow and push them down for after dinner.

"Shit," I say. "I forgot to bring a dessert."

He laughs. "I have some extra snickerdoodle bread we can warm up."

"Where'd you get that?"

He rubs a hand along his beard like he's nervous. "I stopped by your parents' restaurant and got some."

My eyebrows hit my hairline, and my heart squeezes in my chest. "You bought some of my treats from the restaurant? I could've made you some."

He shrugs. "I was hungry."

Not only is he supporting my baking, but he's also supporting my parents' dream.

I smile into my wine glass and dig into my pasta. Flavors burst on my tongue, warming me from the inside out. Fresh basil, chocolate-sprinkled tomatoes, and ricotta cheese all melt perfectly together to create my favorite Italian dish.

"This is amazing."

"I'm glad you're enjoying it."

His feet tangle with mine under the table, and a sense of peace overcomes me. Images of us eating dinner together every night, filling the table with a kid or two, maybe a dog, all speed through my mind as he smiles at me. We chat about the bakery opening but stay far away from the hosting gig he's still waiting to hear about. Respecting the fact that he's not ready to talk about it, I move onto telling him about a cake flavor I want to try.

"I bought you something," he says.

"A gift?" I press my hand against my chest, my heart thumping beneath my palm. "For me?"

He sets a wrapped box in front of me and places a soft kiss on my lips. I try to deepen it, but he pulls back too soon with a smile on his face. I squint at him, curious as to what he has up his sleeve.

A laugh rips out of me when I unwrap the disposable camera.

"For when you're ogling me."

"You're funny." I can't keep the grin off my face as I spin the dial and aim it at him across the table. "Smile."

Of course, he scowls, but then I get a genuine smile out of him and I'm scrambling to spin the dial again to capture it.

"Come here." He pats his lap.

I oblige his request and settle onto his legs. He wraps his arm around my waist, and I hold up the camera, taking a picture of us. He steals the camera from me and presses his lips to mine, tongue dipping in to taste the white wine on my breath. I forget about the stolen camera until the flash and click bring my attention to his raised hand.

"That one is for me," he says, spinning the dial.

I turn around in his arms, ready for another picture. He holds the camera out and tells me to smile, but at the last moment, he brings it closer to my chest and snaps the picture.

"That one, too."

I escape from his canoodling and clear the table of our plates while he continues taking pictures of me in domestic bliss. He comes up behind me at the sink, brushing my hair aside as his warm lips kiss up the side of my neck.

"I'll warm up the world's best snickerdoodle bread and meet you in front of the fireplace."

Chapter Forty
Tilly

Orange flames crackle, wafting the slightly pungent odor of burning wood toward me and Archer cuddled up on the new couch. The stem of my wine glass shimmers as I twist it and relax into the warmth of his embrace. With his arms around me, I'm filled with a burst of confidence to tackle almost anything, even the conversation I'm terrified to have.

"What are you thinking about?" Archer's breath skates down my neck, and he presses a kiss into my hair. "World domination via baking?"

I throw my head back and laugh, accidentally spilling Archer's beer all over us.

"Oops, sorry." I rise from the couch, trying and failing to keep the beer from soaking into the back of my dress. Archer rips off his shirt, and my tongue peeks out to moisten my lips. His abs call to my fingers, begging them to run along the hardened pillows of muscle.

"If you wanted me to get naked, all you had to do was ask." He blots at the back of my dress, chuckling as he tries to sop up the beer.

"In your dreams, bucko." I give him a peck on the lips and push him toward the kitchen. "Why don't you get us fresh drinks and I'll steal a shirt and sweats from your closet."

He leans against the door frame, thumbs hooked through his belt loops and a sly smile on his face. "We could forego the clothes and wrap up in blankets."

"Nice try. We have stuff to talk about, and you're not going to distract me with Satan's washboard."

His dark chuckle follows me up the stairs, and I head into his bathroom to slip out of my clothes and throw them into the hamper. After staying here off and on for the past couple weeks, I'm familiar with the layout of the room, the long dresser covered with teakwood scented cologne and deodorant, the little bowl of candies he hides behind the TV. It's comfortable and inviting, a place where I could get used to spending more time.

I slip into a hoodie and a pair of sweats from his closet before I freshen up and head back into the room. An open notebook lies on his side of the bed, and a forgotten longing to know what he's writing moves to the forefront of my mind. He's always writing in the book, and any time I've asked him what it contains, he brushes me off like it's a secret.

If it was a secret he wouldn't have left it out in the open in a place he knew you'd see it.

My conscience battles itself as my feet move closer to the bed. I'm aware I'm about to cross a line, to delve into the barred off crevasses of Archer's mind, and that I may not like what I find, but the tugging in my chest feels urgent.

Listening for any movement on the stairs, I sit on the edge of the bed and consider my options. I can leave and pretend like I never saw the book, but the uneasiness that floods my system every time I see him writing inside it, every time he brushes off my curiosity about why it seems like an extension of him, makes me rethink.

Self-preservation wins out, and my hands shake as I lift the book and begin to read.

Air slowly seeps out of my lungs when I realize he's writing letters to his brother, and a wave of embarrassment washes over me. I start to close the book, to put it back where I found it and pretend like I didn't cross a line, but my eyes snag on the familiar letters of my name and I'm sucked back into the bubble of curiosity.

Archer is guarded—a closed book I'm dying to read. Seeing my name on these pages makes me want to know what he's writing about me—about us. Is he as happy as I am that we've started seeing each other? Worried we're going to fail at our second chance? Insight into his mind is something I can't pass up.

A knot of dread ties itself in my stomach, and tears burn at the backs of my eyes, pushing through wet eyelashes as I stifle the urge to crumble. Flipping through the pages, learning each new tidbit of information, is like giving my heart tiny paper cuts, bleeding me dry.

Within fifteen minutes, the world Archer carefully created around me shatters as I read about our interactions from his point of view, now shedding a different light on the biggest moments in my life.

I stare down at my empty finger and realize Jessie asked me to marry him with a ring he didn't pick out, that my favorite piece of jewelry, the bracelet I wear daily, was chosen by a man who stood on the sidelines instead of getting onto the field and fighting to win my heart. Was my relationship with Jessie even real? Or was Archer constantly behind the scenes pulling the strings attached to my heart like a puppeteer.

Archer purposefully pushed me away, made it a point to put distance between us by snide comments and making me feel like our friendship in college meant nothing to him.

He was a coward.

Still is.

Clearing away the tears with the sleeve of Archer's hoodie, I continue reading, allowing the facade of my entire relationship with Jessie to break into tiny shards. My throat constricts, and ropes of anguish wrap around my heart while I read about the night of Jessie's proposal then land on the day after his funeral.

The bakery isn't even technically mine. It's still—has always been—Archer's.

My hands ache, skin burning with betrayal as I stare at my now bare finger and imagine the ring I took off before I walked into this house ready to give Archer my heart. It was supposed to signify a promise to love each other, to honor and to cherish, but nothing about the situation makes me feel as such.

Emotions war inside my head. A part of me is...touched he's written about me all these years, but the feeling of betrayal is all encompassing.

A sharp gasp has me lifting my head, tear-stained eyes locking on Archer in the doorway. His mouth is pressed tight together, hands fisted at his sides like he's upset. I almost laugh. Almost tell him he has no leg to stand on if he feels betrayed. He's spent the last five years making me feel like I didn't matter because he wasn't brave enough to fight for me back then, because he let his own superstitions and self-deprecation make him think he wasn't good enough for me.

"Tilly." His voice breaks like the panic has finally set in and he's realized I now know he's a fraud.

"Why?" It's all I can choke out around the pain wreaking havoc on my throat and chest. "How could you lie to me?"

He drags his hands down his face, shoulders lifting with a deep inhale. I close my eyes, ignoring the downturned corners of his lips, not caring if he's hurting at this moment.

My heart plummets into my stomach when he crosses the threshold toward me.

"Look at me," he urges. "Please."

I shake my head, tears leaking down my cheeks as I keep my eyes firmly pressed together.

"Tilda."

"Don't call me that."

Delicate but strong hands grasp my chin, and air from his heavy breathing coasts over my tear-stained cheeks. I can feel him crouch down, settling in the area in front of me.

"Please, look at me," Archer begs.

I open my eyes wide and look up at the ceiling, trying to muster the courage to look at him. Cursing the emotion seeping out of me, I blink the tears away and focus on his green eyes. They're red, glistening with unshed tears.

"Did he ever love me? Or was this some game to you guys?"

He shakes his head. "Don't do that."

"Do what?" I yell.

"Question the love he had for you."

When he reaches for me, I smack his hand away. "Why not? Every moment, every gift, everything's tainted."

He squeezes his jaw. "Jessie loved you with all his heart, Tilly. There wasn't a day that went by that he wasn't telling me about the things he wanted to do for you, the plans he had for a family with you."

"Stop," I choke out, pressing my hand against my chest, trying to squash the blooming pain.

"No," he replies. "You need to hear this."

He paces the floor, running his hand through his hair with each pass.

"You were everything to him. The sun rose and set in his world around you. He was proud to call you his wife, so thankful you chose him to spend your life with."

"But I didn't, did I?" My lips pull back into a sneer. "You guys chose that for me."

All the fight drains out of him, and for the first time I finally see the truth he's never wanted to show me.

Chapter Forty-One
Archer
Five years Ago - Night of Finals

Tears and squeals of joy echo through the university corridors, the celebration of finals being over and the holiday break breathing new life into the campus. Jessie's shoes scuff along the linoleum flooring as we walk down the hallway toward the parking lot, a lightness to our step that wasn't there three hours ago when we stepped into the Chemistry lab for our final.

"Think you passed?" he asks, unlocking his Beemer.

My eyes bounce around behind him, waiting for the moment Tilly finishes and steps out of the building.

"Yeah, totally." I cross my arms and lean against my truck. "If we failed, Tilly will kill us."

"I'd rather she kiss me," he says beneath his breath.

I've grown used to the little comments he makes about her, the times he mentions how beautiful she looks or brings her a coffee when we're in for a long study session. It's infuriating, but I can't pretend like I haven't been doing the same things in hopes she'd notice and maybe want a replay of the karaoke night hallway. We've been ships passing in the night with finals happening, but in the back of my mind I wonder if she's avoiding me because she regrets the kiss. It's been a week since I felt her soft lips against mine, and I'm not ashamed to say I haven't been able to concentrate on anything except that moment.

I shove my hand in my jeans pocket, fingers sliding against the smooth surface of my brother's poker chip. It's been a constant source of stress and anxiety, and somehow also gives me peace when I have it on me. Sebastian didn't go anywhere without his lucky chip, and every decision he allowed it to make brought him success. If only some of that would rub off on me.

"Here she comes," Jessie says.

My attention shifts to the dark-haired beauty dressed in rainbow parachute pants and a cream sweater walking out of the building. Her hair is in a messy bun contained by a lemon scrunchie, and her wide smile strikes me in the chest.

She's effervescent.

"Where are we celebrating?" She stops in front of our cars with an arched brow.

"Why don't we go to your parents' restaurant for a nice dinner?" I suggest.

Her eyes light up. "That's a perfect idea. I have some desserts to drop off anyway. Let's meet at six o'clock?"

"Great idea," Jessie says, but I detect a hint of jealousy in his voice.

"You boys go home and get dressed up," she says. "At night there's a dress code, so I want you in your finest for our celebration."

Like soldiers being sent off by their drill sergeant to clean toilets, we salute her and get into our cars. I roll my window down to ask Jessie if he wants to ride together but he's already backing out. My eyes follow Tilly as she walks to her Corolla, dancing to music that isn't playing. I chuckle and shift into reverse, heading off to my apartment.

I shuffle through my clothes and realize my closet is filled with too many flannel shirts and cowboy boots and not enough nice dress clothes. I have the navy suit my father forced me to wear to my sister's Match Day, and even though that feels too formal, everything else is too relaxed for the restaurant.

I dust off the suit, leaving the jacket, and grab the brown Oxfords from the floor before I head into the shower. Being in school for construction management doesn't afford me many opportunities to dress up, but I'm thankful for my dad's insistence I have at least one nice suit for special occasions.

My phone vibrates across the sink top, Jessie's name glowing on the fogged-up screen.

"Sup?" I ask, combing my hair.

"What are you wearing?" he asks.

Nora's voice sounds in the background as dishes clank around. I'm sure she made dinner already but won't chastise him for missing it in favor of going out with us. She loves Tilly, too.

"The navy suit I wore to Claire's Match Day. You?"

"Black dress shirt and khakis."

Silence encompasses the phone, and the weirdness of calling to check up on the other's outfit choice isn't lost on me. We're both looking to impress Tilly, and I know after tonight there will be a different dynamic to our friendship. Jessie is my best friend, my brother. He nearly sacrificed his own life to save me, and I'll be forever in his debt. But I'm not sure I'm ready to give up my chance at a happily ever after.

"All's fair in love and war," Jessie chirps. "Let's meet at the restaurant's bar for a drink before dinner."

"See you there." I snort and hang up.

Finding a parking spot at five o'clock on a Friday night is a struggle as I pull into the restaurant's lot, eyes scanning the rows for Tilly's or Jessie's car. Taking a lint roller to my pants before I get out of the car helps calm the anxiety flooding my system. Tonight could change everything.

Tonight could be the beginning of the rest of my life with the woman I've fallen for, or it could end up a dumpster fire with me embarrassed.

I touch the poker chip in my pocket to make sure it's still there. My shoulders ease down from my neck, the smooth surface reminding me Sebastian's always with me, encouraging me, as I walk inside.

Chatter fills the area around the bar, men in business suits wheeling and dealing over top-shelf liquor, figuring out a way to screw the working class. I order a Jack and Coke and wait for Jessie to arrive.

He walks in a few minutes later, hair perfect, pleats pressed. He's got this air about him, this confidence I've never quite figured out how to attain. Envy rises in my chest at how relaxed he is, how he exudes this friendly, outgoing personality that has people wrapped around his finger.

"Sup, Arch?" He signals to the bartender. "I'll have a tall Guinness."

We find a spot where we can see Tilly walk inside. Our bodies are angled just so, eyes flitting to the door every time someone arrives. Even though tonight is a big night, it's nice to have a beer with my best friend.

"Did Nora ream you a new one for coming in drunk the other night?"

"You know damn well she did." He laughs. "She made me clean the kitchen and organize the garage during the Cowboys v. Buccaneers game."

"Oof." We clink beers in a moment of silence for the ending of that game. "You ready for your interview next week?"

He shrugs. "It'll be a good foot in the door, but you know me, always looking to move up."

"You're gonna be running that company soon enough." And he will. Everything Jessie puts his mind to, he completes.

We fall into easy silence, and the tick of the clock seems to resound inside my head, drowning out the cacophony of voices in the bar. Tension hangs in the air, and subconsciously my thumb swirls around the smooth chip in my pocket to quell the rising pressure in my chest.

Light spills into the room when the door opens, and I swear the entire bar quiets when Tilly walks into the room. Her hair is pulled into a low ponytail, and curls cascade down her back. My pants strain as I take in the tight black dress hugging her curves, ending just below her knees, highlighting the yellow polka dot high heels she's wearing. I'm sure if I could take my eyes off her, I'd see a version of Jim Carrey during the club scene in *The Mask* on every male face in here, eyes popping out, mouth frozen open, heart beating out of their chest.

"You look beautiful," Jessie says, breaking the ice.

"Absolutely stunning," I add.

Her cheeks pink, and she swipes a loose tendril of hair behind her ear. "Thanks, guys. Y'all clean up well, too."

Drinks paid for and forgotten on the bar top, we accompany Tilly to the host stand where she hugs the bubbly girl. My heart beats all over my body as we follow behind her, both struggling to keep our eyes from being glued to her perfect ass.

The host seats us at a table Tilly's dad reserved for us. "Your server will be with you in a moment."

Nervous energy streamlines through my body. Adjusting the utensils keeps me focused in the short moments as we wait for the server. A warm hand wraps around mine, pulling my eyes from the crooked fork.

"Thanks for being my partners this semester," Tilly says, eyes bouncing between Jessie and me. Her hand is covering his too, and my jaw tenses at the surge of jealousy that rushes through my body.

"No way. Thank you for partnering with us," I say, emphasizing the 'you' portion of my statement.

Jessie nods. "He's right. We couldn't have survived this semester without your magnificent brain."

The server comes over and Tilly removes her hands from ours to order. I immediately miss the warmth of her touch. My eyes lock on Jessie across the table, and I can tell he's feeling the same by the way he's staring at his hand. How did I not notice how apparent his attraction to her has become? Was I so blinded by myself falling for her that I neglected to see my best friend was in deep too?

"I'll have the white," Tilly says, handing back the menu.

On autopilot, Jessie and I repeat our orders from the bar. Tilly doesn't notice the tension at the table, or at least she doesn't mention it as we wait for our drinks. Her dad stops by to say a quick hello but is drawn away by the line at the door. Tilly bites down on her lip and focuses on the menu, ordering the moment the server comes back to the table.

After a round of appetizers and chit-chat, we move onto plans for the next year.

"What classes are you taking next semester?" Tilly asks.

Jessie sets down his beer. "I have my last semester of upper-level business classes."

"I have industrial internships to complete." I leave out the fact that I'll be working for one of Dad's friends on their new hotel. I'm already feeling the pressure of his expectations, and even though I could've gotten my own internship, some things aren't worth the fight. I've tried to keep the peace between us for the sake of mine and Claire's relationship, and to be honest, I know his connections can help bolster my resume.

She smiles and lifts her wine glass. "To finishing our degrees."

We clink glasses, and I notice the small frown that touches her cheek right before she tilts the glass to her lips, draining it in one gulp.

"What are your plans?" Jessie asks, not picking up on the fact that she doesn't want to talk about it.

Her delicate fingers dance along the rim of her glass. "I'm still waiting to hear back if I got into culinary school." She shrugs and pastes a smile onto her face. "Until then, I'll keep baking for the restaurant."

The server drops off our food, and we dig in, chatting about our holiday plans. Before I know it, the restaurant has cleared out except for a few people at the bar. Tilly's dad comped our meal, which had to be at least two-hundred dollars with all the alcohol we ordered and the expensive entrees.

Jessie's eyes meet mine when Tilly goes to the back to chat with her dad for a few minutes. Watching as she disappears out of view, my heart lurches into my throat.

"I want to ask her out," Jessie says, staring at his half-empty glass.

Anger simmers beneath my skin. "So do I."

The proverbial gauntlet has been thrown, and we're two cowboys on opposite ends of a small western town, hands ready to draw our weapons. With a glance in the direction of the kitchen where Tilly is, my heart thrums inside my chest.

"What do we do?" Jessie asks, bringing my attention back to him.

My hand moves to the poker chip in my pocket. All the biggest decisions in my life have been made with a flip of this chip in hopes that my brother would guide me toward the right answer, to the things I deserve.

I remove the chip from my pocket and stare down at it, battling with my own inner demons.

"What are you doing?" Jessie's brows cinch, his lips pinched together.

All the debasement from my parents, the underhanded comments about not deserving what I have, what I took from my brother, come barreling back in, and it's clear in my heart that Tilly probably wouldn't choose me. Why would she want someone whose own parents despise him? Someone who knew his brother was struggling and didn't get him the help he needed before it was too late. I can barely take care of myself and my emotions, and Tilly deserves much better than me.

A calmness settles over me, and in that instant, I realize that if Sebastian thinks I deserve a shot at Tilly he'll make it so the poker chip lands in my favor. I hold my breath as I fling the chip in the air.

The soft clink of it against the table sets my stomach at the top of the highest roller coaster drop. Every muscle is tense, robbed of the air I'm holding in my chest, willing the chip to be on heads.

Jessie's sharp inhale is all the confirmation I need. I don't even look at the chip. I can't bear to see my unworthiness staring back at me from the table, a constant reminder I'm not good enough, undeserving of love.

Swiping the chip back into my pocket, I stick my hand out to Jessie. "Treat her right, or I'll break every bone in your body."

Reluctantly, I meet Jessie's eyes. I expected him to have a shit-eating grin on his face, but he doesn't. His expression is earnest and sincere.

"I will."

I nod, emotions strangling my words. The taste of copper fills my mouth, and I realize I'm biting on my cheek to stem the gutted feeling wreaking havoc on my stomach. "Good."

A few awkward moments of silence pass between us before Tilly bounces over to the table. "Ready to go dancing?"

Her smile rips my paper thin heart, and I momentarily consider forgetting everything I just said to Jessie and going after the girl of my dreams. Instead, I place my napkin on the table, and infuse my voice with a chipperness I don't feel. "I've got some stuff to do in the morning, so you guys go ahead without me."

I don't miss Jessie's nod to me, like he understands I'm accepting this as the new status-quo. I hate it, but in my heart of hearts, all that matters is that Tilly is loved and taken care of, and I know she will be with Jessie. I just have to find a way to sever the ties binding my heart to hers.

Chapter Forty-Two
Tilly

Archer's leaning against the dresser, fingertips pressed into his eyes like he can't believe I'm upset. Like it's a surprise to him that I would've wanted to make my own decision about my life rather than them making it for me by him backing off and giving me the cold shoulder. My skin is flushed, stomach curling in on itself, and I can barely contain the vomit threatening. I rise from the bed and head to the door.

"It wasn't like that, Tilly."

I stop and turn. "Are you sure? Because to me it seems like my two friends flipped a poker chip to see who would get me, as if I was some prize to win."

"You are a prize, damn it." He moves from the dresser, and I retreat, back touching the door jamb. His forefinger and thumb softly grasp my chin. "You're the most amazing woman I know. You're funny, talented, smart, hard-working, and beautiful. Any man would be lucky to have you, so yes, you are a prize."

I rip my chin from his touch. "Then why didn't you just tell me how you felt? Why take the choice away from me? Was I just another conquest to you? Another warm body for a good time? How could you..." I struggle not to burst into tears as my muddied, panicked thoughts collide with one another. "How could you make me believe there could've been something more between us when there's been nothing but lies?"

He carves a hand through his hair. "I love you, Tilly. I have loved you since you walked past my car on campus, since you walked into the Chemistry lab with your funky clothes and space buns." He grips his hair, a look of exasperation on his face. "And I have loved you every day since. There's nothing I wouldn't do for you, but I won't let you believe it was all a lie."

Doors slam inside my head, preventing the words he's saying from reaching my mind and heart. If he loved me, he should've manned up and asked me out himself. He couldn't have treated me the way he did if I meant anything to him like he wants me to believe.

I push the emotions away and maintain an even tone to my voice. "I'll buy you out of your lease with the landlord. Send me the bill for the months the building was empty."

The last thing I need is to worry that the one good thing to come from this situation, my bakery, could be taken away from me. The money from Jessie's life insurance is more than enough to cover that time, and as long as I hustle I should be fine without having to take more from the policy.

"No." His voice is strained, the muscles in his neck and jaw taut.

I hate that I want to reach out and console him, hate that I opened my heart to the one person who's caused me to question myself over the years, and yet I still want to kiss the hell out of him.

"Have your lawyers send me the paperwork *and* the bill."

"Not a chance, Tilly. It was supposed to be a gift."

"You've already given me enough *gifts*," I grit out, shoulders heavy with sadness. "I don't need you to take care of me. It's over. We got it out of our system and can move on."

He doesn't stop me as I take off my bracelet and exit the room, but his words spear through my chest when he says, "You'll never be out of my system."

Suppressing the urge to look back, I go downstairs and grab my purse, leaving the warmth of the house and welcoming the brutal lick of November winds. A cauldron of pain boils in my chest, hot tears leaking down my cheeks as I start the engine and head toward home.

Home. The word sends a spear of pain through my ribcage.

I doubt it'll ever feel like home again.

A mile down the road I have to pull over. My chest aches, tears blur my vision, and the vomit that was kept at bay comes barreling up my throat, forcing me to open the door to expel the contents of my stomach. On the dashboard, my phone continues to vibrate. I know it's most likely Archer begging me to come back, but I can't. I need to get as far away from here as possible.

***

I fan out the blanket I found stuffed inside my trunk and sit in front of Jessie's gravestone, staring ahead at the words etched into the marble slab in front of me.

The words *loving husband* stick into my heart like a hot poker, prodding at the pulverized organ in my chest. I want to laugh, want to feel something other than betrayal, but all I can think about is the letters Archer wrote to Sebastian.

After all these years, I finally understand why Archer felt indebted to Jessie. How if it wasn't for him, Archer could've been the one dead on the pavement. And all of our lives would've been different or may not have intersected at all. Would I have still met Jessie in Chemistry class? Would he have raised his hand, like Archer did, to ask the teacher if he could be my partner? Too many emotions pelt me as I stare into the headstone, wishing I could punch it to smithereens.

They both lied to me.

And even though I understand why Archer treated me the way he did, why he needed to push me away, I still can't fathom the fact that he chose to give up instead of fighting all those years ago. For assuming what my choice would be and letting our lives play out this way because of a stupid poker chip. I can't help feeling like the choice of who I wanted to pursue me was stolen right out of my hands.

I glare at the gravestone, hands digging into the loamy soil surrounding me. "How can you tell if our love was true if you didn't give me the chance to truly pick you?"

"You would've chosen him," a voice answers me, and I startle, nearly breaking my neck when I whip around and find Shantel leaning against another headstone behind me, orange sunlight cresting over the horizon behind her.

"What are you doing here?" Wiping snot and tears away, I look back at the headstone in front of me, willing the words to come from Jessie. From the man I thought loved me.

"Archer called and said you needed me, but he didn't tell me what happened."

I scoff. "I wonder why."

She rolls her eyes, a small smile on her face. "When I couldn't find you at the house or the bakery I came here. Figured you might be in a weird headspace."

"Something like that. I guess arguing with your dead husband about his decisions is kind of a weird spot to be in."

"You know, Jessie might've been the one to ask you out, but you had the opportunity to say no, to tell him you were interested in Archer, but you didn't."

Her truthful words slam into me, and shame rises in my chest.

"He was the person your heart wanted back then, even if you can't see it right now. You guys were meant for each other for the time he had left on this earth."

I gnaw on my cheek, begging my brain to be silent. For years, I thought I was destined to be alone, that everyone I loved would eventually leave me. Mom died too young, and Dad preferred to work rather than be around me, and then Jessie died. I didn't want to open my heart to that kind of pain again, but Archer beat down the door and set up shop. Then, he demolished any trust we built by not being honest about our interactions.

He broke down my walls and kept his up.

"How didn't I see that they were both interested?"

She shrugs. "You saw what you were meant to."

"Did you know Archer had feelings for me the entire time I've been with Jessie?" My stomach lurches, and I cover my mouth to stop anything from coming out. "How did Jessie feel about it?"

She sighs. "I'm pretty sure everyone knew but you."

It's a gut-punch to realize everyone saw it but me. I want to be angry at her for knowing about Archer's feelings and keeping it a secret, but I know she was in a difficult position.

"It's easier to see things when you aren't involved, and as for how Jessie felt? He knew Archer would never cross that line, and that you wouldn't either."

"But I did," I whisper, emotions tightening my throat.

A firm tap against my thigh brings my attention to Shantel crouching beside me. She stares at Jessie's headstone with a small smile and nods like they've had some secret conversation. Most times when I've visited his gravesite I've done nothing but cry, but this time I came angry, ready to smash the headstone to pieces with the anvil of hurt anchored in my chest.

"No, you didn't. You loved Jessie with all of your heart. And now that he's gone—" she pauses then squeezes my shoulder, "—you have space for Archer."

I shake my head, not ready to admit I'm too scared to let him love me. How could I ever measure up to the woman he's built up in his mind? He doesn't know I spend an hour every day hyping myself to wear the clothes I love, or that for years I've thought I would never be a good enough baker to have my own bakery. He doesn't know that I sometimes fall into spells when the grief hits so hard I can't get out of bed for days, barely managing to bathe myself. He only sees the best parts of me, not the ugly ones.

"Let's get some breakfast." Shantel holds out her hand, urging me to get off the dewy ground.

"I can't." I run my hands down my face, clearing the remnants of my breakdown as I hop up. "I've got to find another carpenter to help with the bakery and get a lawyer."

"A lawyer?" She stops me from walking toward my car. "For what?"

"To take over the lease from Archer."

"I'm confused," she says, bumping my shoulder. "But, we can talk about it over mocktails and bacon."

Hand latched on the door, I pin my shoulders back, chin raised high. "Nothing to talk about. We got it out of our systems and can move on."

I thought it would get easier each time I said it, but the knife in my chest twists every time the lie comes from my mouth. As much as I hate to say it, I doubt I'll ever get Archer out of my system. And maybe that's my penance. I chose to fall in love with my husband's best friend, chose to let myself crave his touch, his lips, and his laughter, and now I'm suffering the loss...again.

Chapter Forty-Three

Archer

Present

Beer bottles clink and roll around as I manage to sit up and take in my surroundings. It's dark, and when my hands meet the cold floor, I shiver as the frigid air leaks beneath the office door. I couldn't sleep in the bed where she belonged beside me, nor on the couch where we should've been laughing, cuddled up together by the fire.

I let her believe she wasn't worth the fight.

Heat wasn't a luxury I deserved last night.

My spine cracks when I get off the ground and flip the switch, fluorescent light burning my eyes. Out in the main garage, I prattle about, organizing things to try and keep my mind off the woman I should've woken up beside.

The metal worktop vibrates as my phone buzzes, jangling wrenches and bolts along the surface. Outside of calling Shantel last night to check on Tilly after she refused to answer my call, I haven't talked to anyone. I couldn't even tell Shantel how bad I messed up. She made me promise to give Tilly the space to deal with what happened.

Dark clouds move quickly overhead when I open the garage doors. A gust of wind pushes me back inside, a warning of an incoming storm. I laugh at the irony. My life has turned into a hurricane of bad decisions, and those decisions ruined everything.

I ruined everything.

My hands itch to grab my keys, to drive to Tilly's house and beg her to forgive me, but I don't. I knew years ago I wasn't good enough for her, that she deserved more than I could ever give her. My parents' words echo inside my head. *It should've been you.*

And this time I agree.

I've done nothing but bring hurt to those around me.

My brother was hurting, and I knew I shouldn't have pulled over at that gas station. Even though I couldn't have saved Jessie from his aneurysm, I caused him pain by treating his wife awfully because I couldn't stomach being around her.

And I hurt Tilly.

Out of all of those people, Tilly is the hurt I wish I could take back. She let me climb the walls of her heart and find a morsel of peace I've needed for years. And I threw it all away by being dishonest, by not owning up to my choices in the past so we could have a future.

Can I fix what I've broken?

Thunder rumbles across the sky, and a stampede of feelings crowd my chest. I shut the garage door and grab my phone and keys. If I have any chance of fixing this with Tilly, I can't let more time pass between us.

Rain pelts the windshield as I head down my driveway. Something stops me at the edge of the road, a warning sign blaring in the distant corners of my mind. I pick up my phone, eyes landing on a voicemail from the number I recognize as the HGTV producer's.

Air leaks from my parted lips and a weight settles in my stomach. I shift my car into park with shaky hands and press redial.

"Gideon Roberts."

I clear my throat. "Mr. Roberts, it's Archer Wilson."

"Archer," he exclaims, clapping in the background. "Glad to hear from you."

I imagine him, heels kicked up on the desk, leaning back in his cushy office chair with a pen in his mouth while my whole world is crashing down around me.

"The casting director loved your interviews, but we've decided to..." My mind fills in the words, *go with another host*, and my shoulders fall. I clench my fist around the steering wheel, and slump into the seat to finish listening to the cordial conversation. "...want to start shooting ASAP. Are you still interested in hosting?"

I rear back, confused by what he's asking. They want me to host? Host what?

"I'm sorry, Mr. Roberts, you cut out," I lie, hoping he doesn't catch onto my distraction. "Can you repeat that?"

"The network changed direction with the type of show you'll be hosting. They want *Stud Finders* to be a reality show where carpenters and interior designers redo a house while trying not to fall in love. It'll debut in spring."

A reality dating show? That's not the type of hosting I expected, but it's still a foot in the door.

"Still interested?"

"Absolutely." My voice rises in pitch, heartbeat racing.

"We need you in Knoxville at the beginning of the week to go over contracts and legalese. You get the gist."

"Okay." This is what I've been waiting for, the break I've needed to get out of this town, away from all the destruction I've caused.

"Great," he replies. "Kelly will send you the flight and hotel details right now, and I'll see you on Monday."

The phone disconnects before I have a chance to find my words. I drag my hands down my face, put the truck in reverse, and head back up the driveway. Days ago my life was calm and easy. I hadn't received a call about the hosting gig yet, but I had the woman of my dreams. I could stay here in this city, under the scrutiny of my parents, running my construction business and hardware stores and not long for anything else. But now, everything has changed.

I can't go to Tilly and ask her to take me back when I don't know if I'm staying.

If I leave, I can save us both the heartbreak.

Inside the house, I plop onto the couch and run my hands through my hair. Long gone is the warmth of the fireplace, and Tilly's filled wine glass still sits on the table, a dried ring around the bottom. I sink into the cushion and close my eyes, letting my mind wander.

Shantel told me I need to give Tilly time to deal with her feelings about us, but with the job offer on the table, I've got a lot to think about too. As if on cue, my phone dings with an email. I swipe the screen and scan through the details from Gideon's secretary. My flight leaves in two days, and once I have more information about the job I can come to Tilly with a plan.

If she'll forgive you.

***

Clumps of freshly mowed grass pepper the country club parking lot as I pull up to the back entrance and off load the heavy slab of wood. I hadn't planned on taking other jobs while I finished what needed to be done at the bakery, but when Mr. Kennedy told me he'd pay top dollar for a Wilson original counter, I couldn't turn it down.

"Is that the new bar top?" Mr. Kennedy comes inside from the golf course, slicking back his hair and putting on his hat.

I smooth a hand over the lacquered wood, chest puffing up with a bit of pride. "It is. What do you think?"

He takes in the gold logo in the center of the top, the sprawling black letters of the club's name etched into the wood grain, the built-in coasters, and slats for bar mats and caddies to rest. His smile is wide, and when he claps me on the back I hear a door opening somewhere in the back of my head. Impressing the owner of The Dominion isn't a small feat, and it's one more step toward my name becoming my own, no longer associated with surgeons and doctors.

"It's magnificent," he says, waving over one of his golf buddies to show him. "I have another project you might be interested in, too."

"Okay, great I—"

"But we can talk about that after your brother's event tomorrow or sometime next week," he says, extending his hand.

Words freeze on the tip of my tongue, and I almost ask him to repeat what he said. An event? For Sebastian? I slip my phone out of my pocket and check my calendar. It's empty, and a quick check of my texts with my mom shows no mention of the event.

"Okay." I turn away to gather my thoughts. "I'll be out of town until Wednesday."

My swallow is pained, and I glance around the room looking for answers to questions I didn't know I needed to ask. Why are they having an event for Sebastian? And why didn't they tell me about it?

After saying goodbye to Mr. Kennedy, I hop back into my truck and head to the one place I hope I'll get a straight answer.

Claire's Hill Country estate is small in comparison to my parents' 6,500 sq. foot house, but it's not humble by any means. I could fit two of my houses in here, plus the three-car garage. She's lounging in front of a fire, eyes trained on the cooking show on the TV, when her maid lets me in.

"Hey sis." I sit beside her, legs stretched out before me. "Where's Ben?"

"He got an emergency call." She shrugs, shoving a handful of popcorn in her mouth. Her husband is one of Texas's top plastic surgeons, and more often than not his 'emergencies' consist of rich women or men who have messed up their noses by drunkenly faceplanting into the ground.

"Ah, I see." I lean back, crossing my arms behind my head. "So about this event for Sebastian…"

Her munching comes to a halt, eyes wide and pinned on the screen. "What about it?"

My elbows move to my knees, fingers steepled in front of my lips. "Why didn't you tell me about it?"

She blows air through her nose, reaching forward to grab the remote to pause her show. Her teeth saw into the bottom of her lip, eyes downcast as she turns to me.

"What do you want me to say, Arch?"

I thrust my hands through my hair, agitation needling my spine. "How about the fucking truth for once?"

"It's a memorial walk for Sebastian followed by a dinner at the club." She collapses into the couch like telling the truth zapped every ounce of energy she had. "Dad set it up."

My stomach is a yo-yo of emotions, anger rising and falling with each twist of the knife in my chest. "And he didn't want me there."

She nods. "I'm sorry. You know how he is. How he's always been."

I rise from the couch, intent on leaving.

"Sebastian was his pride and joy," she reminds me.

"He'll never stop blaming me, so why do I keep trying?"

"He doesn't blame you." Her wavering voice betrays her.

"We both know that's not true."

I head off toward the front door, but her small voice reaches into my chest and rips out my heart. "Do you blame him?"

Fury floods my system, heating my skin. "Do I blame Dad for blaming me?" I scoff. "Sounds like you're blaming me too."

"Arch." She sighs. "Don't do that."

My shoulders tense, muscles aching with the restraint not to punch something. Sebastian hid his addiction well. Our parents were willfully ignorant, and Claire was away doing her residency, so she didn't see the toll Dad's expectations were taking on him. I've always stayed mum, kept the details of Sebastian's last moments to myself so his reputation wasn't tarnished, so our family name wasn't dragged through the mud, but I can't take the look of shame on my sister's face.

I hang my head and lean against the marble island. "Sebastian couldn't handle not meeting Dad's expectations."

Claire pads over to the doorway, arms crossed over her chest as she listens. I squeeze my jaw, hating I'm about to shatter the facade she had about our brother.

"He started taking uppers from a classmate so he could stay up studying all night."

She shakes her head, disbelief written all over her face. "No, Seb was fine. I spoke to him a few times a week."

"But you didn't *see* him," I reply. "You didn't see the blown pupils, the constant irritable attitude when he went days without sleep before his first final, or hear him talk about how worthless he felt when he didn't ace a test and Dad gave him a stern talkin' to." Overcome with emotion, I slam my hand on the countertop, startling her. "You weren't here for any of that."

Her jaw is clenched, tears sliding down her face. "You're lying. You just don't understand the type of commitment and dedication it takes to be a doctor."

The temerity of her statement leaves me gutted. "I do understand," I reply. "I watched you and Seb run yourselves into the ground, and that's how I knew it wasn't for me." I pull in my lips, debating whether or not to divulge what I've kept secret from her. "The night he died he asked me to go to that gas station. He went to score *drugs*. And when the dealer thought Seb shorted him, he pulled a gun. Jessie had a split second to decide who to save. Can you imagine that? Having to choose who to save between your two best friends? I'm only here because Jessie chose me, and Sebastian is gone because he chose to let the weight of Dad's expectations take him so far down a path he couldn't come back from."

"Get out." Her voice cracks as she points toward the door.

"I'm done caring about being worthy of your guys' love. You can all go fuck yourselves."

Pride fills my chest as I head to my truck. I've needed to have that conversation for years, and I only wish my mom and dad were there to witness it. No matter, I'm sure Claire will fill them in now that I'm gone.

My hands shake once I'm on the road, the adrenaline wearing away with each mile I travel. The rock I've thrown into the calm waters of the Wilson family will cause waves, but I hope that when everything settles Claire will finally see our parents, and herself, for who they truly are.

I never want to take my life for granted again. All the things I've told myself I don't deserve, the things that would make my life complete, are within my grasp if I get out of my own way. My chest is lighter as I drive home to pack my suitcase for my flight to Knoxville. A few days away should help me clear my head and work out a plan to get Tilly back.

If she'll have me.

Chapter Forty-Four
Tilly

Beeping sounds from a reversing truck pull my attention to the street out front. The delivery man hops out of the cab with a clipboard and heads to the back to open the trailer. I dust off my hands, leave the contact paper in the bakery case meet him at the door.

"I've got a walk-in freezer build for Archibald Wilson?" he says, flipping through his paperwork.

Hearing his name steals the breath from my chest. It's been five days since our blow-up, and I haven't spoken to or seen him. I sent him one text on Saturday to let him know I needed space and time, and he didn't send any the rest of the days. I guess he put as much effort into fixing things with me that he wanted to, and he showed me I was right in thinking I was just another conquest, a box to check off.

"Tilda St. James," I say, hoping and praying my name is on the order sheet as well. Even though Archer owns the space, I'm still the one that paid for the freezer, so it damn well should be.

"Gotcha," he says, holding out his pen. "Sign here, please."

I scribble my name and back out of his way. He grabs a dolly and a few minutes later is backing down the ramp with my freezer. I should feel giddy that the last big item I needed to open is finally here, but I don't.

All I feel is unsatisfied and empty.

It takes a few hours for the walk-in freezer to be built, but once the delivery driver leaves, I plug it in and get back to organizing the shelves.

Most of my list is checked off, but I still have menu boards to do, a bakery case to clean and redecorate, and flyers to disperse. Grand opening is in less than two weeks, and I need to get the word out about my bakery. Archer took some flyers with him to his hardware stores last week, and the managers told him a lot of people seemed excited to try my desserts.

Imposter syndrome weighs on my chest, and the thought sends me back to being a teenager at the school bake sale.

No one wanted to try the tropical coconut brownies or the martian cookies I made, and when my mom saw I was the only one without people at my table, she whispered words of encouragement into my ears as she paid for a cookie for herself to eat.

They don't have sophisticated palates like us, she'd say. And while she was right most of the time, she's no longer here to give me the encouragement I need. I shake off the unwelcome doubt and piddle around the shop before I head off to do baby stuff with Shantel.

"Hey girl, hey," Shantel yells from the side of the car.

"Ready to fill up this registry?" I ask, sliding into the passenger seat.

We zip down the highway, passing the massive cowboy boots in front of North Star Mall. Now that Thanksgiving has come and gone, the boots are lit up with Christmas lights, inviting everyone in to get their shopping finished before the holiday season begins. This will be my second Christmas without Jessie, and the thought of spending it alone strangles me as we step into the baby store.

"I wanna look at the swaddles and bassinets first," she says, heading down the aisle.

After perusing bibs and highchairs, pack and plays, nipple guards and breast pumps, we hand over the handheld scanners and leave to meet Nora for dinner. Shantel's energy is antsy as she fiddles with the radio, the air conditioner, and the windows, and I can't help but wonder what's going on.

"You okay?" I ask.

She nods. "Yup."

I narrow my eyes. "Shantel?"

"Mmhmm?"

"What's going on?"

She chews on the skin of her fingers, leaning forward to look at the light. "Nothing's wrong."

Knowing she'll never come out and say what it is, I figure a change of subject is in order. "Have you and Malik thought about names for the baby?"

"Archer's going to be at dinner," she blurts out.

Well, that's a change of subject if I've ever heard one.

"Okay," I say, heart pounding in my chest. "That's fine."

"You don't sound fine."

"I'm totally fine." I cringe at my high-pitched voice.

She laughs. "Really? Because your voice sounds like you've joined Alvin and the Chipmunks."

I clear my throat. "It's fine…I'll be fine."

"Mom just wanted to forget all the chaos and celebrate tonight before he leaves."

The seatbelt nearly garrotes me as I lurch forward, eyes wide and pinned on her. "Before he leaves to where?"

Breaths coming in short bursts, I search my brain for any memory of Archer saying he's leaving and find none.

"Where's he going?"

She clamps down on her lips and blows out a breath through her nose. "He didn't tell you?"

"We're not really on speaking terms right now." I sigh. "Tell me what?"

"He got the job in Tennessee."

My shoulders slouch with the rest of my body. "Oh."

She flicks on her blinker, pulling slowly into the parking lot. Archer's green truck is here, and immediately the appetite I worked up by perusing the aisles of Buy Buy Baby, vanishes. Shantel puts the car in park and turns to me.

"They called him on Saturday morning."

The day after my entire world exploded.

Swallowing shards of glass, I paste on a smile. "That's great news."

My chest aches, stomach writhing as I try to work through this new revelation. Just last week I thought me and Archer were solid. We had finally abolished the line we drew between ourselves and come to a place where I thought we could move forward in a relationship, but within three days everything came crashing down. It's almost like the universe was conspiring against us from the start.

After reading his letters to Sebastian, realizing how much weight he's had on his shoulders since his brother passed, I know this job is the break he needs. He shouldn't have to give up anything when he's given so much already.

At first I was angry, devastated to learn that Archer had mentioned the bakery to Jessie, offering up the place he wanted to open another hardware store, to make my dream come true. That there were moments in my life that were made special because of Archer, despite how much he tried to make it seem like I didn't matter. Everything he's done for the past five years seems like it's been to show me love without me knowing it, but I don't know how to reconcile that with feeling like my agency was stolen away—that I'm living a parallel life to the one I could've had if I knew all the information.

"Let's go eat." I open the door and get out.

Shantel catches up to me after locking the car. "Are you going to say something to him?"

"No." I shake my head. "He's free to leave whenever he wants."

"But what about you guys? Are you going to do long-distance?"

I release the hair tie holding my bun in place and run my fingers through the tangles before swiping them behind my ear. If I let her see I'm upset about how things turned out with Archer, she'll tell him not to leave, and I can't bear the weight of him trying to come up with an excuse for why he *has* to leave. I always knew it would happen, knew I'd fall for him and then he'd be taken from me. I guess I didn't expect it to happen so soon.

"No. We had a moment, and now it's out of our system."

A throat clears behind us, and I spin on my heels and take in the outline of Archer's tall, broad frame, a bouquet of flowers at his side. Nora comes up behind him and waves like they both didn't hear me downplay what happened between me and Archer.

His green eyes land on me, searing my skin with a single glance. My chest tightens as I give him a weak smile and embrace Nora. Less than three months ago I couldn't bear to be touched, but Archer refused to let me fall deeper into the depression and forced me to come back to the land of the living. I can only thank him by letting him finally live his dream, even if it means I'm not part of it.

"Ready to eat?" she asks.

I nod, not trusting my voice to speak. Archer holds the door open for us, and his presence is a block of heat behind me as we walk to the table. He hasn't said hello yet, and the now crinkled bouquet of flowers laying on the table makes me think he absolutely heard what I said. Not that it matters. Even though he ghosted me after apparently being in love with me for years, I still want to see him finally do something for himself.

"Congrats on the job." I unroll the napkin and lay it across my lap.

He coughs and reaches for his water, eyes narrowing at Shantel. "Thanks, I was going to call you tomorrow."

I want to say 'don't bother' but my tongue won't form the words. He's already seen, already dug too deep into my wounds, and he apparently saw I wasn't good enough, or I was too broken for him to put back together, and decided to leave before he had to let his walls down and show me he wasn't perfect either.

"How's the bakery coming along?" Nora asks, oblivious to the tension at the table.

Did he not tell her what happened? Archer looks to me, green eyes filled with something I can't place. Remorse? Exhaustion? My gut tells me to make it clear there's nothing else keeping him here, that he's free to go and that I'll be fine without him. The thought leaves a sour taste in my mouth.

"It's going great. The freezer was delivered this morning and I have another carpenter coming to finish some last-minute things."

"That was quick." Archer clamps down on his lips like he didn't mean to say that.

His words puncture my chest like a snake bite, venom seeping into my veins.

"Yeah, well you told me from the beginning you were leaving, so I had to figure it out myself," I say, snarkiness coating each word.

"Guys," Shantel chastises, eyes flitting to the server standing at the outskirts of our table. "Can we order our meal before the arguing begins? Baby wants food now."

I give the server my order, gritting my teeth against the words I want to say. Nora is quiet across the table, the corners of her mouth downturned, hands clasped in her lap. My body aches with the tension seizing my muscles. Why did I let my walls back down? Why did I think Jessie was telling me it was okay to pursue the stupid feelings I had for his best friend? Part of me wonders if he's up in Heaven laughing at us both, wondering how we could ever think it was a good idea to cross that line.

Dinner passes with no more words between me and Archer. He tells Nora about the job, how it starts filming next week in Knoxville, and how the network is planning to keep him on as a regular guest for their other home improvement shows and reality programs. With each new revelation, embarrassment warms my face. How could I think I'd be enough for him to want to stay here? To give up his dreams for? My shoulders droop as a picture of the little girl who was never good enough for anyone pops up inside my mind.

"Can I talk to you for a minute?" Archer asks, knocking his boot against the bench outside after dinner.

"For what?" I bite out.

Nora and Shantel head toward the cars, leaving us to speak in private.

"Tilly." He sighs, running a hand through his hair. "Please don't do this."

I scoff. "Do what, Archer? You're leaving, just like I knew you always would."

"That's not..."

"Not what?" I ask. "The truth? Not what's happening? Save it, Arch. I should've taken you at your word when you said it at the beginning instead of thinking I was enough to keep you here." I know I should stop speaking, stop letting the word vomit spill out of me, but I can't. "We had a good time, the sex was fantastic, but that's all it was. A good time."

I feel the words land on their target, and I'm immediately disgusted with myself for diminishing what happened between us to a simple 'good time,' but the words are already out, and I can't force them back inside. My heart tries to remind me of the pure love that was written in his journal, but my head reminds me of all the reasons I'm not right for him. The reasons I wasn't enough for him to fight for back then.

Before I allow my mind free reign, I shove the thoughts back into a box and square my shoulders. I've spent too long thinking I'm not good enough for people, and right now, all that matters is I'm good enough for me.

White clouds puff out of Archer's mouth as he sighs. "Can you just stop for a minute—"

"Sure." I roll my eyes and snuggle into my cardigan, bracing against the slight chill.

He holds up a finger and walks to his truck. I bounce on my heels and try to see what he's reaching inside to grab but can't see over his dashboard. It takes a moment, but when he shuts the door and makes it back to me, he has a large manila envelope in his hands.

"Here's the paperwork for the bakery."

My heart plummets, throat tightening when he places the paperwork in my hands. I open the clasp and pull out the contract. Reading is made harder by the burning tears at the backs of my eyes. My mouth is dry, palms sweaty as I shove the papers back inside the envelope. Words evade me as tears press against my eyelids, and all I can manage is a nod and a faint smile.

Archer grabs my hand and squeezes, and I feel that touch inside my chest like his hand is wrapped around my heart. He leaves me standing in front of the restaurant gutted and broken.

Chapter Forty-Five
Archer
Present

"Promise to call if you need anything." Nora stands in front of my door, arms outstretched. Her gray hair is pulled back, the wrinkles at the corners of her eyes more prominent now that they're wet with tears.

"I promise." I pull her into a hug, resting my chin on her head, the soothing scent of her rose perfume comforting me. The thought of leaving spears through me, and I imagine the ache in my chest is what a son feels like leaving his mother.

In a sense, Nora is my mother.

She's been there for me throughout my whole life, been the source of encouragement I needed when my own parents couldn't be bothered, and I never once doubted she loved me like her own. I don't feel that way about my own mom, and I didn't tell her or anyone else I was leaving because it wouldn't matter to them anyway.

"How long will you be gone?" Shantel sniffles. "Are you going to move there permanently? Will you be home for Christmas?"

Her tears give me pause. I'm not sure if it's because of the hormones from the baby or if she's actually going to miss me, but I've never seen her so emotional.

She's losing another brother, my conscience reminds me, causing a flame of regret to burn in my chest.

"I'm not sure yet." I pull her to my side. "I'll have a better idea of what's to come once I'm there, but I know I have a few weeks of non-stop shooting."

Her lip pokes out like it's not the answer she wants, and to be honest, I'm not sure it's the answer I want to give. I hate the idea of being away during the holidays. I love Nora and Shantel, they're my family. But I can't pretend all is well, that inside I'm not heartbroken because of what happened with me and Tilly, and the longer I stay here, the harder it gets to not beg her to understand the position I was put in, the reasons I didn't challenge Jessie for a chance at loving her myself.

"Are you going to say goodbye?" Shantel asks.

I know she's talking about Tilly, but the muscles in my throat constrict even thinking about saying goodbye to the woman I've spent years loving, the woman I'm leaving behind for an opportunity of a fresh start.

"I'll let you know when I land." I give them both another hug and get into my truck.

Shantel's frown of disappointment follows me as I get onto the interstate. Aware of the time it'll take me to get through San Antonio's small airport, I chance a drive down to The Pearl toward the bakery and pull onto a side street.

One last look, I tell myself.

If she's in there I'll stop and say goodbye.

The poker chip stares back at me from the cup holder, a beacon of change just out of reach. Ever since Sebastian died, this chip has been a constant in my life, a compass pointing me which way to go. Most of the time it's pointed me in the right direction, but occasionally it's been a thorn in my side, giving me an answer I didn't want, like when it made me believe I didn't deserve Tilly.

Staring at it now, I want to laugh at the hold it has on me. The sheer insanity that makes me grab it and flip it into the air, hoping it lands on what I want it to so that I can pretend it's the universe and not me telling myself I don't deserve everything I want.

Disgust infiltrates my bloodstream, and I lose the battle I'm fighting. My thumb thrusts the chip into the air, and I ask myself one last time if I deserve Tilly. It lands on my thigh, and the weight of its answer burns through my jeans.

Heads.

I close my eyes against the tears threatening to overtake me and punch the steering wheel, angry at my brother, my family, and myself for making me feel this way, for not fighting for the things I've wanted.

A knock at my door startles me, and I curse myself for stopping on this side street when I see it's Deidre at my window. It takes everything in me not to give her the finger and tell her to screw off, but I know her anger was borne out of insecurity I created in her.

"You okay?" she asks, forehead creased when I roll down the window.

I nod and clear the tears away with my sleeves. "I'm fine."

"Here, you need this more than me." She hands me a coffee with a surprisingly warm smile on her face. "What's wrong? Why are you...sulking in your car?"

I give her a side eye as if she deserves any explanation after the way she acted.

"Oh, come on, Archer. I apologized."

I grunt. "Not to the right person."

She sighs. "I'll apologize to her the next time I see her."

I shake my head. "No, she deserves it now."

"Fine," she huffs. "Trouble already in lover's paradise?"

There's no bite to her words, but a hint of amusement. I don't reply.

"She'll come around eventually."

I rub my forehead, confused as to why she thinks I'd discuss anything about Tilly and me with her. She mistakes it as confusion of who she's talking about.

"Tilly." She shrugs. "She'll get past all the bullshit and realize you guys are meant for each other."

I blink, confounded by her words. "Are you okay?"

She laughs. "I'm fine, Archer. I knew years ago Tilly would always be the one for you. I guess I just wanted to hurt you like you hurt me before you figured it out, but I know that's just as shitty."

I curl my lips over my teeth. Part of me feels bad for leading Deidre on for so long, but back then I didn't realize I'd never get over Tilly. At first, I thought I could force myself to get over her by sleeping around, and when that didn't work, I tried dating someone long enough that the feelings would vanish. That didn't work either, and I ended up hurting a good woman.

"I'm sorry."

She shakes her head. "I knew what I was up against when I started dating you, and it's my fault for trying to come between what was meant to be."

Her words float over me, searching for a place to land, but I brush them away. If it was meant to be then it would've worked out between us. Noting the time, I thank her for the coffee and let her know I've got to catch my flight.

***

Whoever invented headphones is now at the top of the list of my favorite people. The noise canceling feature gives me peace as I'm surrounded by people rushing to and from their gate, each worrying they're about to miss their flight as Christmas music blares through the airport speakers. I stretch out on the seat, watching as the planes land and take off again, hurtling people toward their destinations.

I grab my ticket from my carry-on to ensure I'm at the correct gate. The black writing pulses like a warning, reminding me I'm headed to a new place. A place where no one knows me or has opinions about my last name and what I might or might not be responsible for. A place where I can become someone else.

"Excuse me." A woman taps my shoulder. "Is this seat taken?"

I shake my head, moving my bag off the seat. There are plenty of other seats she could've sat at, but within seconds her daughter is glued to the window, watching the airplanes take off. My chest tightens when I see the little girl's tiny space buns and polka dot boots.

As if on cue, my music app decides to play a song from the CD Tilly gave me years ago. I've listened to this CD more often than I want to admit. It's been a comfort, a reminder of the times we jammed out to music while studying. A reminder that she was thinking about me, even if she didn't know I couldn't stop thinking about her.

Unbidden, her face from the other night pops into my head. She looked devastated after I gave her the contract, but I couldn't bear to stand there and not embrace her any longer. She made it clear that what happened between us was nothing more than a fling, but her comments about not being enough to stay for have been niggling at the back of my mind. Did she not read how hopelessly in love with her I was? *Still am.* How even though she didn't know it, she was part of every decision I made. When I could've moved away and opened my construction business elsewhere, it was her that kept me here.

I don't know how to convince her she was everything I wanted, everything I dreamed for, when I did such a good job of convincing her for so many years she wasn't what I wanted.

And now she's pushing me away.

Like I deserve.

"Flight 61414 to Knoxville will start boarding in five minutes," a woman's amplified voice speaks through the intercom system.

I gather my bags and get in line. Passengers around me tell their loved ones goodbye, and my fingers itch to call Tilly, to tell her I'll do whatever it takes to fix what was broken between us if she'll give me the chance, but I know it won't matter. I messed up by not being open about the things I was struggling with and being honest about the circumstances of how our friendship crumbled. Had I known I'd lose her for good, I would've cherished the moments I had with her more, savored each laugh, kiss, and touch she blessed me with during our time together.

Heading down the gangway, I pull my phone out of my pocket. My fingers hover over the screen, unsure what to say. Even though I'm sure she'll delete it, I send her a text wishing her a good grand opening, and as the flight attendants do their last-minute checks, I tack on an 'I love you' for good measure.

Chapter Forty-Six
Tilly

Christmas is supposed to be the most amazing time of the year. It's supposed to be filled with beautiful lights, warm nights by the fireplace, and thankfulness for everything you've been blessed with throughout the year, not sadness. I walk through The Pearl, taking in the magnificent Christmas tree lit up with a million tiny lights, the kids running around the Astroturf, and the fountain lit up blue to pretend like it's actual snow, and I remind myself that it's okay that I'm one of a small group of people who experience the Christmas season differently.

I used to love caroling with my mom, baking cookies on Christmas Eve, and staying up late to watch multiple runs of A Christmas Story with a mug of hot cocoa, snuggled between my parents. Some of those same traditions transferred over to my relationship with Jessie and his mom and sister, but now that he's gone, the place where my Christmas spirit lived feels...vacant.

"Ho, ho, ho," a volunteer Santa crows as I pass him in my oversized black sweater and black yoga pants. It's a week before Christmas, and I'm sure I look like the grim reaper of the ghost of Christmas past. The bubbly, quirky Tilly I was two weeks ago is gone. An oppressive weight came with the season change, and it's settled into my bones.

Feeling sorry for the old man stuck out in the cold, nary a flurry in sight, I grab a couple dollars from my purse and shove them into the red donation bucket. He slides a small candy cane into my hand, and I promptly pass it off to a little kid as I make my way to the bakery.

Lights flicker to life when I open the back door and flip the switch. The kitchen area is spotless, neatly organized, with each shelf properly labeled. It's the only part of my life that feels...right. I toss my purse onto the table and preheat the oven before checking on the cooler and freezer, ensuring their temperature held over the weekend.

I pull the small tray of coconut cinnamon rolls I made yesterday from the rack and place them on the table. A warmth rises in my chest as I grab the ingredients to make the pineapple icing. Baking is my happy place, where my creativity flows freely without opinions or discouraging words.

The oven dings, and I push the cinnamon rolls inside, setting the timer before I walk out to check the front. Multi-colored lights reflect into the bakery from the lamppost outside, garland strung across the poles lining the sidewalk. The colors dance along the floor as the breeze whips them back and forth, and there's a soft trumpet playing somewhere close, its sad tune echoing down the empty road.

I rest against the windowsill, exhausted from putting the finishing touches on the bakery. Having to hire another contractor was the most difficult part about getting this place ready. There weren't many things left to finish outside of a few shelves and anything the inspector found that wasn't up to code, but not having Archer here to go through things with me was terrifying.

The mayor stopped by to look at the place, telling me he's glad Archer finally got the place up and running because the other people on the street were breathing down his neck to sell the boarded-up eyesore to someone who'd open something inside. Knowing this place used to be a restaurant that Archer bought to use as a hardware store before he gifted it to me for my bakery, I understand their frustrations. The plywood was bringing down the look of the entire street.

The timer goes off, and I head into the back to pull out the cinnamon rolls. As they cool, I go through the list of businesses I'd like to drop off flyers at or trade marketing with. Most of them are offices I expect might want to order cakes for birthdays or business meetings, and a few event planners that cater to weddings. Getting the word out about my bakery is the priority right now, and even though I'm excited for the grand opening, I can't find a blip of happiness.

Archer's texts appear in my mind, and I bring it up on my phone, touching the screen as if I can feel the words on my skin.

I hope your grand opening goes well.

I wish things were different.

I love you.

Emotions choke me as I spread the pineapple icing over the rolls, wiping away tears with the sleeve of my sweater. Everything in this bakery reminds me of him, of what he did for me. The punny light he hung, the sign he made me that sits above the shop, the bakery case he drove hours away to buy me then fucked me against like it was his dying wish. His touch is ingrained into every fiber of my being, and my bakery.

All these things were showing me that he truly knew me, that he truly loved me, and I threw it all away because he was too scared to tell me, to fight for me all those years ago. Because his parents, and even me, made him feel so unworthy of love that when it finally came time for him to have it, he didn't feel like he deserved it.

Gulping down air, I sob and slide down to the ground, curling into a ball as a blast of nausea rolls into my core. My stomach twists with the realization I threw away my second chance at true love. That all the time we spent working on this bakery wasn't enough to keep us together, to show us that we were exactly right for each other.

***

"It smells in here."

I pop my eye open, cursing the sliver of light landing directly in my pupil as Shantel drops something onto my dresser with a clink and plops onto the bed beside me.

"No one asked you to break into my house," I say, pulling the covers over my head.

She rudely steals the covers, bunching them on the other side of the bed. Her belly is rounder since I last saw her, and I reach out, waiting for her to tell me if I can touch the cute bump. She scootches closer, grabbing my hand and laying it directly where the baby is softly kicking. She's not far enough along for me to feel the gymnastic tumbling the baby likes to do, but knowing there are little flutters and kicks going on beneath my hand brings me a tiny bit of joy.

"You haven't left this house in days." She rises from the bed and opens the curtains. Like a vampire, I shriek at the sudden glaring light, waiting for it to melt my skin and leave me nothing but bones. She laughs and rolls her eyes. "You're so dramatic."

"What do you want?" I groan, sliding out of bed and heading to the bathroom. A wave of dizziness makes my steps falter. I press my hand against the cool marble sink top and curse myself for not eating yesterday.

She follows, leaning against the door jamb with her arms crossed. "You didn't come to Sunday dinner." She looks around with a frown on her face. "And it looks like you've been in bed for a few days. What gives? Are you sick?"

I drag a brush through my tangled hair and shrug. "I'm fine."

She moves quickly, grabbing the brush from my hands. I'm stunned, momentarily worried she's going to hit me with it, but she takes my hair in her hands and starts to brush it. I sag with relief, closing my eyes as the knots come undone.

"It's okay to need someone to take care of you," she whispers.

My throat aches, and I press my hands onto the sink top, willing the anxious energy away. "I know."

"But do you?" she replies, eyes challenging me in the mirror.

I look away from her penetrating stare. I'm not sure what she expects me to say. It's Christmas season, without Jessie, and the man I thought I'd found a second chance with is a thousand miles away. I can barely manage to look at the bakery without breaking into tears. I'm constantly sick to my stomach, and I can't stop crying. The solace of my home is where I needed to be.

Alone.

"What do you want me to say?" I ask.

She walks over to the shower and turns it on, steam filling the air within seconds. I've never been more thankful for the on-demand water heater Jessie had installed before he died.

"Get in, then we'll talk."

Like a child, I nod and return to the bedroom to find clothes. My bracelet sits atop the dresser, the mixing bowl charm lying flat where Shantel must've dropped it. A small smile takes over my face. When I found the gift after the wedding, Jessie didn't know where it came from, but I thought maybe he had bought it and forgot about it. After reading Archer's journal and finding out it came from him, I realize I should've known.

The thought stabs me in the chest where my already broken heart is hanging on by a thread, and I shove the bracelet into the drawer and grab some clothes.

Hot water beats against my back, loosening the tense muscles in my neck. I squirt the body wash onto my loofah and the scent of apples fills the air. My stomach tumbles like a washing machine, and I press my hand against my breastbone, trying to calm my speeding heart. Vomit threatens, and I lean against the cool tile wall until the sensation abates.

When I first lost Jessie, I didn't eat for days. It took Nora and Shantel rallying around me, forcing me to finally nibble on some crackers. Even after I started eating, the loss still kept my stomach on a constant roll of nausea and hollowness. I wonder if my body is responding the same way because it remembers what it feels like to lose love. I've heard it said that grief is the price we pay for loving one another, but I feel like I've overpaid on my account. I'm due for a refund.

I hold my breath and wash the soap out of the loofa. The fresh steam quells the uneasiness swirling in my stomach. I shut off the shower and towel myself dry before I slip into a fresh set of pajamas and throw my hair into a messy bun.

"What are you wearing?" Shantel asks when I walk into the kitchen, grabbing a glass of water.

"Clothes?"

She laughs and cracks an egg into a bowl. "Go change, we have flyers to hand out."

My finger dances around the rim of the glass, eyes cast downward. "I'm going to sell."

An egg falls to the ground, cracking and spewing albumen across my kitchen floor. I hurry to clean up the spill with paper towels, and Shantel stands still with her eyes trained on me.

"No, you're not."

I sigh, emptying the trash into the bin. "I can't do it."

"It'll get easier once you're open and busy."

The invisible wound in my chest reopens when I think about opening the bakery alone. He was supposed to be here with me. His touch is everywhere, and nowhere at the same time. I can't look at the shelf he spent an hour redoing because I put it together wrong, or the stupidly cute sign he bought that pulls together the funky style of the place, and I definitely can't look at the bakery case without thinking about his body pressed against mine.

If I can't have him, then I don't want that bakery location.

Resolution settles in my gut.

"What are you thinking?" she asks, whisking another egg as the pan heats.

"What do you mean?"

She smiles. "You have that look in your eye like you're about to do something wild."

I laugh, but she's right. She's known me long enough to see when something is percolating inside my mind. I pushed Archer away because I was scared I wasn't enough, and that I was too much at the same time. I didn't give him a chance to truly show me he was serious about us, and instead of trusting his words from the book, I turned it around on him and made him feel like a cheap fling to me. I closed the door on my second chance, and it's up to me to pry the door back open and put myself out on a limb.

I grab my laptop, restarting it as Shantel pours the eggs into the pan. The sizzling and popping of the oil is the background to my airline deep-dive, which takes less than five minutes.

"Are you going to visit him?" Shantel sets the plate of eggs in front of me.

I catch a whiff of something rotten, and my stomach roils. A sharp intake of air doesn't clear the nausea and I'm out of my seat, headed toward the trash can to dry heave. Bile burns my esophagus because I haven't eaten anything.

"Oh my gosh. Are you okay?" Shantel rubs my back as my stomach continues to constrict.

A minute passes, and the wave is gone. I step back from the trash can, and Shantel hands me a napkin to wipe off my face. I blink a few times to clear the tears from dry heaving and sit back at the table.

"Tilly." Shantel's voice is deep, a command. "Look at me."

My cheeks heat, embarrassed by the state of my appearance and life. I should probably see a therapist again, but they'd probably commit me when I tell them even the smell of food reminds me of the losses I've endured. I'm sure Shantel can see my cheeks stained with pink as I look up and into her eyes.

Without a word, a smile cracks her face, and she lunges toward me.

Chapter Forty-Seven
Archer
Present

Spotlights move across the studio, highlighting the audience gathered for the *Stud Finders* episode. Assistants stand off to the side holding massive white applause and laughter signs, switching off when either emotional reaction is needed from the crowd.

When Gideon told me the new contract was for a reality dating show, I wanted to tell him no. I didn't work my butt off running my construction company and hardware stores to host a dating game. But after reading through the benefits package and deal memo, I realized the money from this gig could help me fund the workshop I wanted to open. Surprisingly, networks will pay more money for a reality show where interior designers and carpenters try to work together without falling in love than they do for people looking to bless a friend with a redone bathroom.

You and Tilly could've been the poster children for this show.

"Cut," the producer yells, drawing my attention to the wings of the stage.

The contestants begin to filter out, but two remain off to the side quarreling over their vision for the project. Bliss Calloway, an interior decorator for some large hotel chain, was paired up with Canon Martin, an easygoing small-town carpenter, and they've done nothing but bicker.

It reminds me of how Tilly and I would get over certain things pertaining to the bakery.

My chest constricts when I think about her putting the finishing touches on the bakery case we made love against, filling the shelves she tried—and failed—to put together. Her opening is in a few days, and I wish I could see the line that's going to form around the corner.

She's going to be successful, and she deserves everything she has coming her way.

I know it with every fiber of my being.

If only she knew I'd give anything to be back there with her, rooting her on and watching her make her dreams come true.

But you can, my conscience reminds me.

I crack my knuckles and push away the thoughts. Even if I could fly out tomorrow, she wouldn't want me there. And I don't blame her. She was worried she wasn't enough to make me stay, that I was going to leave her like everyone else did, and that's exactly what I ended up doing. I proved her right, and now I'm where I was meant to be, miserable but successful.

"Archer," Gideon calls from the wings of the stage.

I shove my hands in my pockets and head his way, stopping momentarily to say hello to one of the producers. Gideon smiles like a Cheshire Cat as I approach.

"They love you," he exclaims.

"Who?" I ask.

His hand clamps onto my shoulder and he leans in. "The network. See that woman over there?" He points to a redhead in a pink business suit talking with the director. "That's Allie Marin, the network CEO."

I shrug, but my insides are twisting with curiosity. "Okay, and?"

"She thinks you're charismatic," he says, accentuating the word. "Wants you to be our new Ty Pennington."

The comparison steals the air from my lungs. Ty was the reason I became a carpenter, why I started a construction business. Extreme Home Makeover made me want to be able to change the lives of the people around me by making their dream houses come alive. Being compared to him is the highest compliment I could've received.

"What does that mean for me?" I ask.

"I assume you'll be pulled into another contract meeting to see what shows you'll be able to participate in."

His words fill me with unbridled ambition, renewing my hopes that people will no longer associate me with the Wilson surgeons, but with my career as a staple on the home improvement network circuit.

"Wow, that's amazing." I drag a hand down my beard, stunned into silence.

"You might want to get an agent to handle this stuff, maybe think about buying another house here for when you're shooting."

The mention of buying another house gives me pause. "What do you mean for when I'm shooting?"

He laughs. "Well, you know how these things go."

I don't.

"Humor me," I say.

"You'll shoot this show and be required to be here for any re-shoot necessary, but you'll be able to go back home once this contract is finished. Assuming you're going to get picked up for a second season of Stud Finders or another show, then you'd come back to the studios to shoot on another schedule."

In my rush to get to Knoxville in time for shooting, I never once thought about what happens after the show ends. Normally I'd think through everything, read every line of the contract, twice, make sure all my ducks were in a row, but I was so hellbent on getting as far away from the mistakes I made, from Tilly, I didn't do my due diligence in asking the important questions. Thankfully, I haven't found an apartment yet, and the network is paying for my hotel and food expenses while I'm here, so I haven't had to worry about that.

I was thrown into the lion's den when I got here, and immediately started shooting the next day. I didn't have time to think about anything but retaining all the important information about where I was supposed to be at what time, and who not to look directly in the eye when I spoke to them.

Gideon walks away, prattling on as I absentmindedly toy with the chip in my pocket. Its presence used to soothe my nerves, but recently all it's done is remind me of the woman it took away from me. The woman I made feel like she wasn't enough for me to stay because I thought my stupid brother was telling me she deserved better.

I pull it out of my pocket and stare down at it. I close my eyes, wistfully imagining Sebastian is right beside me. But he's not. And the chip in my hand is nothing but a reminder of all the loss I've experienced. The truth of that statement hits me directly in my chest and I stumble backward.

I collapse into a chair, resting my elbows on my knees and my head in my hands. I gave up everything I had, everything I could've had with Tilly, love, marriage, a family, because of this stupid chip.

My phone vibrates in my pocket, and I slip it out and see Shantel's name on the screen.

Shantel: Can you come home soon?

As if the universe had a front seat to my breakdown, I reread the words with a sense of peace.

Home.

Where Tilly is.

I pocket my phone without answering Shantel. There's no point in responding to her until I know if what I'm thinking about doing is possible. With a renewed spirit, I walk up to Gideon. "My shots are done for the day, and you don't need me tomorrow, right?"

He nods, gaze focused on something through the camera lens. I see him catching a spat between Bliss and Canon, and even I can see the sexual chemistry sparking between them.

"The next two days are all day shoots for the contestants at the house. You're back on Thursday for the next elimination."

I stifle the urge to jump into the air and instead clap him on the back. "Great, I'm going to grab my stuff and head out then."

He mumbles an approval and waves me off, zooming in on the fiery couple at the table saw. Within seconds, I cue up all available flights back to San Antonio. If I can get a flight out tonight or tomorrow morning, I'll be able to be there for her opening day.

During the cab ride, I find a five a.m. flight out of Knoxville tomorrow morning that arrives at nine am. My fingers have never tapped a screen as quickly as they did buying the ticket back home.

I empty my pockets and place the poker chip beside my wallet on the sink top before undressing for a shower. My stomach hardens when I think about continuing to let it make decisions for me when it's done nothing but bring me heartache. Sebastian will always be a part of me, but I don't need his chip to make my decisions anymore. I feel confident in the path I'm taking by going home to grovel and ask Tilly to take me back.

I'll attend the opening day of Tilly's bakery and convince her that I'm not going to leave until we figure out a way to move forward together. Until I convince her she's my beginning and my end, the one I want to spend my life with, the woman I want to be the mother of my kids and the matriarch of *our* family. A family that accepts, forgives, and encourages one another.

Tomorrow my new life begins.

Chapter Forty-Eight
Tilly

"You're pregnant," Shantel squeals.

Every muscle in my body tenses, and I jerk my head back. "What?"

"Have you taken a test yet?"

A coldness settles into my bones. "I'm not preg...No."

Suddenly, there's not enough air in the room and I'm gasping for any morsel my lungs can get.

"Tilly," Shantel says, voice high pitched. "We're pregnant together!"

My vision swims, brain fuzzing out on every thought trying to ram through my mental block.

Pregnant?

I can't even say I'm surprised by how much sex we had after that night at the barn, but I've always known my ovulation cycle. How could I get pregnant if there wasn't supposed to be an egg in there?

How am I going to tell him?

A million questions batter my weary mind, and I rest my head on the cool island to catch my breath.

"Fuck."

"No, no, no," Shantel says, arm laying over my shoulder. "He's going to be so happy, Tilly."

"You don't know that." Tears drip onto the countertop, and I reach for a napkin to wipe them away. "He left."

She shakes my shoulders. "He has loved you since the day he met you, Tilda St. James. And he might have left, but he didn't want to. You didn't give him any reason to stay. You were too scared to tell him you loved him too. Too scared to give him your heart again, but it's not too late."

"He's going to be so mad." My stomach clenches with the thought. We never spoke about kids and whether he wanted to have them. With how he was raised, I'm not sure he'd want any himself.

"Stop assuming what he's going to be." She takes my computer. "Let's get you to Knoxville to find out."

"I can't go there now." I try to take the computer back, but she pushes me away.

"You were planning to go there anyway. Nothing has changed."

I throw my hands in the air. "Everything has changed!"

"You're being dramatic, and that's my area of expertise. You're going to get your baby daddy and bring him back here."

I get up from the island and go outside to think in peace. My hand automatically moves to my stomach, and I savor the brisk air, willing it to calm my nerves. I've always wanted kids, but Jessie and I never got that opportunity.

Oddly enough, it feels like everything, and nothing, has changed since this revelation. Even though it's terrifying to think about, I can see how good of a father Archer would be to our kid. How good of a husband he could be if I let him.

If he still wants me.

Thoughts of what to do about our life speed through my mind. Would Archer move back here? Would I move? Can I find another bakery space there?

Swallowing past my dry throat, I decide to go through with my plan of selling the bakery. Even if he wants nothing to do with me, with our baby, I still can't handle being there without him.

"I bought your tickets to Knoxville," Shantel says when I come back inside. "You leave tomorrow morning."

I lean my head on her shoulder. "Why am I such an idiot?"

"Don't talk about yourself that way." Shantel grabs my purse and places it into my hands. "Let's go get a test to confirm."

Three pregnancy tests and a sweet potato later, I stand in front of the bakery with a sense of unease. I've wanted this my entire life, and now that I finally have it within my grasp, it doesn't feel like I expected it to. Without Archer in my life to celebrate with, nothing feels...right.

I press the red and white For Lease sign onto the bakery window. Tears stroll down my cheeks as I back away, hoping someone who has a dream of having their own bakery buys the building instead of another restaurant or overly priced hot yoga studio.

I tug my cardigan closer, walking down the sidewalk and into The Pearl's square. The ding of the holiday bell brings my attention to the rotund Santa, his cheeks rosy and beard slightly yellow. He's not the same Santa from the other night, but I'm sure the little kids standing in line to greet him don't notice. They're too excited for him to make their dreams come true.

I wonder if he can make mine come true.

My eyes fall to my stomach, and a wish forms in my head. I'm sure that Santa knows my Christmas spirit is lacking, but hopefully he'll renew it by making one wish come true. I wait patiently behind kids hopped up on sugar from the cookies and candy canes being passed out in the square. When it's finally my turn, I forgo the picture opportunity and lean into Santa's ear to tell him my wish. With a smile and a squeeze of my hand, he nods and tells me he'll do his best. I want to tell him I'm not holding my breath, but I'll take all the luck I can get at this point.

***

"Shantel will drop off the cakes to you at ten." I pull my carry-on behind me, talking to my dad as I dodge travelers arriving at the gate and try to find a seat. At five am, getting through security was easy, but the line at Dunkin' held me up an extra thirty minutes, and I barely made it to the gate on time.

At least I'm caffeinated.

"Okay, sweetheart." He sighs, and I know it's not the end of it. "Are you sure you want to do this?"

"Yes, Dad."

"But the bakery was your dream."

I swallow, massaging the tense muscles wreaking havoc on my neck. Dad was surprised, and a little angry, to hear I wanted to put the bakery up for sublet before it even opened. All the hard work and money Jessie and Archer spent getting it ready would be lost if I couldn't find another renter, and I'd be essentially selling my dream for a chance at a relationship with someone who left me. I didn't tell him that I pushed him away, that I made it near impossible for him to want to stay when I told him we were nothing but a fling.

"If I'm meant to have my own bakery there will be other opportunities."

His voice lowers, takes on a menacing tone. "He better be worth it."

"He is," I reply, sure of my words. I may not have made him feel worth it, but I know with my entire soul he is worth more than a building. More than a dream.

"If you say so." He exhales, and Gloria calls his name in the background. "I've gotta go, but let me know when you land sweet pea. Love you."

"I will. Love you, too."

I hang up with him and pull up the text from Shantel with Archer's hotel information. I didn't let him know I was coming because I was scared I'd blurt out that I'm pregnant before I had a chance to see him. To see the reaction on his face to truly know how he feels about it, about me.

I fire off a text to let her know we're boarding and power down my phone. It's a four-hour flight, and I'm sure I'll be on pins and needles the entire time. Hopefully when I arrive, I'll finally have figured out a plan to fix things.

Chapter Forty-Nine
Archer
Present

Loud snoring and a sweaty head interrupt my viewing of the latest Marvel movie. I push the man's head back onto his headrest and turn up the volume on my earbuds. Air blasts into my face from the nozzle above me, and I welcome the chill as I contemplate what I'm going to do when I arrive back home. I didn't tell anyone, not even Shantel, that I was coming home. I figured it'd be a great surprise to show up for Sunday dinner after I've fixed things with Tilly.

Sweat forms on my hands the closer we get to the ground, and as the wheels touch down, I know it's not turbulence or the pilot's landing that's making me nauseated.

It's her.

It's finally being closer to my happily ever after.

Assuming Tilly will forgive me.

The thought strikes me beneath my ribcage. Tilly has no reason to forgive me for bailing on her, for fucking up a second chance to choose her over my fears. She never responded to the message I sent before I left, but I know she saw it.

I slide my sweaty palms over my jeans, staring at the cracked pleather of the seat in front of me as people exit the plane.

What happens if she won't forgive you?

What if she doesn't want you anymore?

I pinch the skin at my neck as my throat constricts. That can't happen. This can't be the end of our journey together when we just started.

I'll do whatever it takes to prove to her that we belong together. I may not have fought back then to make sure she knew what was inside my heart, but I won't make that mistake again.

My skin tingles, heart racing as I call an Uber to the bakery. It's still early, but if I know Tilly, she'll already have the doors open. I rest my head against the seat and close my eyes, trying to hype myself up for seeing her again.

"That'll be twenty-six-dollars," the driver says, hand outstretched.

I pay him and slide out of the car, smoothing my slick hands down my jeans. I had him park on the next block, so I have time to gather my thoughts. My phone vibrates inside my pocket, but I'm too focused on my mission to allow anyone to interrupt my grand gesture.

I round the corner and almost plow into a few people gathered by the shop, hands cupped around their face looking into the windows. Elation fills my chest, and I can't contain my smile. Tilly's dreams are finally coming to fruition.

"What the hell?" someone says, face scrunched up as they walk away.

My phone continues to vibrate in my pocket, but I'm busy watching the small crowd with long faces dispersing from in front of Tilly's bakery. I quicken my pace, curiosity pushing me forward until I'm standing in front of a large red and white sign with the words 'For Lease' written across it.

The thud of my stomach has the effect of a shotgun going off, and all the proverbial crows flap their wings in effort to get away, taking my breath with them.

She's not opening the bakery?

My attention moves to my no longer vibrating phone, and I see messages from Shantel but swipe them away. I bring up Tilly's number and press call.

She doesn't answer.

I shoot off a text to her and bring up the message thread I have with Shantel. Multiple messages stare back at me, and my stomach twists as I read each one.

Where are you?

Are you at the set?

Tilly flew all the way there to see you, the least you could do is answer your messages!

Realization dawns on me. I never texted Shantel back after she asked me to come home soon. She didn't know I was coming. *Fuck.* Hands shaking, I dial Shantel's number. One ring passes before her exasperated voice is in my ear.

"Where the hell are you?"

"I'm here," I yell back. And because there are more important things to do than yell at my pseudo-sister, I add, "Tilly's not opening the bakery?"

"What do you mean you're here? You're supposed to be in Knoxville!"

Her screeching makes me pull the phone away from my ear. When she's finally calmed down, I take a moment to gather my own thoughts.

"I came back to surprise her...to try and win her back."

She growls at me. "Damn it, Arch. What kind of Hallmark shit you trying to pull here?"

My laugh is wooden. "You told me I needed to come back."

"I didn't mean today." She sighs heavily and says something to Nora in the background. "Sorry, I should've been more clear. Baby brain."

I lean against the door, struggling to gather my thoughts. Tilly flew all the way to Knoxville to see me, and I came here for the same reason.

"You could've given me a heads-up she was planning to come, you know. Text her and tell her to come home."

"She's calling me," she says. "I'll call you back."

The line cuts off before I have a chance to say anything else, and I stand in front of the bakery that should be open and busy serving customers. I cup my hands and peer into the shop. Everything inside is ready. The tables are set up, the boxes are put together and on shelves, and the only thing missing, other than Tilly, are her sweet treats.

A plan formulates in my head, and without a second thought I rip down the for-lease sign and shoot off a bunch of texts to Shantel, Nora, and Tilly's father.

I may not have gotten to tell the woman I love that she's more than enough, but I'll be damned if I don't show her.

***

Grocery shopping with Mr. St. James is something I never thought I'd be doing, but as we traverse the aisles gathering ingredients to make Tilly's recipes, I find his presence slightly calming. With a list in hand, he hums merrily, tossing a few bars of unsweetened chocolate into the basket.

"Are you going to marry my daughter?" he asks, adding a bag of flour.

Stunned by his question, I stop mid-stride. Adrenaline courses through my veins thinking about Tilly in a white dress, standing across from me, this time with me as her groom. Would I marry her? In a heartbeat. Would she marry me? Doubtful.

"If she'd have me, absolutely."

He continues down the aisle as if he didn't ask me a heart-stopping question. My skin is tingling, head swimming in the clouds.

"Her dreams have to be important to you," he mumbles. "She's lost too much already."

I stop him, my hand resting on his forearm. "That's why I'm here doing this. I won't let her give up because I was an idiot."

"This is all fine and dandy, but what happens when you leave? Will she have to move with you? Give up her bakery and her dreams again?"

I shake my head. "I'll do whatever she wants me to."

The words leave my mouth without another thought, and in my heart of hearts, I know it to be true. If Tilly asked me to stay, to give up the carpentry show, I would.

I know this is a conversation I should be having with Tilly, not her father, but I need him to know I'm serious about his daughter. I've always been serious about her. And it's time I make sure she knows it too.

"Archer?" a woman's voice stops me.

A cold sensation overtakes me and I'm frozen as I stare at my mother at the end of the aisle. Why is she here? She has maids that cook for her. She tilts her head, looking at Mr. St. James with a hint of confusion in her eyes.

"Why haven't you answered my calls?" she asks, pushing her cart toward me.

Tilly's dad and I share a look before he saunters off to get the rest of the ingredients needed to start baking.

I sigh and cross my arms. "I've been busy."

"Too busy to call your own mother back?"

I clamp my lips over my teeth, anger simmering at the surface, ready to boil over. As much as I want to call her out on being a shitty mom, now is not the time.

"I bet you call Nora back when she calls," she mumbles.

I guess this is the time.

The lid covering my emotions blows off, and heat flares in my chest.

"I absolutely do call Nora back." My voice raises. "You want to know why?"

"Archibald," she chastises.

I'm vaguely aware of all the eyes on us, but I'm done letting her make me feel bad for her lack of parenting and motherly qualities.

"She's the only mom I've known since I was a child. You and Dad were so busy trying to be the best surgeons, you didn't even bother being good parents."

"We were great parents to you," she whisper-yells. "You had a roof over your head, food in the fridge, and more toys than anyone could ask for."

Unchecked anger rises, and I tamp it down. I step closer to her and lower my voice. "If you think that's all it takes to show a kid love, then you're more delusional than I thought."

"Well, your sister and brother felt loved."

"Don't you bring them into this." I bend down, pointing my finger in her face. "You're the last person that should ever be commenting on the love you gave to Sebastian. You sat by while Dad put so much pressure on him that he turned to drugs."

The crack of her hand echoes through the baking aisle, the sting of the slap warming my face. "I did not."

Her lip is quivering, hand drawn to her chest like even she can't believe she just hit her own child.

"I'll tell you like I told Claire. Sebastian's death is on you and Dad. You can blame me all you want for your missteps as parents, but I'm done hearing them. I'm done allowing you guys to make me feel like I don't deserve everything I've worked for, everything I've built from the ground up."

"Oh that's grand."

"If you can't see how you failed me as a mother, then I don't want you in my life."

She sneers. "You think being a parent is so easy, but just wait until you have your own kids."

"I can't wait to have my own kids, because they sure as hell will know that they're loved and won't be blamed for their parents' mistakes." Spittle flies out of my mouth, and I inhale a short breath. "And they won't be scared to tell me they need help because my expectations mean more to them than their own mental health and wellbeing. I'll encourage my kids to go after things they love rather than pushing my own dreams on them like you guys did."

Her mouth pops open and closed like a fish, a flush rising to her cheeks.

"Save it," I say. "I'm done listening."

I turn and walk away, searching for Tilly's dad. Like I expected, my mother doesn't follow, doesn't try to make excuses for her actions. My chest is lighter as I approach the checkout station, proud of myself for standing up to her.

"Everything okay?" Tilly's dad asks.

I nod and give him a pained smile as I pull out my card and hand it to the cashier.

Making dozens of cookies and treats was not how I expected to spend this morning, but if I can somehow get Tilly's bakery up and running before she gets back, then I have to try.

I can't let the woman of my dreams give up on her own.

Chapter Fifty
Tilly

If I had a needle and thread, I'd be working on an Archer voodoo doll during this flight. To think I flew the entire way there assuming he'd be in his hotel suite, but he's back in Texas doing God knows what during his two off days. You think he would've called, maybe apologized for the confusion or at least offered to meet me when I got home, but nope. Nada. I even messaged him after I realized what happened, but he hasn't read any of my texts.

When the hotel concierge couldn't contact Archer to ask if he could give me his room number, I called Shantel. She couldn't get a hold of him either, so I went down to the studios to see if I could find him there.

A beautiful red-haired woman kindly let me know Archer wasn't there but that they were *so blessed* to have such an amazing carpenter on their show. Her pointed glances at my left hand made it clear why she was overly sweet in the beginning and then changed her demeanor once her eyes settled on my ringless finger. After talking to her, I didn't want to talk to anyone and decided to turn off my phone.

"Pretzels or peanuts?"

Pulled from my reeling by a bag of salty peanuts, I smile and take it, pushing the image of the woman from my mind. The loud crunch of the bag garners me dirty looks from the passenger across the aisle trying to sleep, and a whiff of the nutty goodness makes my stomach grumble loud enough to rival the engines.

I stare out the airplane window at the fading orange light, but it gives me no peace, and as we descend into San Antonio, the disappointment of my grand gesture settles into my bones. I could've stayed, waited until he came back, told him I want to make things work, but if it was meant to be then it would've worked out.

As the wheels touch down, every nerve I channeled into anger comes rushing back in with the jingle of my phone going off airplane mode. Texts from Dad and Shantel overflow my inbox, and my breath vanishes when my eyes snag on Archer's name. I sit back in my seat, hands shaking as I click his text.

Archer: Come home to me.

Tongue pressed against my cheek, I rest my head on the seat and try to calm myself down. I tried to go to him, and he wasn't there. Why is he even in San Antonio? He hightailed it out of there the minute things didn't work with us, and now he wants me to come home to him? The emotional whiplash makes my head spin.

Ignoring the anger, I concentrate on the underlying message. Where is home anymore? I thought I'd found it in the bakery, thought I'd found it with Archer, but neither of those worked out how they were supposed to, and each time my heart broke a little more.

A buzz in my hand draws my attention.

Shantel: Come to the bakery.

My heart rate skyrockets. Why does she want me to meet her there? Did something happen? Did it get broken into?

Me: What happened?

Three dots appear, dancing on the screen.

Shantel: There's something weird going on...Need you here.

A lump takes residence in my throat. Once I'm off the plane, I dial her number and it goes directly to voicemail. My fingers tremble as I try my dad. Same thing. With a deep breath, I dial the last number I want to.

It goes directly to voicemail, too.

My hand clenches around the phone, wishing I could break it into tiny pieces.

I quickly make my way down to the arrivals exit and hail a cab. The less than ten-minute drive takes forty minutes during rush hour on Interstate 410, and when we get close to the bakery the traffic is completely grid locked. Fearing the worst, I pay for my fare and speed toward the bakery, my heart in my throat.

A line around the corner stops me as I approach the street. People have their cameras out, taking pictures of the line and of themselves, the local news station has set up, and I'm terrified to see why. Has the bakery been burned to the ground? A glance at the clear sky quells my unease about a fire, but the closer I get, I realize the line is coming *out* of my bakery.

I move closer. "What's going on?"

"Grand opening of this new hot spot called Tilly's," a college-aged kid in a flannel shirt and beanie says.

Grand Opening? Tilly's? What the hell.

I basically levitate to the front of the shop.

"No jumping the line," someone yells as if we're standing in line for a club instead of a bakery. A laugh bubbles out of me when I squeeze through the doorway with my carry-on suitcase and find Dad, Gloria, Shantel, Nora, and Archer behind the counter.

"What the hell?" My voice squeaks, barely heard over the din of the bakery.

Like magnets, Archer's eyes lift to mine, and a smile cracks his now bare face. It's been years since I've seen him clean shaven, and the snare drum inside my chest crescendos.

"Attention everyone," Archer yells. "Welcome to the Grand Opening of Tilly's bakery. Here's the woman of the hour!"

My skin heats with all the eyes that shift to me, and applause and whoops of congratulations fill the air. Stunned, I struggle to find words to convey the sheer insanity of all of this. The bakery case is filled with treats I didn't make, there's a line of people out the door that I didn't invite, and the man I've fallen in love with is standing behind the counter when he should be in Tennessee.

Dizzy and confused, I find a seat and plop my purse on the table. My mouth is dry as Archer makes his way over to me with a bouquet of flowers in his hand.

"How?" I ask, breathless. "Why?"

He takes my hand, pulling me from the chair and handing me the flowers. "Because this is your dream."

My eyes fall to the aromatic sweet alyssums he gathered in purple, pink, and white. A nudge on my chin, and green eyes pierce the Teflon armor of my heart.

"I want to be the man who makes all of your dreams come true, Tilda St. James."

Breath rushes out of me, and I close my eyes as his lips meet mine. Loud hoots and hollers echo in the tiny bakery, but I'm reduced to goo as Archer wraps his arms around my waist and pulls me closer. My brain lags to catch up, and I push him back a step, touching my fingertips to my lips.

"But why?" I ask.

He runs a hand through his hair, and the eyes on us seem to narrow as if the entire store is on bated breath waiting to hear his answer.

"Because I made a mistake in leaving."

I scoff, but immediately feel bad because I pushed him away. If it wasn't for me, maybe he would've stayed here.

No, I tell myself. I pushed him away because he needed to follow his dreams. He's given so much up for everyone else, and it was time for him to take care of himself.

"I didn't stay to fight for you, like I should've all those years ago. I can only apologize for that, but I'm here right now."

"What about your job?"

"Forget the job," he says, moving closer and taking my hand. "There are other jobs out there, but there's only one you."

A chorus of 'awws' starts around the room, and my eyes lock on Nora and Shantel at the counter boxing up cookies. Their smiles warm my heart, and a small nod from Nora giving her blessing fills my chest with happiness. As if recognizing the moment for what it is, my stomach spins and a wave of nausea hits me.

"But..."

"Enough, Tilda." Archer's deep voice sends a chill down my back. "No job, no poker chip, no nothing, will take me from you. I'm yours if you'll have me."

"Say yes!" a few customers yell, and I almost want to laugh at how cheesy we probably look, me with my carry-on luggage, and Archer confessing his love.

"I love you, Tilly."

"I'm pregnant."

Oh, fuck. I didn't mean to blurt that out right here.

Everyone's sharp gasps make it seem like we're in the theaters and they're watching a movie. Archer's eyes are wide, mouth slightly parted. The silence seems to stretch, and a flush creeps up my neck. This was definitely not the time or place I should've told Archer something so...earth shattering.

"Sorry," I mumble. "I didn't mean—"

My feet leave the floor, and Archer spins me around, his smile so wide I'm worried his face is going to crack.

"Really?" he asks.

My voice is nowhere to be found, but the nausea in my stomach is ever-present and it's slowly creeping up my chest. I press against his shoulders, willing him to put me down before I throw up all over him in front of the entire store.

He sets me down and holds me at arm distance, eyes filled with excitement. "Really?"

I press my hand against my stomach and nod. "Yes."

He pulls me into his arms, burying his face in my neck. His hand moves down to my stomach, and I hold my breath as he says, "I love you...both." His eyes meet mine. "I'm ready to leave all the baggage behind us and move forward together if you are?"

Tears leak down my face, surely brought on by the raging hormones. With a laugh, I wipe them away and nod. "I'm so ready."

I drag my suitcase behind the counter and after greeting my family, I fall in line beside them, boxing up the rest of the orders and rubbing elbows with some of the business owners around. Apparently, flyers went out this morning to the three major college campuses downtown and to the surrounding buildings naming my bakery as the newest hot spot to check out. The news caught onto the hullabaloo and followed everyone over.

"I can't thank you guys enough for everything you did today," I say, wiping down the counter and bakery case.

"It was all Archer's idea," Dad says, pulling me to his side and kissing the top of my head. "Congratulations, pumpkin."

I lean into his embrace. For so long there was distance between us, and I'm grateful to Gloria for helping us bridge the gap.

"Don't forget Sunday dinner." Nora rests her feet at a table across the way. "And you're making the desserts because I'm desserted out."

Everyone laughs, and we share a collective sigh. One by one they leave, and as the day comes to a close, a sense of completion comes over me as I flip the lock and turn off the neons. Finally able to catch my breath, I take a moment and go to the kitchen. It's a mess of sprinkles, icing, and flour, but I'm astounded by the love the community and my family showed me today by getting my bakery opened.

The door swings open, and my heart pitter-patters inside my chest when Archer steps through. He's wiping his hands on an apron, eyes lit with desire.

Chapter Fifty-One
Tilly
One Year Later...

Wind wraps my hair around the top of Jessica's bottle and nearly rips it from her mouth as I struggle to close the window. Her rosy cheeks bounce as she sucks, and I snuggle her closer as I move around the house, trying to gather everything we need for Sunday dinner. Shuffling a diaper bag, car seat, and a baby on your own isn't ideal, but Archer's flying back tonight after shooting the reunion show of Stud Finders.

The season ended with the two breakout stars of the show, Canon and Bliss, at odds with each other, and everyone is dying for any tidbit of information. I try to keep up with the shows Archer is on, but half the time I fall asleep after pumping breast milk, or I'm too busy at the bakery. Now that we've started taking on wedding cake clients, I had to hire another assistant to help with the regular orders we get weekly. I couldn't be more thankful to the businesses around The Pearl for constantly keeping me busy with lunch time cupcake orders and the occasional birthday cake, but I'm ready to expand.

Jessica coos and promptly follows it up with a loud belch once I put her on my shoulder. She's been a rough sleeper, but when Archer is home, I don't hear a peep, almost like she can't sleep soundly when Daddy is away. I can relate. Thankfully, he's home for the holidays, and he's taking a break from the shows to focus on expanding the construction businesses here.

I never expected my obsession with yams would bring me this beautiful bundle of joy, but apparently, they are known to increase fertility and cause multiple ovulation, which is why I thought I was safe when our bakery case bang session ended with a ripped condom. Either way, I'm thankful for the blessing of this amazing family.

My phone vibrates along the new countertop. After moving in last year, Archer and I decided to renovate his house and expand the kitchen and garage so we could occasionally work from home. While my house was beautiful, it was mine and Jessie's. Archer and I needed a fresh start if we were going to be able to make this work, and for Jessica to grow up in a house that wasn't rife with bad memories for me.

"Hey Shantel." I answer the phone and put Jessica into her car seat.

"On a scale of one to ten, how much do you love me?"

Pots clang loudly in the background, and I immediately recognize the laughing accompanying the banging as Shantel's son, Tanner. I never thought I'd be pregnant at the same time as my sister-in-law, but crazier things have happened.

I laugh. "I love you a billion million, why?"

There's a crash in the background and a chorus of 'no, no, no' but Shantel's back on the line within seconds. "Sorry, Tanner was...on the steps. I need you to stop by the bakery."

I sigh, wrapping my arm through Jessica's seat and heading out to the car. "You forgot to pick up the pie, didn't you?"

Her pause is all I need to know I'm spot on.

"I'll do the dishes this time," she pleads.

I secure Jessica's seat and get in the front. "You'll do them the next two times," I counter.

She growls. "Fine."

I laugh and hang up with her, focusing on the road ahead of me.

Christmas lights swoop between the lamp poles, and the tinny ding of a bell steals my attention. The same Santa from last year stands in the middle of The Pearl's square, ringing his bell in front of a donation bin. He stops to take pictures with a family and, wrapping Jessica's cover around her tighter, I get in line behind them. Last year, I made a wish I never imagined would come true, but it did. This year, I just want to say thanks.

After visiting with Santa and snagging a candy cane, I head toward the bakery. The December wind brushes along my bare legs, and I curse myself for wearing a dress instead of comfy leggings. At least I have earmuffs and a scarf, and a small baby who makes things ten times hotter, or else I'd be a popsicle.

I wiggle my keys out of the side of the diaper bag, insert them into the keyhole, and find the door is already unlocked. I pause on the threshold, sorting through last night, trying to remember if I locked the door. My heart thumps as I peer inside the dark bakery, careful not to make any noise.

Twinkling lights come on, and the sight of Archer in a suit steals my breath. He's leaning against the countertop, legs crossed in front of him with a box in his hands. His head snaps up when I come in, a smile cresting his freshly shaved face. My body flushes, and Jessica stirs in my arms.

"What's all this?" I ask, breathless.

He comes toward me and drops down to one knee. It's in this moment I note the soft piano music playing in the background, the pictures of us strung along those twinkling lights he's hung on the shelves.

"Tilda St. James," he says, taking my hand and causing a shiver to speed down my spine. "You cake my breath away."

"Arch." I laugh, and tears form in my eyes.

"And I know we've hit a lot of speed bumps over the years, most of them created by me, but there's no one else I'd want to travel this road with. Will you marry me?"

He opens the box, unearthing a stunning white gold diamond band. I gasp at the beautiful woven pattern, and Jessica's tiny eyes open, her arms reaching out for Daddy.

"Yes."

His eyes light up. "Yes?"

I nod and let the tears stroll down my cheeks. He places the ring on my hand and pulls me in for a heart-stopping kiss. Tiny arms latch onto his neck, and Jessica moves into his arms, curling up in her favorite place. Her piercing green eyes and dark hair are an exact replica of Archer's, and I can't help falling even more in love with him when I look at her.

We've been through more than most couples, but our foundation was built on friendship and developed into something more. Our lives have been interwoven from the beginning, and even though we couldn't see it, we were meant to be entangled for life in one way or another. I'm lucky to have found love once, and I'm blessed to have found it twice.

Leaning into his embrace, I look into the eyes of the man who was patient with me as I struggled, who listened when I wasn't speaking to him, the man who made every single one of my dreams come true.

"Arch," I say, tilting his head toward me. "You cake my breath away, too."

Chapter Fifty-Two
Epilogue

Dear Seb,

Today, the spot beside me was empty. The spot where you would've stood, had you still been alive. I can imagine it now. You, in your black suit, winking at a girl in the audience you planned to woo later that night, fumbling when the pastor asked you for the ring in your pocket. It'd probably be as funny as it was watching Jessica with her space buns toddle down the aisle in her lime green dress, stumbling side to side as Tilly coached her down the path.

It was a small wedding, exactly how Tilly and I wanted. Pink-and purple-colored flowers filled the short aisle leading to the arbor I built out back, and each table had a plate filled with little desserts Tilly baked. Your niece drew pictures we framed as table numbers, and to be honest, I think with her illegible handwriting, she may be following in your footsteps as a doctor.

Nora, along with Shantel and her family, Tilly's father and girlfriend, and a few friends I made from the reality show were the only ones in attendance. I haven't spoken to Mom, Dad, or Claire since I told them why you were really there at that gas station, and to be honest, I don't think I ever will again. I know people always say you'll regret cutting ties with family, regret all the things you didn't say or the time you'll miss with them, but I won't. I have an amazing family, one who loves me, who is supportive and *encouraging, and will never make me feel like I'm less than. I only wish you were here to be part of that family.*

I still have your poker chip. Well...kind of. I wanted to throw it in the garbage disposal and grind it to pieces, but Tilly reminded me it's all I have left of you. But that's not entirely true. I have memories, good ones, of us growing up, laughing together, spending time with you and Jessie after school. Memories I look back on often as I consider begging Tilly for another child.

Jessica is two years old now, and I don't want her to grow up without a sibling. I want her to have someone to play with, someone she can teach things like you taught me, someone she can run to when things get rough and she needs to talk. That's what these letters to you have always done for me. I know it's not the same, but having you to talk to, even though you can't talk back, has helped me get through a lot, helped me let go of the heavy burdens I've been carrying around for too damn long.

Anyway, Tilly surprised me by taking the picture of you and I from on top of the fireplace and having someone woodwork a frame where your poker chip would fit, and she placed it on a chair in the front row along with a candle. She wanted to make sure I knew you'd always be there, even if you weren't actually here. I know what you're thinking, 'she's amazing, and hot,' but too bad, bro, she's taken. She's mine, and I'm never letting her go.

-*Arch*

Thank You

Thank you readers!

With so many books out there, it means a ton to me that you've chosen to spend your time reading my book.

Reviews help books find their readers, so I'd love it if you could leave one for You Cake My Breath Away on Amazon, Goodreads, and/or anywhere else you tend to buy books!

If you want to stay updated on new books and giveaways, you can sign up for my Substack.

To connect with Tobie:
www.Tobiecarter.Com
Instagram- @tobiecarter.writer
TikTok-@authortobiecarter
Threads-@tobiecarter.writer

Acknowledgements

There are no words meaningful enough to thank everyone who helped bring this book to fruition. For the most part, my acknowledgements section stays the same because I'm surrounded by such amazing people who are willing to read and critique multiple versions of my messy books, but I always try to name everyone who has a hand in my books!

Now, to thank some very special people!

First, to God for blessing me with a never-ending well of stories to write.

Second, to my amazing husband who supports and encourages me daily to chase this dream!

Yaya & Nonna, my two moms. I wrote this book after you both lost kids, and I lost two brothers. Though I can only imagine the grief you carry with you daily, I tried to capture the strength you've both exuded in the face of immense loss. You two are my heroes.

Michelle. Mich. My sister. I'm sorry I made you read this book umpteen times before publishing it. As always, you are the Wizard behind the curtain helping me cut and chop so the readers don't have to endure clunky sentences and repetitious words. I'm forever grateful to have you in my life. I love you! P.S. #LOAMY.

Kelly. My co-host for the #ThrillsandChills chat and another writing sister. Thank you for reading this story a million times. I mean, it's been like three years since I first wrote it and you've read it at least ten or more times. That's friendship right there. Thank you for your constant encouragement and support of my writing. You're my hype woman and one of my absolute best friends!

My Twisted Sisters. Thanks for not killing me on our writing retreat(reader, see the note in GNOME ONE LIKE YOU)

Marysa. My ride or die. Your insight is always a fresh breath of air into the dusty pages of the stories I send you. Thank you for always telling me like it is, and making sure my men grovel in the best way possible. P.S. We need to get some more pineapple cilantro sherbet.

Ingrid. Thank you for always being available for an encouraging word and for letting me send you a million GIFs at random moments. I'm counting down the seconds until we're in the same place so that we can wrangle Michelle into a writing retreat!

I was blessed to have a ton of friends who read multiple versions of this book, and even though I'm sure I'll forget to name a few, I'm at least going to try- Maritza, Farrah, Scarlette, Elizabeth, TT Lex, Bethany, Etta, and so many more. Also, to Alexandria and Daisy for the last minute beta reads! All of you are rockstars.

And to my three reasons for never giving up, my babies. You kiddos show me that life is worth living, that every day brings something new, and that no matter how dirty I think something is, you can make it dirtier. Thank you for always being ready with a hug and a kiss for Mommy. I love you.

Also By Tobie Carter

THE BOTTOM LINE- Available on KU

Workplace Romance
Rivals-to-lovers
Mental Health Rep
Grumpy but lovable Pop-Pop
Steamy Swim Lessons
Complicated Family Dynamics

GNOME ONE LIKE YOU- Available on KU

Second Chance Romance
Forced Proximity
Fake Dating
Brother's Best Friend
Only One Bed
Meddling Nana
Naughty Uses for Decorations

About the author

Tobie Carter is a fiction writer of contemporary romance stories that speak to the heart of the reader and leave them with a story that lingers in their mind long after finishing. Her stories are fast-paced, angsty, high heat, and feature relatable characters who refuse to settle for less than they deserve. She lives in Central Texas with her husband and three young children.

Made in the USA
Coppell, TX
04 February 2026